Three Complete Novels

BARBARA CARTLAND

Three Complete Novels

BARBARA CARTLAND

A NIGHT OF GAIETY

A DUKE IN DANGER

SECRET HARBOR

WINGS BOOKS
New York • Avenel, New Jersey

This omnibus was originally published in separate volumes under the titles:

A Night of Gaiety, copyright © 1981 by Barbara Cartland.
A Duke in Danger, copyright © 1983 by Barbara Cartland.
Secret Harbor, copyright © 1982 by Barbara Cartland.

This 1994 edition is published by Wings Books,
distributed by Random House Value Publishing, Inc.,
40 Engelhard Avenue, Avenel, New Jersey 07001,
by arrangement with the author.

Random House
New York • Toronto • London • Sydney • Auckland

Printed and bound in the United States of America

Library of Congress Cataloging-in-Publication Data

Cartland, Barbara, 1902–
    [Novels. Selections]
    Three complete novels / Barbara Cartland.
        p.   cm.
    Contents : A night of gaiety -- A duke in danger -- Secret harbor.
    ISBN 0-517-11929-3
    1. Historical fiction, English. 2. Love stories, English.
  I. Title
  PR6005.A765A6   1994b
  823' .912--dc20   94-17415
                                                        CIP

8 7 6 5 4 3 2 1

CONTENTS

A NIGHT
OF GAIETY

Author's Notes

I knew many of the Gaiety Girls when I came out in the 1920s. One dear friend was the Marchioness of Headfort, who was Rosie Boote. She came from Tipperary and her father had been a gentleman of independent means. She first appeared in *The Shop Girl* in 1895. She worked hard, never slacked, and never gave an indifferent performance.

The Marquis of Headfort had a prominent place in the Irish Peerage and was very popular at Court. His family strenuously opposed the marriage; but Rosie stepped into her high position with such grace and charm that everyone loved her. She and her husband were very happy.

I knew the Countess Poulett, who was Sylvia Storey, and the lovely Denise Orme, who married first Lord Churston and as her third husband the Duke of Leinster, but my greatest friend was the fascinating Zena Dare.

She married the Hon. Maurice Brett, and one of their duaghters was one of my bridesmaids. After her husband's death, Zena went back on the stage and played in *My Fair lady* for nine years, as the mother of Professor Higgins, without missing a performance.

She only gave up when she was over eighty but still slim, lovely, fascinating, and carried herself magnificently, like a goddess—or should I say, a Gaiety Girl?

CHAPTER ONE

1891

"*I*s that all?" Davita asked.

"I am afraid so, Miss Kilcraig," the Solicitor replied. "It is extremely regrettable that your father was so extravagant during the last years of his life. I am afraid he ignored any suggestions from me or my partners that he should economise."

Davita did not reply because she knew that what Mr. Stirling was saying was that this last year her father had been so intent on drinking away his sorrows that he did not heed anything anybody said to him.

More than once she had tried to talk to him about their financial position, but he would always tell her not to interfere, and now that he was dead, what she had feared had happened.

The bills had mounted and mounted.

They had been bad enough before her Stepmother had left, but afterwards her father had seemed to enjoy throwing his money about in ridiculous ways, or else being too sodden with whisky to know what he was doing.

But even in her most depressed moment, Davita had not imagined that she would find herself with just under two hundred pounds and literally nothing else.

The Castle which had belonged to the Kilcraigs for several hundred years had been mortgaged up to the hilt, and what was left of the furniture had now been sold.

The better pieces, like the paintings and some rather fine gold-framed mirrors, her father had already sold soon after he married Katie Kingston.

This past year when her father had become more and more irresponsible, Davita had often thought that she should hate her Stepmother, but instead she could not help feeling that in many ways there was a good excuse for her behaviour.

After her own mother had died three years ago, when Davita was only fifteen, her father had found the loneliness intolerable, and he had gone off first to Edinburgh and then to London in search of amusement.

Davita had thought even then that she could understand that her father had often craved for the gay life he had known as a young man in London before he had inherited the Baronetcy and come to Scotland to marry and what people called "settle down."

Because he had been very much in love with his wife, he had found it tolerable to live in an ancient, crumbling Castle with a thousand unproductive acres of moorland and only a few neighbours.

Somehow he and Davita's mother had managed to amuse themselves, fishing in the river, shooting over the moors, and every so often going off on a spree to Edinburgh and even occasionally to London.

But her mother worried because these trips cost money.

"We cannot really afford it, Iain," she would say when her husband suggested they should leave Davita in charge of the servants and have what he called a "second honeymoon."

"We are only young once," he would reply.

Then her mother would forget her qualms of conscience, there would be a scuffle to get their best clothes packed, and they would drive away looking, Davita thought, very much like a honeymoon couple.

Then her mother had died one cold winter when the

winds blowing from the North Sea and down from the snow-peaked mountains seemed to catch at one's throat.

Her father had been so distraught that it had in fact been a relief when he said he could stand the gloom of Scotland no longer and intended to go South.

"Go to London, Papa, and see your friends," Davita had said. "I shall be all right, and when I am older perhaps I shall be able to come with you."

Her father had smiled.

"I do not think you would be able to accompany me to any of my old haunts," he had said, "but I will think about it. In the meantime, get on with your lessons. You might just as well be clever as well as beautiful."

Davita had flushed at the word because she thought it a compliment, but she knew that she did in fact resemble her mother, and no-one could ever deny that Lady Kilcraig had been a very beautiful woman.

When Davita looked up at the portrait of her mother which hung over the mantelpiece in the Drawing-Room, she would pray that she would grow more and more like her.

They had the same colour hair with its fiery lights, and it was certainly not the ugly, gingery red that was characteristic of so many Scots. It was the deep red of the first autumn leaves which seemed to hold the sunshine.

Her eyes, again like her mother's, were grey in some lights and green in others, and, where Davita was concerned, they were clear and innocent as a trout-stream.

Because she was very young she had a child-like beauty. It may have been the curves of her face or the softness of her mouth, but there was something flower-like about her which belied her red hair and the green of her eyes.

"With your colouring," her father once said, "you ought to look like a seductive siren. But instead, my sweet, you look like a fairy-child who has been left behind amidst the toad-stools where the fairies dance."

Davita had always loved it when her father talked to

7

her of the myths and stories that circulated amongst the Scottish crofters.

They had learnt them from the Bards, and in the long winter evenings they told their children tales of the feuds between the Chieftains, interspersed with legends, superstitions, and stories which were all a part of their being "fey."

It had been so much a part of her own childhood that she often found it difficult to know where her knowledge ended and her imagination began.

Her mother added to her fantasies because her parents, both Scots, came from the Western Isles and her grandmother had been Irish.

"Your mother brought the leprechauns with her!" her father would sometimes say teasingly, when something vanished mysteriously or her mother had a presentiment that something strange was going to happen.

Davita had not been able to comfort her father in his grief, and now she imagined that she had been partially to blame for the fact that, desperate in his loneliness, he had married again when he was in London.

It had seemed inconceivable that he should have chosen as his second wife a Gaiety Girl, but when Davita saw Katie Kingston, which had been her stage-name, after the first shock of finding that any woman had taken her mother's place, and an actress at that, she had liked her.

She was certainly very attractive, although her mascaraed eye-lashes, her crimson mouth, and her rouged cheeks had been somewhat of a surprise in Scotland.

But her laughter and her voice, which had a distinct lilt in it, seemed to vibrate through the house like sunshine coming through the clouds.

Then, as might have been expected, Katie began to be bored.

Davita could understand that it had been one thing in London to marry a Baronet with all the leading actors and actresses of the Gaiety present, but quite another to have no audience but a few crofters, a stepdaughter, and a husband who, now that he was home, occupied most of his hours with sport.

"What shall we do today?" she would ask Davita as she sat up in the big oak four-poster bed, eating her breakfast and looking somewhat disconsolately out the window at the moors.

"What do you want to do?" Davita would ask.

"If I were in London," her Stepmother replied, "I'd go shopping in Bond Street, promenade down Regent's Street, and then have lunch with an admirer at Romano's."

She gave a little sigh before she went on:

"Best of all, I would know that at six o'clock this evening I should be popping in at the stage-door and climbing up to my dressing-room to put on my make-up."

There was a yearning note in her voice which Davita began to listen for, and it would intensify as she went on to relate what it was like behind the scenes of the Gaiety.

Katie was already thirty-six—which was another reason why she had married while she had the chance—so she had seen many of the great changes that had taken place at the Gaiety over the years.

"You've never seen anything like it," she told Davita once, "when Hollingshead, who was the Boss in those days, installed electric light at the Theatre."

Katie's blue eyes were gleaming as she went on:

"It was nine o'clock on August second in 1878 that the current was switched on. Lamps sizzled and flickered, then it brought the crowds hurrying into the Strand to look at the Gaiety."

It was not only the Theatre she described to Davita; she would tell her about the Stage-Door Johnnies, young men who would arrive in hansoms, "all dolled up" with their evening-dress capes, their silk Opera-hats, white gloves in their hands, and patent-leather boots shining like jet.

"They were all waiting after the Show to take us out to supper," Katie would say rapturously. "They sent flowers that filled the dressing-rooms and often gave us expensive presents."

"It must have been very exciting!" Davita would cry breathlessly.

"There's never been actresses anywhere in the world that had the glamour and the allure of us Gaiety Girls!" Katie boasted. "The newspapers say that we're the 'Spirit of the London Gaiety incarnate,' and that's what we are! The Guv'nor knows that we bring in the Nobs to the Theatre, so he doesn't economise on us, oh no! Only the best for a Gaiety Girl!"

Katie would show Davita her gowns that she wore on stage, some of which had been a present from the "Guv'nor," George Edwardes, when she left.

They were all made of the most expensive silks and satins, her petticoats were trimmed with real lace, and her hats were ornamented with the finest ostrich-feathers obtainable.

"We Gaiety Girls are famous!" Katie boasted.

Davita began to understand that what Katie was saying was that whether a man was rich or poor, young or elderly, to take a Gaiety Girl out to supper, to drive her home in a hansom, or to propel her in a punt at Maidenhead was to touch the wings of ecstatic romance.

What Katie did not tell Davita, Hector, who had been her father's valet for years and was now getting old, added after she was gone.

"Ye canna cage a song-bird, Miss Davita," he had said with his broad Scots accent. "Them Gaiety gals are not like th' other actresses. Th' gentlemen go mad over 'em and it's no surprising."

"Are they really so lovely, Hector?" Davita asked curiously.

"They be chosen for their looks," Hector said, "but some o' them are canny as weel, and there's nothing of the old Music Hall aboot them."

It took Davita some time to understand that the women who performed at the Music Hall were often coarse and vulgar, while the Gaiety Girls were ostensibly ladylike and refined.

Not that she found Katie particularly refined when she compared her with her mother.

At the same time, she could understand that it was her *joie de vivre* which her father had found fascinating and which had made him determined that he would not return to Scotland without her.

While Katie was struggling to adjust herself to her new life—Davita knew she had at first made a real effort —it was Violet, her daughter, who faced facts fairly and squarely when, six months after the marriage, she arrived to stay.

If Davita had thought her Stepmother attractive, she found herself staring wide-eyed at Violet.

She learnt that there were always eight outstandingly beautiful girls in every Gaiety production who moved about the stage wearing gorgeous gowns but were not performers in any other way.

They were not part of the *corps de ballet,* nor did they have anything to say; they just looked and were beautiful.

Violet was one of these, and when she appeared in Scotland she seemed to Davita like a goddess from another planet.

She had fair hair and blue eyes like her mother, her features were perfect, and when she smiled it was as if the *Venus de Milo* had suddenly become human.

"Why, I could hardly believe my eyes when I got your telegram!" Katie exclaimed, flinging her arms round her daughter.

"We've got a fortnight's holiday before we start rehearsals for the next Show, and I thought I'd come and see you. I've brought Harry with me. I hope you can put us up?"

Harry was an exceedingly handsome actor, and Katie made him as welcome as her daughter.

"He's getting on a bit," she said to Davita when they were talking about him. "He wants to 'go straight' rather than keep to the Juvenile leads which entail so much singing and dancing."

Harry had done well and had been billed as leading-man in the last three Shows at the Gaiety, besides becoming a draw at the Music Halls.

He seemed to have more to say to Katie than to her daughter, and it had been left to Davita to entertain Violet.

"Do you like the Theatre?" she had asked.

Violet's blue eyes lit up.

"I adore it! I'd not leave the Gaiety if a Duke asked me to run away with him, let alone a Baronet!"

She spoke without thinking, and added apologetically:

"I suppose I shouldn't have said that."

"I understand," Davita said with a smile.

"I don't know how Mum sticks it," Violet went on. "All this space!"

She looked out over the moors.

"I like to see houses out the window. You must be cut off here in the winter."

Davita laughed.

"You will be back in London before that."

"I sincerely hope so!" Violet exclaimed fervently.

"Your mother is very happy with my father," Davita said quickly, "although she misses London sometimes."

"I'm not surprised!"

Violet made herself very pleasant and Davita liked her.

Actually there was not very much difference in their ages, because Violet, having been, as Katie said "a little mistake" when she was only seventeen, had just passed her eighteenth birthday.

Davita could never quite understand what had happened to her father, Katie's first husband, whose name had been Lock.

"Good-looking he was," Katie had once said reminiscently, "with dark eyes that always seemed to have a smouldering fire in them, and that's why the audience went mad about him! But Lord knows he was dull when he got home! I was very young and very stupid, but Violet's got her head screwed on all right. I've seen to that!"

Davita did not quite understand the innuendoes in this conversation, but she gathered that Mr. Lock had left Katie before Violet was born.

Although she had never seen him again, he had not died until three years ago, leaving Katie free to marry Sir Iain Kilcraig.

"It must have been very difficult for you bringing up Violet all by yourself," Davita said sympathetically.

"I was lucky, I had very good—friends," Katie said briefly, and left it at that.

Violet learnt to fish while she was staying in Scotland. She soon picked up the art of casting and was thrilled with the first salmon she caught.

Davita persuaded her to walk up to the top of the moors and for a short time she forgot that she was an actress from the Gaiety Theatre and became just a young girl enjoying the exercise and, when it grew hot, paddling with Davita in the burns.

They went riding on the sure-footed small ponies that Davita had ridden ever since she was a child, talked to the crofters, and shopped in the village which was over two miles from the Castle.

It was only afterwards that Davita realised that while she was enjoying her time with Violet, Katie was spending her time with Harry.

Her father had been busy because it was the lambing season and he always made a point of assisting the shepherds. Moreover, unfortunately as it turned out, there was a run of salmon, which meant that the fishing was good, and he had spent a good part of each day by the river.

Even so, Davita thought that what happened was inevitable and it was only a question of Katie finding the right moment.

Soon after Violet had returned to London and Harry went with her, Katie disappeared.

She left a note for her husband saying that she had an irresistible urge to see her friends, and she had not told him so to his face because she could not face a scene! She promised to write to him later.

When she did write, and the letter arrived just as Sir Iain was determined to go and find her, it was to say that she was sorry but she could not leave the stage.

She had the chance of going to America with a part on Broadway, and it was something she could not refuse.

It was Hector who revealed that that was where Harry also had gone.

"He talked aboot it a great deal, Miss Davita, while I was putting out his clothes. He said it was the chance of a lifetime an' something he'd no intention o' missing."

In a way, Davita could understand that it had been the "chance of a lifetime" for Katie as well, but her father behaved at first like a madman, then settled down to drown his sorrows.

He died of pneumonia, caught because he had fallen into a ditch on his way back from the village where he had gone to buy more whisky.

He had apparently been so drunk that he lay there all night, and in the morning a shepherd found him and helped him home. But the cold he caught turned to pneumonia, and when Davita called the Doctor there was nothing he could do.

Davita now realised with a shock that she had been left penniless, although it was satisfactory that Hector had been provided for.

Her father had left him a small croft with a pension, separated from everything else which had been pooled to meet his debts.

When Davita looked at the bills she had been appalled at what her father had managed to spend in London during the time he had spent there after her mother's death.

There were bills for champagne, for flowers, for gowns, hats, furs, sun-shades, all of which she presumed he had given to Katie.

There was also an account from a Jeweller's, and bills for his own clothes which seemed astronomical.

Again in her imagination she could understand that her father would have wanted to be smart, dashing, and young, as he had been in the days before he first married.

Then he had his own hansom-cab always waiting for him, belonged to the best Clubs, and dined every night, naturally not alone, at Romano's, Rules, or The Continental.

But now Davita was alone, and it was frightening to think that everything that was familiar, everything that had been her background ever since she was a child, was no longer hers.

Mr. Stirling put into words the question that was in her mind.

"What are you going to do, Miss Kilcraig?"

Davita made a helpless little gesture with her hands, and the elderly man watching her thought how young she was and how very lovely.

It struck him that she was like a beautiful, exotic flower, and he had the uncomfortable feeling that she might not transplant.

"Surely you must have some relations?" he asked gently.

"Papa's sister, who was older than he was, is dead," Davita answered. "I had a Great-Aunt who lived in Edinburgh, but she died a long time ago, and I never remember meeting any of Mama's family because they lived so far away."

"You could write to them," Mr. Stirling suggested.

"It would be very embarrassing if I tried to foist myself on them," Davita answered, "and I do not think they are well off."

When she thought about it, the Western Isles seemed to be in another world.

"You cannot stay here," Mr. Stirling said, "so I am afraid you will have to find either a relative with whom you can live, or some sort of employment."

"Employment?" Davita queried. "But I am not certain what I could do."

"One of my partners might be able to suggest something," Mr. Stirling suggested. "There must be employment in Edinburgh for a young lady like yourself, but for the moment I cannot think what it could be."

"It is very kind of you to think of it," Davita said with a smile, "but although Papa always insisted I should be well educated, it seems extraordinary that nothing I have learnt seems likely to be saleable."

Davita gave him a brief little smile as if she was determined to make light of her difficulties.

"Of course the best thing would be for you to be married," Mr. Stirling said.

"That would be rather difficult," Davita replied, "as nobody has asked me."

That, she thought, was not surprising, since there were no young men in the vicinity, and she had never stayed in Edinburgh for any length of time, nor, after her mother's death, had she made contact with the few friends they had there.

"I tell you what I will do," Mr. Stirling said. "I will have a talk with my wife and the wives of my partners. Perhaps you could look after children or something of that sort."

"It is very kind of you," Davita replied, "very, very kind, and I am most grateful."

"You will be hearing from me."

The carriage was waiting to drive him to the Station, and as he drove away, raising his old-fashioned, low top-hat, Davita thought he looked like one of the Elders of the Church, and her heart sank.

She could imagine all too clearly what his wife and the wives of his partners would look like, and she was quite sure they would disapprove of her because she looked

16

so young, just as they disapproved because her father had married a Gaiety Girl.

She knew that the stage was considered extremely disreputable, especially in Scotland, and she could almost see the ladies in Edinburgh wringing their hands in horror because she had been associated with anyone so reprehensible as an actress from the Gaiety Theatre.

'What am I to do? What *am* I to do?' she questioned.

Because she was frightened for her future, she went in search of Hector.

He was packing up her father's clothes, and as she entered the bedroom he looked up from the leather trunk beside which he was kneeling to ask:

"Has the gentleman gone, Miss Davita?"

"Yes," Davita answered, "and as we both expected, Hector, he brought bad news."

"I was afraid o' that, Miss Davita," Hector said, "an' it's awful hard on ye."

Davita had no secrets from Hector, he knew her financial position, and he had in fact explained a great deal to her before Mr. Stirling had arrived.

"When everything is cleared up," Davita said, sitting down on the edge of the bed, "I shall have precisely one hundred ninety-six pounds, ten shillings!"

"Well, that's better than nought," Hector remarked.

"Yes, I know," Davita replied, "but it will not last forever, and I shall have to find work of some sort, Hector. But what can I do?"

"Work, Miss Davita?"

Hector sat back on his heels and it was obvious that this had not occurred to him before.

"Either that, or live on air, which I do not believe is very substantial fare," Davita said.

"Now suppose for th' time being ye have me croft, Miss Davita?" Hector said. "I've still got a few years o' work left in me, an' . . ."

Davita gave a little cry and interrupted him before he could say any more.

"Do not be so ridiculous, Hector!" she said. "It is

17

sweet of you, and just like your kind heart, but you know as well as I do that you should not go on working any longer, and Papa was sensible enough to give you a croft and leave you enough money so that you will not starve."

She paused to say in a more practical tone:

"All the same, there will be work at the Castle to employ you for a few days a week, which will provide you with the luxuries you could not otherwise afford."

"I don't need much, Miss Davita," Hector replied, "and there's always a wee rabbit or a grouse up th' hill."

Davita laughed, and they both knew he intended to poach what he required.

"If it comes to that," he said, "there'll be enough for two. I'm not a big eater."

"You are the kindest man in the world," Davita replied, "but we have to be sensible, Hector. I cannot stay with you for the rest of my life, and at eighteen I have to learn to look after myself."

She gave a little sigh.

"Not that it would be very exciting being in Edinburgh with Mrs. Stirling!"

"Is that what he suggested?" Hector enquired.

"Something of the . . . sort."

She knew by the expression on the old man's face that he was thinking, as she had, that Mrs. Stirling would disapprove of her father having died as he had, and more especially of Katie.

Davita felt she could almost hear the whispers:

"You can't touch pitch without being defiled!"

"Those who sup with the Devil should use a long spoon!"

She wanted to cry out that she could not bear it, and she felt she would be quite incapable of controlling young children and making them obey her.

"Oh, Hector, what shall I . . . do?" she asked.

Then as she looked down at what he was packing she saw in the trunk a picture of Katie.

It was in a silver frame and Hector had laid it on top

of one of her father's suits and obviously intended to cover it with another so that there was no possibility of the glass breaking.

Davita had heard from Katie all about the photographic beauties whose faces filled the illustrated papers and show-windows.

Katie had been photographed for advertisements and, like Maude Branscombe, who had been the first of the beauties, had posed for a religious picture.

"Very pretty I looked," she had told Davita, "wearing a kind of nightgown with my hair hanging over my shoulders, and clinging to a cross!"

Then she had laughed the light, spontaneous laugh which had always delighted Sir Iain.

"I wonder what some of those old battle-axes who took my picture into their pious homes would feel if they knew it was a Gaiety Girl they were pressing in their Bibles or hanging on the wall!"

Katie had laughed again.

"That picture brought me in a lot of shiny golden sovereigns, and that's what mattered!"

It was then, looking at Katie's photograph, that Davita had an idea.

What was the point of being looked down on and perhaps despised in Edinburgh?

If she had to work, she was much more likely to find it in London than anywhere else.

She would go to Violet, who had been very friendly all the time she was staying with her, and in fact at times she had seemed almost like the sister Davita had never had.

She remembered too that Violet had said to her:

"You're very pretty, Davita, and in a year or two you'll be stunning! If you take my advice, you'll not waste yourself in this dead-or-alive place."

"But this is my home!" Davita had said.

"Home or not, the moors aren't going to pay you compliments, and the only kisses you'll get will be from the wind, which anyway will ruin your skin!"

Davita had laughed, but when Violet had gone she had missed her.

It had been fun to have another girl of almost the same age to talk to, while she knew that her father, when he was with Katie, found her rather an encumbrance.

Afterwards, when he was sober enough he clung to her because there was no-one else.

"If you think I want that woman back, you are mistaken!" he would say angrily. "I'll show her I can do without her! This is my home, and if it is not good enough for her, she can go and jump in the sea for all I care!"

His violent mood would then give way to self-pity and a little while later he would cry:

"I miss her, Davita! You are a good child and I am fond of you, but a man wants a woman in his life, and she was so pretty! I liked to hear her laugh. I wish you had seen her on the stage; I could not look at anybody else when she was there."

He would go on and on for hours, until once, without thinking, Davita had said:

"Why do you not go to London, Papa? It would cheer you up."

Her father had turned on her angrily.

"Do you suppose I have not thought of that? Do you suppose I wish to be stuck in this benighted place? Dammit all, London would help me to forget—of course it would—but I have not the money. Do you understand, Davita? I have not a penny to my name!"

Davita could almost hear him now, shouting the words at her, and they seemed to be still echoing round the room.

Then as Hector put a neatly folded suit over Katie Kingston's photograph, she made up her mind.

"I am going to London, Hector!" she said quietly. "If Miss Violet cannot help me to find work, then I will come back."

The train in which Davita was travelling from Edinburgh was uncomfortably crowded for the first part of
the journey.

Then gradually, as passengers got out at every stop,
Davita found herself alone, with the exception of one
other woman, in the carriage marked: *"Ladies Only."*

It was Hector who had insisted she should travel Sec-
ond-Class.

"I think it is too extravagant," Davita had said, thinking how long her money had to last.

"I'm not having ye, Miss Davita, going off on yer own
in a Third-Class carriage with th' type of scum that's
sometimes in 'em!" Hector replied.

Although Davita knew he was talking good sense, she
parted reluctantly with what seemed to her a lot of
money, and left Hector to find her a corner seat and
make sure her trunk was placed in the Guard's-Van.

As she waved him good-bye she felt as if she was leaving behind her in Scotland not only everything she
loved but also her childhood.

Now she was on her own, grown up, a woman who
should take care of herself, but somehow she had not
the least idea how to set about it.

Then she thought that if things got too frightening,
she could go back to Hector and stay with him in his tiny
croft until she could start again.

It consisted of only two rooms, one up and one down,
but she knew it would not worry Hector to sleep in the
lower room while she occupied the only bedroom.

He would look after her as he had looked after her
father from the time he was a boy, and her mother when
they were married.

But Hector was growing old, and she had to be sensible and start to find her own way in the world, as many
other young women had done before her.

But deep down inside she was frightened, and she

found herself wishing, as she had so often before in her life, that she had been the boy her mother had expected, who was to have been called "David," which was a family name, instead of being a girl and an only child at that.

She had brought with her the only possessions she owned, and they filled exactly two trunks.

After her mother's death she had fortunately kept her clothes and altered them to fit herself.

But she was quite sure, even though they were made of good materials and some of them came from the best shops in Edinburgh, that by now they would be out of fashion.

Katie's clothes had of course been very different.

At the same time, while she had been living with them Davita had taken the opportunity of altering some of her mother's gowns to make them more fashionable.

Katie had also occasionally thrown a gown at Davita and said:

"Here, you take this! I'll never wear it again, and although it's too big for you, the stuff's good—the Guv'nor saw to that!"

Davita had managed to make herself two gowns out of Katie's cast-offs, but the third was of crimson taffeta, which was a hopeless contrast to her hair.

She did not dare spend one penny of her precious inheritance on clothes, so she merely wore a travelling-gown and cape which had belonged to her mother, and changed the ribbons and feathers from one bonnet to another to make what she hoped was a suitable ensemble in which to appear in London.

As the train drew nearer and nearer to the Metropolis, Davita became more and more frightened.

She had never been to London before, but from all she had heard about it, she suddenly felt that she had made a mistake and would much better have stayed in the world to which she belonged, however lonely it might have been.

Her father had extolled London as if it were a

Paradise of gaiety and excitement, with dashing, handsome men and beautiful, alluring women.

But he was a man, and from some of the things Katie had told her, Davita had been well aware that for a woman without money life could be a struggle with a lot of danger about it that she did not completely understand.

"I had a hard time on me own with Violet to look after, and no job until I got back my health and strength, and my figure too, when it came to that."

"Surely your husband . . . ?" Davita began.

"He'd gone—scuttled!" Katie said. "He was the sort who never ought to have got married. I was a fool to listen to him, but when you're in love . . ."

She had spoken derisively, then with one of her lilting little laughs she had added:

"I never learn, do I? Here I am at thirty-six, letting me heart rule me head once again, and where's it got me? To bonnie Scotland, and not so bonnie from what I've seen of it!"

Davita had laughed, but she had thought then that there was a little note of desperation in Katie's voice, which had worried her.

Katie had left for America with not only her experience of the stage to help her but also Harry.

Afterwards, Davita thought she might have expected that Katie was infatuated with the handsome actor, from the way she looked at him all the time he had been staying with them.

She had thought innocently that it was because he was a great actor and, as Violet had described him, a "star."

But after Katie was gone she supposed that the expression in her blue eyes had been one of love, and she thought the way Harry had looked at her had explained why the women at the matinees had watched him breathlessly and found their hearts beating quicker.

Katie would be all right, Davita thought, and wondered how she could let her know she was now a widow.

Then she remembered that she was going to see

Violet, who would undoubtedly know where her mother was to be found.

Again Davita felt a little quiver of fear.

Suppose Violet did not want her? Suppose she was angry with her for coming South without waiting for a reply to her letters?

Davita had written to her ten days ago, but she had not actually expected Violet to answer, because she remembered her saying several times when she had been staying with them:

"I can't bear writing letters or anything else for that matter! I learnt enough at School to read, but writing's hard work, and besides, I can't spell!"

"Better not let the Guv'nor hear you talking like that!" Katie had exclaimed. "You know he likes his girls to be ladylike, and ladies always say 'thank you' properly."

"I don't know what you mean by 'properly,' " Violet had replied. "I'd rather say 'thank you' with a kiss than write."

Katie had laughed.

"That's a different thing! But if a Duke asks you out to supper, you can hardly send him a kiss to say 'yes.' "

"I manage!" Violet answered, and they both had laughed.

Davita thought now that if Violet refused to have her, she would have to try to find a Domestic Bureau.

She remembered her mother talking about them once and saying that servants in the South and in Edinburgh could be obtained from Bureaus which brought employers and employees together.

"What a strange idea!" Davita had exclaimed. She had been very young at the time.

"Not really," her mother had answered. "If you want a Cook, for instance, you can hardly put a notice-board outside your house saying 'Cook Wanted.' "

"If you did, you might get hundreds and hundreds of applicants for the position!" Davita had laughed.

"And that would certainly be a nuisance," Lady

Kilcraig had replied with a smile. "So, grand ladies go to a Bureau when they want a Cook, a house-maid, a Governess, or a footman, and the servants sit on hard benches hoping someone will require their services and pay them well and be kind masters."

Davita remembered at the time thinking it was a strange way of doing things, but now she told herself that that was what she would have to do—sit on a hard bench until somebody came in who said:

"I want a young, inexperienced girl with no particular talents, but I will pay her and be kind to her if she will come into my employment."

"That would certainly have to be a very eccentric and very exceptional sort of person," she told herself.

She felt panic rising within her as they passed through the suburbs and she realised they would soon be steaming into St. Pancras Station.

It was Hector, who had travelled a great deal in his life, who had made the journey far more comfortable than it would have been otherwise.

He had packed her a small picnic-basket with enough food to ensure that she would not be hungry before she reached London.

He had even provided her with a bottle of cold tea, saying it was nicer than water, and if she tried to buy food in the Stations she might get involved with rowdy or unpleasant men.

He had also made her take a rug to cover her knees in case she was cold at night. It had been difficult to sleep because of the noise and the movement of the train, and she knew how sensible he had been.

Now she put on her bonnet, tidied her hair, and wished she could wash before she went in search of Violet.

She knew, as it was getting late in the afternoon, that the sooner she reached her destination the better.

Fortunately, Violet had given her her address when she had said good-bye at the Castle.

"If I've left anything behind, be a sport and post it to

me," she said. "I lost one of my brooches at the last place I stayed and they never sent it on to me."

"Do you mean they kept it?" Davita asked in amazement.

"I wouldn't be surprised."

"Well, I promise anything I find I will post to you at once!"

Davita had written down Violet's address, and although she had found nothing to send on, she had kept a note of it.

Now she remembered that it was some time ago and perhaps Violet would have gone elsewhere.

It was the first time this idea had suggested itself, and Davita was more frightened than she had been before.

As the train steamed into the Station and drew up at the platform, she felt it was impossible for her to leave the carriage.

Then a porter was shouting at the window and she forced herself to ask him to find her trunks for her. He picked up her picnic-basket and the small bag in which she had carried the few things which would not fit into her trunk, then set off in the direction of the Guard's-Van.

Carrying her rug over one arm, with her handbag in the other, Davita followed him down the platform, feeling that there were far too many people and the noise was deafening.

Then, the porter having kindly looked after her, Davita found herself driving away from the Station in a four-wheeler, her trunks perched on the top of it, with a rather tired horse carrying her through the crowded streets.

"I am here!" she said to herself. "I am in London, and please . . . please, God . . . take care of me!"

CHAPTER TWO

*T*HE HOUSE LOOKED rather dingy and gloomy on the outside and Davita told herself it was because she was not used to London houses.

She asked the cabman who had climbed down from his box to wait, and went up two steps to raise the knocker which she noted needed polishing.

There was some delay before the door was opened, and a rather blowsy but pleasant-looking woman stood facing her.

"Could I please . . . speak to . . . Miss Violet Lock?" Davita asked in a voice that sounded somewhat hesitating.

The woman smiled.

"I thinks yer must be the friend her's expectin' from Scotland," she said with a Cockney accent.

For a moment Davita felt such a wave of relief sweep over her that it was difficult to speak. Then she said:

"Yes . . . I am . . . Is Miss Lock . . . here?"

"You've just missed her, dearie, she's gorn to the Theatre," the woman replied. "I'm Mrs. Jenkins, an' I gathers I'm to expec' a new lodger."

"I should be very grateful if I could stay here," Davita replied.

The Landlady had already pushed past her to shout to the cabby outside:

27

"Bring 'em up t' the Second Floor back, there's a good man!"

Davita thought the cabman grumbled at the instructions, but she did not wait to hear as she followed Mrs. Jenkins up the stairs.

They were narrow and the carpet was worn, but she could think of nothing but the joy of knowing that Violet had expected her and she was not, as she had been half-afraid, alone in London with nowhere to go.

When they reached the second floor, Mrs. Jenkins opened a door at the back and Davita almost gasped as she saw the tiniest room she had ever been expected to sleep in.

There was just room for one bedstead and a rather rickety-looking chest-of-drawers. There was a rag-mat on the soiled linoleum.

"It's a bit small," Mrs. Jenkins said, which was an understatement, "but yer friend's next door, and I feels yer'd rather be near 'er than up another flight."

"Yes . . . of course," Davita said quickly, "and it was very kind of you to think of it."

Mrs. Jenkins smiled at her.

"I tries to 'elp," she answered, "an' I never tikes a lodger in what ain't on the boards. Yer're the exception, but wiv yer looks yer'll soon find yersel' a place at the Gaiety."

She looked at Davita appraisingly as she spoke, taking in the red hair under her bonnet, the clear petal-like skin, and her large, rather frightened eyes.

"Yer're pretty enough—I'll say that for yer," she said. "Can yer dance?"

"I . . . I am afraid not," Davita answered. "And I would be far too nervous to go on the stage, besides . . ."

She was just about to say that it was something of which her mother would not have approved, then she thought it would be a mistake to do so.

Mrs. Jenkins laughed.

"If yer gets the chance, yer'll jump at it!"

28

Davita did not have to reply, because at that moment the cabman, breathing heavily, came up the stairs with one of her trunks on his back.

It was impossible for him to get it into the room unless they both moved into the passage, and when finally he brought up the other trunk, Davita thought she would have to climb over them to get into bed.

Then, having paid the cabman, as she stood looking rather helplessly at her trunks, Mrs. Jenkins said:

"Now what yer'd better do, dearie, is change yer clothes, clean yerself up a bit, nip round to the Theatre, an' tell Violet yer're 'ere."

"G-go to the . . . Theatre?" Davita questioned.

"Yeah. Billy'll get yer a hackney-carriage when yer're ready, an' yer tell 'im to go to the stage-door. Yer'll find 'er in 'er dressing-room. The Show don't start for another 'our."

Because Mrs. Jenkins spoke so positively, Davita did not dare to argue with her.

Instead, as the Landlady went down the stairs, she obediently took off her travelling-gown and cape, and found in one of her trunks a pretty afternoon-gown which was not too creased.

It had belonged to her mother, and she had altered it to look a little more fashionable, copying one of the gowns which Katie had brought North with her.

When she was ready, Davita looked very pretty. Katie had told her that everybody in London always wore a hat in the evening unless they were going to a Ball, so she took one from her hat-box.

It was a hat which Katie had given her and which she had thought she would never wear because it was far too smart and over-decorated for Scotland.

Even now she hesitated after she had put it on, thinking as she looked at herself in the mirror that if she appeared in the Kirk in such a creation, the Congregation would either be scandalised or would laugh at her.

Quickly she removed two of the ostrich-feathers, and when she thought she looked comparatively ordinary and her appearance was unlikely to cause comment, she picked up her handbag and went rather nervously down the stairs.

She had difficulty finding Mrs. Jenkins. Then, hearing a noise from the basement, she descended to find her in a large, dark kitchen, cooking on an old-fashioned range.

"Excuse me . . ." Davita began nervously.

Mrs. Jenkins turned round.

"Oh, there yer are, dearie," she exclaimed, "quicker'n I expected!"

"Do I . . . do I look . . . all right?" Davita asked hesitatingly.

"O' course yer do!" Mrs. Jenkins replied. "A bit plain for th' Gaiety, but London'll soon smarten yer up, don't yer worry about that!"

She suddenly shouted so loudly at the top of her voice that Davita jumped.

"Billy! Where are yer? Come 'ere! I wants yer!"

There was no response for a moment. Then just as Mrs. Jenkins opened her mouth to shout again, a strange-looking, under-sized man, with arms that were too long for his body and a leg that limped, came to the door on the other side of the kitchen.

"Wot yer want?" he asked.

"Sleepin' again?" Mrs. Jenkins demanded. " 'Ow often do I have to tell yer, there's work to be done?"

"I were working," Billy answered sullenly.

"Well, work yerself out the door an' find a cab for this young lidy."

Billy looked at Davita with what she thought were bright, rather intelligent eyes which belied his appearance. Then he gave her a grin.

"A'noon, Miss."

"Tell the driver to take 'er to the Gaiety—to the stage-door!"

As Billy passed Davita and started up the stairs ahead of her, Mrs. Jenkins shouted:

"An' mind 'e don't over-charge yer. Ninepence is th'

right fare from 'ere to th' Gaiety, an' threepence for th' tip."

"Thank you for telling me," Davita said, and hurried up the stairs after Billy.

The Gaiety was ablaze with lights. Katie had told her that it was the first Theatre in London to have electric lighting, and although it was what Davita had expected, it seemed dazzling.

The stage-door, the cabby told her, was down an alley-way at the side of the Theatre.

Davita expected to see young men in top-hats outside it, but there were only a few poorly dressed people, obviously waiting to see the actors and actresses arrive.

Then she told herself that of course the "Stage-Door Johnnies" would not be there until after the Show.

There were a number of messenger-boys arriving with magnificent baskets and bouquets of flowers, and she followed them nervously through the open door.

Inside, there was what looked like the Ticket-Office in a Railway-Station, and behind the counter was an elderly man with grey hair, surrounded by the flowers for the actresses.

On the walls of the tiny room, which was no bigger than a cupboard, there were pictures of Gaiety Girls and the leading actors and actresses.

Despite the warmth of the evening, there was a fire, and the moment Davita appeared, the old man left it to say politely:

" 'Evening, Miss, an' what can I do for you?"

"Could I please see . . . Miss Violet Lock?" Davita asked.

The elderly man looked at her keenly.

"Is she expecting you?" he enquired.

"I . . . I think so," Davita answered. "She knew I was coming to . . . London from Scotland."

The elderly man raised his eye-brows.

An old sea-captain, Tierney, unlike many stage-door keepers, was always polite and never forgot a message. He knew almost by instinct who could go in and who

31

should not. Davita was not aware of it, but for the moment he could not place her.

She was obviously not one of the girls who were always trying to sneak in and get an autograph or a souvenir from one of the actors they admired, nor did she look as if she wanted a part.

As if she was suddenly aware of his hesitation, Davita said:

"I am a . . . sort of . . . relative of Miss Lock."

Old Tierney smiled.

"Then you'd better go up and see 'er," he said. "Third door at the top of the First Floor. If she doesn't want you, you're to come back down again. You understand—Miss?"

The "Miss" came after just a slight hesitation, as if Tierney had suddenly decided she was entitled to it.

"Thank you very . . . much," Davita said breathlessly.

Then she was climbing an iron staircase, thinking as she did so that whatever the Theatre was like in the front, at the back it was not very prepossessing.

It was also rather frightening because it was so busy.

As she went up the staircase, several people passed her in a hurry, going either up or down, in various stages of dress and undress which made her want to stare at them curiously.

When she reached a long corridor with doors opening off it, she could hear the chatter of voices and laughter, and when a door opened she had a glimpse of several women in various stages of undress.

She hurried to the door that had been indicated.

She knocked, but because she was nervous it made very little sound.

The voices she heard inside did not stop talking.

Then she knocked again, and this time somebody called out: "Come in!"

She opened the door and found herself facing a long room in which there were a number of women, each, to Davita's startled gaze, more beautiful than the last.

Several were sitting in front of mirrors, applying grease-paint to their faces, two were struggling into very elaborate, brightly coloured gowns, helped by two elderly women.

One at the far end of the room was being laced into a very tight corset, and with a leap of her heart Davita recognised Violet.

She moved forward, and as she did so the woman nearest to her said sharply:

"Shut the door behind you!"

Apologetically, Davita obeyed, and as she did so Violet recognised her.

"Davita!" she cried.

Because there was a warmth in her voice which Davita recognised, she hurried across the room to fling her arms round her.

"I am here, Violet! You were expecting me?"

"I got your letter and I knew you'd turn up sooner or later," Violet said. "I suppose Ma Jenkins sent you here?"

"Yes, she did. And she has given me a room."

"That's all right then."

As Violet spoke, she turned her head to look back at the dresser who was lacing up her corset, and said:

"Here, Jessie, not too tight! I can't breathe!"

"You don't have to!" Jessie answered.

"If I faint on the stage, it'll be your fault, not mine!"

With barely a pause between the words, Violet went on to Davita:

"Let's have a look at you! Goodness, I wish I had a complexion like yours! I suppose you'll say it's all that Scottish air. Well, there's too much of it for my liking!"

"Oh, Violet, you did not mind my coming, did you?" Davita questioned. "I had nowhere else to go, and I have to find employment of some sort."

"You said in your letter your father was dead. Didn't he leave you anything?" Violet enquired. "What about the Castle?"

"It was . . . mortgaged," Davita said in a small voice,

feeling embarrassed at talking so intimately when there were other people round her.

But the other women were paying no attention, chatting amongst themselves as they continued to apply cosmetics to their faces or were buttoned into their gowns.

The woman who was dressing Violet now produced the most beautiful dress that Davita could possibly imagine.

It swirled out from her tiny waist in elaborate frills ornamented with roses and bows of silk ribbon.

The bodice, however, seemed to Davita almost embarrassingly low, and she thought that if she had to wear such a gown she would feel extremely shy.

Roses decorated the small sleeves and the décolletage, and there were roses, tulle, and feathers on the magnificent hat which the dresser was setting in place on Violet's fair, elaborately arranged hair.

She sat down on a chair in front of the mirror to put it on, and Davita exclaimed:

"How lovely you look, Violet! I am not surprised that people flock to the Theatre to see you."

"And a few others," Violet said, "but wait 'til you see the Show!"

"I would love to do that," Davita answered. "Do you think it would be possible for me to get a seat in the Gallery, or somewhere cheap?"

Violet looked at her as if she were joking. Then she said:

"I'm not having that! Not when you've come all the way from Scotland to see me!"

She thought for a moment. Then she said:

"I know. I'll put you in the Box with Bertie. He ought to be here by now."

"No, no. Please do not trouble," Davita said quickly. "I do not want to be a nuisance to anybody. Perhaps I can wait here until you are ready to leave."

Violet laughed as if she had made a joke.

"If you're suggesting that when I leave here I'll be

going straight home, then that's where you're wrong, Miss Innocent!"

She looked at the dresser who was arranging her hair.

"We don't go home after the Show, do we, Jessie?"

"Might be better if yer did occasionally!" Jessie answered tartly. "All these late nights'll make yer old before yer years, yer mark my words!"

Violet laughed spontaneously, just as she had when she had been in Scotland with Davita.

"I've got a bit of time left to get my 'beauty-sleep,' as you call it," she answered, "when nobody asks me out to supper."

As she spoke, Davita realised that she had been very stupid.

She had somehow thought that when she stayed with Violet they would be together and she would go back with her to her lodgings.

Now she knew that, looking so lovely, Violet would have a "Stage-Door Johnny" waiting to take her to the places her father had mentioned—Romano's or Rules—and there would certainly be no point in her waiting.

"I am sorry, Violet," she said quickly. "I did not mean to be a bother coming here. I will go back and we can talk tomorrow."

"You'll do no such thing!" Violet said.

She turned her face first one way, then the other, looking at her reflection in the mirror. Then she said:

"That's all right, Jessie. Now nip down and find out if Lord Mundesley's in his usual Box, and if he is, ask him to come through the stage-door and speak to me for a moment."

"The Guv'nor don't like gentlemen coming through 'fore the interval!" Jessie said.

"I know he doesn't," Violet replied, "but I've got to introduce His Lordship to my friend, haven't I? Go on, Jessie, and hurry up!"

Jessie flounced off with rather a bad grace and Davita said anxiously:

"Oh, please, Violet, I shall be all right. I can see the Show another night."

"What's the point of waiting?" Violet asked. "Let's have a look at you."

She turned round from contemplating her own reflection to look at Davita.

"Your gown's not bad," she said. "It's a bit dowdy, and it's not right for the evening, but you'll pass."

Her eyes rose a little higher and she said:

"I remember that hat. What have you done with the feathers?"

"It was so kind of your mother to give it to me," Davita said apologetically, "but it looked rather overpowering on me."

"She owed you something, didn't she," Violet said with a touch of humour in her voice, "nipping off like that. Your father must have been a bit upset."

Davita drew in her breath, remembering how dreadfully upset her father had been; in fact, after he'd lost Katie he'd been incapable to cope with life at all.

"Yes, he minded very much," she said in a low voice.

"I'm sorry," Violet said casually, "but after all, she'd never have stuck all that empty space for long. I had a letter from her—it must be three months ago—and she was doing all right."

"On Broadway?" Davita asked curiously.

"No, she was on tour," Violet replied. "I gather she'd left Harry for someone else."

For a moment Davita was too shocked to reply.

It seemed bad enough that Katie should have left her father to go to America with another man, but that she should have already left him seemed both incredible and positively wicked.

Then Davita told herself that she had no right to judge anybody, and she was honest enough to know that Violet was right. Katie could never have stayed in Scotland for long, especially when there had been no money to buy her all the pretty things that she expected.

"Do you really mean you've got no money?" Violet asked suddenly.

"Very little," Davita replied. "My father's Solicitors suggested they might get me a job looking after children in Edinburgh, but I thought I could find something I would like better in London."

"With your looks, you don't want to be cluttering yourself up with other people's children!" Violet said scathingly.

Then she smiled.

"You leave it to me, Davita. I'll look after you and see you have a bit of fun for a change!"

She put out her hand in a slightly protective manner to pat Davita on the arm.

"You gave me a good time when I came to Scotland," she said, "and I'll do the same for you."

There was a sudden rat-tat on the door and a boy's voice called:

"Ten minutes, lidies!"

Violet rose from the chair.

"Where's that Jessie?" she asked.

As she spoke, the dresser came wending her way through the other women towards her.

"You've given him the message?" Violet asked.

"Yus, but yer'll have to hurry if yer're going to see 'im."

"I know! I know!" Violet replied. "Come on, Davita!"

She walked across the room like a ship in full sail and Davita followed her.

They went down the iron staircase, which now seemed even more crowded with people than it had been before.

They greeted Violet admiringly or jokingly.

Then when they reached the Ground Floor, Davita heard Violet speak to somebody and saw that standing just in front of the door that obviously led into the Auditorium was a man in evening-dress.

He looked, she thought at first, very magnificent with

his stiff white shirt and tail-coat, a tall, shiny top-hat on the side of his head.

Then at a second glance she realised that he was older than she had expected. He had heavy moustaches and side-whiskers, and his figure had thickened as if he was approaching middle-age.

However, Davita could see that he was a gentleman, and the voice in which he spoke was cultured, which was made all the more obvious because Violet's voice was, Davita had noticed before, at times slightly common.

"Hullo, Bertie!"

"You sent for me, my fair enchantress," Lord Mundesley replied, "and of course to hear is to obey!"

"I haven't got much time," Violet said quickly, "but this is the daughter of my Stepfather, if you can work that out, and she's just arrived from Scotland and wants to see the Show. She's never been in London before, so look after her for me—and no tricks!"

"I do not know what you mean!" Bertie said in affronted dignity which was obviously assumed.

Then he swept his silk hat from his head and put out his hand.

"How do you do? Perhaps the alluring Violet will introduce us a little more elegantly."

"I expect you'll introduce yourself, Bertie!" Violet said. "This is Davita Kilcraig, whose father was the Baronet my mother married."

"And left!" Lord Mundesley added.

"All right, so she left him," Violet retorted, "but that's none o' your business and it wasn't Davita's fault neither!"

"Of course not," Lord Mundesley agreed.

He was still holding Davita's hand, which made her feel a little embarrassed.

He was about to say something when a boy's strident voice called: "Three minutes, lidies!" and Violet gave a little cry.

"See you after the Show!" she said, and picking up her skirts with both hands ran back up the staircase.

"We had better go to the front of the house," Lord Mundesley said to Davita.

He opened a door for her, and, because he obviously expected it, Davita preceded him down some steps and found herself in the Auditorium of the Theatre.

The noise of the audience seemed to hit her almost like a wave, then there was a kaleidoscope of colour, and, as women passed her being shown to their seats in the Stalls, the fragrance of exotic perfumes.

"This way," Lord Mundesley directed.

Davita climbed a small staircase which was very different from the iron one behind the scenes. The walls were painted in an attractive colour, it was lit with electric light, and there was a thick carpet under her feet.

A moment later she found herself in a Box draped with red velvet curtains and with seats covered in red plush.

Lord Mundesley seated her on his right so that she had the best view of the stage, and he sat in the centre of the Box, picking up a pair of Opera-glasses which rested on the ledge.

Davita stared about her with an excitement that made it impossible to speak.

She had several times been to a Theatre in Edinburgh, but it had been nothing like as large and certainly not as colourful as the scene before her now.

Everything seemed to sparkle, and the crimson and gold of the Boxes, the splendour of the dropped curtain, and the lights were only part of the background for the audience.

Never had she imagined it possible to see so many attractive, beautiful women and distinguished-looking men congregated together in one place.

Then, as she was staring almost open-mouthed at the people being packed into the Stalls, at the Royal Circle filled without an empty seat to be had, and the Gallery sloping up to the ceiling and apparently just as full, the lights were dimmed.

The Orchestra that had been playing softly swelled in

a crescendo until the sound seemed to vibrate through the whole Theatre and become part, Davita thought, of her very breathing.

Then she forgot everything except the excitement of seeing for the first time in her life a Show at the Gaiety.

Because she had of course been interested in what was being produced at the Theatre in which first her Stepmother had played, and then Violet, she knew that the Show she was about to see was called *Cinder-Ellen Up-Too-Late*.

The Lead had originally been played by Nellie Farren, one of the great stars of the Gaiety, but now she had left because she had rheumatic trouble which made it impossible for her to carry on.

The few newspapers that Davita had read in Scotland which reported what was happening in London had all declared what a tragedy it was for the Gaiety that one of the greatest Leading Ladies they had ever known should have been forced to retire.

Hector, who had often seen Nellie when he was in London with her father, had told her with what for him had been fulsome praise of her achievements and her courage.

"Her wouldn'a gi' in wi'out a struggle," he had said to Davita, "an' it'll be awful hard for 'em to find someone to replace her."

"I would like to have seen her," Davita had said, thinking it was something she would never be able to do any more than she would ever see the Gaiety itself.

Yet here she was, watching a new edition of the Show, and she was aware that Lottie Collins, who had been in the Gaiety chorus and was the well-known skipping-rope dancer, had now taken over the Lead.

It was difficult, however, to think of anything but the beauty of the stage-sets and the dancing of the *corps de ballet*.

And of course there was the elegance of Violet and the seven other girls like her as they came onto the stage, looking so exquisitely beautiful that she thought

that every man in the Theatre must fall in love with
them.

Just once when Violet was on the stage, Davita
glanced at Lord Mundesley sitting next to her and
found, to her surprise, that he was looking not at Violet
but at her.

She wanted to tell him how much she was enjoying
herself, but she thought she should not speak, and instead gave him a shy little smile.

Then her eyes went back to the stage.

There was an amazing performance from Fred Leslie,
and Davita was to learn later that he was a unique draw
of the Show.

Then after several dancing-sequences and some very
comic performances, Lottie Collins came onto the stage
dressed in a red gown and a big Gainsborough hat, with
her blonde hair streaming over her shoulders.

She sang softly, almost timidly, it seemed to Davita,
making a great play with a lace handkerchief.

She sang the verse of a song in the manner, although
Davita did not know it, of a Leading Lady in a Light
Opera, quietly, simply, and perhaps rather nervously:

> *"A smart and stylish girl you see,*
> *The Belle of High Society,*
> *Fond of fun as fond could be—*
> *When it's on the strict Q.T.*
> *Not too young, and not too old,*
> *Not too timid, not too bold,*
> *But just the very thing I'm told,*
> *That in your arms you'd like to hold . . ."*

Then suddenly, so suddenly that Davita started, the
chorus crashed out, wildly, boldly, and noisily, and the
first boom was accompanied by the bang of drums and a
terrific crash of cymbals which seemed almost to break
the ear-drums.

Then, with one hand on her hip, the other waving
her handkerchief, Lottie appeared to go mad.

41

Her voice and those of the chorus seemed to grow louder and louder:

"Ta-ra-ra-boom-de-ay,
Ta-ra-ra-boom-de-ay,
Ta-ra-ra-boom-de-ay,
Ta-ra-ra-boom-de-ay!"

The whole Theatre was filled with it, and as her hair streamed the hat bobbed, her short skirts whirled and showed her white petticoats. She was primeval, Bacchic, with all the fury of wild abandon that was associated with a Gypsy dance.

As Davita found it difficult to breathe and impossible even to think, and she could only stare in astonishment, the refrain grew wilder and wilder and the drums, the cymbals, and the wild dancing swept the audience off their feet.

There was a last *"Ta-ra-ra-boom-de-ay"* that finished with the whole audience shouting and applauding, the gentlemen shouting "Bravo! Bravo!" while those in the Gallery were screaming their heads off.

It was not what Davita had expected. It was not anything she could have imagined in her wildest dreams would occur at the Gaiety.

Only as the curtain fell and the applause gradually subsided did she look at the man sitting next to her. His eyes were still on her face and he was smiling as if at her surprise.

Because she felt he was waiting for her to speak, she said in a hesitating little voice:

"I . . . I had no idea . . . that . . . anyone could . . . dance like that."

"Were you shocked?"

"N-not . . . really."

"I think you were," he said with a smile. "Lottie is rather overwhelming when she lets herself go."

"How . . . how can she do that . . . every night?" Davita enquired.

Lord Mundesley gave a laugh.

"That is what acting is all about. Come, let us go and see Violet. We are allowed to go behind during the interval."

He led the way and they had to push through crowds of people moving from their seats and also a number of men who were walking in the same direction as themselves through the small door which led behind the scenes.

It took them some time to climb the staircase, and now in the dressing-room the eight girls who shared it were already holding Court.

Davita noticed there were dozens more bouquets than there had been before the performance began, and each beautiful Gaiety Girl, looking more attractive than the last, was receiving her admirers.

Violet was already talking to two gentlemen when Lord Mundesley and Davita joined her.

"What did you think of the Show?" Violet asked Davita.

Because she did not reply, Lord Mundesley answered for her.

"She was stunned and a little shocked!"

"Shocked?" Violet questioned. "Well, I suppose Lottie would seem a bit of a firebrand to anyone who'd just come off the moors!"

"Of course! Your friend is Scottish!" one of the gentlemen ejaculated. "I should have known it, with that colour hair."

"It's not out of a dye-bottle, if that's what you're insinuating!" Violet said sharply.

"I would never be so ungallant as to suggest anything of the sort!" the gentleman replied.

"I want to talk to Miss Violet alone," Lord Mundesley said in a proprietary manner which made the two gentlemen who were there before him move off to speak to the other girls.

"Bertie, you're being bossy, and I don't like it," Violet complained.

"I only want to ask you if Miss Kilcraig is coming to supper with us," Lord Mundesley said. "In which case, I will have to find somebody to partner her."

"No . . . no, please," Davita said quickly in an embarrassed tone. "You have already been kind enough to let me share your Box, but as soon as the Show is over I will go back to my lodgings."

"There is no reason for you to do that," Lord Mundesley replied. "In fact, I think as this is your first night in London it would be a great mistake. Do you not agree, Violet?"

Davita thought uncomfortably that Violet hesitated a moment before she said:

"Of course! I want Davita to come with us. She's staying with me, isn't she?"

"Very well," Lord Mundesley said. "Shall I ask Tony or Willie?"

Violet glanced at him provocatively, Davita thought, from under her dark, mascaraed eye-lashes before she said:

"How about the Marquis?"

The expression on Lord Mundesley's face changed.

"Do not mention that man to me!"

"I heard his horse had beaten yours today."

"Damn him! That is the third time, and it has made me hate him even more than I did before!"

There was something ferocious in the way Lord Mundesley spoke, and it seemed to Davita to be almost as violent, though in a different way, as the dance she had just witnessed.

Violet laughed.

"Why waste time hating him? He always seems to get the better of you!"

"You are deliberately trying to make me lose my temper!" Lord Mundesley said aggressively. "You know what I feel about Vange."

"Well, for Heaven's sake, don't tell me," Violet said. "I've listened to Rosie crying her eyes out all the afternoon."

"Are you telling me he has broken off with her?"
Lord Mundesley enquired.

"Chucked her out, bag and baggage, from his house
in Chelsea, and told her she was lucky to be able to keep
the jewellery."

"He is intolerable!" Lord Mundesley ejaculated. "I
loathe him, and a great many other people feel the
same."

"Rosie for one!" Violet said. "But it's her own fault for
losing her heart. I told her what he was like when they
first started."

"You were not the only one," Lord Mundesley said.
"Rosie is a silly little fool, but one day I will see that
Vange gets his just deserts. Then we will see who has the
last laugh!"

Davita knew by the expression on Violet's face that
she was about to make some mischievous reply, when
there was a knock on the door and the call-boy's voice
chanting:

"Ten minutes, lidies! Ten minutes!"

There were cries from all the women, and the men
moved towards the door.

Before they had even reached it, the dressers were
undoing the elaborate gowns at the back and a change
of clothing had begun.

Davita gave Violet a smile before she hurriedly followed Lord Mundesley out of the dressing-room and
into the corridor, and only as they reached the Box
again did she say to him:

"Please . . . Lord Mundesley . . . let me go back to
my lodgings afterwards . . . I do not want to be a . . .
nuisance."

"You are certainly not that," Lord Mundesley said,
bending towards her, "and quite frankly, Davita—and I
hope I may call you that—I find it entrancing to watch
you experience for the first time the delights of London."

He paused before he added softly:

"And there are many more delights I want to show you!"

There was something in the way he spoke which made Davita feel shy.

She was not quite certain why, but she thought perhaps it was because he seemed so old, experienced, and worldly-wise, while she was exactly the opposite.

He was obviously Violet's "young man," if that was the right term, and because she had no wish to talk about herself, she asked:

"Who is the gentleman who has made you so cross?"

"The Marquis of Vange!" Lord Mundesley answered. "A most unpleasant character, and a man you must studiously avoid."

"In what way is he so wicked?" Davita asked.

Lord Mundesley smiled.

"That is the right adjective to describe him, and make no mistake, Davita, he is the villain in a plot which is unfolding before your young, innocent eyes! There is, of course, also a hero, and I hope you will realise, my pretty little Scot, that that is the part I wish to play."

Davita stared at Lord Mundesley incredulously, feeling she must have misunderstood what he said.

Then as once again the expression in his eyes made her feel extremely embarrassed, it was a relief when the lights went down and the curtain rose.

CHAPTER THREE

❧

$\mathcal{D}$AVITA LOOKED ABOUT her with a feeling of excitement.
'So this,' she thought, 'is Romano's!'

It was not very far from the Theatre, and, as she had
expected from all her father and Katie had told her, the
moment they were bowed into the Restaurant by a dark,
suave little man who was Romano himself, the atmosphere seemed to be filled with laughter.

It was an oblong room with dark red draped curtains
and plush sofas, and most of the tables were already
filled with women who, like Violet, appeared over-
whelmingly beautiful.

The décolletages of their gowns were extremely low,
their waists so small that a man's two hands could easily
meet round them, and they were as colourful as the
flowers that decked their tables.

Suspended over some tables were blossoms fashioned
like bells which bore the names of famous actresses.

Lord Mundesley was shown to a table for four, and
Davita and Violet sat on the comfortable sofa while the
two men sat opposite them.

Davita realised that Violet was not important enough
to have her name on a flower-bell, but she could see one
on which was emblazoned "Lottie Collins," and two others with "Linda Verner" and "Ethel Blenheim," who
were also stars in *Cinder-Ellen Up-Too-Late*.

Everything was so glamorous that Davita told herself

47

she looked a positive country mouse beside the other women, and a Scottish one at that.

At the same time, she was thrilled at the chance of seeing Romano's and was glad that after so much anticipation she was not disappointed.

People were arriving all the time, and while Lord Mundesley ordered supper, a bottle of champagne in an ice-bucket was brought to their table immediately.

Davita looked round wide-eyed, hoping that if she never had the chance of coming here again, she would always remember what it looked like.

The fourth member of the party was a fair-haired young man who, she thought as they were driving there in Lord Mundesley's very comfortable carriage, seemed rather stupid.

However, she learnt he was the son of a Duke and his name was Lord William Tetherington.

He was obviously very enamoured of Violet and never took his eyes from her as she sat opposite him.

The next table was empty and it remained so until they had almost finished their meal.

Then as Lord Mundesley lit a cigar and sipped a glass of brandy, Romano escorted a tall, dark man to the empty table.

He was alone and therefore sat down on the sofa to look round him in what Davita thought was a somewhat contemptuous way, as if he thought the place was not good enough for him.

At the same time, he was extremely good-looking, and he had an air of authority which Davita somehow expected an important English gentleman would show, even though she had seen very few of them.

Then she realised that while she was staring at the newcomer, Lord Mundesley had stiffened and there was a frown between his eye-brows.

He had been very genial until then, making them laugh and paying Violet extravagant compliments, though at the same time Davita realised he was continually looking at her in a manner which made her feel shy.

Then she heard Lord William say:

"Congratulations, Vange! I thought your horse would win, so I backed it heavily!"

Davita gave a little start.

Now she realised that the newcomer was the Marquis of Vange, whom Lord Mundesley hated so violently and had disparaged several times during supper.

As if the Marquis was suddenly aware of who was at the next table, he replied to Lord William:

"I am afraid you cannot have got a very good price, as it was favourite." Then, turning to Violet, he said: "Good-evening! I was thinking tonight when I watched you on the stage that I have seldom seen you look lovelier!"

"Thank you," Violet replied.

Davita was surprised to see that after all she had said about him, she showed no animosity towards the Marquis, and in fact she gave him her hand and looked at him coquettishly from under her mascaraed eye-lashes.

The Marquis turned towards Lord Mundesley, and, seeing the scowl on his face, he said with a mocking smile:

"I suppose, Mundesley, you expect me to apologise for beating you by a head?"

"I have my own opinions as to how that was possible," Lord Mundesley replied disagreeably.

"Are you suggesting that either I or my jockey was breaking the rules?" the Marquis enquired.

Now there was a hard note in this voice that was unmistakably a challenge.

As if he realised he had gone too far, Lord Mundesley said quickly:

"No, of course not! I was naturally disappointed."

"Naturally!"

There was no doubt, from the expression on the Marquis's face, that he was well aware of Lord Mundesley's feelings.

Then he saw Davita, and she sensed that in some

strange way his eyes took in every detail of her appearance and he was surprised that she was so badly dressed.

A waiter was at his side, waiting for his order, and he turned to take the menu in his hand.

"Damn! He would be sitting next to us!" Lord Mundesley said in a low voice to Violet.

Then, as if he thought he had been indiscreet, he deliberately addressed Lord William in honeyed tones, as if to bridge over the uncomfortable moment.

To Davita it was all rather fascinating and like seeing a play at the Theatre.

As the Marquis sat alone eating his supper and making no effort to speak to them again, it was as if his very presence brought a feeling of constraint to their party.

Violet had just begun to point out some celebrities in the room when an extremely beautiful young woman, whom Davita realised she had seen in the same dressing-room as Violet, crossed the Restaurant to stand beside the Marquis.

For a moment she did not speak. Then as he looked up at her she said:

"I want to talk to you. I *must* talk to you!"

He did not rise to his feet but merely looked up and said quietly but distinctly:

"There is nothing for us to talk about, as you well know."

"I have a lot to say."

She spoke with an hysterical tone in her voice, and Violet bent forward to say to her quietly:

"Please, Rosie, don't be stupid."

Davita realised that this was the Rosie whom Violet had been talking about to Lord Mundesley.

She looked so beautiful that Davita wondered how the Marquis could resist her. But Rosie ignored Violet and said:

"If you won't listen to me, I'm going to kill myself! Do you hear? I'm going to kill myself now—at once! Then perhaps you'll be—sorry!"

As she finished speaking she burst into tears, and as

they ran down her pink-and-white cheeks she repeated brokenly:

"I—I'll kill myself—I'll kill—myself!"

Violet jumped up from her seat and put her arms round Rosie, and as she did so she gave Lord Mundesley a frantic glance, imploring him to help.

"You can't make a scene here!" Violet said. "Come on, Rosie dear, it'll be best if you go home."

"I don't—want to go—home," Rosie tried to protest through her sobs.

But with Violet on one side of her and Lord Mundesley on the other there was nothing she could do but let them draw her away from the table towards the door.

Only as they moved away did Lord Mundesley say over his shoulder:

"Order my carriage, will you, Willie?"

Lord William hurried to obey, and Davita was left alone at the table, wondering if she should follow them but feeling that she would only be in the way.

She was staring at their backs as they moved rather slowly towards the door of the Restaurant, since Rosie was obviously resisting being taken away, when the Marquis remarked:

"I suppose I should apologise."

Davita realised he was speaking to her and turned her head to look at him, her eyes very wide and astonished at what had just taken place.

As if he understood her surprise, he said:

"I can assure you, this is not a usual occurrence at Romano's. I have the idea this is your first visit."

"Yes . . . I only . . . arrived in London . . . to-night."

She thought it would be correct and would show good breeding to speak quite calmly and not to appear upset by what had happened. But her voice sounded very young and breathless.

"Where have you come from?" the Marquis enquired.

"From . . . Scotland."

"Then I can understand that for the moment everything seems strange, but you will get used to it."

He did not sound as though he thought that was a
particularly enviable prospect, and Davita, again trying
to behave normally, replied:

"I have always heard about . . . Romano's . . . and
the . . . Gaiety . . . but they are very much more
. . . exciting than I . . . ever imagined they would
. . . be."

"That, of course, is a matter of opinion," the Marquis
said cynically. "They are certainly the best that London
can provide."

He spoke as if other countries could do better, and
Davita felt that if he disparaged both the Theatre and
the Restaurant, it would somehow spoil it for her. So she
asked:

"Have you had a great deal of . . . success with your
horses this . . . season?"

"I have been lucky," the Marquis replied. "You sound
as if you are interested in racing."

Davita smiled.

"I am afraid I have never seen an important race,
only those that take place in Edinburgh, and the Stee-
ple-Chases which my father sometimes . . . arranged
when he had a good horse."

As she spoke, she thought that the Marquis would
certainly think this was not particularly interesting, and
she added quickly:

"But I think a Thoroughbred is the most beautiful
animal in the world!"

"I agree with you there," the Marquis said, "and from
the way you speak, I presume you enjoy riding."

"Whenever I have the chance," Davita answered. "My
father considered me a good rider, although of course
he may have been prejudiced."

"One could hardly blame him for that."

As the Marquis spoke, Davita thought that he looked
her over in the way a man might take in the good points

of a horse. His eyes seemed to linger for a moment on her hair. Then he said:

"I see your escorts are returning, in which case I will bid you good-night, and hope that you will be sensible enough to return to Scotland as quickly as you can!"

He rose to his feet as he spoke, and Davita was so surprised by what he had said that she could find no words with which to reply.

The Marquis moved away to speak to somebody on the other side of the Restaurant as Violet sat down beside her and Lord Mundesley took the seat opposite.

Davita realised that Lord William was not with them, and, as if she had asked the question aloud, Violet said:

"Willie's taking Rosie home."

"I could have done that," Davita said quickly. "Why did you not send for me?"

"She'll be all right with Willie," Violet replied, and Lord Mundesley added:

"We have no wish to lose you, my pretty little red-haired Scot!"

There was a note in his voice and a look in his eyes which now made Davita feel not only uncomfortable but that in some way she was being disloyal to Violet.

"As we are now three," Lord Mundesley said, "there is room for me to sit between you, which will be much more comfortable, and I shall also be extremely proud to be a thorn between two such exquisite roses!"

Once again Davita felt as if she were taking part in a Theatrical performance and that Lord Mundesley was over-acting.

When he sat between her and Violet she felt as if he encroached on her, and although she tried to squeeze herself away from him, she was very conscious of his closeness.

Once or twice, as if to emphasize what he was saying, he put his hand on her knee and she could feel his fingers through the thin silk of her gown.

It was a relief when Lord William returned.

When he did, he sat down in a chair opposite them and said before anyone could speak:

"I want a drink—and a strong one! I must say, Violet, you make me do some damned uncomfortable things!"

"Is she all right?" Violet asked.

"I left her with Gladys, who lodges in the same building, and she said she would look after her."

"I thought Gladys was away," Violet said, "or I'd have suggested it myself."

"She has just returned," Lord William replied, "but I gather she will not be staying for long. I think Sheffield intends to marry her."

Violet gave a cry of delight.

"Do you mean that? Oh, I *am* glad! It'll be wonderful for Gladys if she pulls that off!"

"Do not count your chickens," Lord Mundesley interrupted. "Sheffield's father will cut him off with the proverbial shilling if he marries an actress."

"If that's true, it's extremely unfair!" Violet said hotly. "After all, Belle married the Earl of Clancarty and they're happy enough."

"After some ups and downs!" Lord Mundesley said.

"Every marriage has them!" Violet snapped. "What we've got to do is to find Rosie a nice husband."

"I can assure you it will not be Vange," Lord William said.

"He's behaved abominably," Violet exclaimed, "but then, he always does!"

"I know what you feel about Vange," Lord William replied, "but if you ask me, he should not have got involved with her in the first place. I know Rosie is beautiful, but the way she went on in the carriage when I was taking her home made me think she is a little unhinged."

"She is a bit hysterical," Violet agreed.

"Well, I cannot see Vange putting up with that sort of thing, and what is more, women, however beautiful, never look their best when they are crying."

"You are quite right," Lord Mundesley agreed. "I like a woman to laugh."

As he spoke, he turned his head to look at Davita and said:

"I expect a great many people have told you that you have a laugh like the chime of silver bells, or perhaps like a little song-bird."

"Nobody has told me that before," Davita replied with a smile, "but I am glad you do not think my laugh is like the sound of a grouse flying down the hill, or like the noise the gulls make when they come in from the sea in bad weather."

"I assure you that everything about you is entrancing!" Lord Mundesley said in a low voice.

Davita felt his knee pressing against hers.

On the drive home, which was very late—in fact it was the early hours of the morning—she found it hard to stay awake.

They did not have a long way to go, but Lord Mundesley insisted on sitting between her and Violet on the back-seat, and to her consternation he put his arms round both of them and said:

"Now, my sweet girls, tell me if you enjoyed this evening and how soon we can repeat it."

"I reckon we ought to take Rosie out with us next time," Violet replied.

Davita had the idea that it was not something she really wanted but was an excuse to exclude herself.

Then she thought that perhaps she was being over-sensitive, but she had noticed a cold note in Violet's voice when they had gone to the cloak-room so that she could collect her wrap before they had left the Restaurant.

"It has been a wonderful, wonderful evening!" Davita had exclaimed.

"I'm glad you've enjoyed yourself," Violet had replied, "but you don't want to believe everything His Lordship tells you."

"No, of course not," Davita had answered, "but it was kind of him to be so polite."

Violet had given her a rather sharp glance and asked:

"Is that what you call it?"

Now as they drove along she suddenly said:

"I've got an idea!"

"What is it?" Lord Mundesley enquired.

"It's a way you can get even with the Marquis, if that's what you want."

"Get even with him?" Lord Mundesley echoed. "I want to knock him down—annihilate him! I would shoot him, if it were not for the thought of facing the hangman."

"Then listen to me . . ." Violet began.

She put her arm round Lord Mundesley's neck to pull his head down so that she could whisper in his ear.

Davita knew she must not listen, so she bent forward, trying to free herself from Lord Mundesley's arm round her waist, and said to Lord William:

"There are so many things I want to see while I am in London that I do not know where to begin."

"I will show you some of them with pleasure," Lord William replied.

"I did not mean that," Davita said quickly. "I was just thinking that it would be very exciting to go sight-seeing, but first I have to find myself some sort of employment."

"Are you thinking of going on the stage with Violet?" Lord William enquired.

Davita shook her head.

"I knew tonight it would be something I could never do. To begin with, I have no talent, and for another, it would frighten me terribly!"

"All you have to do is to look beautiful, and that should not be difficult," Lord William said.

"I have no intention of going on the stage," Davita said firmly. "There must be other things I can do."

"My mother was saying the other day that there are

only two careers open to a lady," Lord William replied, "either to be a Governess or a Companion."

Davita thought that was the same idea that Mr. Stirling had suggested.

"There must be others," she said.

"I expect there are," Lord William said vaguely, "but if you ask me, you would have a far better time if George Edwardes could find a place for you."

Davita felt there was no point in reiterating once again that she had no wish to go on the stage, but before she could speak, Lord Mundesley exclaimed:

"My God, Violet! I believe you have something there! It is certainly an idea!"

"Well, think it over," Violet answered.

As she spoke the horses came to a standstill and Davita saw that they were outside Mrs. Jenkins's tall, dingy house.

"Good-night, Bertie," Violet said to Lord Mundesley, "and thanks! You're always the perfect host, as you well know."

"Good-night, my dear. I will be in touch with you tomorrow, and I will have a word with Boris. He's the man we want for this."

"Yes, of course. The Marquis would never refuse one of the Prince's parties," Violet replied.

So they were back talking once again about the Marquis, Davita thought, as she followed Violet out of the carriage, and she had a feeling, although she could not be sure, that they were plotting something against him.

Lord Mundesley kissed Violet good-night in the small, dark hallway, and Lord William also kissed her on the cheek.

"You have been rather unkind to me this evening," Davita heard him say. "Will you have supper with me tomorrow?"

"I'll think about it," Violet replied.

She looked at Lord Mundesley as she spoke, but he was raising Davita's hand to his lips.

"Good-night, and thank you very, very much," she

said. "It was the most exciting evening I have ever spent."

She did not wait for his reply because when he had kissed her hand she had been half-afraid that he would try to kiss her cheek, and she knew she had no wish for him to touch her.

She had in fact hated the feeling of his lips on her skin.

As she reached the turn in the stairway she looked back to see that Violet had not followed her but was talking to the two men.

She was speaking in a low voice and very earnestly, and both Lord Mundesley and Lord William were listening to her intently.

Davita could not be sure, but she felt that once again they were talking about the Marquis.

'It is ridiculous for them to hate him so violently!' she thought, and remembered how he had advised her to return to Scotland.

It was none of his business, but she went on thinking of what he had said even when she was in bed, and so tired after such a long day that she expected to fall asleep immediately.

Instead, in the darkness she kept seeing the Marquis's handsome face, his cynical, almost contemptuous expression, and that penetrating look in his eyes.

To her surprise, when he had told her to go back to Scotland she had felt as if he was speaking sincerely and was really thinking it was the best thing for her.

Then she told herself quickly that there must be a very good reason for Lord Mundesley and Violet to dislike him so much.

Rosie obviously loved him, and he must have done something to make her fall in love with him so frantically.

Thinking back, Davita remembered Violet saying that the Marquis had turned her out "bag and baggage."

She wondered what that meant and why he should have done such a thing.

Had she been staying with him as his guest? And what had Violet meant when she said the Marquis had remarked that she was lucky to be able to keep the jewellery?

Davita remembered her mother saying that no lady accepted presents from a gentleman unless she was engaged to marry him.

It was then that she understood.

Of course! The Marquis must have asked Rosie to marry him, then perhaps because they had quarrelled the engagement had been broken off.

That was why Violet had said they must find her a husband, and Lord Mundesley had said sarcastically that the one person who would not marry her would be Vange.

It struck Davita that Rosie must have been very stupid to have lost the Marquis once he had asked her to be his wife.

She was well aware that because actresses had such a bad reputation it was unusual for them to marry into the aristocracy.

But it had happened, as when her father had married Katie King, and, as Violet had mentioned this evening, another Gaiety Girl, Belle Bilston, had married Lord Dunlo, who afterwards had become the Earl of Clancarty.

Katie had told her that they lived in Ireland and had twin sons, and she had laughed when she said it.

"That's something your father and I aren't likely to have, so don't worry that you might lose your inheritance."

Davita had assured her at the time that she had not thought of such a thing, and, thinking of it now, she could not help feeling that she would have had a small inheritance indeed if she had had to share the one hundred ninety-nine pounds with twin half-brothers.

Katie had mentioned another Gaiety Girl called Katie Vaughan, who she had said was the biggest star the Gaiety had ever known, and she had married the Honourable Arthur Frederick Wellesley, nephew of the great Duke of Wellington.

"But that marriage," she had said in her gossipy way, "ended upside-down in the Divorce Courts."

'That might have happened to Papa,' Davita thought, 'if he had wanted to re-marry after Katie had left him.'

Instead he had just taken to drink, and she wondered if the Gaiety Girls did in fact make such very good wives.

She was just dropping off to sleep when it seemed she could almost hear the Marquis's voice saying:

"Go back to Scotland!"

※

The next morning Davita awoke at what seemed to her to be a disgracefully late hour, and she sat up staring at the clock beside her bed incredulously to find it was a quarter-to-ten.

'Violet will think I am very lazy,' she thought.

Then she knew she was being foolish because Violet certainly would not yet be awake.

However, she washed herself in the cold water that was in a china ewer in the corner of her tiny room, extracted a day-gown from her trunk, and went downstairs to the kitchen.

Mrs. Jenkins, with her hair in curling-rags, was cooking on the range.

"Good-morning, Mrs. Jenkins," Davita said.

"I suppose you're looking for breakfast," Mrs. Jenkins replied. "Well, yer're a bit early, but I'll see wot I can do."

"Early!" Davita exclaimed.

Mrs. Jenkins laughed.

"Those as come 'ere from the country all starts by appearing at the crack o' dawn. Then they soon gets into the Theatre ways. Yer'll find yer friend Violet won't open her blue eyes 'til after noon, and then only if she's lunching with one o' the 'Nobs.' "

"I would love some breakfast, if it is no trouble," Davita said. "I am hungry."

"Then sit down and I'll fry yer some eggs," Mrs. Jenkins said. "Yer'll find a pot of tea on the stove. There's a cup and saucer in the cupboard."

Davita fetched the cup and saucer, poured the tea out of the brown china pot, and found that it was so strong that it would be impossible to drink it unless she added some hot water.

Fortunately, there was also a kettle boiling with which to dilute what seemed more like stew than ordinary tea, and in a cupboard she found a jug filled with very thin, watery-looking milk.

Because she was genuinely hungry and had drunk very little champagne last night, she ate a hearty breakfast for which she thanked Mrs. Jenkins profusely.

"Don't thank me," the Landlady replied, "yer're payin' for it, as yer'll find when you gets the bill at the end o' the week!"

She thought there was a frightened expression in Davita's eyes, and added kindly:

"Now don't yer fret yerself, child. I'll not over-charge yer. And one day yer might find yerself in the lead an' drawing two hundred pounds a week like Lottie Collins."

"Two hundred pounds a week!" Davita exclaimed.

She began to think that perhaps she was being stupid about not going on the stage. Then she remembered Lottie Collins's performance, and knew that Lord Mundesley had been right. It had indeed shocked her!

Even though she was acting, for a woman to appear so abandoned, so out of control, had made her feel ashamed.

She knew in her heart that she wanted to be like her mother, soft, sweet, feminine, and at the same time intelligent and able to do almost anything well.

That was not to say that riding, fishing, shooting, and making a house a happy place were accomplishments for which anyone would employ her.

Then uncomfortably she knew the answer.

What her mother had been was a very accomplished wife, and Mr. Stirling had been right when he had said she ought to get married.

'Perhaps I shall meet someone here in London,' she thought, and knew, although she had no reason for thinking so, that it was unlikely.

She was quite sure that whatever Katie might have said about Gaiety Girls getting married, the men she had seen last night were out to enjoy themselves and were not looking for a wife amongst the glamorous, lovely actresses they escorted to Romano's.

They were fascinated, amused, and certainly entertained by the charmers sitting under the flowery bells inscribed with their names, or leaning towards them across the table in a manner which made the lowness of their elaborate gowns seem somewhat immodest. But that did not mean marriage.

"Besides," Davita said to herself, "if I married into that sort of life, I would be like a fish out of water."

As if it was something somebody had said aloud, she knew she would never marry any man unless she loved him.

When Lord Mundesley had put his arm round her she had felt a little shiver of distaste go through her, and when he had kissed her hand good-night she had wanted to snatch it away from him.

Why did she feel like that, when he had been far more affectionate towards Violet and had kissed her on the lips?

Davita shuddered as she thought of how unpleasant it would be to feel his mouth touch hers, and she told herself, although she knew it was very stupid, that she hoped she would never see him again.

'I will have to find out about a Domestic Bureau today,' she thought, and said aloud to Mrs. Jenkins:

"Is there a Domestic Bureau near here where employers engage staff?"

Mrs. Jenkins turned from the stove to ask:

"What do yer want a Domestic Bureau for?"

"I have to find myself some work, Mrs. Jenkins."

"Yer mean yer're not planning to go on the stage like yer friend?"

Davita shook her head. Then she said anxiously:

"You would not refuse to keep me because I have said that? I know you only take Theatrical people, but I am very happy here with you."

"Don't fret yerself," Mrs. Jenkins replied. "I'll not turn yer away. I can see yer're a lidy without knowing who yer father was. But wot sort of work was yer planning on gettin'?"

"I really do not know," Davita replied. "It is . . . difficult. I have no experience and everything I have been taught seems particularly unsaleable."

She thought Mrs. Jenkins looked at her in a rather strange way before she replied:

"Perhaps Violet'll 'ave some ideas on the subject. She can look after 'erself, that one can!"

"She is so beautiful," Davita said. "I can understand her getting good parts in the Theatre, even if she does not act."

Mrs. Jenkins did not reply but returned to her cooking, and Davita went on as if following the train of her thoughts:

'Perhaps she will get married . . .'

She stopped as she thought she had been very stupid.

Of course Violet would marry Lord Mundesley!

She had made it very clear that he belonged to her, and he certainly had behaved in a very possessive manner. Why otherwise should she have kissed him?

"You see, Mrs. Jenkins," she said, "if Violet gets married, then I should have to find someone else to be with, and . . ."

"What makes yer think she's likely to be married?" Mrs. Jenkins interrupted.

"I was thinking that perhaps she is secretly engaged, although she has . . . not told me so, to Lord Mundesley."

Mrs. Jenkins gave a short laugh without much humour in it.

"Now yer're barking up the wrong tree," she said. " 'Ow d'yer expect Violet to marry Lord Mundesley, when he's married already!"

✿✿✿

Later that day, when she was shopping with Violet, who was ordering herself a new gown and a hat to go with it, Davita told herself that she had been very stupid.

It had never struck her for one moment that Lord Mundesley, and perhaps a great number of other men amongst those she had seen last night, were enjoying themselves without the company of their wives.

She supposed she was ignorant in such matters because her father and mother had always been so happy together, and it had never entered her head that there could be anyone else in their lives.

Her first feeling had been one of indignation that Lord Mundesley should behave as he did, kissing Violet and flattering her when he had a wife all the time.

Then she felt very lost and ignorant and even more afraid of the glittering world in which she found herself than she had been before. She wondered if Lord William was a married man, or the Marquis.

But if the Marquis was married he could not have been engaged to Rosie. In which case, why had he invited her to stay in his house in Chelsea, then turned her out?

It all seemed incomprehensible, and although Davita longed to ask Violet a lot of questions, she felt it was impertinent and she might resent it.

So instead she tried to concentrate on the gown which Violet was choosing in what seemed to Davita a large and impressive shop in Regent Street.

Finally when Violet was satisfied that she had found what she wanted, she ordered some alterations to be made and insisted that the dressmaker added more lace and ribbon to the already elaborate dress.

Only when she had finished did Davita ask:

"What are we going to do now?"

"We'll have some tea at Gunters in Berkeley Square," Violet answered, "and while you're enjoying one of the best ice-creams you've ever tasted in your life, I want to talk to you."

She spoke in a mysterious manner which made Davita look at her apprehensively, but she did not say anything as Violet, dressed once again in her own gown, pinned her hat covered in flowers on her fair hair with jewelled hat-pins and picked up her handbag.

"The gown will be ready tomorrow afternoon, Ma'am," the dressmaker promised, "and may I add that it is always a great pleasure to have the privilege of dressing you, Miss Lock."

"Thank you," Violet replied.

"I went to the Gaiety the other night for the fifth time! I thought you looked wonderful, you really did!"

"Thank you."

"Shall I send the gown to the same address?" the dressmaker enquired.

"Yes, please."

"And the bill as usual to Lord Mundesley?"

Violet nodded.

As they walked away, Davita felt as though somebody had struck her a sharp blow on the head.

The person who was paying for the gown was Lord Mundesley, who was a married man, and Davita was certain that the bill would be astronomical.

It was something that would have shocked her mother considerably, and Davita was not quite certain whether she should tell Violet she thought it wrong, or say nothing.

Then she remembered the bills her father had run up, which she had found after he had died.

Of course the gowns and dozens of other things he

had ordered had been for Katie, whom he had married, which was a very different thing.

But even that was wrong, for a man to dress a woman before she was actually his wife.

'I wish somebody could explain it to me,' Davita thought unhappily.

Then she told herself it was something that need not concern her, as long as she behaved in a way that she knew was right and of which her mother would have approved.

They drove in a hackney-carriage to Berkeley Square, where on one corner of Hay Hill was a bow-fronted shop filled with small tables.

It was quite early in the afternoon, but there were a number of people already seated, and when Violet had ordered two strawberry ice-creams Davita understood why.

They were more delicious than anything she had ever eaten, and when she said so, Violet smiled at her enthusiasm.

"I thought you'd enjoy them, and now it's time to have a little chat. I want to have a rest before I go to the Theatre, and if we start talking then, I shan't get a chance of some shut-eye."

"What do you want to talk to me about?" Davita asked.

"Yourself," Violet said. "You told me you came here to get some work, and I'd like to know what your father left you."

"Exactly one hundred ninety-nine pounds, ten shillings!" Davita answered. "But out of that I had to pay my fare to London, so it will not last forever."

"You're not carrying it with you?" Violet asked.

"I would not be so stupid as that. I put most of it in the Bank, and I have a cheque-book of my own!"

"A cheque-book's all right," Violet remarked, "but the Bank-balance is nothing to write home about it; it's got to last you to your old age."

"That is what worries me," Davita said, "and now you

understand why I have to find something to do, and quickly."

"I don't mind telling you it's what I suspected," Violet said. "Ma always was extravagant and I guessed she'd clean your father out before she left him."

"Why did you think that?" Davita asked.

She had the awful feeling that Violet was about to say: "because she always did," but instead there was an uncomfortable silence until Violet replied:

"I just knew your father wasn't a rich man."

Davita ate a spoonful of the ice-cream before she said in a low voice:

"Everything had to be sold, and all I possess is now in my two trunks."

"I don't suppose that's worth much, judging from the wardrobe I've seen so far," Violet remarked.

Davita flushed.

She was not going to explain that the dress she was wearing had been her mother's.

She knew only too well how dowdy it must appear to Violet, in her fashionable, expensive clothes which had been paid for by Lord Mundesley.

"Now if you ask me," Violet was saying, "you've as much hope of finding anyone to employ you as flying over the moon. You are too young, for one thing, and for another it'd be just sheer waste of your looks."

Davita stared at her in surprise, and she said almost angrily:

"Come on, Davita! Don't play the idiot with me! You're as aware as I am that with your red hair and your baby-face, most men are ready to fall flat at the sight of you."

"I am sure that is not true."

"It's too true for my liking," Violet said somewhat tartly, "but never mind that. What I want to do is to set you up one way or another, either with marriage, which is difficult, or with money, which is easier."

"What . . . do you mean . . . easy?" Davita enquired.

"I'm not going to say too much now," Violet said, "but I want you to promise to trust me and leave me to look after you."

She paused before she went on:

"I'm fond of you, Davita. You know as much about life as a chicken that's just popped out of the egg. But as there's no-one else, it's got to be me!"

"I do not wish to be a nuisance to you."

"I know that," Violet answered, "but it's my duty to see that you aren't reduced to the same state as Rosie."

Davita stiffened.

"I hope I never behave in such an uncontrolled manner," she said, "but I was very, very sorry for her."

"She only had herself to blame," Violet replied. "She's the whining, complaining, possessive sort, which would bore any man after he'd got used to her face."

Davita thought that was rather hard, but she said nothing, and Violet went on:

"Now, you're different. That young spring-like look would charm the wisest old pigeon off the tree. But if it's my pigeon, it's something I've got to prevent."

"I do not . . . understand."

"That's all the better!" Violet replied. "What you've got to do is promise me that whatever happens, you'll do what I tell you and say nothing I wouldn't want you to say in front of other people."

Davita continued to look puzzled and Violet went on:

"What I'm asking you to do is to believe that I'm doing everything in my power that's in your best interests. Is that clear?"

"Y-yes . . . of course . . . I am very grateful," Davita answered. "It is just that I do not . . . understand . . ."

"You don't have to," Violet said.

She put up her hand to call the waiter.

"Come on, I must go home now or I'll look hideous, and we are going to a party."

"A party?" Davita exclaimed.

"Yes, a really good one given by a friend of mine, and you'll enjoy it. Have you got a decent evening-gown?"

"I do not know what you would think of it," Davita answered.

"What's wrong with it?"

"Nothing . . . it is . . . white."

"White?"

"It was my mother's wedding-gown, which she altered and sometimes wore on special occasions."

"Well, that's exactly what you want," Violet exclaimed. "A wedding-gown. It couldn't be more suitable!"

CHAPTER FOUR

THEY DROVE BACK to their lodgings, and while Davita was longing to ask Violet a hundred questions, she had the feeling that she would not answer them.

At the same time, she was very touched that Violet should be so concerned for her.

After all, she was well aware that she was somewhat of an encumbrance, and she told herself that she must try to find a job on her own and not impose on Violet.

'She is right,' Davita thought, 'I am ignorant of the world, but how could I be anything else after living in Scotland and seeing so few people?'

Of one thing she was determined—she would not be critical of Violet or her friends.

It was nothing to do with her if Violet liked to be

friends with a married man, and even less her concern
that they should hate the Marquis and plot against him.

When she thought of last night, it seemed to her a
whirligig of colour, noise, and laughter. At the same
time, the Show itself had been an excitement which she
felt she would always remember.

The glamorous actresses, the beauty of the girls like
Violet, and the laughter evoked by Fred Lacey were all
like something out of a dream.

"Goodness, I'm tired!" Violet said suddenly, breaking
in on her thoughts. "It's all these late nights. Thank
goodness I can get nearly two hours' sleep before we
have to go to the Theatre."

"Am I to come with you?" Davita asked.

"Of course you are!" Violet said. "You can sit in the
dressing-room—or, if you wish, in the Box with Bertie."

There was just a pause before the last few words, and
Davita said quickly:

"I will sit in the dressing-room. After all, I saw the
Show last night."

She thought Violet seemed relieved, and she certainly
smiled before she said:

"You're a sensible girl, Davita. The trouble is, you're
not only pretty but something new, and there's not a
man alive who doesn't like a novelty."

Davita looked at her in surprise, not understanding
what she was talking about, but because she wanted to
please Violet she said:

"I am so grateful to you for being so kind to me. If
you had sent me away last night, I do not know what I
should have done."

"Leave everything to me," Violet said in a brisk tone.
"I've said I'll look after you and I will."

The cab drew up outside their lodgings, Violet paid
the cabby, and Billy opened the door to them to say with
a grin:

"There be some flowers oopstairs for yer. No guesses
who sent 'em!"

"I've told you before not to read the cards on my flowers," Violet said sharply.

"Oi didn't 'ave to," Billy answered. " 'Is Nibs sent 'is footlicker wi' 'em!"

He spoke as if he was glad to score off Violet, but she merely tossed her head as if he were beneath her notice and went up the stairs.

Davita followed her and Violet opened the door of her bedroom, which was a large, well-decorated room at least six times the size of Davita's.

Inside there was a basket of purple orchids that made her exclaim with astonishment:

"I have never seen anything so exotic!"

There were several other floral arrangements in the room, which Davita could not help thinking looked very different from the rest of the house.

The large bed had a pink satin cover on it trimmed with lace which matched the pillow-cases, and there were a number of satin cushions on the *chaise-longue* and on two comfortable arm-chairs arranged on either side of the fireplace.

There were white fur rugs on the floor, and the tas-selled pink silk curtains were very different from the roughly made Holland ones which covered the windows of Davita's room.

What made it different from any other bedroom Davita had ever seen were the photographs which were arranged on the mantelshelf, the dressing-table, and on every other piece of furniture.

Stuck on the wall on each side of the mantelpiece were press-cuttings.

These of course all referred to Violet, and the photographs were mostly of her, although some of them were of other actresses, and one or two of men.

They were all signed, and Davita thought she would enjoy looking at them when there was time.

But Violet said now:

"Undo my gown for me, and the quicker I can get

between the sheets, the better. I forgot to tell Billy to knock on my door at five-thirty. Will you remind him?"

"Yes, of course I will," Davita replied as she undid Violet's gown.

She hung it up in the wardrobe, and by the time she had put away her hat, Violet had covered her hair with a net to keep it tidy, slipped into her nightgown, and was in bed.

Davita drew the curtains and as she left the room she fancied that Violet was already asleep.

She thought she would go into her own room and take off her bonnet.

Then when she opened the door she had a shock, for perched on top of one of her trunks, because there was nowhere else to put it, was a basket nearly as large as the one in Violet's room, but instead of orchids it was filled with white roses and lilies.

She was staring at it in astonishment, thinking it must really have been meant for Violet, until seeing the card attached to the handle she pulled it off and read:

To a very bonny lassie from a most admiring
Mundesley

Davita drew in her breath.

It struck her that Violet would be annoyed at Lord Mundesley spending so much money and paying so much attention to her.

She looked at the card, read it again, and wished it was possible to send the flowers back without Violet being aware that he had given them to her.

'I shall have to thank him,' she thought, and she wished again, as she had last night, that she need not see him again.

Then she remembered Violet's message and hurried down the stairs to find Billy.

She reached the last flight and saw him speaking to somebody at the front door. As she came down into the Hall, she could see that it was a servant in livery.

Billy turned round and saw her.

"Ah, t'ere y' are, Miss. Oi were comin' to find yer."

"I was coming to find you," Davita replied. "Miss Lock says please remember to knock on her foor at five-thirty."

"Oi'll not forget," Billy answered. "An' t'ere's some-un 'ere as wants t' speak t' yer."

"Speak to me?" Davita questioned in surprise.

She saw that the servant was no longer standing in the doorway but was outside in the street where there was a closed brougham.

"Who is it?" she asked.

"Oi were just told 'twas a gent'man as wants to 'ave a word wiv yer."

Davita stood irresolute.

It would only be one of two gentlemen, and if it was Lord Mundesley she had no wish to speak to him.

Yet she knew it would be rude to refuse, and it flashed through her mind that while she must thank him for the flowers, she would ask him not to send her any more.

Billy was holding the door open for her, and she walked down the steps and across the pavement to where a footman was standing with his hand on the carriage-door.

When she reached it he opened it, and Davita could see, as she had feared, Lord Mundesley sitting inside.

He bent forward and held out his hand.

"Get in, Davita. I want to speak to you."

"I was just . . . going to . . . lie down."

"I will not keep you long."

Because she did not know what else she could do, Davita put her hand in his to let him draw her into the carriage. As she sat down beside him, the horses started to move and she asked:

"Where are you taking me? I really have to go back."

"We are merely moving a little farther up the road so that we can talk without being observed," Lord Mundesley replied.

She knew without his putting it into words that what he meant was so that Violet would not see them.

He was looking very smart with a carnation in his button-hole and a large pearl tie-pin in his cravat. He also seemed large and overpowering, and the way he was looking at her made Davita feel shy.

Because she was nervous she said quickly:

"I must . . . thank you. It was very kind of you to send me those . . . beautiful flowers. At the same time, I want to ask you . . . not to send me any . . . more."

She thought he might ask her why, but instead he said:

"Are you afraid Violet will be jealous? That is something I wish to talk to you about."

As she spoke, the horses came to a standstill. Davita now realised he had been truthful when he had said they would only go a little way up the street, and she asked more calmly:

"What do you want to talk to me about?"

"The answer to that is quite simple," Lord Mundesley said. "You, and of course myself."

Davita looked at him in surprise and he said:

"You must be aware, my lovely little Scot, that you captivated me from the moment I set eyes on you, and I have a proposition to make."

"A . . . p-proposition?" Davita stammered.

Although Lord Mundesley had not moved while he was speaking, she felt, as she had last night, that he was encroaching on her and instinctively she moved as far as she could away from him to the farther corner of the carriage.

Even so, he still seemed unpleasantly near.

"I understand from Violet," Lord Mundesley went on, "that you have come to London in search of employment. Although I could quite easily arrange for George Edwardes to find you a place at the Gaiety, I do not think you are really suited for a life on the stage."

Davita gave a little sigh of relief, thinking her apprehension had been quite unnecessary and Lord

Mundesley was in fact trying to help her in a practical manner.

She turned her face to him eagerly.

"I am so glad you said that, because not only am I quite certain that I would be a failure if I went on the stage, but it is not the sort of life I would like, and Mama would have disapproved."

"Your mother is dead," Lord Mundesley said, "so whether she approves or disapproves of what you do is not likely to concern us."

Davita was puzzled.

She did not understand why he should say such a thing.

"At the same time," Lord Mundesley continued, "your mother would, I am sure, not wish you to endure a life of hardship or have none of the luxuries and comforts to which anybody as pretty as you is entitled."

He paused, and as Davita did not speak he went on:

"What I want to suggest to you, Davita, is that you let me look after you. You will find me a kind and generous man, and I think we could be very happy together."

Davita's eyes opened so wide that they seemed to fill her whole face. Then she asked in a voice that was barely audible:

"What are you . . . suggesting . . . what are you . . . s-saying?"

"I am saying, my dear, that I will give you a comfortable little house in Chelsea, all the beautiful gowns you want, and a great number of other things that will make you happy."

For a moment Davita found it hard to breathe, for she was so shocked and horrified at what he had suggested.

Then as she opened her lips to speak, Lord Mundesley put out his arms and drew her against him.

At his touch she started to struggle violently.

"No! No!" she cried. "How can you think of . . . anything so wrong . . . so wicked? You are a . . . married man, and what you are . . . suggesting is a . . . sin against your wife . . . and God."

She was so vehement that now it was Lord Mundesley's turn to be surprised.

He still had his arm round her, but there was an astonished expression on his face as she tried to push him away from her.

"Now listen to me, Davita . . ." he began, but with a sound that was almost a scream Davita interrupted:

"I will not . . . listen! Let me . . . go! I do not . . . want to hear any . . . more!"

She twisted herself from him, bent forward to open the carriage-door, and sprang out into the road, so intent on escaping that she did not realise that Lord Mundesley was making no effort to stop her.

Then she was running down the pavement towards the door of her lodgings, and when she got there she found to her relief that the door was open as Billy was just taking in a parcel that had arrived from a trades-man.

Davita ran past Billy and pounded up the stairs as if all the devils of hell were at her heels.

When she reached her own room on the Second Floor, she rushed in, slammed the door behind her, locked it, and, edging her way round her trunks, threw herself down on the bed.

"How . . . dare . . . he? How . . . dare he . . . suggest such a . . . thing!" she panted.

Her heart was beating suffocatingly, and as she ran away from Lord Mundesley her bonnet had fallen from her head and was suspended by the ribbons which had been tied under her chin.

She flung her bonnet on the floor and lay face-down-wards, her face in the pillow.

So that was how men behaved in London! Now she understood not only what Lord Mundesley was suggesting to her, but what had happened to Rosie.

How could she have known, how could she have guessed, that Rosie had been the Marquis's mistress and he had thrown her out "bag and baggage" not because they were engaged to be married but because she was a woman for whom he had no further use.

It was so shocking, so degrading, and Davita had never imagined she would come in contact with anything so evil.

She had vaguely known that there were women who in the words of the Bible "committed adultery" and to whom nobody respectable would speak.

There had been a girl in the village who had run away with a Piper who was married and could not marry her.

Davita had heard the servants talking about her, and when she asked her mother what had happened, she had explained gently and carefully that the girl had lost the love and respect of her parents and of everybody else.

"Why should she do such a thing, Mama?" Davita had asked.

"Because she was tempted," her mother had replied.

"I do not understand," Davita had protested, "why she should want to be with a man who cannot marry her."

"These things happen, dearest," her mother had said, "but I do not want you to think about it now. It is something which is best forgotten."

But because the servants had not forgotten and had gone on talking about Jeannie, it had been impossible for Davita not to be curious.

"I always knew she would come to no good," she could hear them saying to one another. "She'll rue the day she trusted a man who'd throw her aside when he's had all he wants of her."

Davita wondered what he had wanted, but she knew if she asked questions nobody would explain.

She heard two years later that Jeannie had had a baby and, having been deserted by the Piper, had drowned herself and the child.

It was then that she had exclaimed to her mother:

"How could such a terrible thing happen? And why did Jeannie not come home?"

"If she had, they would not have let her in," her mother had replied.

"So you mean that her father and mother would have let her starve?"

"It is something I would never be able to do myself," her mother had admitted, "but I know Jeannie's parents. They are respected members of the Kirk and very strait-laced. They would never forgive their daughter for bringing disgrace upon them."

Davita tried to understand. At the same time, because Jeannie had been young and attractive, she felt it was a terrible thing that she should kill herself and her baby and that no-one should be sorry that she had done so.

Now she thought with a kind of terror that that might happen to her.

How could a gentleman like Lord Mundesley suggest that he should give her a house in Chelsea, and that while he had a wife somewhere else, she should live with him and be his mistress?

It was a degradation she had never imagined for one moment would ever be suggested to her, and she thought how shocked her father and mother would be if they knew.

She was sure that her father, if he were alive, would be prepared to knock Lord Mundesley down because he had insulted her.

Then suddenly she stiffened as she thought of the way Lord Mundesley had spoken to Violet and how he had kissed her good-night.

Could it be possible that Violet was already his mistress?

Then she told herself with a feeling of relief that the answer to that idea was "no."

If she was, Violet would not be living here but in Chelsea, and although he might have suggested it to her, Violet had obviously refused.

The feeling of relief was like a warm wave sweeping through Davita and clearing away the feeling of shock.

Violet was a good girl. Violet would not, Davita was sure, contemplate anything so wicked.

Then why had Lord Mundesley suggested such a thing to her after knowing her for such a short time?

She could not understand, except perhaps that Violet, intending to be kind, had painted such a bleak picture of her future with no money and no job that he had made the suggestion because in his own way he wanted to be kind.

Davita could still feel his arms pulling her against him, and she had the feeling that if she had not struggled, he might have kissed her.

"I hate him!" she said aloud, and knew there was something unpleasant about him that was difficult to put into words.

'I shall never see him again!' she thought.

Then she knew that she would have to do so if she went to the party tonight.

"I will stay here. I will stay at home," she decided firmly, and got up from the bed to pick up her bonnet and put it tidily away.

Then as she did so she realised that if she told Violet she was not going to the party with her as they had planned, she would have to give a very good explanation as to why she had changed her mind.

What could she say that would not upset Violet?

It was obvious, although she had not said so, that Violet thought Lord Mundesley was her admirer and in a way her property.

Looking back, Davita could remember dozens of little words and gestures that proclaimed all too clearly that Lord Mundesley had devoted himself to Violet.

Now, disloyal and unfaithful—although that was hardly the right description considering that he was married—he was ready to transfer his affections to her.

'I cannot tell Violet that!' Davita thought in a panic. 'It would upset her, and she has been so kind to me.'

She looked round the tiny room, feeling as if the walls whirled round her as she tried to think what she could say and what she could do.

Then she knew, almost as if somebody was saying it aloud, that it would be extremely unkind if she let Violet know what had happened.

'Sooner or later she will find out for herself what he is like,' Davita thought, 'but I must not be the person to tell her so.'

She sat down on her bed and tried to think clearly and she sent up a prayer to her mother for help.

"I am in a mess, Mama," she said. "Tell me what I should do. Tell me how I can avoid Lord Mundesley without hurting Violet, who has been kind . . . very, very kind."

She almost expected to hear her mother answer, and gradually a plan came to her mind.

She would have to go to the party tonight rather than make Violet suspicious, and she was quite sure that Lord Mundesley would not tell Violet what he had suggested.

Tomorrow, first thing, she would go to a Domestic Bureau and take a job, any job that she was offered.

Davita gave a little sigh.

"I am sure that is the right thing to do," she told herself.

It was reassuring to think that if her first job was an unpleasant one, she had enough money to support herself while she waited for another.

The idea that she would be alone and frightened came insidiously into her mind, but she swept it aside.

The only thing that mattered now was to get away from Lord Mundesley.

"Once I am gone, he will think only of Violet again, and if I do not give her my address there will be no chance of his trying to get in touch with me," Davita decided.

To her surprise, she found herself wishing she could ask the Marquis to advise her. She had thought of him during the night and how handsome he had looked despite his cynical and contemptuous air.

He had told her to go back to Scotland, and he had been right: that was what she ought to do.

Perhaps he had guessed that Lord Mundesley or some other man like him would make such horrible suggestions to her simply because she was with the Gaiety Girls.

"He was right, absolutely right. I should not be here," Davita said to herself.

Because she was upset and still shocked by what had happened, when a little later she went to do up Violet's gown before they went to the Theatre, the latter exclaimed:

"You look very pale, Davita! It must be your gown, but I should have thought white would have suited you with your red hair."

"I think I am just a little tired," Davita replied. "Is this gown all right?"

Violet turned to look at her.

"It's really rather pretty in its own way."

Davita herself had always thought it very lovely.

It was made of Brussels lace and her mother had always told her that because it had come from the best shop in Edinburgh, it had caused a sensation at home in the Western Isles when she had worn it to marry Sir Iain Kilcraig.

"They had never seen anything like it, Davita," she had said with a smile, "and neither had I. My Godmother gave it to me because she was so pleased I was marrying such a distinguished man, and when it arrived a week before my marriage, people came from all over the island to look at it!"

"You must have looked lovely on your wedding-day, Mama," Davita had remarked.

"If I looked lovely it was not because of the gown," her mother had answered, "but because I was so happy. I loved your father, Davita, and he was and is the most handsome man I have ever known."

The lace had a fragility about it, and to Davita it had an almost fairy-like loveliness that made her feel like a Princess in a fairy-story.

It was the first time she had had the opportunity of wearing it, and she felt, because it revealed her neck and white shoulders, that for the first time she was really grown-up.

"I must behave as though I am," she admonished herself, "and not allow Lord Mundesley to upset me!"

It was an easy thing to say, but when after the Show was over she followed Violet downstairs to where he was waiting at the stage-door to escort them to his carriage, she felt a quiver of fear inside her and knew it was impossible to look at him.

Lord Mundesley, however, was completely at his ease.

"Violet, you look more adorable than usual!" he said as he kissed her hand.

"Why didn't you come round at the interval, Bertie?" Violet asked.

"I had some friends to see," Lord Mundesley replied, "and although they wanted to meet you, I wished to keep you to myself."

The way he spoke made Davita think he was deliberately warning her that he was ready to reassure Violet that he belonged to her if she had by any chance tried to make trouble.

She longed to tell him that she would not lower herself to do anything so unkind or spiteful, but she knew that the only dignified way to behave was to ignore what had happened, and she therefore said nothing.

As they drove away from the Theatre, Lord Mundesley made no effort to sit between them as he had the night before, but sat on the seat opposite.

Nevertheless, Davita, without even looking in his direction, was aware that his eyes were on her face and she turned deliberately to look out the window.

"Everything's arranged, is it?" Violet asked.

"You can be sure of that," Lord Mundesley replied,

"and Boris thought it a huge joke, as I thought he would."

"You are sure that 'You-Know-Who' will turn up?"

"I am sure of it. He intends to discuss the sale of a couple of horses with Boris, and they are bound to have a somewhat spirited argument over the price."

Violet gave a little laugh.

"Horses are always more irresistible than a woman!"

"But not where I am concerned," Lord Mundesley said with a caressing note in his voice. "You look very beautiful tonight. That gown certainly becomes you."

"I'm glad you like it," Violet replied. "I bought it especially for you."

'And he paid for it!' Davita added in her mind, but told herself it was vulgar even to think such things.

She wished she were not going to the party. She wished almost wildly that she were back in Scotland.

Then she told herself with a sudden pride that she would not let Lord Mundesley's infamy defeat or depress her.

This was an adventure, and only if things became too unbearable would she surrender to the inevitable and return to Scotland.

"Davita's wearing her mother's wedding-dress," Violet said unexpectedly.

Lord Mundesley gave a short laugh.

"If there is one thing I love about you, Violet, it is your sense of humour."

"But it's true!" Violet objected.

Lord Mundesley laughed again and Davita thought he was laughing at her mother, and hated him more violently than she had before.

She wished there was a way in which she could warn Violet that he was a man to be avoided.

"Here we are!" Violet exclaimed a little while later. "I can't understand how the Prince when he comes to London always manages to rent the largest and finest houses."

"He managed it because he can afford it," Lord

Mundesley answered. "He is paying an enormous rent for this house which he has taken over for the Season. In fact, the Duke said the offer was so astronomical that he could not afford to refuse."

"Well, quite frankly," Violet said, "I'm looking forward to seeing the inside of Uxminster House. All the Duke would be likely to offer me is the outside of his front door!"

Lord Mundesley laughed.

"That is true enough. Uxminster is a dull old fossil. No Gaiety Girls for him!"

"Well, thank goodness the Prince is different!" Violet said as the carriage-door was opened and she stepped out into a blaze of light.

Uxminster House was certainly very impressive as they walked up a red-carpeted staircase to the First Floor, and Davita was glad that she had come after all.

This was the sort of house she had always hoped she would see in London, with family portraits and tapestries on the walls, and huge crystal chandeliers sparkling in the light of hundreds of candles.

To her surprise, they were not shown by a very smartly liveried servant into a room on the First Floor which she could see through an open door was large and extremely impressive.

Instead, they were taken along a corridor and shown at the end of it into a smaller room where they were greeted by their host.

The Prince was a middle-aged Russian, distinguished, bearded, with twinkling dark eyes, and as Davita looked about her it seemed to her almost as if she were back in Romano's again.

The room was massed with flowers, but far more glamorous than any blossoms were the guests, some of whom she recognised as having come from the Gaiety as she and Violet had.

Lottie Collins was there and several other Leading Actresses, all flashing with jewels and wearing gowns that were as spectacular as those that they had worn on stage.

As the evening wore on, Leading Ladies from other Theatres, many of whose names Davita recognised, although not their faces, arrived for the party.

Champagne was being handed round, and about twenty minutes after they had arrived they went into a Dining-Room which led off the room in which they had been received and which was arranged like a Restaurant.

There was a table in the centre, at which the Prince sat with a dozen of his guests, and in addition there were small tables for six, four, and even two. The only light was from the candles on the tables, which gave the room an air of mystery.

At the same time, there was an atmosphere of irrepressible gaiety enhanced by the music.

There were two Bands: one played dreamy, romantic waltzes; the other, a Gypsy Orchestra, wild, passionate, exciting, made the heart beat to the clash of the cymbals and the throb of the drums.

To Davita it was very exciting, and as the Prince introduced her not to one young man but to half-a-dozen, she thought what an excellent host he was, and how because she was never without a partner it was easy to keep away from Lord Mundesley.

In fact, he made no effort to talk to her either intimately or otherwise, but devoted himself to Violet, and when the dancing started he apparently had no wish to leave her for anybody else.

Supper was over before the curtains at one end of the Dining-Room were drawn back to reveal a Dance-Floor.

Those who wished to do so could continue to sit at their tables, drinking or eating, but still could get up and dance as it suited them.

To Davita's delight, the men to whom the Prince had introduced her were only too eager to ask her to dance with them.

Up until now, although she had had dancing-lessons

occasionally in Edinburgh, because her mother had said it was essential that she should be a good dancer, she had danced at home only with her father.

Now for the first time she was able to dance with not one young man but a dozen, and she found it an exhilarating experience.

"You are as light as thistledown," one told her as she was swept round the room to the strains of a Strauss waltz.

It was so thrilling that she forgot her fears about Lord Mundesley, and it was only when she was being whirled round the floor by a tall young man who she learnt was in the Brigade of Guards that she saw the Marquis seated at a table beside her host.

She had not seen him arrive, and she was quite certain he had not been there at supper.

But now, looking as usual cynical and contemptuous of everybody round him, he was beside the Prince, a glass of brandy in one hand and a cigar in the other.

As she looked at him she found that he was looking at her, and she felt that in some way he had mesmerised her into being aware of him.

She almost missed a step, then heard her partner say:

"You have not given me an answer to my question."

"I am sorry," Davita replied. "What was it you asked me?"

"Who are you thinking about?" her partner enquired. "Whoever it is, it is not me."

"I am sorry," Davita said again.

He smiled at her, saying:

"I forgive you. How could I do anything else when you look so lovely?"

Davita did not feel either shy or embarrassed as she had when Lord Mundesley had paid her compliments.

Then once again she was glancing across the room at the Marquis and wondering why Violet and Lord Mundesley had been so keen for him to come to the party when they hated him so much.

"This is my night of gaiety," she told herself.

About two hours later, as she waltzed round the room Davita realised she had not seen Violet and Lord Mundesley for some time.

Then as she looked for them she saw that they were at the far end of the Supper-Room, talking earnestly to the Prince.

'What are they plotting?' Davita wondered.

She was sure that if it was against the Marquis, he would not be affected by it because he was far stronger than they were! Then she wondered what she meant by that.

The dance came to an end and the Prince rose to his feet.

"I have something to say to you," he said in his deep voice with just a slight foreign accent, which made it sound very attractive.

The ladies all flocked towards him, looking as they moved in their full frilled skirts like the flowers that decorated the room.

"What is it, Your Highness?" one of them asked. "Have you a surprise for us?"

"Several, as it happens," the Prince replied. "For one, there is a Cotillion when you will all get very attractive prizes."

There was a cry of delight at this, and one woman said effusively:

"Darling Boris! You are always so generous!"

"I think we both are, Dolores, in one way or another!" the Prince replied. There was a shriek of laughter at the repartee and Dolores laughed too.

"Before the Cotillion," the Prince said, "as it is my birthday, we must have a little celebration."

"Your *birthday!*"

There were shrieks from everyone.

"Why did you not tell us?" "Why did we not know?" "We would have brought you a present!"

"All I need as a present is that you are all here," the Prince replied. "I intend to cut my cake, then you shall drink my health in a very special wine that comes from my own vineyard in my own country."

As he spoke, servants came in carrying an enormous iced cake on which flared a number of candles.

They set it down on a small table in front of the Prince, and as they did so Davita felt her hand taken by Violet.

"Let us get near so that we see," she said.

She pulled Davita through the guests until they stood at the Prince's side.

"I want my friend from Scotland to see this ceremony, Your Highness," Violet said to him. "Everything's new and exciting to her and this is something she mustn't miss!"

"Of course not," the Prince answered, "and I hope, Miss Kilcraig, you will wish me happiness in the future."

"Of course I will!" Davita answered.

The Prince smiled at her, and picking up a knife with a jewelled handle was ready to cut the cake.

"I must blow out the candles first," he said, "and for as many as I extinguish, I shall have as many happy years."

"No cheating!" somebody shouted.

"That is one thing I never do," the Prince replied.

He drew in his breath and with one terrific blow extinguished every candle on the cake.

There were shrieks of delight, then everybody clapped.

"Now wish!" Violet said.

"That is what I am doing, but of course what I wish must be a secret!"

He inserted the jewelled knife into the cake and cut it, then as the servants took it away, others brought huge trays on which there were glasses of wine.

One servant brought a gold tray on which there were only three glasses and presented it to the Prince.

"Now these," the Prince said, "are for myself and my two special guests this evening."

He picked up the glass on the right and, turning to the Marquis, who was at his side, said:

"Vange, you and I have been competitors on the race-course and at times in the race for love. I would like you to drink my health, and may we have many more years ahead of us as competitors and—friends."

"You may be sure of that, Your Highness," the Marquis answered, "and I promise I shall always do my best to defeat you!"

"And I promise I shall strive indefatigably to be victorious!"

There was a roar of laughter at this, then the Prince lifted the left-hand glass and the middle one.

Then to Davita's utter surprise he turned to her and said:

"There is an old superstition in my country that a red-haired woman presents a challenge which all men find irresistible. May I ask you, Miss Kilcraig, as I think you are the only red-headed person present, to drink my health, and I hope that the future will prove a challenge both for me and for yourself!"

Davita took the glass from the Prince's hand and said a little shyly:

"I . . . I hope I may bring Your . . . Highness both a challenge and good luck."

"Thank you."

The Prince raised his glass.

"Let us all drink to the future," he said, "and, in the fashion of my country—no heel-taps!"

Everybody raised their glasses.

"To Boris!" they cried, "and to the future!"

Davita put the glass to her lips, and despite what the Prince had said, she was about only to sip the wine when Violet beside her whispered:

"You must drink it down! Otherwise it's an insult!"

Because she thought that to disobey such an instruction might draw attention to herself, Davita tipped the glass upwards and felt the liquid, which was soft, sweet, and tasted of strawberries, slip down her throat.

She was grateful that it was not the rather harsh, fiery wine she had expected.

Then as she turned her face to look at the Prince, she suddenly felt as if the whole room were moving.

At first it was just a movement like the waves of the sea. Then it seemed to accelerate and whirl as the Gypsy music was whirling, growing wilder and more insistent!

The sound became deafening and with it was a darkness which came up from the floor to cover her. . . .

CHAPTER FIVE

DAVITA REALISED THAT her head was aching and she must be very tired.

Her mouth felt dry, and vaguely she wondered if she had drunk too much champagne the night before.

Her eyes felt heavy and seemed to be throbbing, and it was with an effort that she managed to open them.

Then she knew that she must be dreaming, for beside her on the bed, and she thought it was in her lodgings, was a man!

She could see his white shirt and his dark head, and when she shut her eyes to try to make herself wake up, she could feel again the dryness of her mouth and the pain in her head.

Suddenly there were voices and laughter and she opened her eyes to see Violet in the doorway of a strange room and beside her Lord Mundesley.

For a moment their faces swam in front of her eyes,

and there was another face too, and she was sure that she was having a nightmare.

Then Violet was saying angrily:

"Really, My Lord! It is disgraceful of you to behave in such a manner to my poor little friend who has only just arrived from Scotland!"

It was then Davita realised that Violet was not looking at her but was speaking to somebody beside her.

Slowly, because she was so frightened that it was almost impossible to move, she turned her head.

The man she had seen in what she thought was a dream was the Marquis!

Now in a horror that made her feel spellbound she was aware that they were lying on a huge canopied bed, with silk curtains falling from a gold corola, side by side on lace-edged pillows.

"I must wake up, I must!" Davita told herself.

But the Marquis did not disappear. He was there in his white shirt without his evening-coat, and he was real . . . real!

As if he was as bemused as she was, he lay very still for a moment. Then slowly he raised himself on the pillow, saying as he did so:

"What the devil is all this about?"

Only when he was sitting up on the bed did he see that Davita was beside him, and as he looked at her Violet said again:

"You have behaved disgracefully! I cannot allow my friend's reputation to be injured, so you will have to make reparation!"

Without saying anything, but with an expression of anger and contempt on his face, the Marquis rose from the bed and Davita felt sure that he was feeling as strange and as hazy as she was.

He picked up his evening-coat, which was lying on a chair, and as he started to put it on Lord Mundesley said:

"It is checkmate, Vange! There are only two things you can do—marry the girl, or pay up."

Davita drew in her breath.

It was gradually percolating through her befuddled mind what had happened. She remembered the toast on the Prince's birthday, and the way she had been forced to drink the whole glass of wine because Violet had said that otherwise it would be an insult.

Suddenly she understood. She had been drugged! She remembered the room seeming to swing round her before she was overwhelmed by a darkness which rendered her unconscious.

The same thing must have happened to the Marquis, and this was what Violet and Lord Mundesley had been planning: to discredit him, to pay him out for beating Lord Mundesley's horses at the races and for treating Rosie in the way he had.

But why should she be part of the plot?

She knew she must tell the Marquis that it was nothing to do with her.

But because her lips were so dry, although by now she was sitting up, it was impossible either to move or to speak.

She could only watch what was happening, finding it hard to breathe.

The Marquis had put on his evening-coat, and now as he pulled his lapels into place he said in an icy voice:

"Let me make it clear that I will not be blackmailed!"

"I think you might prefer it to being sued for breach of promise," Lord Mundesley said with a sneer.

The Marquis did not reply, and with what Davita felt was an unassailable dignity he started to move towards the door. Then Violet said:

"As Davita is not lucky enough to have any jewellery to keep, I should imagine a sum of—say—five thousand pounds would mend a broken heart."

The Marquis by now had reached the door of the bedroom, and as he went to open it Lord Mundesley said mockingly:

"It is no use, Vange! You are caught—hook, line, and sinker! We have a photograph, in fact several, of you together with this poor, innocent child, and let me point out she is not a Gaiety Girl but respectable and innocent —or rather she was!"

The Marquis walked three paces back to face Lord Mundesley.

The two men confronted each other and Davita saw that the Marquis's fists were clenched and she thought he would strike Lord Mundesley.

With an effort she found her voice.

"N-no . . . please . . . ! This is . . . wrong . . . very wrong . . . I . . ."

Before she could say any more, Violet was beside her.

She caught hold of her arm, digging her fingers into the softness of the flesh as she said in a hissing whisper:

"Be quiet! Don't say anything!"

"B-but . . . I . . ." Davita began, then realised that neither of the men had paid any attention to her interruption.

"I know only too well why you have done this," the Marquis was saying, and his voice was low and controlled.

"You have had it coming for some time, Vange," Lord Mundesley replied. "This time I have slipped under your guard and the only thing you can do is to pay up. As Violet says, it will cost you five thousand pounds to buy the photographs from me."

The way he spoke was even more unpleasant than what he said, and once again Davita knew that the Marquis was considering knocking him down.

Then, as if it was beneath his dignity, he said:

"Go to the devil!"

Then he walked from the room, slamming the door behind him.

For a moment there was silence. Then Violet gave a little cry and asked:

"Have we won?"

"We have!" Lord Mundesley replied. "He will pay up because there is nothing else he can do."

He walked to the end of the bed and, resting his arms on it, leant forward to look at Davita.

"Well, my pretty little Scot," he said, "I have done you a good turn. With five thousand pounds in your pocket, there will be no need for you to go looking for employment for some time!"

As he spoke, Davita was vividly conscious of the look in his eyes, which made her shrink away from him as she had done in his carriage.

She was not only afraid of him, but she hated him so violently that for the moment she was aware only of a disgust which made her feel sick.

Then it swept over her with horror that she had been humiliated and made a participant in Lord Mundesley's and Violet's plot to extract money from the Marquis.

However, some instinct of self-preservation warned her not to say so at this moment, and she merely turned her face towards Violet, saying desperately:

"I . . . want to . . . go . . . home!"

"That is where I'll take you," Violet answered.

She helped Davita off the bed, but when her feet touched the floor she felt as if the room were still swinging round her and she staggered.

"You're all right," Violet said. "You'll soon sleep it off."

She put her arm round Davita's shoulders to lead her towards the door.

"I will help you," Lord Mundesley said.

Davita shrank away from him as Violet said:

"Leave her alone! She's all right. Just see that the coast is clear. She won't want to talk to anybody at the moment."

"Oh . . . no . . . please . . . !"

"Don't worry," Violet said as Lord Mundesley went ahead of them. "Nearly everyone's left by now, and the rest are too drunk to know whether it's Christmas or Easter!"

"What . . . about the . . . Prince?"

Davita vaguely remembered seeing him peering through the door when she first woke up.

"He thinks it's a fine joke!" Violet replied. "He won't talk, and most of the others didn't realise what had happened. We got you out quick and up the stairs while the rest of the party were toasting their host."

"How . . . could you . . . do such a . . . thing?" Davita asked.

"I'll tell you later."

They reached the stairs and Davita was walking more firmly but she still held on to Violet's arm.

Lord Mundesley's carriage was at the front-door, and as they drove away she leant back and shut her eyes, determined not to talk about it to him.

However, she was obliged to listen to him chuckling and gloating over the Marquis's discomfort in what she knew was a most unpleasant manner.

"I never thought to catch him at such a disadvantage!" Lord Mundesley said in a self-satisfied voice. "Violet, my pet, you are a genius!"

"I'm not worrying about your revenge," Violet replied, "and I couldn't care one way or the other if the Marquis has better horses than you. What I did was to help Davita. She'll be all right now and will need assistance from *no-one* . . ."

There was an accent on the last word that made Davita think Violet was aware of the proposition Lord Mundesley had made to her.

Then she told herself it was impossible, but unless she was blind Violet must have noticed the way he looked at her, which had been very revealing.

'I hate him! I hate him!' she thought, and did not open her eyes until they reached their lodgings.

Then her hatred of Lord Mundesley gave her a burst of energy which enabled her to hurry past him as he assisted first Violet and then herself to alight and be halfway up the staircase before they had reached the hall.

As she turned to climb the second flight, she glanced

down to see Lord Mundesley pulling Violet into his arms, and she wondered how she could allow anyone so revolting to kiss her.

It was an inexpressible relief to reach her own bedroom and take off her mother's gown, feeling she had besmirched it and would never wear it again, before Violet came into the room.

"Now don't be upset, Davita," she said in a coaxing tone. "I know it was a bit of a shock, but when you get the Marquis's cheque tomorrow, you'll thank me from the bottom of your heart."

"I will not . . . take his . . . money," Davita said in a low voice.

"Don't be such a little fool!" Violet said sharply. "You know as well as I do you've no alternative, unless you're prepared to accept the suggestion which I suspect Bertie's prepared to make you."

Davita drew in her breath.

"I'm not half-witted," Violet went on. "I know he fancies you, even though he may not have said anything yet."

Davita hoped the relief these last words gave her did not show on her face, and Violet went on:

"Not that I'd mind losing him as much as all that— there's plenty of others! But I know Bertie, and he'd soon tire of you after he got what he wants."

This was the phrase that Davita had heard in her childhood, and it made her think of Jeannie and how she had killed herself and her baby because the Piper could not marry her.

"How can . . . you be so . . . friendly with him . . . Violet?" she asked. "He is . . . a married man."

Violet laughed.

"I'm not expecting Bertie or any of his kind to marry me," she said, "but he gives me a good time, and he's generous when it comes to gowns and sables. There's a dozen like Willie, bless their hearts, but they haven't got two pennies to rub together."

"But it is . . . wrong," Davita murmured.

Violet gave a little laugh and turned her back.

"Undo my gown, there's a dear, and stop worrying your head over me. I've saved you from being faced with the eternal question of 'starvation or sin,' and that's all that need concern you for the moment."

Davita unbuttoned her gown and Violet with difficulty moved round the tiny room towards the door, saying as she went:

"Good-night, and tell them downstairs that no-one's to wake me 'til I call. I'm dead on my feet!"

As she shut the door behind her, Davita put her hands over her face and sat down on the bed to try and think.

❦❦❦

It was ten o'clock before Davita had finished her packing and asked Billy to carry her trunks downstairs and fetch a hackney-carriage.

She knew that Violet would not wake for at least another two hours, and by that time she would have disappeared.

This was the only thing she could do, for she was certain that however much she protested, however much she swore she would not take the Marquis's money, Violet and Lord Mundesley would compel her to do so.

The mere idea of accepting even a farthing from him was so humiliating that she could almost hear her mother telling her that she must go away and hide rather than be involved in what the Marquis had said so truly was blackmail.

Davita was aware that blackmail was a crime punishable by law, but although the Marquis had been contemptuous of the manner in which he had been tricked, she was quite certain that he would not wish to face a scandal.

"What must he think of me?" she asked. "Does he think I was a party to what was happening?"

Then she thought despairingly that that was what he must think. Why it should matter to her if the Marquis disapproved of her personally she did not know—but it did!

Because Lord Mundesley was his implacable enemy, Davita was sure that he would not hesitate to allow the photographs that had been taken of them in bed to be printed in the more scurrilous newspapers.

She remembered how her father when he returned from London had brought home a number of newspapers which he told her not to read.

Curious, because they were lying about in his study she had glanced at them, seeing that they were mostly concerned with scandalous stories about the aristocracy and were, she was sure, an effort by the Radicals to discredit the Government and the Conservative Party.

When she thought about it, she realised that if she accepted Lord Mundesley's proposition of installing her in a house in Chelsea, his plot to get at the Marquis would have been dropped.

"But how could he think I could do anything not only so wicked but so . . . disloyal to . . . Violet?" Davita asked herself.

The more she thought about it, the more despicable Lord Mundesley's behaviour appeared.

It was he who had arranged with the Prince that she and the Marquis should be drugged at the party and carried up to the bedroom in his house.

At the same time, because she attracted him, he had been prepared, if she agreed, to call it off at the last moment, drop Violet, and make her his mistress.

It was obvious, Davita thought, that he had not offered Violet a house in Chelsea.

Then she told herself that she was disparaging her friend even by thinking she would sink so low with any man, let alone Lord Mundesley.

Yet Violet accepted expensive gowns from him and, on her own admission, sables.

"I do not . . . understand," Davita complained, and did not want to.

As the night wore on she felt less woolly-headed, more alert, and it was only an hour after she got to bed that dawn broke.

She got up, packed her trunks, and strapped them up as they had been when she arrived from Scotland.

Then she dressed herself in the same garments which had belonged to her mother and in which she had travelled down from the North, and put on the plain but pretty bonnet with the ribbons that tied under her chin.

When she looked at herself in the mirror she saw that there were lines under her eyes and she was very pale.

Otherwise, the horrors of the night appeared to have left little mark on her, although she thought that if her hair had turned white she would not have been surprised.

Then she remembered how before they had drunk the toast to the Prince and he had cut his birthday-cake, the evening had seemed so glorious and exciting.

"My night of gaiety," she told herself, "and I shall never have one again."

She knew that the whole idea of the Gaiety Theatre with its lovely girls was typified by Lottie Collins's dance when she sang: *"Ta-ra-ra-boom-de-ay!"*

First there was her demure appearance in her red gown and Gainsborough hat, and the shy, sweet little verse, before unexpectedly and with a wild abandonment came the chorus.

That was the reality of the Gaiety Theatre and the so-called Gaiety Girls, Davita thought, and the impression they evoked of being refined and ladylike was merely superficial.

"I will never see them or the Theatre again," she told herself, as her hackney-carriage drove away from Mrs. Jenkins's lodging-house.

She had paid for her bed and board, and only when she told her what she owed did Mrs. Jenkins say:

"Violet never tells me yer was leavin' today."

"It was all arranged last night," Davita answered.

"Well, I hopes yer're going some'ere nice, dear," Mrs. Jenkins replied. "With yer face, yer'll have to look after yerself, an' don't forget I told yer so."

"I will remember," Davita replied, "and thank you very much for being so kind to me."

She told the cabman in Mrs. Jenkins's hearing to drive to Waterloo Station, but as soon as they reached the end of the road she put her head out the window, saying she had changed her mind.

"I want to go to the best Domestic Bureau in the West End," she said.

For one moment she was afraid he would say he did not know where there was one, but after a moment he replied:

"Yer means th' un in Mount Street?"

"That is right."

The horse did not hurry itself, and as they journeyed there Davita planned what she would say.

Nevertheless, when they drew up outside the building that had a shop on the Ground Floor with a door at the side of it marked: *Mrs. Belmont's Domestic Bureau,*" her heart was beating in a frightened manner.

She asked the cabman to wait and he grunted a reply. Then she went up some narrow, rather dirty stairs and opened a door on the small landing at the top of them.

Inside there was a narrow room which was exactly what her mother had told her to expect.

On each side of it were long wooden benches on which several servants were seated.

At the far end there was a high desk where there was a strange-looking woman wearing what appeared to be a black wig.

She had a large nose and her thin face was wrinkled with lines, but her eyes were sharp and shrewd and she looked at Davita a little uncertainly as she walked up to her.

As she reached the desk there was a pause before the woman asked:

"What can I do for you—Ma'am?"

There was a distinct pause before the word "Ma'am," and Davita knew she was making up her mind whether she was an employer or an employee and had come to the conclusion that she was the former.

"I am looking for a position as a . . . Companion," Davita replied.

She tried to make her voice sound firm and confident, but there was a decided tremor on the last word.

Mrs. Belmont's attitude changed immediately.

"A Companion?" she repeated. "Have you any experience?"

"I am afraid not."

"I imagined that was the case," Mrs. Belmont observed in a hard voice. "And I'd have thought you were far too young for that sort of position."

Davita had decided in the carriage what she should say, but it was difficult to speak because she felt Mrs. Belmont was already dismissing her. However, she managed at length to articulate:

"My mother . . . Lady Kilcraig, when she was . . . alive, always told me that if ever I . . . needed a position . . . I should apply . . . to you."

There was a distinct pause.

"Did you say your mother was a Lady of Title?" Mrs. Belmont enquired.

"Yes. My father was Sir Iain Kilcraig of Kilcraig Castle, Kirkcudbrightshire, Scotland."

It was obvious that Mrs. Belmont's attitude had changed once again.

Now she looked at Davita as if she hoped to find something in her appearance to recommend her. Then she looked down at the huge ledger which stood open on her desk.

Without speaking she turned over several pages.

Then a mousy, middle-aged woman who had been sitting behind her and whom Davita had not noticed before came to Mrs. Belmont's side to whisper in her ear.

Davita heard her say:

"She wants someone immediately and there's no-one else we can send."

Mrs. Belmont turned over another page of the ledger.

"She's too young," she replied out of the side of her mouth.

"But she might fill the gap," the mousy woman replied.

Mrs. Belmont looked at Davita again and made up her mind.

"I've just one place where you might be suitable," she said. "You'd better give me your particulars."

Davita gave her name, but when Mrs. Belmont asked her age she hesitated. Then, fearing that eighteen would sound much too young, she said:

"I am twenty . . . nearly twenty-one."

"You certainly don't look it!" Mrs. Belmont remarked.

"I know," Davita agreed, "but I shall become older in time."

Mrs. Belmont did not smile, she merely noted Davita's age in her ledger.

"Address?" she queried.

"I have only just arrived from Scotland, and I have at the moment no address in London."

"Then you can leave for the country immediately?"

"That is what I should like to do."

"You have your luggage with you?"

"Yes."

Mrs. Belmont had a long conversation with the mousy woman. Then she said:

"Have you enough money to pay your own fare to Oxford?"

"Yes, I have," Davita replied.

"Very well, then," Mrs. Belmont said. "I will send a telegram to say that you are arriving at Oxford on the next train from Paddington. They'll be able to find out which it is and you'll be met at the Station. Your fare will be refunded to you."

"Thank you."

Mrs. Belmont was writing in an untidy, uneducated hand on a card.

It took her some time, and when she had finished she passed it to Davita.

"This is who you're going to as Companion," she said, "and I hope, Miss Kilcraig, you'll do everything in your power to give satisfaction. If you return with a bad reference, it would be very difficult for me to place you in another position. Do you understand?"

"Yes, I understand," Davita answered, "and thank you very much for helping me."

"I don't mind telling you," Mrs. Belmont went on, "that I'm taking a risk in sending anyone so young to the Dowager Countess. She's very particular. In fact, I've supplied her with no less than four Companions this last year, and none of them have settled down or been satisfactory."

"Was it because they wished to leave, or because they were dismissed?" Davita asked.

"I don't think there's any need for me to answer that question," Mrs. Belmont said in a lofty tone. "You just do your best, Miss Kilcraig, and remember that as you're so young and inexperienced, you've a lot to learn."

She held out the card and Davita took it from her.

She looked at it, saw that written on it was *The Dowager Countess of Sherburn, Sherburn House, Wilbrougham Oxfordshire.*

"Thank you," she said after she had read it. "Thank you very much."

"Now remember what I've said," Mrs. Belmont warned. "The young never listen to advice, but I expect your mother'd want you to listen to me."

"I will certainly try to please the Countess," Davita promised.

But as she drove towards Paddington Station she was

thinking of the four Companions who had failed in the last year to satisfy the Dowager.

Yet nothing mattered for the moment except that she was escaping from Violet, from Lord Mundesley, and from the intolerable position in which they had placed her.

They were not likely to guess where she had gone, and even if Violet was curious enough to make enquiries at various Domestic Bureaus, she would doubtless "let sleeping dogs lie," and be content that she had Lord Mundesley to herself.

"Besides, she will be angry with me for not accepting the Marquis's money," Davita told herself, "and she would never understand why I was not grateful to her for worrying about me."

Violet was willing to accept money and clothes from Lord Mundesley and doubtless from other men, and it would be impossible to explain to her why she could not do the same.

"I am much poorer than Violet, with no salary coming in every week," Davita reasoned. "But she, like her mother, is prepared to take anything anyone will give her. I am different."

She knew that even if she was starving and down to her very last penny, she would not, after what had happened, accept help either from Violet or from Lord Mundesley.

He at any rate would expect a return for his money, and she knew what that was!

'I hate him!' she thought again.

She knew that if it had not been for him, the fairy-like illusion that the Gaiety had brought her the first night she had watched the Show would not have been transformed into something ugly and unpleasant.

Davita could not bear to let her thoughts linger on the moment when she had awakened to find herself lying on the bed with the Marquis.

He was so magnificent that it hurt her to think how he had been treated and how bitterly he would resent it.

It would inevitably make him even more cynical and contemptuous than he was already.

"But I will not think about him or the Gaiety or Lord Mundesley any longer!" she told herself.

She tried instead to recall the fairy-stories that had been so much part of her life when she had been in Scotland.

She remembered the tales that her father had related to her of Scottish gallantry, the feuds between the Clans, the superstitions that were so much part of the High-lands.

That was what had been real to her before first Katie and then Violet had come into her life.

She felt now as if they deliberately prevented her from being a happy child and had turned her into a grown-up woman for whom fairy-land could have no reality.

She had a long wait at the Station, and all the time she was trying to think herself back into the happiness and contentment she had known when she walked over the moors, fished in the river, or rode with her father.

Then inevitably when the train carried her nearer and nearer to Oxford she felt apprehensive.

Fortunately, Mrs. Belmont's telegram had reached its destination promptly, for there was someone to meet her at the Station.

As Davita stood feeling alone on the crowded plat-form, a footman in a smart livery with a crested top-hat looked at her, decided she was not the person he was meeting, and would have walked on if she had not said nervously:

"E-excuse me . . . but are you from . . . Sherburn House?"

"That's right, Ma'am. Can ye be Miss Kilcraig?"

"I am!"

"I've been sent to meet ye," the footman said, "but I were expectin' someone older."

Davita thought with a lowering of her spirits that this was what his mistress also would be expecting.

The footman collected her trunks and made the porter carry them outside the Station to where there was waiting a brake drawn by two horses.

It was too large for one person, but Davita thought perceptively that it was the type of vehicle which would be used to convey servants, and as she climbed into it, she was thankful that for the moment she was the only occupant.

They drove out of the town and were soon in narrow, dusty lanes bordered by high hedges, and Davita looked round her with interest because the countryside was so different from Scotland.

There were small villages with usually in the centre a village green, an ancient Inn, and a duck-pond.

They drove for what seemed a long time before finally the horses turned in through some impressive lodge-gates and started down the long drive.

Now at last Davita had a glimpse ahead of the house and realised it was very large and impressive, although she thought it was not very old and the architecture was decidedly Victorian.

She had always been interested in buildings, and her father had taught her a great deal about those in Edinburgh, including the Castle which overshadowed the city and had always seemed to Davita very romantic.

She had also studied books on English Architecture and she thought now that it was disappointing that she had been in London for so short a time that she had not seen any of the sights.

Even to think of what had happened instead made a little shudder run through her, and the large and imposing mansion which seemed to grow bigger and bigger the nearer they drew to it seemed a place of safety and security after her experience of the Gaiety and those who frequented it.

The brake did not drive up to the front door with its long flight of stone steps.

Instead, Davita was taken to a side-door which she

told herself with a smile was obviously the right entrance for anyone of so little importance as a paid Companion.

Here she was met by a liveried footman.

"I suppose ye're th' lady we're expecting?" he said.

"I am," Davita replied, and waited for the inevitable reaction.

"Ye look too young to be a Companion, Miss. All th' others had one foot in the grave!"

He obviously intended to be friendly, and Davita laughed.

"I think it will be a long time before I have that."

"Certainly will. This way, Miss. I'll take ye up to 'er Ladyship."

He led the way as he spoke up what Davita was sure was a secondary staircase.

When they reached the landing they turned into a corridor that was wide and very impressive with high ceilings painted and gilded.

The furniture was magnificent and so were the paintings, and Davita hoped that she would have time to see everything in the house before she was dismissed.

'I am obviously going to be much too young,' she thought despairingly, 'but perhaps I can manage to last a week or so.'

The footman ahead of her stopped in front of two massive mahogany doors.

He knocked on one of them and it was opened by an elderly woman wearing a black gown but with no apron, and Davita supposed she was a lady's-maid.

"What do you want?" she asked in a rather disagreeable voice.

Then before the footman could reply she saw Davita and said:

"Are you Miss Kilcraig who we're expecting?"

"Yes, I am," Davita replied, wondering how often she would have to answer the same question.

The lady's-maid looked at her critically, but she did not say anything. As the footman walked away, Davita entered a small vestibule with several doors leading out of it.

"Wait here!" the maid commanded.

She went through the centre door and Davita heard her speaking to somebody. Then she opened it, saying:

"Come in! Her Ladyship'll see you."

Feeling as if she were a School-Girl who had been sent for by the Head Mistress, Davita walked into a large room full of light from the afternoon sunshine.

To her surprise, it was a bedroom with a huge four-poster bed against one wall.

Sitting in the centre of it propped up by pillows was an old lady who seemed to Davita quite fantastic in her appearance.

Her white hair was elegantly arranged on top of her head, and beneath it was a face that had once been beautiful but was now lined and very thin.

But what was so extraordinary was the amount of jewellery she wore.

There were ropes of magnificent pearls round her neck, there were diamond ear-rings in her ears, and above her blue-veined hands her slim wrists were weighted down with bracelets.

The bed-cover was of exquisite Venetian lace and she wore a lace dressing-jacket to match it, but it was almost obscured by her jewels.

Davita stood just inside the door.

Then the Dowager Countess said sharply:

"What have they sent me this time? If you are another of those nit-wits who have been popping in and out of here like frightened rabbits, you can go straight back on the next train!"

The way she spoke sounded so funny that Davita instead of being frightened wanted to laugh.

"I hope I will not . . . have to do . . . that," she said.

Then quickly she remembered to add "Ma'am" and to curtsey.

"So you have a voice of your own. That is something!"

the old lady said. "Come here, and let me have a look at you."

Davita obeyed, moving closer to the bed.

The Countess stared at her. Then she said:

"You are nothing but a child! How old are you— sixteen?"

"I told Mrs. Belmont at the Domestic Bureau that I was nearly twenty-one," Davita said.

"And how old are you really?"

"Eighteen . . . but I desperately wanted . . . employment."

"Why?"

"For one reason . . . because I wanted to get . . . away from . . . London."

"What has London done to make you feel like that?"

"Things I would rather not . . . speak about, Ma'am," Davita replied, "but I only came . . . South three days ago."

The Countess looked down at something that lay on her lace cover and Davita realised it was a telegram.

"Your name is Kilcraig," she said, "so I suppose you are from Scotland?"

Davita nodded.

"My home was near Selkirk, which is not far from Edinburgh."

"And why did you leave?"

"Both my father and mother are . . . dead."

"And have left you with no money, I suppose?"

Davita did not think it was strange that her whole life story was being extracted from her in a few words.

"That is why I have to find employment," she said. "Oh, please, Ma'am, let me try to do whatever you want. I will make every effort to be satisfactory."

"You are certainly not what I expected," the Countess remarked.

"I can only hope I will not be another . . . rabbit to be sent back on the . . . next train."

"I think that is unlikely," the Countess said. "Now, suppose you let Banks show you to your room, and then you can come back and tell me all about yourself, as I am certain you are anxious to do."

There was something a little sarcastic in the way she spoke, and Davita said quickly:

"I would much . . . rather hear about you, Ma'am, and this enormous . . . exciting house."

"From the way you speak," the Countess said, "I imagine your own home was much smaller."

"It is a crumbling old Castle," Davita replied, "but very, very old."

The Countess laughed.

"I get the implication. Sherburn was built only forty years ago. I suppose that is what you are hinting at."

"I would not have been so . . . impertinent as to . . . hint at it," Davita answered, "but I am glad to think I was not . . . mistaken when I first . . . saw it."

The Dowager put out her hand and picked up a small gold bell that stood on a table beside the bed.

She rang it and the door opened so quickly that Davita suspected Banks had been listening outside.

"Take Miss Kilcraig to her room, Banks," the Countess commanded. "She can come back when she has taken off her travelling-things."

"Very good, M'Lady."

Davita remembered to bob a curtsey before she followed Banks from the room, and she was almost certain that the Countess smiled at her.

As they walked down the corridor she said to the lady's-maid:

"Please, help me. I would like to stay here, but I am very afraid I shall be too ignorant and inefficient."

Banks looked at her in surprise.

"Most of them thinks they knows everything!"

"I know nothing," Davita replied, "and I am quite prepared to admit it!"

There was just a faint smile on the elderly woman's thin lips.

"Her Ladyship's not easy," she said, "and if you ask

me, she doesn't need a Companion. I can do all she
wants, if it comes to that."

Davita understood that this was a bone of contention,
and she suspected that Banks had had a great deal to do
with the Companions being dismissed almost as soon as
they arrived.

"I promise you I will not get in your way," she said,
"and perhaps I could help you if you would tell me if
there is anything you want me to do. I can sew quite
well, and I have always pressed my own clothes."

The maid looked at her with what Davita thought was
a far more pleasant expression.

At the end of the corridor she opened a door and
Davita saw it was a nice bedroom with a high ceiling.

It was well furnished. Already her trunks had been
brought upstairs and placed on the floor, and there was
a young housemaid starting to unpack them.

"Emily'll help you to unpack," Banks said, "but she's
too much to do to give you much attention otherwise."

"I can look after myself," Davita said quickly, "and it
is very kind of Emily to help me."

She paused before she added:

"I am afraid there is rather a lot in the trunks. They
contain everything I possess in the world now that my
. . . father is . . . dead."

She could not help there being a little quiver in her
voice on the last words, and Banks asked:

"Has he been gone long?"

"Just over a month," Davita replied. "And my mother
died some years ago."

"You just have to be brave about it," Banks remarked.

Then, as if she felt she was being sentimental, she said
sharply to Emily:

"Now hurry up, Emily. Get everything straight for
Miss Kilcraig."

She would have left the room if Davita had not said:

"One thing I would like to ask . . . although it may
seem rather . . . an imposition."

"What is it?" Banks asked in an uncompromising voice.

"Would it be possible for me to have something to eat? Just some bread and butter would do. I did not like to leave the Waiting-Room at Paddington Station before the train came in, and I have had nothing to eat since breakfast."

"Good gracious! You must be starving!" Banks exclaimed. "What you want is a cup of tea and something substantial with it."

"I do not want to be a bother."

"It's no bother," Banks answered. "Nip downstairs, Emily, and see if you can find something for Miss Kilcraig to eat. Don't be long about it. Her Ladyship's waiting for her."

Emily sprang to her feet to do as she was told, and as she left the room Davita said:

"Thank you very much. You are very kind to me, but I do not want to be a nuisance and keep asking you for things."

"You ask," Banks replied. "I'll tell you when you're a nuisance, and it may be a long time before you are."

She actually smiled before she left the room, and when she had gone Davita went to the window to look out at the view over the Park and the lake.

Then she gave a little exclamation of pleasure.

She had escaped! She was free. She had left Violet, Lord Mundesley, and the Gaiety behind her, and she was here!

Because it was in the country, even though it was very different from Scotland, it seemed like home.

She could see stags moving under the trees in the Park, there were birds flying overhead, and the sun was shining on the lake as it did on the river near the Castle.

It was all so different from London, and she clasped her hands together.

"Oh, please, God, let me stay! Please, God, do not let the Countess send me away."

It was a cry that came from the very depths of her heart.

Then, because she realised time was passing, she hurriedly untied her bonnet and began to take off her travelling-gown.

CHAPTER SIX

DAVITA SHUT THE book with a snap.

"How could she have died at the end?" she asked, and there were tears in her eyes.

The Countess smiled.

"Most women like a good weep at the end of a story."

"I am sure that isn't true," Davita replied. "I want everyone to live happily ever after."

"I know you do, dear," the Countess said, and her voice was soft. "Perhaps one day you will find happiness."

"I hope so," Davita answered. "Papa and Mama were very happy until she died."

There was a little tremor in her voice because it was always hard for her to speak of her mother, and to think of what had happened when Katie had left her father always upset her.

She did not realise that her eyes were very expressive, and the Countess said quickly:

"Anyway, you have made me happy."

"Have I really?" Davita asked.

"Very happy," the Countess replied. "I feel sometimes that you are the daughter I never had."

Davita gave a little cry of delight.

"You could not say anything which would please me more, because I feel that you are like the Grandmother I never knew. I would have loved to have had a Grandmother!"

"Then that is what I am quite content to be," the Countess replied.

Davita smiled at her radiantly, but before she could say anything the door opened and Banks came in.

"Now, M'Lady," she said briskly, "time for your rest, as you well know, and Miss Davita should be outside in the sunshine putting roses into her cheeks."

Davita laughed.

"If they were there, I am sure they would clash with my hair."

Banks did not reply but she was obviously suppressing a laugh.

"Before I go out," Davita said to the Countess, "I intend to choose a book in the Library with a happy ending. That is what we both want to listen to."

She did not wait for an answer but hurried from the bedroom.

When she had gone, the Countess began to take off her strings of pearls and said:

"That is a very sweet child, Banks. I am so glad she came here."

"She's one of the nicest young ladies I've ever met, M'Lady," Banks replied. "None of those other complaining women ever offered to help me as Miss Davita does."

Running down the stairs, Davita thought with delight that she had nearly an hour and a half to do all the things she wanted to do.

As soon as she had chosen a book in the Library—she was determined she would not read the Countess another unhappy one—she would walk down to the lake, and she wished as she had wished before that her father could watch the trout with her.

'Perhaps one day I might suggest that I fish for them,' she told herself.

Then she decided she would not wish to kill anything, not even a trout.

After that she would go to the stables. She drew in her breath with excitement as she remembered that the Countess had offered to give her a new riding-habit. It should be arriving any day now.

Ever since she had come to Sherburn House three weeks ago, every moment had seemed more thrilling than the last.

Davita sometimes thought it was as if she had come home and Sherburn House belonged to her.

Then she knew she felt this because in her dreams she, or her fanciful heroines who were a part of herself, always had a background which only a grand house could provide.

The paintings, the furnishings, the miniatures, the painted ceilings, and the huge State-Rooms were all part of her dreams, and sometimes she wandered through them pretending that she was in fact a Countess of Sherburn, and the history of the family was her history too.

She had seemed to fit in from the very moment she arrived. Not only did she amuse the Countess, but the servants liked her, and, although she was quite unaware of it, everyone treated her as if she were an entrancing child whom they wished to spoil.

"The Chef has made this pudding especially for you," the Butler would say at luncheon or dinner.

The housemaids would tidy her room and press her dresses and the grooms would keep carrots and apples ready in the stables for her to give to the horses.

"I am so happy," Davita would say to herself when she went to bed.

In her prayers she would thank God not only that she was happy but that she was safe.

115

"No-one can find me here," she would say reassuringly to herself, almost every hour during the first week after she arrived.

Then, because there were so many new things to occupy her mind, she began to forget abut Violet and Lord Mundesley and even the Gaiety.

In retrospect it became a dream that had ended in a nightmare, and even her thoughts shied away from recalling the terrible night when she came out of a drugged sleep to find the Marquis on the bed beside her.

The Library of Sherburn House was very impressive, most of the volumes being old and very valuable.

But the Countess's eldest son, to whom the house belonged, had collected quite a large number of modern books when he was at home, and Davita felt grateful to him for affording her such a choice.

The Countess had had two sons, one of whom had been killed fighting in what she described as "one of Queen Victoria's little wars."

The elder, the Earl of Sherburn, was now Governor of Khartoum in the Sudan. Because he was so often abroad, having been Governor in other places before this appointment, he had persuaded his mother to live at Sherburn House and "keep it warm" for him.

"The servants have all been with us for years," she told Davita. "We really would not know what to do with them if my son closed the house, and quite frankly I am happy to live in what was my home for so many years."

"It is a very lovely home," Davita replied, "even though it is a modern building."

"Built onto an ancient foundation," the Countess said sharply.

Her eyes were twinkling because the age of Sherburn House was a joke between her and Davita.

Now Davita ran to the far end of the Library where the modern books had been neatly arranged and catalogued by the Curator.

She took one down from a shelf and put it back again.

Then she pulled out another one by Jane Austen, wondering if it would amuse the Countess or if she already knew it too well.

She was turning over the pages when she heard someone come into the Library and thought it must be Mr. Anstruther, the Curator.

She was just going to ask him if the Countess had read *Pride and Prejudice* recently, when she looked round and was suddenly rigid.

It was not Mr. Anstruther who was walking slowly from the doorway towards the mantelpiece, but the Marquis!

For a moment she thought he could not be real and she was imagining him, because he looked just as handsome, imperious, and cynical as he had been in her thoughts.

Then he saw her, and he was obviously as surprised as she was.

After a silence which seemed to last a long time, in a voice that did not sound like her own Davita asked:

"Can you . . . are you . . . looking for . . . me? Why . . . are you . . . here?"

The Marquis did not reply, he merely walked nearer to her until he was standing facing her.

"I should be asking that question," he said. "Why are you in the house of my Great-Aunt?"

"Your . . . Great-Aunt?"

Davita repeated the words under her breath, and then she said almost frantically:

"Please . . . please do not . . . tell her about . . . me. If you do, she will . . . send me . . . away. I am so happy . . . here and . . . safe. Please . . . please!"

Even as she pleaded with him she thought it was useless and she would have to leave. Yet she knew that if he made her go, it would be like being turned out of Paradise.

"I heard you had disappeared," the Marquis said slowly, "but I certainly did not expect to find you here."

"Who . . . told you I had . . . disappeared?"

"The Prince, as it happens. I am sure your friend Violet was waiting to accept my money on your behalf."

Davita gave a little cry.

"How could you think . . . how could you . . . imagine I would . . . touch any of your . . . money?" she asked passionately. "I swear to you I had no idea what they had . . . planned or what they . . . intended to do. It was horrible . . . degrading! That is why I ran away . . . hoping they would never . . . find me, and therefore they would not be able to . . . to . . . blackmail you."

She said the dreaded word, and added:

"Perhaps . . . because I was a . . . party to their . . . plot, you will . . . want to send me to . . . prison."

Now she was trembling. Her eyes as she looked up at the Marquis were piteous.

"I think you must be well aware," he said coldly, "that I have no wish for the Police to be involved in this very reprehensible affair. The Prince discovered you had vanished, and I have not communicated with either Violet Lock or Lord Mundesley since the night of the party."

"I am glad . . . so very glad you did not . . . give them any . . . money," Davita whispered. "How did the Prince . . . discover I had . . . gone?"

"He went to your lodgings to apologise to you, as he had apologised to me, that we should have both been embroiled in anything so unpleasant in his house."

The Marquis's voice was hard as he went on:

"Mundesley tricked the Prince by pretending it was just a joke that would have no serious repercussions."

"Lord Mundesley has not . . . still got the . . . photographs?"

"The Prince took them from him and tore them up," the Marquis replied.

Davita felt a wave of relief sweep over her that was so intense that she put down the book she was still holding in her hand and steadied herself against a chair.

Then as the Marquis did not speak, she said in a very small, frightened little voice:

"What are . . . you going to . . . do about . . . me?"

"What do you expect me to do?" he enquired.

"I suppose you . . . will want me to . . . leave," Davita said dully. "Please . . . if so, do not tell your . . . Great-Aunt what . . . happened."

"Why should she not know the truth?"

"Because it would upset and shock her, as it . . . shocked me."

"Do you really mind what she thinks?"

"Of course I do!" Davita replied. "She has been so . . . kind to me . . . so very . . . very kind. Only just now she said I was . . . like the . . . daughter she had . . . never . . . had."

As Davita spoke, the tears that had been in her eyes overflowed and ran down her cheeks. She made no effort to wipe them away and merely said in a broken voice:

"If you will say . . . nothing, I will make some . . . excuse to explain my . . . having to . . . leave."

"What excuse will you give?" the Marquis enquired.

Davita made a helpless little gesture with her hands.

"I could say I must go . . . back to . . . Scotland. But as the Countess knows my home is . . . gone, I would have to . . . think of something very . . . convincing, but I am not . . . certain what it . . . can be."

Now the tears ran from her cheeks down the front of her gown.

Davita groped for her handkerchief which was concealed in her waistband, and she wiped them away, thinking despairingly as she did so that once again she was alone and frightened.

Unexpectedly the Marquis said:

"Suppose we sit down and you tell me a little more about your circumstances."

Because it was more of a command than a request,

Davita obediently followed him to the ornate marble mantelpiece.

There was a sofa and several arm-chairs grouped round the hearth. She sat down on the edge of the sofa, feeling as if her fairy-tale world had collapsed round her in ruins.

"You tell me you have been happy here," the Marquis remarked.

"Very . . . very . . . happy."

"I have already learnt your father was Sir Iain Kilcraig and Violet was the daughter of your Stepmother. Why did you come to London? Did you intend to go on the stage?"

"No, I never wanted to do that," Davita answered. "Mama would have been . . . shocked at the . . . idea."

"Then why did you not stay in Scotland?"

"I had to find employment of some sort, because there was no money after Papa's debts were paid. I thought it would be easier to find something to do in London than in Edinburgh."

"So you came to ask Violet to help you?"

"There was no-one else," Davita replied. "Mama's relations all lived in the Western Isles and I never met them."

"I learnt your mother was a MacLeod," the Marquis said, as if he had spoken to himself.

Davita wondered why he had been interested, and then she thought in a kind of horror that he had made enquiries about her because he believed she was blackmailing him.

"I never . . . meant," she said in a frightened little voice, "to have . . . anything to do with the . . . Gaiety or . . . someone like . . . like . . . Lord Mundesley."

The way she spoke made the Marquis look at her sharply.

"Why do you speak of Mundesley like that?" he enquired.

"Because he is horrible . . . disgusting, and . . . wicked!" Davita answered passionately.

"What did he do to you to make you feel like that about him?"

Davita did not reply, but the Marquis saw the colour rise in her cheeks.

"I asked you a question, Davita, I want an answer!"

She wanted to say she could not speak of it, but somehow because he was looking at her and waiting, she felt that he compelled her to reply to his question.

"He . . . offered me a . . . house in . . . Chelsea," she said in a voice that was almost inaudible.

"It does not surprise me," the Marquis said. "Mundesley is a bounder and no decent woman would associate with him."

It was what Davita felt herself. Because she was ashamed of what she had had to tell the Marquis, she could only sit with her hands clasped together and her head bowed.

"Forget him," the Marquis said sharply.

"I want to, because he . . . frightens . . . me."

It struck her that if she had to leave Sherburn House, Lord Mundesley might find her again!

She thought the only thing she could do would be to go back to Scotland and stay with Hector until Mr. Stirling found her some sort of employment.

Because the idea seemed bleak and depressing, she lifted her head to look at the Marquis as she said pleadingly:

"How . . . soon do you . . . want me to . . . leave?"

"I have not said that you should do so."

There was just a flicker of hope in her eyes, and then she said, as if it was the other alternative:

"You do not . . . intend to tell your Great-Aunt . . . about me and . . . make her . . . dismiss me?"

"I promise you I will say nothing to upset my Great-Aunt."

"But you still . . . mean me to . . . go away?"

"Not if you wish to stay."

Davita's whole face lit up.

"Do you mean . . . are you saying," she stammered incoherently, "that I can stay here?"

For a moment the Marquis did not answer.

Davita added pleadingly:

"Please . . . please let me. I can only say how very . . . very sorry I am for what . . . happened at the . . . party."

"I believe now that you had nothing to do with it," the Marquis said kindly.

"As I told you, I had no idea . . . what they had . . . planned," Davita answered. "At the same time, I suppose if I had accepted what Lord Mundesley . . . suggested, it would not have . . . happened. Also, Violet was angry because she . . . guessed what he . . . felt about . . . me."

She stammered a little over her explanation. She felt somehow she had to be completely honest with the Marquis.

"Forget it," he said. "One day someone—and I hope it will be myself—will give Mundesley the lesson he deserves. Until that happens, put him out of your mind."

"That is what I want to do," Davita replied simply.

"Then do it!" the Marquis commanded.

"And I can stay . . . here with the . . . Countess?"

"As far as I am concerned. I imagine it is an acceptable arrangement, both for you and my Great-Aunt. She has certainly had a great number of failures with her Companions until now."

"She said they were like . . . frightened rabbits," Davita said with just a faint smile.

"You are not frightened?" the Marquis asked.

"Not of the Countess, only of you. I thought you would be very . . . very . . . angry with . . . me."

"I was very angry," the Marquis answered. "But not particularly with you, especially after I knew you had disappeared."

"You did realise that I had no intention of taking any money from you?"

"I thought that might be the reason you had gone away."

Davita gave a deep sigh.

"I am so glad you thought that. In a way, it makes everything much better, even though I never want to think about it or anything to do with the Gaiety again."

"The Gaiety?" the Marquis said in a puzzled voice.

"It is all part of a . . . world and . . . people that I do not . . . understand," Davita explained. "Katie, my Stepmother, was kind to me, and so was Violet, but at the same time they . . . shocked me."

As she spoke, she thought of Katie going away with Harry, and of Violet accepting the sables and gowns from Lord Mundesley.

"How old are you?" the Marquis asked.

"Eighteen," Davita replied.

"And you had never been away from Scotland until you came South?"

Davita shook her head.

"I had just arrived the night you saw me at Romano's, and everything was very . . . strange."

As she spoke, she remembered that what had been particularly strange had been the way Rosie had behaved. Once again she could not meet the Marquis's eyes, and the colour rose in her cheeks.

"Forget it," he said again sharply, as if he knew what she was thinking. "You should never have got mixed up in the world you call 'the Gaiety.' I can understand now why you want to stay here."

"I may really . . . stay?" Davita asked, as if she were half-afraid that he would change his mind.

"Certainly, as far as I am concerned!"

"Oh, thank you, thank you. You may think perhaps it is an . . . impertinence, but the Countess is like a . . . Grandmother to me and I love being with . . . her. Every day here has been happier than the last . . ."

As she spoke, she saw that the Marquis was looking at her penetratingly.

It was as if he found it hard to believe that, being so young, she was as happy as she said she was, living in the house alone with an old woman and no young people of her own age.

Davita's eyes, however, shone with an unmistakable sincerity.

After a moment he said:

"I came here to ask my Great-Aunt if I may stay the night. I only heard yesterday that there are some horses for sale in the neighbourhood, and I wish to see them. I thought too it was an opportunity to pay my respects to someone I have neglected somewhat remissibly for the last three months."

"I am sure the Countess will be very thrilled to see you," Davita replied, "but she is resting for another hour."

"That is what the servants told me," the Marquis answered. "I was going to read the papers which I understood were here in the Library, and then visit the stables."

"I was going to do that too," Davita said. "I love the horses and I feed them every afternoon."

"Then suppose we go there together," the Marquis suggested. "I have a feeling my cousin's horses are under-exercised and under-fed in his absence. If they are, I shall certainly reprimand his Head Groom."

Davita gave a little cry.

"Oh, you mustn't do that! Yates is such a conscientious man, and I promise you the horses are exercised every morning."

"By you?" the Marquis enquired.

"I have been allowed to help him since I have been here. It was been wonderful for me. I have never ridden such magnificent animals before."

"I see you have made yourself very much at home."

The Marquis's voice was mocking.

"Perhaps you think I am . . . imposing on the

Countess . . . but I . . . swear to you she . . . suggested in the first place I should . . . ride and do all the . . . other things I have been . . . allowed to do."

The Marquis did not reply, and Davita wondered apprehensively if he thought she was pushing herself forward, asking favours to which she was not entitled.

'It is not surprising he disapproves of me,' she thought miserably.

Then the Marquis smiled as he said:

"Come along. What are we waiting for?"

She felt as if the sun had come out.

*   *   *

Later that evening Davita felt as if once again she had stepped into a dream, and that this time there was no chance of it ending in a nightmare.

It had been the Countess who suggested that she should join the Marquis for dinner.

"I am sure my great-nephew would not wish to dine alone," she had said. "And it would be a chance for you to have someone young to talk to."

"Perhaps His Lordship will not want . . . me," Davita said nervously.

"Of course he will want you," the Countess said positively. "He has a reputation of always being surrounded by attractive women."

Davita was quite certain that the Marquis did not think she was attractive. She was not surprised, when she compared herself to the beauty of Rosie, even though he had grown tired of her.

However, there was no reason why she should not do what the Countess suggested, and she was supposed to have met the Marquis today for the first time.

She therefore went to change before dinner, feeling uncertain as to whether or not she was looking forward to the evening.

"Suppose he is bored and is contemptuous of me?" she asked herself.

It was, however, a consolation to feel that she could wear a new evening-gown that she had made herself from a sketch in *The Ladies Journal*.

It was Banks who had found some very pretty material that had been put away years ago in the cupboard and never made up.

It was Banks, too, who had found a sketch of the gown that was described as having come from Paris, and it seemed to Davita as pretty as, if not prettier than, anything that had been worn by the Gaiety Girls.

She had cut it out and made it in the Sewing-Room after the Countess had gone to bed.

Now she was wearing it for the first time and she was glad it looked so very different from the evening-gown in which the Marquis had first seen her.

She could never think of her mother's wedding-dress of Brussels lace without a little shudder.

But her new gown was spring-green gauze, the colour of her eyes, with chiffon drapes round the low back of the bodice, and a sash of green velvet encircled her tiny waist.

Although she was unaware of it, Davita looked the very embodiment of Spring.

Banks brushed her hair for her until the red lights shone like little flames of fire, and when she was ready she went into the Countess's bedroom to say "goodnight."

"Is that the dress you made yourself?" the Dowager asked.

"Banks found the material that you bought in Paris over ten years ago," Davita answered. "Do tell me if you like it."

"It looks very attractive," the Countess replied, "and so do you, my dear. Fetch my jewel-case."

The Countess's jewel-case, large and heavy, was made of polished leather and stood on the dressing-table.

Davita carried it to the bed and the Countess opened it.

Davita thought the flashing jewels that filled it made it look like something out of Aladdin's Cave.

The Countess searched first the top tray and then the second, until at the very bottom she found what she wanted.

"I wore this when I was your age," she said. "Put it on. I want to see it round your neck."

It was a delicate necklace with small emeralds and diamonds fashioned in the shape of flowers.

Excitedly Davita ran to the mirror on the dressing-table and clasped it round her neck. It gave a finish, she thought, to her whole appearance, and also accentuated the whiteness of her skin.

"It is lovely!" she exclaimed. "May I really wear it tonight? I will be very careful with it."

"It is a present."

"A present?" Davita gasped. "I cannot take it, it is too valuable! You must not give me any more than you have given me already."

"I want you to have it," the Countess said. "I shall be very hurt if you refuse to accept it."

"Thank you, thank you," Davita answered. "You are so kind to me. I haven't any words to tell you how grateful I am."

She lifted the Countess's hand as she spoke and kissed it, and then she said:

"One day perhaps I shall be able to repay what you have done for me. I do not know quite how I shall do so."

There were tears in her eyes as she spoke, and the Countess replied:

"Run along, child, and enjoy yourself, you are making me feel sentimental."

Smiling, Davita ran downstairs where she knew the Marquis would be waiting for her in the Blue Drawing-Room. He was looking magnificent as he had the first night she had seen him in his evening-clothes.

Because he had watched her with the usual rather

cynical expression on his face as she walked towards him, he made her feel very shy.

Then because what had happened was too exciting to keep to herself, she said:

"Please look at what your Great-Aunt has just given me. I feel I ought not to accept, but she said she would be very . . . hurt if I did not do so."

Then as she spoke, Davita thought she had made a mistake. Maybe the Marquis thought she was like Violet, getting presents out of men or anyone whose generosity she could impose on.

To her relief, the Marquis merely replied:

"It is certainly very suitable with your green eyes."

"You do not think it . . . wrong of me to accept such a . . . valuable present?"

"I think after what my Great-Aunt said about you to me this afternoon, it would be unkind of you not to do so."

Davita's face seemed to light up as if there were suddenly a thousand lights blazing in the room.

"Now I feel happy about . . . accepting it," she replied. "She is so . . . so kind to me, and I do want to make her . . . happy."

During dinner, although Davita had been apprehensive that she might bore him, there were so many things to talk about that time seemed to speed past on wings.

They first talked of Scotland and the Marquis told Davita how he went grouse-shooting every August and how many salmon he had caught the previous year.

"Ours is not a famous river," Davita said. "But once Papa caught fifteen in a day, and another time I caught ten."

"I call that a very good catch," the Marquis said with a smile.

But she knew he was delighted as a sportsman that his best day had been nineteen.

"I wonder what horses you will buy tomorrow?" she asked as dinner came to an end.

"I will be able to tell you that tomorrow evening," he answered.

"You will come back after the sale?"

"I have no wish to make the journey back to London late in the evening if I am not able to bid early in the day for the horses I want."

"I will be very eager to hear all about your purchases."

"I might even bring them back with me," the Marquis said. "Two of my grooms are meeting me at the sale."

"That would be even more exciting!" Davita exclaimed.

The Marquis smiled a little mockingly.

"I am not certain that is really a compliment."

For the moment she did not understand what he meant. Then she realised that she had implied that his horses were more interesting than he was.

A little shyly, because she was uncertain how he would take the question, she asked:

"Do you . . . like being . . . flattered?"

"Only if it is sincere," the Marquis answered. "Then of course I appreciate it."

"I should have thought it would not matter to you what anyone thought about you."

"Why should you think that?"

"I suppose it is because you seem so important . . . so authoritative and . . ."

Davita stopped, afraid that what she was about to say was rude.

The Marquis did not leave that unchallenged.

"And what?" he enquired.

"I have . . . forgotten what I was going to . . . say."

"That is not true!" he said. "And I would like you to finish the sentence."

As if once again he compelled her, Davita said shyly:

"When I saw you that first night at . . . Romano's I thought that you seemed cynical and a little . . .

129

contemptuous of everything that was going on round you. Was I right?"

The Marquis looked at her in surprise.

"In a sense," he answered. "But I did not realise it was so obvious."

"Perhaps it would not have been to everyone, but you must not forget that the Scots are fey."

The Marquis laughed.

"So you were aware I was feeling at odds with the world—that particular world in which we met."

As she thought he was referring to Rosie, Davita merely nodded her head.

The Marquis seemed to hesitate. Then he said:

"It is not something I should discuss ordinarily with someone of your age, but because you were at Romano's that night and were indirectly involved in a scene that should never have taken place, I will tell you the background of the story."

There was a hard note in his voice, and Davita said quickly:

"There is no . . . reason for you to do so. It is not for me to . . . criticise, but you did . . . ask me what I . . . felt."

"What you felt was perhaps what no-one else would. So I intend to explain to you why I was in such an unpleasant mood."

As he paused for a moment, Davita thought it was a very strange conversation for her to be having with the Marquis. But then the whole evening, she realised, was strange.

They were alone, for one thing, sitting at a candle-lit table in the huge Dining-Room, hung with paintings of the Sherburn ancestors. They were isolated on a little island of light as if they had embarked together on an unknown sea into an unknown future.

It flashed through her mind that that was indeed just what they were doing!

Then she told herself she was being ridiculously

imaginative and she must listen attentively to what the Marquis was saying.

"Because you have been impelled into a world of which most girls of your age and breeding have no knowledge whatsoever," he began, "you were doubtless unaware, even before Lord Mundesley made his objectionable proposal to you, that men as a rule do not marry actresses but enjoy them as companions in a very different manner."

Davita understood that he meant gentlemen took them as mistresses.

She could not help thinking it would have been far better if that was what her father had done rather than marry Katie, who had run away to be the mistress of Harry.

"I thought Rosie very beautiful," the Marquis was saying, "which indeed she is. It was only after she accepted my protection, as it is usually called, that I discovered that she was incapable of being faithful to her protector, even though it is an unwritten law that that is what is expected of a woman in such circumstances."

He spoke in such an impersonal manner that Davita did not feel embarrassed. She was only interested as he went on:

"I found it impossible to continue providing a house for a woman who entertained in my absence a series of ne'er-do-wells who drank my wine and smoked my cigars, and as they did so felt that they were having the laugh of me."

He paused before he continued:

"That is the whole story in a nutshell. Rosie broke the rules of the game, and I brought the game to an end."

"You do not really . . . think she would have . . . killed herself?" Davita asked almost in a whisper.

The Marquis shook his head.

"It is a trick women of her class use very frequently both here and in Paris, to get their own way."

He saw the question in Davita's eyes and added:

"If you feel at all worried about Rosie's future, I

learnt before I left London that she was already very comfortably settled in another house—this time in Regent's Park—which belongs to a member of the House of Lords who is frequently away from London for long intervals."

The Marquis did not give Davita a chance to say anything and merely said quietly:

"Now that I have explained that, the whole subject is a closed chapter. We will neither of us refer to it again."

Davita gave a little sigh.

"I am glad you told me."

"I only wish I did not have to do so," the Marquis said. "Do you remember my advice that night?"

"That I should go back to Scotland?" Davita asked. "What you were really saying is that I should not have come South in the first place."

She glanced at the Marquis a little uncertainly as she said:

"Even after all the . . . awful things that . . . happened . . . I am glad I did. If I had not, I should never have come to Sherburn House and would not be . . . sitting here with . . . you at this . . . moment."

"You are glad you are?" the Marquis enquired.

"But of course I am very glad. It is very exciting for me," Davita answered.

Then as her eyes met his, perhaps it was a trick of the candlelight, but she found it hard to look away.

❦❦❦

The next day the Marquis left early to go to the sale. He sent a message to his Great-Aunt to say he was looking forward to seeing her that evening, and he hoped she had passed a restful night as he had.

Davita was with the Countess when the message was brought to her, and she laughed.

"I am sure it is a most unusual occurrence for my great-nephew to spend a restful night," she said. "From all I hear, if he is not escorting some beautiful actress from the Gaiety Theatre, he is dancing attendance on one of the beauties who surround the Prince of Wales at Marlborough House."

She spoke with a note of satisfaction in her voice, which made Davita feel she was proud that the Marquis could prove himself to be what Violet and Katie had called a "dasher."

This she had learnt was the highest grade a young man about town could reach.

"Then he must have been very bored with me last night," Davita told herself with a sigh.

Nevertheless, the Marquis had not appeared bored. They had sat talking for a long time over dinner and then had gone on talking when they retired to the Blue Drawing-Room.

To her surprise, he had been as easy to talk to on any number of subjects as her father had been before he had married Katie and started drinking.

Davita had gone to bed thinking over what they had said, and had planned what she would say as a challenge when she had the chance to talk with him another evening.

"Even if he was bored," she told herself, "he is coming back tonight, and even if I never see him again, I shall have quite a lot to remember."

It was a warm day, and she went riding for an hour in the morning, while the Countess was having massage on her legs from an experienced masseur who came from Oxford to treat her.

Wearing her smart new habit, Davita could not help wishing that the Marquis could see her and they could ride together.

Then she told herself that wishing things was just a waste of time, and he would doubtless think her a very poor horsewoman beside those he rode with in Rotten Row or in his estate in Hertfordshire.

The Countess had told her how fine it was.

"You would certainly approve of my great-nephew's

house. It was restored in the middle of the Eighteenth Century and a great part of it is much older than that."

"I know I would not love it as much as I love this house," Davita had replied loyally.

"Nevertheless, get him to tell you about it," the Countess said. "He is very proud of his ancestry. I have told him for years that it is time he was married and had a family."

Davita was surprised at the strange feeling the Countess's words gave her. It was almost like a physical pain.

Then she thought wistfully how fortunate the Marquis's wife would be, not because she would have a fine house and a grand estate but because she would be able to talk to him and learn from him so much that was interesting.

'If only he would stay here a week,' she thought wistfully. 'I would be very much wiser and better informed by the time he left.'

She assumed that tomorrow, perhaps early in the morning, he would go back to London and, though she tried not to put it into words, the house would seem empty without him.

There was still tonight, and she wished she had another dress to wear.

'Not that he would notice me if I were dressed up like the Queen of Sheba,' she thought mockingly.

The hours of the day seemed to pass slowly, and when the Countess went to rest, Davita went out into the sunshine.

Instead of going down to the lake as she always did, she went to the stables.

"Have you room for the horses His Lordship may bring back with him from the sale?" she asked Yates, the Head Groom.

"There's places for a dozen more 'orses, Miss," he replied. "But I don't think 'is Lordship'll bring more than two or three."

"I am sure they will be very fine animals," Davita remarked.

"They will," Yates agreed. " 'Is Lordship be a first-class judge of 'orseflesh."

Davita fed the horses as she always did with carrots and apples, and made a fuss of each one.

Then she walked from the stables into the courtyard outside the front door, and down the first part of the drive towards the bridge which spanned the lake.

She stood for a long time, leaning on the greystone to look into the water below and watch the fish flashing over the gravel bottom.

She walked under the shadow of the great oak trees, a little way up the drive, and although she would not admit it to herself, she half-hoped she might meet the Marquis returning from the sale.

She was almost halfway to the lodges when she saw a carriage turn in at them. Her heart leapt; the Marquis was returning, and far sooner than she had expected.

She stood still, watching the horses approach, but as they drew near she was aware that it was not the open curricle that was coming towards her which the Marquis had been driving when he had left that morning.

Instead it was a closed brougham, and she thought with a feeling of disappointment that it must be someone coming to call on the Countess.

Quickly, because the horses were drawing near, she turned and walked away from the drive into the Park.

She heard the horses pass, and deliberately did not look round but went on walking to where she could see a cluster of spotted deer in the shade of one of the larger trees.

She was wondering how near she could get to them without their being afraid, when her instinct, or perhaps her sixth sense, made her aware that someone was behind her.

She had heard no sound because of the thick grass. She turned round apprehensively, then was frozen to the spot on which she was standing.

Striding towards her, florid and flamboyant, was Lord Mundesley!

Chapter Seven

Davita was frozen into immobility as she stared at Lord Mundesley, thinking he could not be real.

But there was no mistaking his swaggering walk, his top-hat set at a jaunty angle, and the carnation in his button-hole.

Only when he reached her side did she think of running away, but then it was too late.

"So here you are!" he said in a tone of satisfaction. "It has taken me a long time to find you; but now I am successful, as I always am."

"What do you want . . . what are you . . . doing?" Davita managed to say, feeling almost as if she had choked on the words.

"I want you," Lord Mundesley replied, "as I always have. If you thought I had forgotten what you look like, you are very much mistaken."

"Leave me . . . alone!" Davita cried. "You have no . . . right here. I have no wish to see . . . you or Violet ever . . . again."

Lord Mundesley smiled unpleasantly, and his eyes, looking at her in a way that always made her feel shy, were now somehow menacing.

Then as if her face, which was very pale, her red hair, and her green eyes moved him irresistibly, there was a note of passion in his voice as he said:

"I want you, Davita! I have wanted you since I first saw you, and I mean to have you!"

She gave a little startled cry, and he went on:

"You do not suppose the Countess of Sherburn, who is a very respectable old lady, would keep you as her Companion if I tell her of your behaviour in London or that you are very closely connected with the Gaiety."

"You are . . . blackmailing . . . me!"

She meant to speak angrily and accusingly because Lord Mundesley frightened her as he always had, but her voice sounded weak, and he could see that she was trembling.

"I have spent a lot of money on detectives who have finally tracked you down," he said. "Now that I have found you, I suggest you behave like a sensible girl and come back with me to London. I will look after you as I always intended to do."

Now Davita gave a small scream, like an animal that had been trapped, and turned to run away. It was too late!

Lord Mundesley reached out, caught hold of her wrists when she was in the very act of moving, and as she struggled to be free, he pulled her relentlessly into his arms.

"Let me go . . . let me go!" she cried.

She knew even as she fought against him that her resistance excited him, and he was also very strong.

"I will teach you to obey me," he said, "and to love me."

"I hate you . . . I hate you!" she tried to say.

But the words were strangled in her throat, because she was aware that his face was very near to hers and he was about to kiss her.

It was then that she screamed again, fighting with every ounce of her strength, but knowing it must be ineffective.

Suddenly a furious voice shouted:

"What the devil do you think you are doing!"

Then she knew that at the very last moment—the eleventh hour—she was saved.

Lord Mundesley's arms holding her slackened, and she managed to twist herself free of him. But because she was breathless and weak from fear, she stumbled and collapsed to the ground.

As she did so, she heard the Marquis say:

"It is time you were taught a lesson, Mundesley, and this time I will see that you have it."

As he spoke he struck out at Lord Mundesley, who stepped backwards to protect himself, while his hat fell off his head.

As he put up his fists to defend himself, the Marquis struck him again. This time he staggered but did not fall.

"Damn you, Vange!" he exclaimed. "If you want to fight, do so, but in a gentlemanly fashion—with pistols."

"You are no gentleman," the Marquis retorted. "And you do not behave like one."

He advanced on Lord Mundesley again, who attempted to fend him off.

But the Marquis slipped under his guard, caught him on the point of the chin, and he crashed to the ground.

For a moment he was stunned, and then as he opened his eyes the Marquis standing over him said:

"Get out of here or I swear you will be carried out on a stretcher!"

Lord Mundesley let out a foul oath.

The Marquis continued:

"I am letting you off lightly because of your age, but if you ever approach Davita again I will thrash you within an inch of your life. Is that clear?"

Lord Mundesley swore again, but the Marquis did not wait to listen to it. He turned to Davita, who was still sitting on the ground with a stricken look in her eyes.

The Marquis pulled her to her feet, and as she swayed weakly against him, he picked her up in his arms and carried her back through the trees to the drive.

She was trembling as he did so, but at the same time

his arms were the most comforting thing she had ever known.

Drawn up behind Lord Mundesley's brougham was the Marquis's chaise.

He put Davita down gently in the seat, got in beside her, and, taking the reins from the groom who had been holding the horses, said:

"Walk home, Jim."

"Very good, M'Lord."

The Marquis drove his horses away down the drive without even glancing in the direction of where he had left Lord Mundesley.

As he approached the lake he did not cross the bridge which led to the house, but instead drove along a grass track which led to the end of the lake where there was a wood.

When they were out of sight of the house, the Marquis drew the horses to a standstill, fixed the reins to the dashboard, and turned to look at Davita.

She was sitting in the corner of the chaise where he had placed her, her fingers clenched together, and there was still a stricken expression in her eyes.

At the same time, she was not trembling so violently.

"It is all right," the Marquis said quietly. "You are safe!"

It was then that Davita gave a little cry and burst into tears.

"He will . . . take his . . . revenge," she sobbed. "He will . . . tell the Countess about . . . me, and I shall . . . have to go . . . away. He will . . . never let me . . . go."

Her words were almost incoherent, but the Marquis heard them. Very gently, as if he was afraid he would frighten her, he put his arms round her and drew her close to him.

She was so distressed she hardly realised what he was doing, and went on crying against his shoulder.

"I told you it was all right," he said quietly.

"Mundesley will do none of those things. I will not let him."

"How . . . can you . . . stop him? He had . . . detectives looking for me. Everywhere I . . . hide, they will . . . find me."

There was a note of despair in her voice, and as she spoke Davita had pictures of herself running . . . running with Lord Mundesley pursuing her as if she were a fox.

"Stop crying," the Marquis said. "I want to talk to you."

It struck Davita that perhaps this was the last time she would ever be able to talk to him.

With what was almost a superhuman effort, she attempted to control her tears, and groped in her waist-band for her handkerchief.

The Marquis took one from the breast-pocket of his coat and placed it in her hands.

Because it smelt of eau-de-Cologne, and because it was his, it made her want to cry again.

She wiped the tears from her cheeks and though they were still swimming in her eyes and her eye-lashes were wet, she looked at him, feeling she should move from the shelter of his arms, but making no effort to do so.

He looked down at her and said gently:

"You look as if you are very much in need of someone to look after you."

Davita shuddered, and he knew she was thinking it might be Lord Mundesley.

"How could I have anticipated that this would happen to you?" the Marquis asked. "And yet I came home early because I had an idea I was needed."

"I needed you desperately," Davita whispered, "and somehow I . . . thought you might be . . . earlier than was . . . expected."

"Was that why you were walking on the drive?" the Marquis asked.

Because he might think it forward of her, she looked down shyly, and could not answer him.

"I came in time," the Marquis said, as if he was following his own train of thought. "And now, as I have said, Lord Mundesley will not trouble you again."

His words brought the fear back, and Davita cried:

"But he will . . . and how can you . . . prevent him when you have . . . gone away?"

"By taking you with me," the Marquis said very quietly.

She thought she could not have heard him aright.

As her eyes looked up at him enquiringly, he said:

"It is too soon—I did not mean to tell you about it yet, Davita, but ever since I first saw you I have been unable to forget you, and I think perhaps you know already that we mean something very special to each other."

For the moment Davita thought she must be dreaming, but then as the Marquis seemed to be enveloped with a dazzling light, she thought that perhaps he was making her the same proposal as Lord Mundesley had.

With an inarticulate little sound she turned her face away from him.

As if he knew without words what she was thinking, he said:

"I am suggesting that the only way you can be completely safe for the rest of your life is to marry me."

For a moment Davita could only hold her breath. Then she said in a voice that did not sound like her own:

"Did you . . . ask me to . . . marry you?"

"I will keep you safe," the Marquis replied, "not only from Mundesley but from anyone like him, and I promise, my darling, one thing I will never allow you to do is to go behind the stage at the Gaiety or have supper at Romano's."

He was smiling at her as he spoke, with a look in his eyes which made him appear no longer cynical or contemptuous but very different.

"It can . . . not be . . . true!"

Davita was trembling, and her eyes were shining as if

the same light she had seen envelop the Marquis was radiating from her.

"I will have to make you believe it," he said, "but first I want to know what you feel about me."

"You cannot . . . marry me," she murmured. "You are so . . . magnificent, as I thought the first time I . . . saw you, and when I thought more about you I knew you were . . . everything a . . . man should . . . be."

"You thought about me?" the Marquis asked.

"How could I . . . help it? And after that . . . terrible party, I thought you would . . . hate me."

"I suspected you could have had nothing to do with such a despicable plot," the Marquis said, "and when you disappeared I was certain of it."

"I wanted to . . . ask you to . . . forgive me long before you came . . . here."

"I will forgive you," the Marquis said, "if you tell me what you feel about me now."

Davita leant forward, and hiding her face against his shoulder she whispered:

"I love . . . you. I did not . . . realise it was . . . love . . . but I kept thinking about you, and when you . . . talked to me last night I knew to be with you was the most . . . wonderful thing that had . . . ever . . . happened to me."

"You will always be with me in the future."

As the Marquis spoke he put his fingers under her chin and gently turned her face up to his. As he did so, he felt her tremble, but he knew it was not with fear.

He looked down at her face for a long moment, as if he wished to engrave it on his memory forever, then as his arms tightened his lips sought hers.

It was as if the Heavens opened, and she knew an inexpressible ecstasy that was beyond all thought or imagination.

The touch of the Marquis's lips seemed to give her all the beauty she had sought in her dreams, all the wonder that she had known could only be found in love, and thought it would never be hers.

He kissed her gently at first, as if she was something infinitely precious, then the softness of her mouth aroused him in a way he had never known before.

His kiss became more possessive, more insistent, and yet Davita was not afraid.

She knew that she belonged to him, and she surrendered herself to his strength and the vibrations which came from him to link with the vibrations from herself.

She felt as if he took not only her body into his keeping, but her heart and her soul. They were his and she knew that her love for him, and his for her, was not only very human but also part of the Divine.

When finally the Marquis raised his head, she said a little incoherently, but with a note of indescribable rapture in her voice:

"I love you . . . I love you!"

"And I love you, my sweet darling," the Marquis replied.

"How can you love me when there are so many really . . . beautiful women in your . . . life?"

She was thinking of the Gaiety Girls as she spoke. Of Rosie and Violet, of Lottie Collins, and also the social beauties that the Countess had said pursued him.

The Marquis held her very closely against him.

"When I first saw you sitting in the Box," he said, "I knew you were different from anyone I had ever seen before."

"In the Box?" Davita asked in a puzzled voice.

"I was looking round the Theatre with my Operaglasses," he explained. "And I saw you watching the Show, with the excitement of a child at her first Pantomime."

"I had no . . . idea you were . . . there."

The Marquis smiled.

"I found you more entrancing than any Show I have ever seen, and when later I saw you in Romano's, I found you were even lovelier than you had appeared at a distance."

"You . . . told me to go . . . back to . . . Scotland!"

"I could not bear you to be spoilt, and to think of you losing that young, untouched look, which is the most beautiful thing I have ever seen in my life."

As if he could not help himself, he bent his head and kissed her again, and as he felt Davita's instinctive response, he said a long time later, and his voice was unsteady:

"I have so much to teach you, my darling, and you have so much to learn about love. Thank God you ran away when you did."

"I . . . thought I would . . . never see you . . . again."

"I thought the same thing—you haunted me. If Mundesley was looking for you, so was I."

He gave a little laugh.

"Fate played into my hands—I found you where I least expected to—in the Library of Sherburn House."

"I thought you would . . . send me . . . away."

"I was overjoyed at finding you. At the same time, I had to make sure that you were not implicated in any way in Mundesley's disgraceful act of vengeance."

"I was so . . . ashamed."

"I told you to forget it! At the same time, my precious little love, we must be thankful that however reprehensible it was to be mixed up with such people, it brought us together."

"You are . . . quite certain that I can . . . marry you?" Davita asked. "Perhaps the Countess and your other relatives will . . . disapprove."

"I think my Great-Aunt will be delighted," the Marquis replied, "even though she will regret losing you, and the rest of my relatives do not matter, although they will be pleased I am doing what they have urged me to do for a long time."

"They . . . wanted you to be . . . married?"

"They wanted me to have a wife and an heir."

Davita blushed and hid her face against him.

"Do I make you shy?" the Marquis enquired.

"Yes . . . but I am also very . . . very proud . . . I still cannot believe that what you are saying is . . . true."

"I will make you believe it," the Marquis said.

Once again he would have kissed her, but Davita put up her hands to stop him.

"There is something I want to . . . say to you."

"What is it?" he asked.

"You have asked me to . . . marry you. It is the most glorious . . . perfect thing which can ever happen, but are you certain . . . absolutely certain that I will not . . . bore you?"

For a moment the Marquis did not answer and she went on:

"It would be an unbearable agony if I lost you now, but it would be worse . . . very much worse . . . if I lost you after I became your . . . wife. In fact, I think then I would . . . really want to . . . die."

As she spoke, she felt she was saying almost the same thing as Rosie had said, and yet it was a cry that came from her heart.

The Marquis gave her such a sense of security that she knew that when she was in his arms she would never feel afraid again. At the same time, he already filled her whole world, and she knew that once they were married he would fill the sky as well.

Without him there would only be darkness!

As if what she was thinking was reflected in her eyes, and the Marquis could read her thoughts, he said:

"It is difficult to explain to you, my sweet, but although I was not really aware of it, I have been looking for you all my life. I thought it was impossible to find a woman who was intelligent enough to stimulate my mind and at the same time be pure, innocent, and untouched, and very different in every way from the women with whom I amused myself."

He drew Davita closer as he said:

"When I saw you at first sitting in the Box, and the next time at Romano's, it was almost as if you were enveloped with light. I knew you were what I had always wanted."

Davita gave a little start when he said the word "light." As if she knew he wanted her to explain, she said:

"Just now when you said you . . . wished to . . . marry me, there was light blazing all round you, and I knew it was the . . . light that came from . . . God."

"My darling—my sweet," the Marquis said in his deep voice. "We think alike. We are perhaps fey about each other, and because of it we know that we belong."

He kissed her again before she could answer, and then as his kiss finished he looked down at her eyes shining up at his, a faint flush on her cheeks, and her lips soft and trembling from his kisses.

"I adore you and I want you," he said. "The sooner we get married, the sooner you will be sure that you are safe, and no-one will ever hurt or frighten you again. Let us go back and tell Aunt Louise that she has to find another Companion."

"I am afraid she will be . . . upset," Davita said.

"She will be compensated in knowing she now has a great-niece," the Marquis smiled.

He picked up the reins. The horses, who had been quietly grazing the grass, began to move.

He turned the chaise round skilfully. Then as they started the drive back alongside the lake, putting one arm round Davita, he pulled her closer to him.

"I love you, my adorable little Scot," he said, "and I know that just as you will never lose me, I will never lose you. We have so many exciting things to do together."

Davita put her head against his arm.

"I am so happy," she whispered, "so wildly, unbelievably happy . . . but it is like walking into a dream . . . and I want . . . you to . . . feel the same."

"I am so happy that I feel I am dreaming," the

Marquis said. "At the same time, when I kiss you I know you are real—very real, and this is only the beginning of our love, which will grow and intensify all the years we are together."

Davita gave a little cry of happiness.

"How can you say such wonderful things to me?"

"It is you who make me say them," the Marquis replied. "In fact I am rather surprised at them myself."

There was just the touch of a mocking note in his voice, but it was very different from the way he had spoken when he was cynical and contemptuous.

Looking up at him, Davita thought the lines had almost vanished on his face, and he looked much younger. Then when his eyes met hers she knew he was very much in love.

They reached the end of the lake, and as the Marquis took his arm from her so that he could drive his horses over the bridge, Davita said:

"When I arrived and saw the house, I felt I could hide here in safety . . . but now I know there is only one safe place . . . and that is with . . . you."

The Marquis took his eyes from the horses to look at her, and as he smiled he said:

"My love will keep you safe, my beautiful one, now and forever."

Then as Davita put out her hand to touch him, she knew they were both enveloped with the light of love, which comes from God and sweeps away the darkness of evil.

A Duke in Danger

Author's Note

The Army of Occupation in France after the defeat of Napoleon presented an enormous problem of organisation. The French thought that the feeding of 150,000 troops would be a miracle, and their attitude towards the force swung from welcome to resentment.

What was more, the French were protesting that they would not pay their indemnity, and Madame de Staël predicted it would be paid "in gold the first year, in silver the second, and in the third in lead."

The occupation finally ended after the Congress of Aix-la-Chapelle in November 1818. But in England there were two different enemies—political agitation and economic distress. The soldiers returning home found that in the country for which they had fought so valiantly, there was no place for heroes.

CHAPTER ONE

❧

1818

THE DUKE OF Harlington arrived at Harlington House in Berkeley Square and looked round him with satisfaction.

The house was obviously in excellent repair, and he viewed with pride the portraits of his ancestors on the walls and up the stairs.

There were also the paintings collected by a previous Duke which included a number of those by French Masters.

He had just come from France, where he had learnt to recognise the genius of the French artists in a way he had been unable to do before the war with Napoleon.

However, he was intelligent enough to realise that since the end of the war he had increased his knowledge of a great number of things in which he had not been interested previously.

A tall, extremely handsome man, his years as a soldier had left their mark on the way he walked, and perhaps too in the expression in his eyes.

Women, and there had been a great number of them, had said to him that he always appeared to be looking for something below the surface and generally to be disappointed.

He was not quite certain what they meant, but he had

learnt to judge men and women by their fundamental personalities rather than by their superficial qualities.

He had indeed owed his very important position in Wellington's Army to his understanding of human nature.

He was not only a leader, but, as someone had once said of him, he had that extra quality of magnetism which is found only in the greatest Rulers.

It was a compliment that had made the Duke laugh when he heard it. At the same time, because he was not in the least conceited, he hoped it was true.

Now as he walked from the Hall into the downstairs Sitting-Room and from there into the book-filled Library, he thought few men could have been as fortunate in life as he had been.

He had survived five gruelling years in Portugal and Spain, then in France and finally at Waterloo, without receiving a scratch, when so many of his friends and contemporaries had been killed beside him.

Then, because of his outstanding ability not only as a soldier but as a diplomat, he had become essential to the Iron Duke during the Years of Occupation.

Looking back on them, they had undoubtedly been troubled times of frustration and political drama that concerned not only Britain but the whole of Europe.

Yet now, though it seemed incredible, it was over, and by the end of the year—it was now three years after Waterloo—the Army of Occupation would have come home.

After all the dramatic discussions, the tension of rising tempers, the decisions made and unmade, combined with the endless tug-of-war between the Allies, the Duke could hardly believe that he was at this moment, a free man.

There was still the Congress of Aix-la-Chapelle which was to take place in October, but the Army was to be out of France by November 30.

As far as the Duke of Harlington was concerned, he had now his own personal problems to settle, for

Wellington had reluctantly allowed him to leave the Army at the beginning of the summer so that he could put his own affairs in order.

It was a pleasant surprise to arrive in London to find that Harlington House at any rate seemed in fairly good shape.

He had sent one of his *Aides-de-Camp,* an extremely trustworthy man, ahead of him, with instructions to see that the staff was notified of his arrival.

He intended to stay under his own roof while he called on the Prince Regent, and if the King was well enough, to call on His Majesty at Buckingham Palace.

It was strange to be back in England after so many years abroad, but stranger still to know that his position in life was now very different from what it had been when he was last here.

Then as Ivar Harling, one of the youngest Colonels in the British Army, he had found a great deal to amuse him, most of which was unfortunately well beyond his purse.

Now as the Duke of Harlington he was not only a distinguished aristocrat with many hereditary duties which had to be taken up, but also an extremely wealthy man.

Letters which had been waiting for him at Paris from the late Duke's Bankers enclosed not only a list of the possessions which were now his but also a statement of the money which was standing in his name.

The amount of it seemed incredible, but as there was still so much to do for Wellington, the new Duke had set his own needs on one side and put his country first.

When he reached the Library, he stood looking at the leather-bound books which made the walls a patchwork of colour and appreciated the very fine painting of horses by Stubbs over the mantelpiece.

The Butler, an elderly man, came into the room.

He was followed by a footman who was carrying a silver tray on which there was a wine-cooler engraved with the family crest and containing an open bottle of champagne.

When a glass was poured out for the Duke, he noticed automatically that the footman's livery did not fit well and his stockings were wrinkled.

It was with some difficulty that he did not point it out to the man and tell him to smarten himself up.

Then as the footman set down the tray on a table in the corner of the room, the Butler hesitated, and the Duke understood that he had something to say.

"What is it?" he enquired. "I think your name is Bateson."

"Yes, Your Grace. That's right."

There was a pause, then he began again a little hesitatingly:

"I hope Your Grace'll find everything to your liking, but we've only had three days to prepare for your visit, and the house has been shut up for the last six years."

"I was thinking how well it looked," the Duke replied pleasantly.

"We've worked hard, Your Grace, and while I presumed to engage several women to clean every room that Your Grace was likely to use, there's a great deal more to be done."

"I suppose since the late Duke was so ill in the last years of his life," the Duke said reflectively, "and did not come to London, you were down to a skeleton staff."

"Just my wife and myself, Your Grace."

The Duke raised his eye-brows.

"That certainly seems very few in so large a house. Yet," he added graciously, "it certainly looks as I expected."

"It's what I hoped Your Grace'd say," the Butler replied, "and if I have your permission to enlarge the staff further, I feel certain we can soon get things back to what they were in the old days."

"Of course!"

The Duke twitched his lips at the Butler's words.

Already references to "the old days" had become a

joke in the Army, in diplomatic and political circles, and, he was quite certain, in domestic ones too.

Every country, and he had visited a great number since peace had been declared, had talked of nothing but the old days and how good things were then, compared to what they were now.

He was quite sure that it was something that would be repeated to him again and again in England.

Then, as if Bateson realised that he had no wish to go on talking, he said:

"Luncheon'll be ready very shortly, Your Grace. I hopes it'll be to your liking."

The Duke thought that the man was almost pathetically eager to please, and when Bateson shut the door behind him he wondered how old he was.

He remembered that when he was a small boy and his father had brought him to this house, Bateson had been there, and he had thought him very impressive with six stalwart footmen behind him as he greeted them in the Hall.

"It was a long time ago," the Duke said to himself.

By now Bateson must be well over sixty, but he could understand that having been in Ducal service all his life, the man had no wish either to make a change or to retire earlier than he need.

The Duke was well aware that there was widespread unemployment in England and it would obviously be difficult for an elderly man to get a job.

Besides which, with men released from the Army of Occupation coming home every month, the situation would become more and more difficult.

He remembered the fuss there had been when the Duke of Wellington had proposed a reduction of thirty thousand men in the Army.

Then he told himself that with the wealth he now owned, there was no need for him to make any reductions in staff; in fact, he would increase it in every house he owned.

When he went into the Dining-Room to eat an

excellent luncheon served by Bateson with the help of two footmen, he decided that his first task, now that he was back in England, should be to visit his new home, Harlington Castle, in Buckinghamshire.

Even now, after he had thought about it for two years, he could hardly believe that it was his and that he was, incredibly and unexpectedly, the fifth Duke of Harlington!

He was exceedingly proud to belong to a family that had played its part in the history of England since the time of the Crusades.

However, he had never in his wildest dreams thought that he might succeed to the Dukedom.

He had always been sensible enough to realise that he was a very unimportant member of the Harlings. His father had been only a cousin of the previous Duke, and there had been three lives between him and any chance of inheritance.

But just as the war had brought devastation and misery to so many households over the whole of Europe, the previous Duke's only son, Richard, had been killed at Waterloo.

Ivar Harling had seen Richard just before the battle, and he had been in tremendous spirits.

"If we do not defeat the Froggies once and for all this time," he had said cheerfully, "then I will bet you a dinner at White's to a case of champagne that the war will last another five years."

Ivar Harling had laughed.

"Done, Richard!" he said. "I have the feeling I shall be the loser, but it will be in a good cause!"

"It certainly will!" Richard replied with a grin; then he had added: "Seriously, what is our chance?"

"Excellent, if the Prussian Guards arrive on time."

Both men had been silent for a moment, knowing that actually the situation was very much more critical than it appeared on the surface.

"Good luck!"

Ivar Harling, turning his horse, galloped to where

Wellington was watching the battle and saw that the Duke had ordered his Cavalry to counter-attack.

Then as he rode to the side of the great man, the Duke turned to his *Aide-de-Camp,* Colonel James Stanhope, and asked the time.

"Twenty minutes past four."

"The battle is mine! And if the Prussians arrive soon," Wellington said, "there will be an end to the war."

Even as he spoke, Ivar Harling heard the first Prussian guns on the fringe of a distant wood.

⋘⋙⋘⋙⋘⋙

When luncheon was over, the Duke suddenly felt as if the house was very quiet.

He was used to having people moving incessantly round him, seeing scurrying Statesmen with worried faces trekking in and out of Wellington's Headquarters in Paris, hearing sharp commands being given at all times of the day and night, and dealing with endless complaints, requests, and reports.

There were also parties, Receptions, Assemblies, and Balls, besides the long-drawn-out meetings at which everyone seemed to talk and talk but achieve nothing.

There had, however, been interludes which were tender, exciting, interesting, and very alluring.

The Duke thought cynically that now that he was who he was, these would multiply and he could come under a very different pressure from what he had endured during the years of war.

He was of course well aware that as the young General Harling, with many medals for gallantry, women had found him attractive.

Those who had congregated in Paris either for diplomatic reasons or just in search of amusement had, where he was concerned, seldom been disappointed.

While they had had a great deal to offer him, he had had nothing to offer them, but after it became known last year that he was no longer just an officer of the

Household Cavalry but the Duke of Harlington, things had changed considerably.

Now he knew he was a genuine catch from the matrimonial point of view.

At the same time, alluring, exquisitely gowned, sophisticated married women would find it a "feather in their caps" to have him at their feet, or, to put it more bluntly, in their beds.

War heroes were of course the fashion, and every woman wished to capture for herself the hero of the hour, the Duke of Wellington, or if that was impossible then the second choice was inevitably the Duke of Harlington.

At times he found it difficult to prevent himself from smiling mockingly at the compliments he received or to suppress a cynical note in his voice when he replied to them.

It was his friend Major Gerald Chertson who had put into words what he had half-sensed for himself.

"I suppose, Ivar," he had said, "you know that as soon as you get home you will have to get married?"

"Why the hell should I do that?" the Duke asked.

"First, because you have to produce an heir," the Major replied. "That is obligatory on the part of a Duke! You must also prevent that exceedingly unpleasant relative of yours, Jason Harling, from eventually stepping into your shoes, as he is extremely eager to do."

"Are you telling me that Jason Harling is heir presumptive to my title?"

"I certainly am," Gerald Chertson replied. "At least he has been boasting of it lately, loudly and clearly all over Paris."

"I have never thought about it, but I suppose he is!" the Duke remarked.

He remembered that Richard Harling had not been the only member of the family to fall at Waterloo. Another cousin, the son of the last Duke's younger brother, had also died early in the battle, although it was not reported until three days later.

On the fourth Duke's death, in 1817, the title would have been his father's, had he been alive. Instead, it was his.

Now that Gerald spoke of it, he recalled that the title would next go to another and more distant branch of the family now represented by Jason Harling.

He was the one relative of whom the Duke was thoroughly ashamed.

He had always been extremely relieved that during hostilities he had not come into contact with Jason.

They had, however, met in Paris after the war had been won.

The Duke thought Jason had always been an odious child, and he had grown up into an even more odious man.

He had seen very little of the war, but he had managed, by scheming and ingratiating himself in a manner which most men would think beneath them, to get himself a safe and comfortable post.

He became *Aide-de-Camp* to an elderly armchair General who never left England until the French had laid down their arms.

The way Jason toadied to those in power made most men feel sick, but it ensured that he lived an extremely pleasant life.

He managed to move in the best social circles, and he never missed an opportunity to feather his own nest.

The Duke had heard rumours of his accepting bribes and of other ways in which Jason took advantage of his position, but he had told himself it was not his business and tried not to listen.

Now as head of the family he knew that he could not ignore Jason as he had in the past, and he had not realised that he was his heir should he not have a son.

Aloud he had said to his friend Gerald Chertson:

"If there is one thing that would make me look on marriage with less aversion, it would be the quenching of any hopes that Jason might have of stepping into my shoes."

"I have heard that he has been borrowing money on the chance of it," Gerald replied.

"I do not believe you!" the Duke exclaimed. "Who would be fool enough to advance Jason any money on the chance of my not producing an heir?"

"There are always Usurers ready to take such risks at an exorbitant rate of interest," Gerald remarked.

"Then they must be crazy," the Duke said angrily. "After all, I have not yet got one foot in the grave, and I am perfectly capable of having a family, and a large one!"

"Of course, it all depends on whether you live to do so."

"What are you insinuating?"

Gerald paused before he replied:

"I heard, but paid no attention to it at the time, that after Richard's death at Waterloo, Jason had a large wager that you would not be a survivor."

"Well, he lost his money," the Duke said sharply.

"I agree that you are now not likely to be killed by a French bullet, but there is always such a thing as an—accident."

The Duke threw back his head and laughed.

"Really, Gerald, now you are trying to frighten me! Jason is far too much of a shyster to soil his hands with murder."

"I do not suppose it would be Jason's hands which would get dirty," Gerald Chertson answered drily. "Do not forget there was an attempt to assassinate Wellington in February."

"That is true. But André Cantillon was an assassin with a fanatical devotion to Bonaparte."

"I know that," Gerald Chertson replied. "At the same time—and I am not trying to frighten you—Jason Harling has a fanatical devotion to himself and his future."

"I refuse to worry about anything so absurd," the Duke said loftily.

However, as he walked from the Dining-Room

towards the Library after an excellent meal, something struck him.

Together with his satisfaction with the house and everything which now had changed his life to a bed of roses from one which at times had been on very hard ground, he felt that Jason Harling was undoubtedly longing for his future to be assured.

"I suppose I shall have to marry," he told himself.

It was a depressing thought, and his mind wandered to the beautiful Lady Isobel Dalton.

She had made it quite clear when he left Paris that as she would be in London next week, she expected to see a great deal of him.

The daughter of a Duke and widow of an elderly Baronet who had died of a heart-attack from over-eating and over-drinking, Lady Isobel was a very gay widow.

She had been one of the many women in Paris—French, English, and Russian—who had been eager to console the war warriors after their long years in the wilderness.

At every party they had glowed like lights in the darkness, and the Duke had found that Isobel's arms encircled his neck almost too eagerly, while her lips invited his even before he had any desire to kiss them.

However, it would have been impossible not to become aroused by the fiery delights which Lady Isobel offered him, and by the flattery with which she made him feel he was the only man in the world.

"I love you! I want you!" she had said a thousand times. "I loved you the moment we met, and now, dearest, you are in a position I never dreamt would be yours. I love you because you will behave exactly as a Duke should."

He was well aware that she pressed herself both physically and determinedly closer and closer to him, and when he had stayed with her after dinner the night before he left Paris, she had made her intentions very clear.

"As soon as you have everything in order, I will join

you," she had said softly. "We will entertain and make our parties the smartest, the most fashionable, and the most influential in the whole of London."

She had given a little sigh before she said:

"The Prince Regent is getting very old, and the *Beau Monde* needs a new leader, and who would look more handsome and more dashing or authoritative than you?"

She paused, expecting the Duke to say that no-one was more beautiful than she was.

But he realised that he was being pushed into declaring himself, and he had not yet made up his mind whether he wished to marry anyone, let alone Lady Isobel.

When he thought about it, he knew it would be a marriage which would please his many Harling relations and be acclaimed as "sensible" by the Social World at large.

Although Isobel could excite and arouse him as few women had been able to do, something which he called his "intuition" told him she was not really the type of woman with whom he desired to spend the rest of his life.

He had learnt in the Army that women were for pleasure and should not encroach too closely on the man's world of living, fighting, and dying for his country.

Lady Isobel was very different from the attractive young Portuguese women who offered themselves to the tired men who needed some respite after the hard fighting in the Peninsular War.

She was different, too, from the attractive, cheerful little French *cocottes* who could make a man laugh, however tired he might be, and even find it a joke that they had picked his pocket just before he left.

But women were women, and while a man must sometimes relax from the hard realities of war, marriage was a very different thing!

As he had travelled back over Northern France and had an uncomfortable crossing on a tempestuous

Channel, the Duke, when he was not thinking of his new possessions, found himself thinking of Isobel.

She was beautiful and confessed her love for him very convincingly.

Yet, there was something stronger than that thought, which he could not understand, and which held him back from asking the question that she was longing to hear.

"I must be with you, Ivar," she had said a thousand times. "I cannot live without you, and I know you would be lost and lonely without me."

It had been easier to cover her lips with his and kiss her than to argue.

The Duke had known when he left Isobel that she was closing up, before coming to London, the house in which she had been living in Paris.

It was part of a deliberate plan, because she was determined with a steel-like will which lay somewhere in that soft, seductive body, that she would become the Duchess of Harlington.

Thinking of her made the Duke feel restless.

He walked to the fireplace and dragged violently at the elegant needlework bell-pull.

He imagined the wire running down the corridor until the iron bell was jerked backwards and forwards in the passage outside the pantry-door, where it was impossible for Bateson and the footmen not to hear it.

He did not have to wait long before the door opened and Bateson, rather breathless, appeared.

"I have changed my mind," the Duke said. "I have decided I will visit the Castle today. It should not take me more than two hours to drive there."

He saw a look of consternation on Bateson's face.

"Has Your Grace informed Lady Alvina of Your Grace's intention?"

"I meant to stay here," the Duke said, "at least until the end of the week, but I will see the Castle and return either tomorrow or the day after."

"I think it'd be wise for Your Grace to warn Her Ladyship of your arrival."

The Duke smiled.

"I expect I shall be comfortable enough, and after such a good luncheon I will not be very hungry for dinner. Congratulate the Cook, Bateson, after you have ordered the Phaeton and the new team of horses which I understand are already in the stables."

As he had no intention of arriving in England without excellent horses, he had asked Gerald, when he left Paris a week earlier, to go to Berkeley Square and see what horses were waiting for him.

"If they are not up to scratch," he had said, "buy me a team worth driving."

As he and Gerald shared a taste in horses, as in other things, he knew he would not be disappointed, and when twenty minutes later he was told that the Phaeton was at the door, he saw that his friend had done him proud.

The four chestnuts were perfectly matched. They were also exceedingly well bred, and he knew he would be able to cover the distance from Berkeley Square to Harlington Castle very quickly.

Unfortunately, at the moment he was not aware of what the record was, and as the groom who was to accompany him had also been engaged by Gerald, it was no use asking him.

Instead, as his trunk was strapped to the back of the Phaeton, he said to Bateson:

"I have told my valet to take the rest of the day and part of tomorrow off so that he can visit his relatives who live in London. I expect there will be someone who will look after me at the Castle."

"I hopes there'll be, Your Grace," Bateson murmured. "But I thinks it's a mistake, Your Grace, not to take your own man with you."

"Nonsense!" the Duke replied. "You are worrying about me unnecessarily, as you did when I was a small boy. I am sure the Castle will be just as I remember it."

He sprang up into the Phaeton and took the reins from the groom.

It was with a feeling of intense satisfaction that he looked forward to enjoying every minute of driving the finest team of horses he had ever possessed.

The Phaeton, which Gerald had also purchased for him, was so light that it seemed almost to spring off the ground as if it had wings on its wheels.

As he drove round Berkeley Square, he would have seen, had he looked round, Bateson staring after him with a look of apprehension on his old face.

He walked into the house and, as he did so, told the footmen sharply to wind up the red carpet which they had put down over the steps and out over the pavement.

Then he went into the kitchen, where his wife was clearing up after the luncheon with the help of two new scullery-maids who had no idea where to put anything.

"Has he gone?" Mrs. Bateson asked.

Bateson nodded.

"He's not to let Her Ladyship know that he's coming."

Mrs. Bateson put down on the table with a bang the heavy brass sauce-pan she was holding.

"We was told!" she said almost fiercely.

"Yes, I know. His Grace had meant to stay here, I understand, for several days, and we'd then have had a chance to inform Her Ladyship."

Mrs. Bateson gave a sigh.

"As it is, there's nothing we can do. I suppose you didn't think to say anything to him?"

" 'Course not! It's not my place."

"He'll have a shock, of that there's no doubt!"

As Mrs. Bateson spoke there was a ring on the bell. Bateson got up slowly from the chair.

"Who can that be?"

"Caller, probably."

"I suppose I'd better go myself," Bateson grumbled. "These young 'uns won't know what to say."

He padded slowly back along the passage to the Hall as if his feet were hurting him.

As he opened the door, he saw to his astonishment that the Phaeton in which the Duke had just driven away was outside.

"What is it? What's happened?" he asked the groom who was standing on the door-step.

"His Grace has left in the Library some papers which he particularly wanted with him."

Bateson smiled.

It was somehow almost a relief to find that his new Master was human and could make mistakes like everyone else.

"Come with me," he said to the groom, and in a dignified manner walked across the Hall towards the Library.

The Duke, holding the reins of his team outside the house, was frowning. He could not think how he could have been so stupid as to leave behind the papers the Bank had sent him with an inventory of the contents of the Castle.

He supposed he had been so busy admiring the house and its contents that it had for a moment slipped his tidy, self-disciplined mind, which usually made him punctilious about the smallest detail with which he was concerned.

However, he had gone only a short distance and little time would be lost.

It was then that he heard a voice. He looked down to see an elderly man with white hair and a somewhat lugubrious face looking up at him.

"May I ask, Sir, if you're the new Duke of Harlington?" he enquired.

"I am."

"I was a-calling to see Your Grace."

"I am afraid you are too late. I am just leaving. I will be back in a few days."

"It's important that I see Your Grace now."

"What is it about?" the Duke asked.

As he spoke he glanced towards the front door, hoping the groom would return and he could be on his way.

With a little hesitation the man said:

"It concerns certain family treasures. I have one here in which I think Your Grace'd be interested."

"Thank you, but I am not buying anything at the moment."

"It is not a question of buying it, Your Grace, but redeeming."

As the man spoke he opened the black bag he was holding in his hand and drew out a large silver bowl. The Duke looked at it indifferently, then noticed the crest engraved on the side of the bowl.

When he looked a little more closely, he was aware that it was an exquisite piece of silver-work which he was almost sure was by Louis XV's famous goldsmith Thomas Germain.

His mind went back to the last time he had dined at the Castle. He could almost swear the bowl had stood on the Dining-Room table between the candelabra.

His father, who was there with him, had remarked that there was no family in the whole country with such a fine collection of silver- and gold-work as the Harlings'.

"Where did you get that?" he said harshly.

Before the man could answer, the Duke added:

"If it has been stolen, you have no right to have it in your possession!"

"I've every right, Your Grace, as I can prove, should you be interested."

The Duke drew in his breath.

"I am interested," he said, "and I want a very good explanation or I shall have you taken in front of the Magistrates!"

The man did not seem unduly perturbed.

At the moment the groom returned, holding the papers in his hand. As he was about to climb onto the Phaeton, the Duke said:

"Hold the horses, I have to see this man before I leave."

As he spoke, he took the papers from the groom and transferred them to the inside pocket of his coat. Then he stepped down onto the pavement.

"Follow me," he said sharply, walking up the steps and into the house.

The man followed him across the Hall and into the Library, and Bateson closed the door behind them.

"Let me see that bowl again!" the Duke demanded. "What is your name?"

"Emmanuel Pinchbeck, Your Grace. I'm a pawn-broker."

"A pawn-broker!" the Duke repeated.

That was something he had not expected.

"Are you telling me this bowl was pawned?"

"Yes, Your Grace, with a great number of other things."

The Duke's lips tightened as he put the bowl down on the table. It was the most beautiful piece of silver-work he had ever seen.

"You had better start from the beginning," he said quietly but with a note of steel in his voice. "Tell me how you came into possession of this bowl. Who brought it to you?"

Without speaking, Emmanuel Pinchbeck drew out a piece of paper from his pocket and handed it to the Duke. It was somewhat soiled but he could read written quite clearly:

I, Emmanuel Pinchbeck, have loaned the sum of thirty pounds on a silver bowl circa 1690 and will keep it in my possession as long as the interest of thirty per cent is paid to me annually by the owner, who accepts the terms of this contract.

In an elegant, educated hand was the signature *Alvina Harling*.

The Duke looked at it and his chin was squared and his lips set in a hard line. He then said:

"How many other things have you besides this bowl?"

"Six small pictures, Your Grace, several miniatures, four more silver bowls, a snuff-box which is very elegant set with emeralds and diamonds, and two gold candelabra worth a good deal more than what they were pawned for."

There was silence before the Duke said:

"Why have you come to me?"

"I've come to you, Your Grace, because on hearing that Your Grace had inherited the title, I thought it would be to your advantage to redeem everything I hold."

There was again silence. Emmanuel Pinchbeck quickly went on:

"Frankly, Your Grace, I needs the money, and the arrangement isn't satisfactory to me as it stands."

"Why not?"

"Because thirty per cent is a good deal lower than other pawn-brokers charge, and I'm unable to sell what has increased in value, not because of their intrinsic worth, but because the price of gold and silver has risen."

"You mean they would be worth more melted down?" the Duke asked.

He spoke with a note of horror in his voice, but Emmanuel Pinchbeck merely nodded.

"Yes, Your Grace. As I said, times are hard, and I can't go on holding all these things indefinitely."

"How long have you held them already?"

"Nearly three years, Your Grace. I'll never get my money back, and as I said, that's not satisfactory. Not satisfactory at all."

The Duke realised that he was serious, and there were beads of sweat on his forehead.

At the same time, he knew that the man was speaking the truth when he had said that thirty per cent was less than many pawn-brokers charged, and it was not satisfactory from his point of view to hold goods that he could not sell.

Because the Duke was a just man, he said:

"I realise that you have been extremely honest in not selling any of these things, especially those which you say could be melted down. I will therefore buy back from you everything that you hold which has come to you from the person whose signature is on this paper."

The old man's eyes seemed to light up and he smiled.

"I'm very grateful, Your Grace. I knew when I heard of your gallantry in battle that you'd treat me fairly and that I needn't be afraid to approach you."

"I am glad you did," the Duke said. "I will now pay you immediately what is owing on this silver bowl. I shall be returning to London the day after tomorrow, at the very latest, and I suggest you bring the rest of the things here to me."

"That's very kind of Your Grace."

"What is the final total on this piece?" he enquired.

Emmanuel Pinchbeck looked at him out of the corners of his eyes before he said:

"It's been with me for two years and two months, Your Grace."

The Duke made a quick calculation and drew from the wallet which he took from the pocket of his coat notes for well over the amount necessary.

He handed them to Emmanuel Pinchbeck, who swiftly put them away as he said:

"I'm extremely grateful to Your Grace. It'll be a weight off my mind and'll certainly make things easier for me financially."

"I shall see you in two days' time," the Duke said. "In case I am held up, send someone to enquire if I am here before you yourself bring the goods."

"I'll do that, Your Grace."

The Duke walked towards the door, and Emmanuel Pinchbeck, carrying the empty bag, followed behind.

Bateson was in the Hall, and the Duke said:

"You will find a piece of silver on my desk. Have it cleaned and put in the safe until I return."

There was a sharp ring in his voice and his eyes were cold as he spoke. Bateson looked up at him apprehensively, opening his lips as if to say something. But it was too late.

The Duke was out of the house, and, seating himself once again in the Phaeton, he took the reins from the groom and the horses moved off.

As he drove away for the second time, Bateson turned to Emmanuel Pinchbeck, who was watching him go, and said fiercely:

"Why did you 'ave to come here making trouble as soon as His Grace returned? Scum like you only do harm in the world!"

"I wanted my money," Emmanuel Pinchbeck replied defiantly. "You've no right to insult me. I've kept my word to Her Ladyship and have sold nothing, even though I could have got a good price for some of them."

"Get out!" Bateson said angrily. "If you'd any decency you'd have waited a little longer. But no, you pawn-brokers are all the same, grab, grab, grab!"

"That's not fair . . ." Emmanuel Pinchbeck began to argue.

But there was no-one to listen. Bateson had gone back into the house and slammed the door behind him.

As Emmanuel Pinchbeck walked away he could hear the bolts being drawn across the door and the key turned in the lock.

Then, as if to console himself, his hand went to his chest and he patted it.

There was a twisted smile on his thin lips as he felt the notes the Duke had given him.

Chapter Two

*A*s the Duke drove out of London and into the countryside he grew angrier and angrier. With all the money his predecessor had when he died, a great deal must surely have been at the disposal of his daughter.

Why then should his Cousin Alvina have dealt with the pawn-brokers?

He could not imagine why she should need money, unless of course there was some man she was supporting of whom her father had disapproved.

The Duke thought cynically that he had a very poor opinion of most women's morals or sense of honour.

He had always, in the back of his mind, despised married women who were unfaithful to their husbands.

There was also something fastidious, or perhaps almost puritanical, in his make-up which made him dislike the idea that he was by no means the first of Lady Isobel's lovers.

He was quite certain, although she had never said so, that she had been unfaithful to her husband while he was alive, and she had certainly made the most of being free after his death.

It was all part and parcel of the pace set by the Heir to the Throne when he was Prince of Wales and his example had been accepted by the majority of those in Society.

When he thought it over, the Duke knew that,

although it seemed impossible, he would want his own wife to be very different.

He had never really thought about marriage before. As a soldier, he had been quite certain he could not afford it.

But now he was in the position of being obliged not only to marry but to find a wife who would both please him and prove suitable as the Duchess of Harlington.

He was well aware that, although it did not always happen, the head of a great family was looked up to and respected in the same way as was the Chieftain of a Scottish Clan.

Before the Duke of Cumberland had defeated the Highlanders and the rule of law in Scotland was revised and restored, the Chieftains had the power of life and death over their Clansmen.

The Dukes of England certainly did not have that, but on their own Estates they were, in most cases, looked upon almost as if they were Kings, and their word was law.

'It is like commanding an Army,' the Duke thought to himself, and remembered how Wellington was admired, honoured, and loved by the men under his command.

He had also known in his Army-life officers who had such powers of leadership that those they commanded were ready not only to serve them but to die, if necessary, in obeying their orders.

He did not boast to himself of having that particular quality, although actually he did possess it, but he had been praised often enough for the fact that his troops were smarter, were finer fighters, and certainly were better disciplined than those in other Regiments.

Discipline had been the key-word in the Army of Occupation, when it had been difficult to keep soldiers who were not fighting from looting or bullying the beaten enemy and invariably causing trouble where women were concerned.

But now that task was over, and the Duke asked himself whether he would ever be able to discipline a woman or force her to obey him as he had managed to do so successfully with men.

He was quite certain that with Isobel it would be impossible, and he knew that she used the passion she aroused in a man as a weapon to get everything she desired, without exerting herself unduly.

His lips tightened as he decided that she would certainly not be able to do that with him.

Yet, he wondered, if it actually came to the test, whether he would not be as compliant as her other lovers had been.

His thoughts then returned to the extraordinary behaviour of his cousin Alvina.

First, he tried to remember what she looked like, but he could not recall seeing her since she was a little girl of nine or ten years of age.

He had spent a great deal of his time at the Castle when he was very young because he and his cousin Richard were the same age.

He had very few memories of Alvina before meeting her at Richard's twenty-first-birthday party.

He remembered thinking then that there was a large age-gap between brother and sister.

But it had been explained to him that the Duchess had unfortunately lost two other children prematurely in the intervening time.

It had therefore been a triumph for the Doctors when the Duchess's daughter had survived. Alvina must by this time, the Duke calculated, be nineteen or twenty.

He wondered what she would look like. The Duke had been a handsome man, and he knew that the Duchess had been acclaimed as being outstandingly beautiful.

He actually found it hard to remember Alvina's face, because on that occasion he had been so amazed by the magnificence of the Castle and the extravagance of the festivities which celebrated Richard's coming-of-age.

Never, even in his later travels, had he seen better or more spectacular fireworks, and he could remember the fantastic decorations in the Banquetting-Hall, which had been filled with distinguished guests.

The ladies had glittered like Christmas-trees with diamonds on their heads, their necks, and their wrists, and the gentlemen, all wearing their decorations, were not eclipsed.

Because the Duke of Harlington was of such importance, there were several guests of Royal rank present, besides nearly all the Ambassadors to the Court of St. James.

He remembered thinking that their gold-braided uniforms, jewelled decorations, and be-ribboned chests out-glittered even the splendour of a full Regimental dress like his own.

Richard had made an excellent speech that night but now lay buried on the battlefield of Waterloo, while he, a distant cousin, was to take his place at the Castle as the fifth Duke of Harlington.

Then as he drove on, having left the suburbs of London far behind, and now moving through the open country, the Duke's thoughts returned to Lady Alvina.

Once again he squared his chin and tightened his lips.

"How could she have dared to pawn anything so priceless as the Germain bowl?" he asked himself.

When the pawn-broker had mentioned that among the other things in his possession there were several miniatures, the Duke had stiffened.

The Harlington collection of miniatures was the most famous in the country.

Some of them dated back to the reign of Queen Elizabeth, and almost every Harling who had owned the Castle had added a miniature of himself and his wife.

The Duke recalled that they decorated the walls of the Blue Drawing-Room, and it had given him intense satisfaction, when he was in Paris, Vienna, and Rome, to realise that none of these three cities had miniatures that could rival the Harlington collection.

He had never expected to possess any one of them or even to have the pleasure of seeing them frequently. But just as the Harlings always believed that the Castle belonged to them as a family, so they thought of its contents.

On his way back from France, the Duke had known that the one thing he wanted to do more than anything else was to see the Castle, live in it, and make it the focal point of his new life.

"Harlington Castle," he repeated to himself, and knew that the name meant more than could possibly be expressed in words.

The way in which his father had talked of the Castle was one of his first boyhood memories, and it had always seemed to him to be inhabited by Knights.

When he had first read the tale of King Arthur and his Knights of the Round Table, he had pictured them living in a Castle that was exactly like the one to which he belonged by name and birth.

Later, it coloured every fairy-tale he read and every history-book he opened.

When he was taught about the Crusades, he imagined very vividly the Knights setting out to attack the Saracens from Harlington Castle.

Queen Elizabeth had stayed there on her travels round England, and she therefore had a special place in his mind because she had feasted and slept as the guest of one of his ancestors.

So it went on through his history-lessons, until, when in real life he was fighting against the domination of Napoleon, he was fighting for England, but especially for Harlington Castle.

Yet, in the moment of his personal victory, when it was now his, he had discovered that there was a traitor in the family, a woman who had dared to take from the Castle some of its most precious treasures to pawn them for money.

'I can only be thankful,' the Duke thought, 'that by some sense of decency, or was it perhaps fear, she has not sold what has been passed down from one Duke to the next.'

He remembered asking his father once, when he was a small boy and they had stayed at the Castle, whether the Duke felt like a King.

"I am sure he does," his father had said with a smile, "but at the same time, just as in the case of the King, the Palace is his only for his lifetime. The Duke must protect it and improve it for the next Duke who will come after him."

Ivar had found it a little hard to understand, and his father had explained further.

"Each Duke in turn is a Guardian or Trustee of treasures which do not belong to him personally, but to the family as a whole. It is his duty not only to leave the Castle as he finds it but also to look after the family and see that they are cared for and do not want."

"He must have a lot to do," Ivar had replied.

"It is a very big task indeed," his father had answered solemnly, "and one in which we can thank God no Duke so far has failed."

From what he could remember of the fourth Duke, he had been an admirable head of the family.

Therefore, it seemed almost unbelievable that his only daughter should have stooped to stealing, for it was little else, the treasures to which generation after generation of Harlings had contributed, and had pawned them to a man like Pinchbeck.

"It is a miracle," the Duke said to himself, "that he did not sell them, although that might perhaps have been difficult."

He wondered what the Trustees had been doing who were supposed to look after such things.

He realised that because he had been abroad so long, he knew nothing about them or indeed who was in charge of the Estates.

He thought, not for the first time, that he should have come home for his cousin's Funeral and taken charge there and then. But the fourth Duke had died in January 1817, and at that time he had been in Vienna.

He had been there on an important mission on

Wellington's behalf, and therefore he had not heard of his cousin's death until he returned to Paris, where he received the letter from Coutt's Bank.

In it they informed him that as he was now the fifth Duke of Harlington, they enclosed a list of all the properties he had inherited and the monies which had been transferred to his name.

However, it had been impossible at that particular moment to go to England.

He had actually suggested rather tentatively to the Duke of Wellington that he should do so, only to be told that he could not possibly be spared.

There was in fact a tremendous row going on over the reduction of troops in the Army of Occupation.

In December of the previous year, Wellington had declared that a substantial reduction in numbers was impossible.

The next month, however, he notified the permanent Conference of four Ambassadors that his opinion had altered and a reduction of thirty thousand men would begin on the first of April.

This meant that an enormous amount of planning would be left in what Wellington described as "the very capable hands of General Harling."

On top of this, Wellington was negotiating the first loan to the French Government by Baring Brothers and Hopes, and he was relying on Ivar Harling's support and persuasiveness, especially in getting the other Allies to accept the idea of a loan handled by British Bankers.

In fact, there was so much controversy and so many delicate negotiations going on that the Duke had realised it was utterly impossible for him to leave Paris, however important it was, from his own point of view, that he should deal with his problems at home.

He had comforted himself with the idea that everything would go on running as smoothly as it had when the fourth Duke was alive.

If there were problems, they could wait and he could deal with them later.

He therefore merely notified Coutt's Bank that he would return as soon as possible, and almost forgot that his own situation had radically changed as he coped with the hysterical French, the feverish hopes of *Madame* de Staël for a free France, and Wellington's unceasing demands upon him.

There had been no more correspondence from the Bank, and he had therefore imagined that everything was well, and that Lady Alvina, who was living in the Castle as she was the fourth Duke's unmarried daughter, would see to everything until he arrived home.

He now thought that perhaps he should have written to her and that he had been somewhat rude not to have done so, but he had received no communication from her or from anyone else.

Therefore, he had confidently believed that no news was good news and that that was what he would find when he arrived at the Castle.

Gerald Chertson certainly had done him a good turn in buying for him such an excellent team of horses which would get him there quickly.

Gerald had left him a note at Berkeley Square, saying that unfortunately he had to go home to see his father, who was ill.

He would, however, be back in London at the end of the week, and would get in touch with him immediately.

The Duke had been disappointed, since he had expected Gerald to be waiting for him when he arrived.

But Sir Archibald Chertson was old and very demanding, and he accepted that there was nothing else Gerald could do.

"As soon as I get back, Gerald and I will enjoy ourselves," he promised himself.

He then remembered Isobel.

As he thought of her he could almost smell the exotic and seductive perfume she always used and feel her clinging arms round his neck, her lips on his.

However, Jason or no Jason, he told himself, he was not getting married until he wished to do so.

What was more, he had every intention of enjoying himself as a Duke, the head of the family and a very rich man, before he settled down.

"I will see Jason when I return to London," he decided. "I will give him a quite generous allowance on the condition that he behaves himself. I expect anyway I shall have to pay off his debts."

He was quite certain they would be out of all proportion, which would anger him considerably.

At the same time, it would be impossible for him to start off as the fifth Duke with a family scandal.

It was about four o'clock when he turned his horses through the impressive, gold-tipped wrought-iron gates which were flanked on each side with a heraldic lion, which was the crest of the Harlings.

The gates were open and he gave a quick glance as he passed through the Lodges on either side. He noticed that one of them was empty.

This surprised him, for he remembered the Lodge-Keepers, who wore special uniforms with crested silver buttons. They had always kept the gates closed but on hearing a carriage approach would hurry to open them.

If the passer-by happened to be the Duke himself, they would sweep their caps from their grey-haired heads with what seemed a courtly gesture, and in the background their wives and daughters would curtsey respectfully.

The Duke had thought it was very much part of the pageantry of the Castle, and he missed it now.

However, there was no point in stopping to enquire what had happened, and he drove down the long avenue of huge oak trees, which seemed even larger and sturdier than when he had last seen them.

Halfway down the drive there was the first sight of the Castle.

It was very impressive and so beautiful that instinctively, without thinking about it, the Duke checked his horses.

Standing on high ground above a lake, the Castle

overlooked the gardens, the Park, and beyond that the rolling country, much of which was thickly wooded.

Originally it had been built for one of the feudal Barons who had been brought under submission at the time of Magna Carta.

But all that remained of the original Castle was a Tower which had been heightened and strengthened with castellated ramparts a century or so later.

Adjoining the Tower was now an enormous edifice, the centre of which was Elizabethan, while other parts were Restoration, Queen Anne, and early Georgian.

It might be a hotch-potch of architecture, but each century had contributed to the impressiveness of the whole Castle, which from a distance gave the impression of being not so much a great fortification as a fairy-tale Palace.

The afternoon sun was shining on the hundreds of windows, and silhouetted against the sky were statues on the roof which the Duke remembered vividly.

Between each one was an exquisite stone vase. He had as a small boy climbed up to see them close to, and they had then seemed enormous.

But now in the distance they too had a fairy-tale quality that once again made him think of Knights in armour, nymphs rising from the lake in the haze that hung over it in the early morning, and dragons living in the dark fir woods and breathing fire at those who disturbed them.

Then abruptly, as if he had no wish to be fanciful or poetical at the moment, his mind came back to Lady Alvina and her perfidy in daring to damage anything so precious as the traditions of the Harlings, all of which were centred in this one great building.

As he drew nearer he noticed, again with a little surge of anger, that there were weeds in the gravel sweep in front of the great flight of grey stone steps which led up to the front door.

He pulled his horses to a standstill and said to his groom:

"The stables are round to the right of the house. Take the horses there. You will find grooms to help you."

"Very good, Your Grace."

The Duke handed him the reins, saying as he did so:

"I will send someone from the house to help take the luggage in through the back door."

The groom touched the brim of his crested top hat. The Duke alighted from the Phaeton and walked up the steps towards the front door.

This was the moment for which he had been longing and waiting. But now that he was here, he half-regretted that he had not informed Lady Alvina of his arrival.

Because Gerald had notified them at Berkeley Square that he was coming home, Bateson had been waiting in the Hall, and two footmen had run the red carpet down the steps and across the pavement the very moment the carriage which had brought him from Dover had pulled up outside.

But here there was no red carpet, and as he reached the door he saw that it was open and for the first time wondered what he would do if Lady Alvina was away.

He then told himself that it would not constitute any problem, because the servants would obviously still be there.

He walked into the huge marble Hall and saw that the stone statues of gods and goddesses were still in the niches, and the wide staircase with its carved golden balustrade was just as impressive as it had always been.

He felt he was being welcomed home.

He stood still for a moment, looking at the tattered flags hanging beside the beautifully carved mantelpiece.

They had all been won by Harlings in battle, and he remembered as a small boy being told where each one had been captured.

Agincourt especially had remained in his mind. He looked at the French flag captured then as if to reassure himself that it was still there.

He walked on through the quiet house, remembering well where each room was and what it was called.

At the top of the long flight of stairs there was on the left the Picture-Gallery, which ran the whole length of the house, and on the right were the State bedrooms.

These included Queen Elizabeth's room, Charles II's, and Queen Anne's, and at the end of the corridor was the Duke and Duchess's Suite, in which so many of his forebears, with the exception of himself, had been born and died.

He remembered that to the right on the ground floor was the very large Dining-Hall in which he had last eaten at Richard's twenty-first-birthday party.

Beside it was a smaller private Dining-Room which had been designed by William Kent, where the family ate when they were alone.

To the left, where he was moving now, was the Library with its first editions of Shakespeare and books that had been collected for centuries, making it one of the finest and most valuable Libraries in the country.

Successively on that side of the house were the Rubens Room, the Library, the Red Drawing-Room, the Green Drawing-Room, and the Blue Drawing-Room.

The Duke's eyes darkened with the thought of the last as he remembered that that was where the miniatures were.

He wondered why the place was so quiet, with no-one about.

He came to the first door, which opened into the Rubens Room, and found that the furniture was covered in Hollands, the shutters were closed, and the darkness smelt musty.

He closed the door and moved to the next one, which was the door to the Library.

Here there was a light because the windows were not shuttered, and as he walked into the room he had the impression, but he could not be certain, that everything looked shabby and, although it seemed incredible, somewhat dusty.

It was then that he was aware of another human being.

It was a servant, and she had her back to him and was dusting somewhat ineffectively with a feather brush the books on one of the higher shelves.

He watched her for a moment and realised that the feather brush, light though it was, was dislodging a great deal of dust.

He suddenly felt he needed an explanation and asked sharply:

"Where is everybody? Why is there no-one in attendance in the Hall?"

Although he had not intended it, his voice sounded in the room almost unnaturally harsh and loud, and the woman at the far end of it jumped as if she was startled and turned round.

She had a duster over her hair and was wearing an apron.

The Duke, walking towards her, said:

"Is Lady Alvina at home? I wish to speak to her."

It was then, as two very blue eyes stared up at him, he had a sudden idea, although it seemed most improbable, that this was not a servant.

When she did not speak, he felt he should introduce himself and said:

"I am the Duke of Harlington."

The woman facing him gave a little gasp and then said in a voice that was barely audible:

"I thought . . . you were . . . in France."

The Duke smiled.

"On the contrary. I have arrived back today."

There was silence, and the woman stared at him as if she could hardly believe what she had heard.

Then at last, finding her voice with difficulty, she said:

"Why did you not let us . . . know, and how . . . could you have . . . stayed away so . . . long?"

It was then that the Duke realised to whom he was speaking, and he said:

"I think perhaps we should introduce ourselves properly. I am sure you are my cousin Alvina."

"Yes, I am," the woman answered, "and I have waited and waited for you until I had given up . . . hope that you would . . . ever return."

There was a desperate note in her voice that the Duke did not miss, and after a moment, and because he knew it was expected of him, he said:

"I must apologise if I have seemed somewhat remiss, but I had urgent duties in France, and the Duke of Wellington would not release me."

He almost despised himself for making apologies, and yet he had the feeling they were necessary.

As if he was determined not to remain on the defensive, he said:

"If you wanted me back urgently, why did you not write to me?"

"I did write to you when Papa died, but there was no answer."

"I never received your letter."

"I did not . . . think that was the . . . explanation."

"Then what did you think?"

"I did not know. I thought . . . perhaps you were not . . . interested. It was . . . stupid of me . . . not to write . . . again."

"I apologise not only for not receiving your letter but also because I should have written to you. I realise that now."

She did not reply, and he smiled.

"My only excuse is that I had really forgotten you had grown up, and I was thinking of you as the little girl I had last seen when I was here at Richard's twenty-first-birthday celebration."

As he spoke he thought it was tactless to remind Alvina of her brother's death, but she said:

"It was kind of you to write to Papa after Richard was killed, but he would not read . . . any of the letters he . . . received or allow me to . . . reply to them."

The Duke did not quite know what to say to this, so, feeling it might be somewhat embarrassing, he walked away from Alvina towards the window, saying as he did so:

"It was impossible for me to return before now. Now that I am here, I realise there is a lot for me to see and a great deal for me to learn."

"A great . . . deal," she said, and her voice seemed to falter.

The Duke told himself that she was afraid because of her behaviour in pawning the family treasures.

When he thought of them, his anger rose in him again, almost like a crimson streak in front of his eyes.

Yet, because he had disciplined himself to have complete control outwardly over his feelings, he merely said in a cold, icy voice:

"What I need to have explained, Cousin Alvina, is why you have dared to pawn some of the treasures in this house, which I thought any Harling would regard as sacred."

As he spoke he thought he heard a little gasp and told himself she was surprised that he had learnt so soon what she had done.

He turned round and saw that she had taken off the duster which had protected her hair and also the apron she had been wearing.

She was very slim, and now he could see that her hair was fair and somewhat untidy. But she looked very young, little more than a child, and certainly not the age he knew her to be.

She was standing very still, holding the apron and the duster in her hand, and she stared at him with an expression in her eyes which he knew was one of fear.

"I cannot imagine," he said sharply, "what your reason could be for behaving in such a dishonourable manner. And I want you, Cousin Alvina, to tell me the truth as to why you were in need of money and for what purpose!"

Once again his voice seemed to ring out a little louder than he had intended.

As she still stared at him, apparently finding it

difficult to answer his question, his anger suddenly boiled over so that he said furiously:

"Were you trying to trick me because you had no wish to see me in your brother's place? Or were you providing for some man who had taken your fancy and of whom your father did not approve?"

He paused to say even more furiously:

"The pawn-broker, Pinchbeck, tells me this has been going on for nearly three years, ever since your father died, and I cannot imagine anything more underhand and deceitful than that you should behave in a manner which undoubtedly would have hurt and dismayed him had he been aware of it! It has certainly disgusted me!"

He finished speaking and waited, and then in a voice he could barely hear Alvina faltered:

"I . . . I can . . . explain."

"So I should hope," the Duke interrupted, "and it had better be a good explanation!"

Again he waited, and Alvina began to say in a choked voice:

"It was . . . because . . . Papa . . ." she stopped.

He then realised that she was trembling as if she could say no more and was unable to hold back the tears that had come to her eyes.

She then turned and ran away from him down the Library and disappeared through the door.

The Duke gave an exclamation which was one of exasperation and frustration.

"Dammit!" he said to himself. "Is that not exactly like a woman? They always resort to tears when they are caught out!"

He did not really know what to do now that Alvina had left him, but he thought he would have no difficulty in finding someone else he could talk to.

He looked for a bell, but there appeared not to be one. So he walked slowly back down the Library, thinking as he did so how badly kept it was and that there was undoubtedly a great deal of dust on all of the books.

The silver grate was almost black and obviously had not been polished for a long time.

He went out again into the passage which led to the Hall. There was still no-one to be seen.

He opened the door of the Blue Drawing-Room, only to see that, like the first room he had entered, it was shuttered and there were covers over the furniture, and again there was that musty smell.

"What the Devil is happening?" he asked himself.

He was just about to walk on farther when he saw a man coming slowly towards him from beyond the Dining-Hall.

The Duke turned and walked back, realising as he drew closer that the man had white hair and was moving slowly because he was old. He thought, although he was not sure, that he recognised his face.

Then, as they met halfway down the corridor, the man peered up at him as if he found it hard to see him.

"Good-day, Your Grace."

"What is your name?" the Duke asked. "I seem to remember you."

"Walton, Your Grace."

"Yes, of course. You were the Butler here when I was a small boy."

"That's true, Master Ivar . . . I mean Your Grace," the old man said. "I were first footman when you came as a child, and then Butler when you stayed 'ere with your mother and father. A fine, upstanding lad you was, too."

He spoke with warmth in his voice as old people do when they reminisce over the past, and the Duke said:

"I am glad to meet you again, Walton, but you must tell me what is happening. There was no-one in the Hall when I arrived."

There was just a faint note of rebuke in his voice, and Walton replied:

"We weren't expecting Your Grace."

"Yes, I know that," the Duke said. "And I know the war has made a great difference to everything in

England, but I did not anticipate finding all the rooms shut up."

"There were nothing else we could do, Your Grace."

"Why not?" the Duke enquired. "Surely you have servants enough to clean them?"

"No, Your Grace."

The Duke stared at the old man and then said:

"Perhaps it would be best for me to have an explanation from whoever is in charge here. I imagine that is Lady Alvina."

"Yes, Your Grace. Lady Alvina's been looking after everything since His Grace died."

The Duke now regretted having caused her to run away so hastily, and he said:

"Well, Walton, as Lady Alvina seems to have disappeared for the moment, perhaps you had better tell me what I should know."

As he spoke he realised that he could hardly stand talking in the passage, so he said:

"Which rooms is Her Ladyship using besides the Library?"

"The Library's usually shut, Your Grace," Walton said slowly. "Her Ladyship was dusting it as she was trying to find a book she wanted."

The Duke thought that would account for the dust and the way his cousin had been dressed.

"Where can I sit?" he asked.

His voice sharpened a little because he was feeling frustrated by the way every question he asked seemed to lead him nowhere.

"Her Ladyship's using the Breakfast-Room, Your Grace," the Butler replied. "It's the only room we've open at the moment."

The old man preceded him very slowly to the small room which faced South where the Duke remembered breakfasting last time he had stayed at the Castle.

Only the gentlemen used to come down to breakfast, while the ladies had preferred to stay in the bedrooms or their *Boudoirs* and had not appeared until much later in the morning.

As Walton opened the door, he recognised the attractive squared room that overlooked the lake.

He remembered that the early-morning rays of the sun used to shine through the windows on the long sideboard laden with silver entree-dishes kept warm with a lighted candle beneath each.

There had been at least a dozen different foods to choose from.

There had been a large circular table in the centre of the room, and the Duke could recall the big silver racks containing toast and a cottage loaf baked that morning in the kitchen ovens.

There had been scones and rolls fresh and warm, together with a huge comb of golden honey and jams and marmalades made in the Still-Room.

There was everything that a man's body could require early in the morning, and for his mind there were the newspapers, freshly ironed in the Butler's Pantry, set on silver stands opposite each place at the table.

He had been fascinated by all the luxury, and he knew vaguely at the back of his mind that he had expected on his return to England to find everything as it had been then.

But the furniture of the room was entirely changed: there was now only one small round table in the window and a sofa and an armchair standing in front of the fireplace.

The long side-table on which the silver breakfast-dishes had been laid had been removed to leave room for a bookcase.

It was a very fine Chippendale piece, yet somehow it seemed out-of-place in this particular room, with its walls covered with paintings by English artists of the Seventeenth Century.

The Duke had noticed with a quick glance that had been trained to be observant that there was a work-box of English marquetry and a *Secretaire* which was covered with papers and with what he thought looked like bills.

There were some small portraits on the mantelpiece and on the side-tables, and there was also a larger one of Richard, painted by Lawrence, over the fireplace.

He had the feeling as he and the Butler entered the room that they were intruding, although he told himself that it was absurd to feel like that.

After all, the place was now his, and Cousin Alvina was certainly not welcoming him with any enthusiasm.

Almost as if he wished to assert himself, he sat down in the armchair beside the fireplace and said:

"Now, Walton, tell me what all this is about. Why is the house shut up? Why are there no footmen in the Hall? And why is Lady Alvina using only this room instead of one of the Drawing-Rooms?"

The old man drew in his breath, and then with a voice which seemed to tremble he said:

"I'm afraid Your Grace doesn't understand."

"I certainly do not!" the Duke said. "And while I think of it, there is one special question to which I want an answer. Why did you allow Lady Alvina to take the silver Germain bowl out of the safe and take it to London, with, I gather, a number of other valuable things?"

There was silence. Then the Duke realised that Walton's hands were shaking in the same way as Alvina's had.

As he could feel his anger rising, the Duke said:

"Tell me the truth. I shall find out sooner or later, and I want to hear it now."

"It's quite simple, Your Grace," Walton said in a quavering voice. "Her Ladyship had no money."

Chapter Three

*T*HERE WAS SILENCE for a moment before the Duke said in surprise:

"What do you mean, no money?"

Walton cleared his throat before he answered:

" 'Twas like this, Your Grace. There was no money to pay wages and pensions, or even to buy food."

"I do not believe it!" the Duke exclaimed. "My cousin left a very large sum when he died."

Walton looked uncomfortable before he said:

"I thinks, Your Grace, that the war upset a great number of people and His late Grace was one of them."

"You mean when His Lordship was killed?"

"Before that, Your Grace. Things began to get much more expensive, and His Grace decided to economise."

The Duke's lips tightened.

It seemed incredible, in view of the huge sum of money he knew was in the Bank, that his cousin should have thought it necessary to economise to the point of considering the wages of his domestic staff.

He remembered now, although it had not occurred to him before, hearing talk of what was happening in England while he was in Paris.

Someone had told him that the Duke of Buccleuch, because of agricultural distress, had left his farm rents uncollected and was not visiting London so that he might have more cash to pay his retainers.

He had hardly listened to what had been said at that moment because he was more immediately concerned with so much that was happening in Europe.

Now he supposed that it had been foolish of him not to have made enquiries if at the Castle, like in other places in England, there were difficulties on the farms as well as the problem of unemployment.

He had read in the newspapers about unrest in the country, and politicians arriving in Paris from England had confirmed it, since wages had been forced down as thousands of ex-soldiers and sailors were released from the services.

There had also been no compensation or pensions for those who had fought so valiantly.

The Duke had put the information at the back of his mind, to be considered later when he returned home, but now he realised that it was an urgent personal problem which he had to face.

Yet, it still seemed incredible that Walton should talk of there being no money, when he knew how much there was available.

"Surely," he said aloud, "the Duke must have been aware of the difficulties, or whoever managed the Estate could have explained it to him."

"There was no-one, Your Grace."

"Why was there no-one?" the Duke asked sharply.

"His Grace quarrelled with Mr. Fellows, who had been in charge for thirty years, just before His Lordship was killed."

"And he was not replaced?" the Duke asked.

"No, Your Grace."

"So who has been managing the Estate?"

"Lady Alvina, and it's been very hard for her, very hard indeed, Your Grace. She had no money to pay the pensioners."

"I can hardly believe it," the Duke muttered beneath his breath.

Then, as if he felt that this was something that he

should discuss with his cousin, not with a servant, he said:

"Who is here in the house at the moment?"

"There's just m'wife and m'self, M'Lord, and Mrs. Johnson, who I daresay you remember, who's been the Cook for over forty years, and Emma, who's getting on for eighty and can't do much."

"Is that all?" the Duke enquired.

"Everyone else was either dismissed on His Grace's orders, or left."

"It cannot be true."

The Duke was silent for a moment, then he said:

"Thank you for what you have told me, Walton. I think I must discuss this further with Lady Alvina. Will you ask her if she will join me?"

There was some hesitation before Walton said:

"I don't think Lady Alvina's in the Castle, Your Grace."

The Duke sat upright.

"What do you mean she is not in the Castle? Where could she have gone?"

Again there was a pause before Walton said:

"I thinks Her Ladyship were somewhat distressed, and I sees her leave, Your Grace."

"I do not understand. Where can she have gone?"

Again there was an uncomfortable silence before the Duke said:

"I am afraid I must have upset her, which is something I should not have done. Please tell me where I can find her."

He spoke in the persuasive manner which invariably enabled him to get his own way when more authoritative methods failed.

However, Walton shuffled his feet.

"I don't think, Your Grace, that Her Ladyship'll want you to find her at the moment."

"I can understand that," the Duke said quietly, "but you are well aware, Walton, having known us since we were children, that Lady Alvina is the one person who can help me to put right what is wrong and clear up what is obviously a mess."

He thought he saw the old man's eyes lighten a little, and then he said:

"Well, it's like this, Your Grace. If I tells you where Her Ladyship is, I'll be giving away a secret which His late Grace didn't know because he wouldn't have approved."

It flashed through the Duke's mind again that perhaps Alvina had some man in whom she was interested, but he merely replied quietly:

"I think you will understand, Walton, that whatever His Grace felt or did not feel about things, now that I am taking his place I shall have to make a great number of alterations. The first one is to restore the Castle to what it was in the old days."

He could not help thinking with some amusement that now he, of all people, was talking about "the good old days." Yet, it was obvious that if things were to be restored as he wanted, he would have to step back into the past for an example of how they should be done.

Still Walton hesitated, until at last he said:

"When His Grace was making economies he turned Her Ladyship's Governess, Miss Richardson, out of the Castle, and as she'd nowhere to go, Her Ladyship persuaded her to live in what had been the under-gardener's cottage."

"Why did she not have anywhere to go?" the Duke asked curiously.

"Miss Richardson's getting on in years, Your Grace, and she has rheumatism, which makes it hard for her to walk quickly or for any distance."

"So you think that Her Ladyship has gone now to Miss Richardson in the under-gardener's cottage," the Duke said as if he was thinking it out for himself.

"Yes, Your Grace."

"Very well. I will go find her."

He rose from the chair and walked towards the door as Walton said:

"Mrs. Johnson, Your Grace, was wondering, if you are staying tonight, what you'd fancy for dinner."

Perceptively the Duke understood that if he wanted dinner, it would be difficult for the servants to provide the sort of meal they expected him to eat, unless he was prepared to pay for it.

"Now listen, Walton," he said. "You have to help me get things back to normal, and I expect you will be able to find some of the old staff in the village or elsewhere on the Estate."

He saw Walton's eyes light up, and he said:

"It may take a little time, but I suggest the first thing you do is get help for Mrs. Johnson in the kitchen and two or three young men to assist you in the pantry."

He knew as he spoke that Walton was finding it hard to believe what he was hearing.

Putting his hands in his pocket, the Duke pulled out his purse, in which there were a number of gold sovereigns.

He then took from the inside of his coat a twenty-pound note, which he put down on the small table where he had laid his purse, and said:

"This will help you get what is needed immediately. Send Mark, my groom, to a farm or the village to purchase meat or whatever Mrs. Johnson requires for dinner. I suppose there are some horses in the stables?"

"Only two that Her Ladyship's been riding, Your Grace," Walton replied. "One's getting very old."

"Mark can ride one of them," the Duke said. "In the meantime, do what you can to improve things immediately, and there is no need to worry about expenditure. I will deal with that."

As he finished speaking and walked towards the door, he was aware that Walton was staring down at what he had left lying on the table as if he could hardly believe his eyes.

The Duke did not go out the front door, which was still open, but down the passage that passed the Dining-Hall and the small Dining-Room.

He then pulled open the baize-covered door which led to the kitchen-quarters.

He came first to the pantry, where he could remember as a small boy he had been given sugared almonds and other sweet-meats by Walton.

The huge safe was still there, and the table on which the silver was cleaned, and there was also the bed that folded up into the wall for one of the footmen who was invariably on duty at night to guard the contents of the safe.

Now everything looked very shabby. The walls were damp and in need of paint, and the floor looked as if it could do with a good scrub.

The Duke walked on past cupboards and doors which he did not bother to open and the narrow staircase which led up to the servants' bedrooms.

Then on his right was the huge kitchen, which he remembered had always been a hive of activity.

The scullions would be turning chickens and great joints on the spit, and Mrs. Johnson and the kitchen-maids would be at the stove. Brass sauce-pans, polished like mirrors, had hung from the walls while the freshly cured hams had hung from a cross-beam.

Now it seemed smaller to him and very empty, and there was only one old woman with bowed shoulders standing near a small fire.

For a moment he found it impossible to recognise the stout, apple-cheeked Cook who had made him ginger-bread men as a small boy and later, when he was going back to School, huge fruit-cakes which had been the delight of his dormitory.

As he entered the kitchen she turned round, and he saw by the expression in her eyes that she recognised him.

"Master Ivar! Be it really you? You've grown into a fine man, there's no mistake about that."

"Thank you, Mrs. Johnson," the Duke replied. "It is nice to see you again."

He held out his hand and felt how cold her fingers were and realised how old and frail she was.

"Walton has been telling me," he said quietly, "that things have been very difficult for you, but that is all over now. You shall have help the moment we can find anyone from the village to come to the Castle."

He heard Mrs. Johnson make an inarticulate little sound and went on:

"I am looking forward to having one of those delicious dishes you used to cook for me when I was going back to Oxford."

"That be a long time ago, Master Ivar . . . I mean, Your Grace."

"A long time," the Duke agreed.

"Things have been bad, very bad these last years."

She gave a deep sigh before she said:

"We'd all have died, every one of us, if it hadn't been for Her Ladyship."

"That is what Walton has been telling me."

"It's true, Your Grace. We'd have been turned away after all these years without a penny, and there'd have been nothing for us but the Workhouse!"

"Forget it now!" the Duke said. "Everything is going to be exactly as it was when I was a boy and there was no war to make us miserable."

"That's the right word—miserable!" Mrs. Johnson agreed. "With that monster in France killing all our young men, His Grace was never the same after His Lordship fell."

The Duke, feeling somewhat uncomfortable at having taken his cousin Richard's place, replied:

"Now we must only look forward, Mrs. Johnson, and I want you to tell the groom I have brought down with me where he can go in the village to find food and help."

He smiled at her as he continued:

"Tomorrow we can make further plans, but for the moment the best thing to do is just to cope with tonight, and actually I shall undoubtedly be very hungry."

He knew that unless Mrs. Johnson had changed very much, this appeal would not go unanswered, and she said in a different voice:

"You'll have the best dinner I can cook for you, Master Ivar, but there's no pretending that I can do it without vittles."

"That I understand," the Duke said. "Leave everything to me."

He walked away, passing the huge larder with its marble slabs on which there used to stand big open bowls of cream.

He remembered too the pats of golden butter from the Jersey herd and cheese which was made fresh every other day.

Then there were sculleries, a very large Servants' Hall, the Housekeeper's room, the boot-room, the knife-room, and various other offices, before he reached the yard.

He did not stop to look round but walked on as he knew this was the quickest way to the stables.

As he expected, he found that his groom was the only person there and had just finished putting the horses into four different stalls.

He saw at a glance that the roof needed repairing and the stable itself was badly in need of paint.

The stalls were comparatively clean, and as he saw the other two horses in them he had an idea that the only person who could have cleaned them was his cousin Alvina.

He told his groom exactly what he had to do, and was pleased to find that the man Gerald had engaged for him was quick-witted enough to realise that there was a crisis and was ready to help in every way he could.

The Duke sent him into the kitchen to talk to Mrs. Johnson, then looked towards the end of the stables where he could see the roof of a house.

He knew this was the Head-Gardener's and opened on the back of the very large, walled Kitchen Garden, which was out of sight of the Castle.

201

It had always provided him and his cousin Richard with apples, peaches, nectarines, green figs, and golden plums.

He had the horrifying feeling now that it would look like a jungle, and he therefore walked past the Head-Gardener's house quickly.

On the far side of it, about fifty yards away, was a very small cottage.

He was certain that this was where one of the under-gardeners, perhaps the most important of them, had lived.

He was sure he was not wrong in recalling that when he was young there was an army of men working in the Kitchen Garden, on the lawns, in the flower-beds, and down by the lake.

When he reached the cottage, he saw that the windows were clean and the small garden between the gate and the front door was bright with flowers.

He walked up the small paved path and knocked on the door, which he noticed needed painting, although the brass knocker had been polished and so had the key-hole.

For a moment there was silence, then he heard the footsteps of someone who walked with a limp crossing the flagged floor. The door opened and he saw an elderly, rather distinguished, white-haired woman looking at him.

The Duke smiled.

"I think you must be Miss Richardson," he said. "I am the Duke of Harlington."

Miss Richardson made a little effort to curtsey, but it was obviously impossible.

She did not, however, open the door any wider, and after a moment the Duke said:

"I think my cousin Alvina is with you."

"She is, Your Grace, but she has no wish to see anyone at the moment."

"I think you will understand, Miss Richardson," the Duke said, "that since I have just arrived and found things are very different from what I expected, the only person who can help me is Lady Alvina."

As he spoke, he had the uncomfortable feeling that Miss Richardson was contemplating telling him to go away and shutting the door.

Then, as if she decided it would be a mistake, she said:

"Would Your Grace be gracious enough to wait a moment while I ask Lady Alvina if she is prepared to see you?"

She lowered her voice before she added:

"She is somewhat upset at the moment."

"It was my fault," the Duke replied, "but I had no idea before I arrived that the Castle would be so different from what it was when I last visited it."

The way he spoke seemed to sweep away a little of what had been an obvious feeling of hostility on the part of Miss Richardson, and she opened the door a little wider.

"Perhaps Your Grace would come in," she said. "And if you do not mind sitting in the kitchen, I will talk to Lady Alvina."

The door was so low that the Duke had to bend his head and once inside he could only just stand upright.

The kitchen was like a small box. However, it was spotlessly clean, and he thought that the walls must have been white-washed by Miss Richardson herself, or else, though it seemed incredible, Alvina.

There was a very primitive stove, a deal table, and two chairs. On one wall was a dresser which held plates, cups, saucers, and three china jugs.

The window was covered by some very old and faded curtains of a rich brocade which the Duke thought must at some time have hung in the Castle.

He sat down on one of the hard wooden chairs while Miss Richardson limped through a door which he guessed led to the Parlour.

Now he was sure that this cottage, like so many of the other workmen's cottages on the Estate, consisted of two rooms on the ground floor, the kitchen and the Parlour, with a scullery at the back, and there would be two tiny bedrooms up the very small, ladder-like wooden stairs.

It was all so primitive that the Duke felt it was an insult that anyone who was refined and educated, as Miss Richardson obviously was, should have to live in such a place.

Yet, if the previous Duke had turned her away, as Walton had said, and she had nowhere else to go, it at least constituted a roof over her head.

He could hear voices in the next room, although he could not hear what they were saying.

Then the door opened and Miss Richardson said in a quiet, controlled voice:

"Would Your Grace come in?"

The Duke rose and again had to lower his head to enter what he thought was the smallest Sitting-Room he had ever been in.

It was so tiny that there was only just room for two very ancient armchairs and a desk which looked as if it might have come out of the School-Room, with a small chair in front of it.

Again, the windows had curtains that had once been of expensive material, and the paintings on the walls were amateur water-colours.

These he suspected had been done by Miss Richardson's pupils, one of them of course being Alvina herself.

His cousin rose as he entered. He saw that she had been crying and her eyes were enormous in her small face.

Because she looked so woebegone and very young, the Duke suddenly felt he had been unjustly brutal, in fact, unsportsmanlike, to someone so vulnerable and defenceless.

As he heard the door close behind him he said, and his voice was very quiet and sincere:

"I have come to apologise."

It was obviously something she had not expected, and

for a moment she looked at him incredulously, but she did not speak.

"How could I have known—how could I have guessed for one moment," the Duke asked, "that your father did not leave you with any money, and that the staff in the Castle should have been reduced to what it is now?"

As if she felt embarrassed, Alvina looked down, her lashes dark against the whiteness of her skin, and he suspected they were still wet.

"Let us sit down and talk about it," the Duke said. "There is so much I want you to tell me, and I can only ask you to forgive me for upsetting you."

He spoke in a way that both men and women found irresistible when he was being diplomatic, and as if she felt her legs could no longer support her, Alvina sank down onto the chair she had just vacated.

The Duke sat a little gingerly in the one opposite.

"Suppose we start at the beginning," he said, "and you tell me why your father would not give you any money when there is in the Bank a very large sum which I have now inherited."

"A large . . . sum?" Alvina asked in a voice little above a whisper. "Do you . . . mean that we are not . . . bankrupt?"

"Of course not," the Duke replied. "Your father died a very rich man. Surely the Solicitors told you that?"

"We have no Solicitors."

"What do you mean, you have no Solicitors?"

He felt that once again he was asking questions too sharply, and he added quickly:

"Forgive me, but I am completely bewildered as to what has happened, and there appears to be no-one but yourself who can tell me anything."

"Papa was so . . . sure that we were absolutely . . . penniless."

"Walton has told me that your father was not at all himself after Richard died," the Duke answered, almost as if he was making excuses.

"That was true," Alvina agreed. "At the same time, even before that Papa had become very alarmed. He kept on talking about economy, and I think perhaps he had always been very cautious where money was concerned. Only Mama insisted on making everything so happy and comfortable for us at the Castle."

"That is how I remember it," the Duke said, "and there were certainly no economies at Richard's twenty-first party."

"Mama planned that," Alvina said, "and when Richard was killed I was so very . . . very glad he . . . had enjoyed it so . . . much."

"I always think of him enjoying life to the full," the Duke said. "When we were at Oxford together he never worried about his studies, although he did quite well. But he took part in every sport, and no party was complete without him."

He saw the expression on Alvina's face and added:

"I saw him just before he was killed, and he was laughing then and made a rather facetious bet with me about the length of the war."

There were tears in Alvina's eyes, which she managed to control before she said:

"Had Richard come . . . home, things would have been very . . . different, but when he died . . . I think Papa . . . died too."

There was silence until the Duke said:

"Tell me what happened."

"As I have said, Papa was already making many economies before that, and afterwards, now that I think about it, he was not himself . . . almost like a stranger . . . and he refused to give me any money."

She paused, then said:

"I know you are angry with me for pawning all those things, but I could not let the pensioners starve or go to the Workhouse. He would not pay the Waltons their wages or even give me enough money to feed them."

The Duke was frowning as he asked:

"Surely there was someone who could have helped

you, even though you had no Solicitors? Walton tells me that there is no Estate Manager, and what happened to the Trustees?"

Alvina made a helpless little gesture with her hands.

"One had died before Richard went to France, another lived until last year and was very old and deaf, and the third, Sir John Sargent, lives in Scotland and never comes South."

"So there was no-one to help you?"

"No-one. I thought of appealing to the family, but Papa had quarrelled with most of them, and when the rest no longer received the allowance he had always given them, they wrote him furious letters, which he refused to read."

The Duke put his hands to his forehead as if he found it hard to credit before he said:

"As you really had no money, I can understand that you did the only thing possible, but I am still finding it difficult to credit that in your position there was no-one who could have helped you."

"I thought and thought of everyone," Alvina replied, "but after Mama died, Papa quarrelled with so many people, not only our relations but everyone in the County. He refused to entertain and just sat reading the newspapers, hoping the war would end and Richard would come home."

As if she thought the Duke did not understand, she added:

"Richard was the only person who could have persuaded Papa to look after the people on the Estate and the family who depended on him. He also would have prevented him from dismissing all the old servants. Papa would not listen to me."

She gave a deep sigh and continued:

"He always blamed me because Mama was not very strong after I was born, and he had so much wanted me to be a boy."

Her voice trembled for a moment and then she said:

"After Richard was killed he hated me, because he had no son to inherit."

She did not say any more, and in some strange way the Duke could almost read her thoughts.

He knew almost, as if she had said it aloud, that she was remembering how her father had shouted at her to get out of his sight because she was alive while Richard was dead.

For the first time since he had come into the room, he looked at what she was wearing and was aware that her gown was worn and threadbare.

Although she may have deliberately worn something old because she had been cleaning the Library, he had the feeling that it was many years since she had spent anything on herself.

Almost as if she, similarly, could read his thoughts, she said as if he had asked her the question:

"I have not been able to spend anything on myself for years, and when my own dresses became too small for me, I wore Mama's. But as I had so much work to do in the house when Papa had sent all the servants away, I would have been almost naked had it not been for Miss Richardson!"

She glanced toward the door into the kitchen and went on:

"She mended my gowns and even made me a new one from material that had been bought when Mama was alive, to be used for muslin curtains."

She tried to smile as she spoke, but the Duke knew it was an effort.

"What gave you the idea of pawning the things instead of selling them?" he asked.

"I am not so stupid as not to realise that everything in the Castle is entailed," Alvina replied, "just as it is in Harlington House in London."

She drew in her breath before she said:

"To be honest, I went through the inventories very carefully, to find out if there was anything that could be sold, but I could find nothing."

"So you went to that man Pinchbeck. How did you hear of him?"

"I often think," Alvina answered in a low voice, "that there is no such thing as chance in life and that everything is meant."

"I have thought that myself," the Duke agreed.

"When Richard was at Oxford he had got into debt, and when he came home to ask for money, Papa was in one of his bad moods and gave him a tremendous lecture on extravagance. He paid up, but Richard found to his consternation one bill he had overlooked by mistake."

Alvina's voice softened as she went on.

"He brought it to me and said:

" 'Look 'Vina,' . . . that was what he used to call me . . . 'I am in a mess and dare not ask Papa for any more, and these people are pressing me.'

"I had no money of my own then, for I was just a child, and then almost as if someone told me what to answer him, I said:

" 'I was reading a book the other day about some shops in London with three golden balls outside them, and Miss Richardson told me they were what are called pawn-brokers.'

"When I said that, Richard jumped up and said:

" 'How could I have been so stupid? You are a clever girl, 'Vina, and that is where my gold cuff-links, my gold watch, and quite a number of things I have of value will be resting tonight.'

"He kissed me," Alvina went on, "swung me round in his arms, and said:

" 'I have the cleverest sister in the world, and a very pretty one, too.' "

"So that is how you know of Emmanuel Pinchbeck," the Duke remarked.

"Richard told me," Alvina replied, "what he had managed to borrow on all his things, and afterwards, when Papa was in a good temper and gave him quite a large sum, he got them all back."

"Well, fortunately enough, you chose an honest pawn-broker," the Duke said. "Pinchbeck has not disposed of anything you left with him, even though he had been tempted to. As soon as I arrived this morning at Berkeley Square he came to see me."

"So that is . . . how you . . . knew," Alvina whispered.

"Yes."

"And it made you . . . very angry."

"Very angry indeed," the Duke said, "because I did not understand."

"And now you . . . do?"

"I can only apologise for misjudging you and for making you more unhappy than you must have been already."

She gave a little sigh which seemed to come from the depths of her heart, then she said:

"Now there is some money in the Bank. What do you intend to do?"

"I intend," the Duke said slowly, "to make the Castle look exactly as I remember it when I last saw you, but I am sure you will tell me that first we have to see to the pensioners, the relations, and anyone else who has suffered since your father, or rather Richard, died."

Alvina gave a little exclamation and clasped her hands together, and once more the tears were glittering in her eyes.

"Do you . . . mean that?" she asked almost in a whisper. "Do you really . . . mean it?"

"Of course I mean it," the Duke answered, "but I cannot do all that has to be done, and quickly, unless you help me."

"Do you . . . really want . . . me?"

He smiled.

"You know the answer to that question, and, quite frankly, I do not know how to begin until you show me the way."

"I have written down in a book everything that I have spent," Alvina said. "You will see, when you read it, that it is not only the pensioners and relations who have suffered, but also the farmers and everyone else on the Estate."

The Duke looked puzzled.

"When the farmers could not pay their rents, Papa wanted to turn them out," Alvina explained.

"So you sold something and let him think the rents had been paid," the Duke said quickly.

She nodded.

"He also wanted to shut up the whole Castle and said that as he was bedridden there was no need for him to keep any of the servants except for his valet. All the rest could leave."

The Duke looked at her incredulously.

"And who was to cook and clean the house?"

"Papa said I could do that."

Seeing the size of the Castle, the Duke could hardly believe that what he was hearing was the truth, and he exclaimed:

"Your father must have been quite mad."

"I suppose he was," Alvina agreed. "He used to get into terrible rages with me simply because I was not the second son he had wanted."

As if the Duke felt it was a mistake for her to think about how the late Duke had hated her personally, he said:

"What happened to his valet?"

"He died two months ago," Alvina replied. "He was very old, and I think he just kept going for my sake and because, like the Waltons, if he left the Castle he would have had to go to the Workhouse or starve."

"I cannot believe it," the Duke said again.

He thought of the value of the paintings, the statues, the furniture, and all the other incredibly rare treasures the Castle contained.

Yet, because the last Duke had obviously been crazy, so many people in it had actually been near to death simply for want of food.

"Of course," Alvina said, "you can understand that I

dared not repair the pensioners' cottages, which are in a very bad state, and I also could not increase their pensions, because I really believed, since Papa kept on saying so, there was no money in the Bank."

She gave a deep sigh and went on:

"But at least they managed on the few shillings I gave them each week, and Papa was not aware that the farmers were begging me every month to help them when they had leaking roofs, cow-sheds which were tumbling down, and implements which they had no chance of replacing."

"It must have been a nightmare," the Duke said sympathetically.

"It was," Alvina agreed. "Every time I took something out of the safe, or a painting from the wall, I felt I was a traitor and was betraying the family trust, but what was more important than anything else was to keep those who were alive from dying."

"Of course it was," the Duke agreed, "and I can only thank you, Alvina, for being clever enough not to sell those things which are specially precious both to you and to me and to all the Harlings who will follow on after us."

His praise brought a flush to her face and she said:

"Do you really . . . mean you can . . . afford to make things . . . right again?"

"I am not going to tell you how much money your father left," the Duke said, "because I think it would upset you, but I suggest we go back to the Castle and start to plan exactly what we shall do, starting from this moment."

Then as he rose to his feet, he had an afterthought and said:

"I think that as I am the new Duke, people in the County may want to meet me. So, if you are staying with me, which I insist you do, you must have a Chaperone."

He knew that Alvina looked at him in surprise, and he said:

"I am sure you will be able to persuade Miss Richardson to come back to the Castle and look after you and also forestall there being any criticism that you are not properly chaperoned."

Quite unexpectedly Alvina laughed. It was a very young and joyous sound, and as the Duke stared at her, she explained:

"I am laughing because everything has been so frightening, so serious, and so utterly and desperately miserable, that it never struck me for one moment that I was a young lady in need of chaperoning."

She laughed again before she said:

"Of course, Cousin Ivar, you are right, and I know Miss Richardson would be only too pleased to come back and leave this pokey little house in which she has been hiding from Papa."

"How could he have sent her away after she had been with you for so long?" the Duke asked.

"She was another mouth to feed, and Papa was quite certain he could not afford it."

The Duke swept away the frown from his face.

"Then I suggest we celebrate the new era we are opening at the Castle, and be wildly extravagant. When we get back, I intend to ask Walton if we have such a thing as a bottle of champagne in the cellar."

"Yes, there is," Alvina said, and now there was a lilt in her voice. "When Papa said Walton was to go, I was so frightened that he might bring in some strange servants who would work for nothing that I made Walton give me the keys to the cellar."

Her voice was serious as she went on:

"I hid them, having heard that the unemployed men wandering about the countryside could cause terrible . . . trouble if they . . . raided a place where there was . . . drink of any sort."

Now the Duke was definitely frowning again. He remembered the marauding bands of French deserters who had caused endless damage in France, and he asked:

"Are you telling me there has been rioting and thieving by the unemployed in England?"

"There have been terrible troubles," Alvina replied. "I do not suppose it was reported in the French papers, or wherever else you have been, but English ones have been full of little else."

She looked at him almost defiantly as she said:

"Do you realise that the men who fought for the freedom of this country, and who were, according to the Duke of Wellington, the finest Army England has ever had, were dismissed without a pension, a medal, or even a thank-you?"

The Duke knew this, but it seemed more poignant now that it was being expressed bitterly in Alvina's soft voice. Then she added:

"Of course they are resentful! Of course they are desperate! And what do you think has been happening to those who were wounded and lost a leg or an arm? They are dying of starvation unless they can steal, and no-one can blame them for their violence in doing so."

Almost as if it were his fault, rather than the Government's, that the soldiers he had commanded and who had fought so valiantly were brought to such a pass, the Duke saw the sumptuous banquets he had attended in Paris and other big cities.

Almost as if she were standing beside him he could hear Isobel's seductive voice thanking him for the orchids he had given her, which he realised had cost enough money to provide ten starving men with a good meal.

Before he could reply, Alvina said more quietly:

"Now that you are home, perhaps you will be able to make those in Parliament and at the head of the Services realise that as far as this country is concerned, peace is worse than war."

As the Duke finished what had been a surprisingly good dinner, waited on by Walton and two young men who had to be instructed *sotto voce* in everything they did, he sat back in his chair and said to Alvina:

"I have enjoyed my meal immensely, and I must not forget to congratulate Mrs. Johnson for remembering that her strawberry tart was always one of my favourite dishes."

"Mrs. Johnson has never forgotten anything about you or anyone else in the family," Alvina said. "When they knew that you were to be the next Duke, they were so glad that if it could not be Richard, it was you."

She took a sip of champagne before she went on.

"I think we were all terrified that it might be Jason."

The Duke was surprised.

"Do you know your cousin Jason?"

Alvina nodded.

"He came here to stay after Richard died, and I knew that as he was looking round he was thinking that with any luck, you would be killed too, and he would become the next Duke!"

She paused before she explained:

"He invited himself, and the manner in which he went from room to room, looking at everything and making, I thought, mental notes on their value, made me very . . . afraid."

"I can understand that," the Duke said. "I have always disliked Jason, and actually I was told just before I left London that he was raising money on the chance of succeeding me in the title before I produce an heir."

Alvina gave a little cry.

"You must be careful, very careful. I am sure he is a wicked, evil person, and he might murder you."

The Duke stared at her for a moment, then he laughed.

"You are talking nonsense. I am quite certain that Jason would not go as far as that, but my friend Gerald Chertson actually warned me he would do anything to further his ambitions."

"I am sure he is absolutely ruthless where his ambitions are concerned."

"How can you be so positive?"

"Perhaps it is because I have been so much alone here. You will think I am over-imaginative," Alvina replied, "but ever since I was a child, I have had instincts about people and I am never mistaken."

"You mean you are clairvoyant?" the Duke asked almost mockingly.

"Not exactly," Alvina answered, "but you know that the Harlings are a very mixed breed and our Celtic blood is very strong."

The Duke raised his eye-brows as she explained:

"My grandmother was Irish, my great-grandmother was Scottish, and actually Mama had a great number of Welsh relations, although I have never met them."

"If it comes to that," the Duke said, "my great-grandmother was Scandinavian, which is why I was christened 'Ivar.'"

"So you are perceptive, too."

"I like to think I can judge a man without having to read references about him, and that if I follow my instinct where he is concerned, I am invariably right."

"And you can do the same with women?"

"If I answer 'yes,' you will be able to retort that I was completely wrong in the way I judged you."

"Did you . . . really think I had taken that . . . money for . . . myself?" Alvina asked in a low voice.

"To be honest, I thought you might be giving it to some man you fancied and of whom your father did not approve."

Alvina laughed.

"That was certainly very far from the mark! I do not think I have seen a young man for years. When Papa decided we were so hard-up that we could not entertain, he refused every invitation he received, and if anyone called, they were sent away . . . usually rudely."

"It must have been very lonely for you," the Duke said sympathetically.

"It would have been much worse if I had not had books to read and dear Miss Richardson to talk to."

She looked at the Duke, and then as she thought he might contradict her, she said:

"She is a very exceptional person. Her father was an Oxford Don who wrote several books on Roman history which were acclaimed by every scholar in the country. The fact that she was capable of helping him with them shows that had she been a man, she would undoubtedly have been an outstanding scholar."

"You were very well taught, then," the Duke said.

"Of course I was," Alvina said, "and thank you for asking her back here. She is very thrilled at the invitation."

"You did ask her to dine with us tonight?" the Duke said quickly.

"I did, but she declined as her legs were paining her so much as they often do at night-time, and when she is in pain she prefers to be alone."

"I see," the Duke said. "We must get someone who specialises in rheumatism, or whatever she has, to see her."

"Do you mean that?"

"There must be some Physician in London," the Duke replied, "who has studied the rheumatic diseases which affect so many older people."

Alvina put her hand palm upwards on the table.

"How . . . can you . . . be . . . so kind?" she said in a low, broken voice.

The Duke put his hand over hers. He could feel her fingers quiver almost as if he held a small bird in his grasp.

"I hated you," Alvina said in a low voice, "first because you had taken Richard's place and then because you did not answer my letter."

"I can understand that," the Duke said quietly.

"And then you were angry with me when you came here and I thought you were heartless and indifferent."

Her fingers tightened beneath his and she said:

217

"Now I am sorry I thought that."

The Duke smiled.

"I think our Celtic instincts have broken down or gone on strike. They were certainly not working efficiently when we first met each other! That is why, Alvina, we have to start again."

"We have started already," Alvina said. "Mrs. Johnson has three girls in the kitchen, and Walton told me before dinner that he had another footman coming tomorrow from the village and other people who used to be in service here with the Harlings for years."

Her fingers tightened again. Her eyes seemed to glow, partly because there were tears in them, and she said in a voice that was very low:

"Thank you, thank you, for being exactly the head of the family we want."

CHAPTER FOUR

DRIVING BACK TO London, the Duke knew that, if he was honest, he had never enjoyed two days more.

Alvina had taken him round the Estate, both of them riding horses from the team that Gerald had bought him, which were not only perfectly broken as carriage-horses but excellent to ride.

After the old and somewhat indifferent horses which were all that Alvina had after her father had disposed of the stable, it was, the Duke realised, a thrill for her to be mounted on such perfect horse-flesh.

He also realised that she rode extremely well, and because she was so happy she looked, he thought, exceedingly attractive.

Her habit was old and worn but had once been well cut, and because she had really grown out of it, it revealed her very slim and very elegant figure.

The Duke had ridden with many beautiful women in Paris when it had been fashionable to appear every morning in the *Bois,* and also in Vienna with the alluring, auburn-haired Beauties who prided themselves on their horsemanship.

Nevertheless, he thought that his cousin could hold her own from an equestrian point of view.

The fact that she was excited by what he was planning to do made her face glow with a radiance which he seldom saw in a woman's face unless he was making love to her.

They had sat up quite late last night, poring over the book in which Alvina had set down all of her expenditures since 1814 when her father first began cheese-paring.

At first, she had merely supplemented what she was given to pay for the food from what had been her dress allowance and from two hundred pounds which her mother had left her on her death.

Then, when her father became more determined that they were going bankrupt, she had started to pay the wages of the older servants whom he insisted must be dismissed.

However, he was by then confined to his bedroom and had no idea that they were still in the house.

"The Waltons, Mrs. Johnson, and Emma were all too old to leave," Alvina said in her soft voice, "but some of the younger ones found other jobs. The footmen had to go onto the land or into the Services and they were very bitter at being turned away."

She sighed as she explained:

"They had lived on the Estate all their lives, and their families had always served the Harlings."

"We can only hope," the Duke replied, "that some of them will be able to come back now."

"It was kind of you to arrange for Mark to take the Waltons and Mrs. Johnson in a carriage to the village."

"They could hardly walk."

Knowing the drive was over a mile long, Alvina gave a little laugh.

"It would certainly have taken them a very long time, and that of course was another reason why it was impossible for them to leave us even if they had wanted to, because Papa thought he had sold all the horses."

"But you managed to keep two," the Duke stated.

"I kept the one I had ridden for years," Alvina replied, "and poor old Rufus, whom no-one would buy. He must be over seventeen years old."

The Duke made no comment because, as he had said so often, what had happened seemed so incredible that now he was just prepared to listen.

He wanted, however, to find out and see for himself exactly what had happened.

When they visited the farms he could understand that no-one with even a shred of decency in them would have turned away the Hendersons because they could not pay their rent.

There had been five generations of Hendersons farming that particular farm, and on other farms it was much the same story.

He was really appalled at the condition that the farms were in. The roofs had not been repaired for years, and many of the outbuildings had collapsed altogether.

"Things were good in the war, Your Grace," one farmer told him, "but soon as it were over, no-one wanted the farmers any longer, and the big harvest of 1815 flooded the market."

The Duke was quick to understand that few farmers had saved money, and, being able to visualise anything but rising prices, they had invested everything they had in their land.

The poor soils they had ploughed in response to the

war-time demand became economically unworkable when wheat prices fell disastrously.

By the time he and Alvina had ridden over only half of the Estate and listened to the despair the farmers expressed, he could sympathise with, although he certainly did not condone it, the fear which had made the last Duke believe he was ruined.

By the mercy of Providence he could repair much of the damage, but he could not help remembering that he could not replace the men who had been killed in battle and who would never return.

He had, however, told his own tenant-farmers that he would lend them money to make improvements without interest for three years, and he also promised he would find out when he returned to London what were the best markets available for the crops they grew.

Their gratitude was pathetic, and as the Duke and Alvina rode away from the fourth farm they had visited, he said to her:

"I hope that I am not being too optimistic and that there will be purchasers for the wheat, oats, barley, and all the other crops."

"What is more important than anything else," Alvina replied, "is that there should be work for the younger men."

The Duke knew this was true.

As he drove back to London, he saw in the villages through which he passed men who looked unmistakably as if they should be wearing a uniform.

They were sitting about on the Village Green or lounging outside the Inn, obviously with time on their hands because they were unemployed.

He thought to his satisfaction that at least he had a great number of vacancies now at the Castle.

The Head-Gardener was too old and too infirm to do anything active, but Alvina was certain that he would be able to direct any men they employed and would be aware of what would grow best in the Kitchen Garden.

He would also know where the strawberry-beds, the

peas, the beans, and the carrots had been planted in the past.

The Duke had thought that the first thing he should do was to find and engage an Estate Manager.

But because Alvina was so involved in this herself, and he knew it would make her happy to re-employ those who had been dismissed, he had thought that could wait until she found it too much for her.

At the same time, the Estate was a very extensive one.

The next day they had visited other farms, inspected an Orphanage which had been closed for three years, and called at the Schools, which were empty and neglected.

There were also several Churches which were either on the verge of falling down or had no incumbent because the reigning Duke was responsible for his stipend.

When they returned to the Castle late in the afternoon, having had luncheon at a village Inn consisting of fresh bread and cheese washed down with home-brewed cider, the Duke actually felt quite tired.

Alvina, however, despite her frail appearance, seemed to be as fresh and as buoyant as she had been in the morning.

He knew she was stimulated and excited by the knowledge that the burden of misery and despair which had rested on her shoulders for so long had now been lifted.

It was after dinner, when it was getting late and they had almost completed their plans for the next few months at any rate, that the Duke had said:

"Now, Alvina, I think we will talk about you. You have set my feet on the right path, so I must do the same for you."

"What do you mean?" she asked.

"I think I am right in thinking that you are nineteen," the Duke said, "and you should have made your début in London last year, but of course you were in mourning. Now, with Berkeley Square at your disposal, you must meet the *Beau Monde* and, of course, the Prince Regent."

He expected Alvina to be excited at the idea, as he thought any young woman would have been, but to his surprise she looked away from him to say:

"I would much rather stay here. I am too . . . old to be a . . . débutante."

"That is untrue," he said. "And although I am very grateful for your help, I cannot allow you to waste your youth and your beauty tending old pensioners and opening Schools for obstreperous children."

Alvina had risen from the chair in which she had been sitting and walked across the Morning-Room to pull aside the curtains over the window.

Outside, it was night. The sky was bright with stars and there was a moon rising over the tops of the oak trees in the Park.

She stood looking out in silence.

The Duke, watching her, thought how slim and exquisite she looked in a white muslin gown which he knew had been made for her by Miss Richardson.

The muslin, which had been intended for curtains, revealed the soft curves of her breasts, but he knew she was in fact too thin, which doubtless was caused by not having enough to eat.

He had learnt that their staple fare had been rabbits which Alvina had paid boys from the village to snare in the Park, and eggs which came from a few old chickens that were cooped up outside the kitchen-yard.

The vegetables, the Duke learnt, had grown untended in the Kitchen Garden but had naturally become more and more sparse as the years went on, so that Alvina had to search for them amongst the weeds.

Because these were such an important part of their diet, she had planted potatoes to supplement what was growing more or less wild.

The Duke wondered why she was not more enthusiastic about the idea of going to London. Then suddenly she turned from the window to say:

"No! It would be a mistake, and if you do not . . . want me here, perhaps you would let me . . . live in one of the . . . cottages. I would be quite happy if Miss Richardson would . . . stay with me."

The Duke stared at her and found it hard to believe what she was saying, before he replied:

"My dear child, Miss Richardson is already an old woman, while you are young, very young, and your whole life is in front of you. Of course you must take your proper place in Society as you would have done had your mother been alive."

"Are you saying in a tactful manner that you . . . wish to be . . . rid of me?" Alvina asked. "Perhaps you are . . . thinking of getting . . . married."

There was just a little pause before the Duke said firmly:

"I have no intention of getting married, not at any rate for a long time."

He knew as he spoke that it was impossible to imagine Isobel caring for the people on the Estate as Alvina had done, nor would she wish, he knew, to spend any length of time at the Castle.

She would want to be at Berkeley Square, entertaining for the sophisticated, witty, pleasure-loving Socialites who were an intrinsic part of her life wherever she might be.

"If you do not . . . mind my being here," Alvina said, "please, can I stay . . . with you? I should feel . . . afraid anywhere else. You must be aware how . . . ignorant I am of the . . . Social World."

"It consists of people," the Duke replied with a smile, "people like you and me, Alvina, and they are not really a race apart, whatever you may have heard about them."

As he spoke, he thought that was not quite true.

No-one could be more different from the people in the cottages and the villages, who he had realised today almost worshipped Alvina, then the gay, irresponsible

Beau Monde, who were selfish, extravagant, and concerned only with their incessant search for amusement.

They would merely find Alvina a badly dressed country girl.

Because the Duke had spent what free time he had with the most exquisitely gowned Beauties in every Capital he had visited, he was well aware how important clothes were to women.

He said now to Alvina:

"You will have to go to London for one thing, if nothing else—to buy yourself new clothes."

He spoke without thinking that it might sound an insult, and seeing a flush appear on Alvina's face he added:

"Perhaps I should have told you before that you are very lovely, but even the most beautiful picture needs the right frame to show it off."

"I have a feeling," Alvina said slowly, "that you are flattering me to get your own way. I am not used to compliments and so I am suspicious of them. Although I would love some new clothes, I am afraid if I move away from here you will never let me come back."

She spoke lightly, the Duke was aware, but there was undoubtedly a quiver of fear beneath the surface.

"I promise you," he said quickly, "that the Castle is your home for as long as you wish to stay here."

"If you . . . marry . . . what then?"

"I have no intention of marrying," the Duke said almost irritably. "At least not for a very long time."

"But you will have to, otherwise Cousin Jason will know he has a chance of taking your place."

"I will deal with Jason myself when I reach London," the Duke said, "and there is no need for you to worry about him any longer."

He spoke with a hint of laughter in his voice, then in a different tone he said:

"For God's sake, stop thinking of everyone but yourself. You have done that for far too long. I can assure you it is quite unnatural for a pretty and very attractive young woman."

He saw the colour come into her cheeks from his compliment, and she turned away to say almost obstinately:

"I do not . . . wish to go to . . . London."

"That is what you are going to do," the Duke said. "I suppose you realise that now that your father is dead, I am not only head of the family but also your Guardian, and you have to obey me."

She turned to look at him, and now there was a hint of mischief in her eyes as she said:

"And if I do . . . not?"

"Then I shall think of some horrendous punishment which will bring you to heel."

"And what will that be?"

"I cannot think for the moment," the Duke replied, "but perhaps I shall cancel the horses I intended to buy at Tattersall's for you to ride, or perhaps, worse, I will forget my plans for the Ball I want to give here in the Castle to introduce not only you to the County and to my friends from London but also myself."

"A Ball?" Alvina repeated almost stupidly.

"A Ball," the Duke said firmly. "And one thing is very important, Alvina, and that is that you should learn to dance gracefully the new waltz which was introduced to London by the Princess de Lieven."

Alvina came from the window to sit down opposite him on the sofa.

"Did you . . . really say a . . . Ball?" she asked. "I think I am . . . dreaming."

"I have every intention of celebrating my home-coming in a spectacular manner."

Actually he had not thought of it until that moment, but he knew that was much the best way to get Alvina involved in the world that he knew was waiting for her outside the Castle after the years of what was virtually imprisonment.

"I would never have thought," she said, "though

Mama talked of it when I was very young, that there would ever be a . . . Ball in the Castle and that I could . . . dance at it."

"It is something I intend to give," the Duke said.

"But the Ball-Room has not been . . . used for . . . years. The walls all want . . . washing down, the floor . . . polished, and I am certain the mice have eaten holes in the . . . chairs and the . . . curtains."

"As I intend to give the Ball in a month or six weeks' time," the Duke said, "you will have to get busy."

Alvina gave a little scream.

"That is . . . impossible! Quite . . . impossible with . . . everything else!"

"Nothing is impossible when one has unlimited money, Alvina, and as you pointed out to me yourself, there are hundreds of men whom we know and can trust, because they are our own people, longing for work."

"Yes . . . yes, of course . . . that is . . . true," Alvina agreed. "But I have to try and . . . visualise how it can . . . possibly be . . . done."

"I am sure I can leave it in your hands," the Duke said, laughing, "and when I return from London in two or three days' time, I shall have found out which are the best dressmakers for you to visit, and will make arrangements for you to come to London with Miss Richardson and stay at Berkeley Square."

"You are going . . . too fast," Alvina protested. "I have already said that I have . . . no wish to be a . . . débutante."

"You can call yourself what you like," the Duke replied, "but just as I have my duties which are obligatory, as you are well aware, as your father's daughter you have yours."

This was irrefutable, and after a moment Alvina said in a very small voice:

"I know you are . . . right, but I am . . . sure I shall make a . . . mess of it all."

"Just as you are helping me not to make a mess of my

inheritance, of which I have already admitted I am confoundedly ignorant," the Duke said, "I will prevent you from making a mess of what is waiting for you in London, and of that I am considerably knowledgeable."

They went on talking for a little while of what they must both do, apart from improving the conditions on the Estate.

Only when they walked upstairs side by side and paused on the landing to say "good-night" as they went in opposite directions did Alvina say:

"You are quite . . . certain that I shall . . . not be completely out-of-place in London and that you will not be . . . ashamed of me?"

"I am quite prepared to bet a considerable amount of money," the Duke replied, "that you will not only be surprised at your success, but in a very short time will begin to think of it as your right."

Alvina gave a little laugh, and he went on:

"You will then, like all women, undoubtedly complain and reproach me for the omissions in your programme for which I am responsible, and forget to thank me."

He was teasing her, but when Alvina looked up at him wide-eyed, she said:

"How could I ever be anything but very . . . very grateful . . . to you? Perhaps one day I shall be able to find a way to thank you."

Then, as if she felt shy, she said hastily before he could speak:

"Good-night, Cousin Ivar."

Then she slipped away from him down the passage towards her bedroom.

'I will make her a success,' the Duke thought. 'She certainly deserves it after all she has been through.'

At the same time, he could understand that the social life he was visualising for her was very different from what she had known previously.

It must have been very restricting for her to live alone at the Castle with her father, who had undoubtedly been mad, and after his death to be left with the fear of starvation and with no-one to advise her as to what she should do.

"It is all my fault," the Duke told himself for the hundredth time. "I should have come back, however much it annoyed Wellington."

But it was impossible to put back the clock, and now he knew his first duty as head of the family was to ensure, after all she had suffered, that Alvina's future would be very different from what it had been in the past.

⚜⚜⚜

When he arrived at Berkeley Square, it was a pleasure that lifted his heart to find Bateson and four footmen in well-fitting livery waiting for him and the Drawing-Room open, cleaned, and polished.

Actually, the whole house seemed to smell of bees'-wax.

The Duke had sent a groom to London the day before to warn Bateson of his arrival. The man was middle-aged, and Alvina had said that he had worked at the Castle before he joined the Navy.

He had then returned home to find time heavy on his hands because there was nothing for him to do.

The Duke, using his instinct, was sure that the man was trustworthy and good with horses.

He therefore engaged him immediately and told him to look round locally to find two other grooms whom he would recommend as men he would be willing to work with.

He had known by the way the man squared his shoulders and seemed to grow taller that he had given him back his self-respect after three years of idleness.

When he had sent him to London, he was certain that the instructions he gave him would be punctiliously carried out.

In fact, as soon as he entered the Drawing-Room, Bateson said to him,

"Major Chertson called this morning, Your Grace, to say that he had received your note and would be delighted to have luncheon with you today."

The Duke looked at the clock, and realising there would be three-quarters-of-an-hour before Gerald arrived, he decided there were quite a number of things he could do while he waited.

By the time Gerald Chertson appeared, he had written a pile of letters which lay on his desk in the Library. Some of them were to be delivered by hand and some were to be posted.

Gerald came hurrying into the room, and as the Duke rose to meet him he felt that almost a century had passed since they had last talked together, before he had set off for the Castle, furiously angry because of what he believed to be his cousin Alvina's treacherous behaviour.

He told Gerald all about it while they drank a glass of champagne before going in to luncheon.

Then in front of Bateson and the footmen they discussed mostly the improvements necessary on the Estate and the horses he wanted to buy at Tattersall's.

"I always knew you were a good organiser," Gerald said after the Duke had talked for a long time, "and as you appear now to have a campaign of your own on your hands, I can imagine that it will not only give you pleasure but will be very good for you."

"What do you mean by that?" the Duke enquired.

"I often thought when we were in Paris that you were too comfortably in the saddle as the great man's special envoy, with the red carpet rolled out before you wherever you went, and you did not have to fight for what you wanted."

"Fight? I have done damn little else for the past nine years," the Duke said.

"I do not mean that sort of enemy, you fool," Gerald replied. "I mean fighting for yourself and getting what you need personally, which is a very different thing."

"I suppose you are right," the Duke agreed. "I do not see very much difference, except that it is rather like starting with a lot of raw recruits and wondering if they will ever turn into the excellent soldiers you want them to be."

"You will do it," Gerald said, "but I am intrigued about this cousin of yours. Tell me about her."

The servants had now left the room, and the Duke said:

"That is where I am going to need your help. You have been in London far more than I have, and you are of course very knowledgeable as to what she should and should not do."

"Before you go any further," Gerald said, "you will have to find her a Chaperone who will introduce her to the right hostesses and of course get her accepted at Almack's."

"I have already arranged . . ." the Duke began.

"If you are thinking of the Governess, forget her," Gerald said. "What you want is someone of distinction who is respected by all the best hostesses. Surely there is one of your relations who can fit that bill?"

"I have actually been considering who could present her," the Duke said.

"You need someone to do a great deal more than that," Gerald answered, "and it must naturally be someone with an impeccable reputation."

The Duke knew quite well that Gerald was subtly warning him against Lady Isobel, and when he thought about it he knew she was one person whom he had no wish for Alvina to meet.

He had put her at the back of his mind while he was in the country and had deliberately refrained from asking Gerald whether she was back in England.

Now, as if there was no need to ask the question, his friend said:

"Isobel arrived from Paris yesterday. She is staying at her father's house in Piccadilly and is expecting you to dine with her tonight."

"Why did you tell her I was back?" the Duke asked sharply.

"I did not have to tell her, she knew."

"How could she have known?"

"She sent a servant, I gather, to call here to enquire when you were expected, and since you did not tell your Butler to keep it a secret, he naturally gave the answer."

"Dammit!" the Duke said beneath his breath. "I really do not have time for Isobel at the moment."

"You will find that Isobel has very different ideas."

"She will be disappointed."

That, however, was easier said than done.

Before the Duke had time to send a note to her father's house to say he was unavoidably prevented from dining with her that evening, it was too late.

When he returned to Berkeley Square, having spent the afternoon visiting the Prince Regent and being enthusiastically received at Carlton House, he saw a carriage outside his house.

It was emblazoned with a very impressive coat-of-arms, and he knew that Isobel was waiting for him.

There was nothing he could do, because he was well aware that Isobel would continue to wait however long he remained away.

Bateson told him she had been in the house for over an hour, and he went into the Drawing-Room.

As the door closed behind him she rose from the chair in which she was sitting by the fireplace.

He had to admit she looked very lovely. She had discarded her thin cloak and also her bonnet, which was trimmed with a dozen small ostrich-feathers.

Her fashionable gown was almost transparent and revealed the perfection of her figure.

The Duke had only a glimpse of it before she ran down the room, her arms outstretched.

She threw herself against him and lifting her face to his looked up at him, her dark eyes filled with an expression of desire which he knew only too well.

Then, before he could even speak, her lips were on his.

She kissed him as he should have kissed her, passionately, demandingly, insistently.

As he felt her soft body press closer and closer to him, it was impossible for him not to put his arms round her.

It was only when she set him free that he managed to say:

"I did not expect you to arrive from France so soon."

"But you are glad I am here. Tell me, dearest, that you are glad to see me!"

He was aware that the seductive note in Isobel's voice was somewhat contrived, but, at the same time, as her arms tightened round his neck he was aware that she was genuinely excited by his closeness and the kisses she had given him.

"Oh, Ivar," she went on before he could speak. "I have missed you. Paris was ghastly without you, despite the fact that the Prince de Conde paid me extravagant compliments and I had a dozen invitations for dinner every night."

With difficulty the Duke managed to extricate himself from her clinging arms, and walked towards the fireplace, saying as he did so:

"I am not surprised, Isobel. You are certainly in very good looks."

"Every man I meet tells me that," she said a little pettishly. "I want you to say that you have been dying without me."

"I am afraid that would not be true," the Duke replied, "for the simple reason that I have been busy."

"Too busy to think of me?"

Again she did not wait for him to answer, but said excitedly:

"Oh, Ivar, now that I am here, there are so many things for us to do together! Although I wanted to dine alone with you tonight, I think we will have to go to Carlton House."

The Duke smiled.

"I have just come from the Prince Regent and he has made my attendance at dinner a Royal Command."

Isobel laughed.

"I thought he would do so. I dined with him last night and told him as a dead secret how much we mean to each other."

The Duke stiffened.

"I think that was a mistake."

"Why?" Isobel asked. "Everybody I have met has spoken to me of their delight that you are now the Duke, and of the wonders of your Castle."

She looked round the room and said:

"And this house is perfect for what we want in London. I have already seen the big *Salon* upstairs, and we can have at least one hundred and fifty people at our parties without it being a squeeze."

The Duke frowned.

"I can hardly believe that you inspected my house, Isobel, when I was not here to show it to you."

"Darling, do not be so stuffy!" she replied. "I wanted to be quite certain that we should be happy here, although of course we would be happy anywhere. At the same time, I must have the right background in order to play the perfect hostess."

The Duke was silent for a moment while he sought for words to inform Isobel that he had no intention of marrying anyone at the moment.

But the door opened and Gerald came in.

"I thought I should have to apologise for having kept you waiting," he said, "but Bateson tells me you have only just returned."

"That is true," the Duke replied.

Gerald crossed the room to raise Isobel's hands to his lips, saying:

"I thought I might find you here."

"I have been waiting for Ivar for over an hour," Isobel replied, "but as I have just said, I have not wasted my time."

"What have you been doing?" Gerald asked, as she obviously expected him to.

"I have been finding out that the house is perfect for

us to entertain in, and I can see myself so clearly receiving our guests at the top of that very attractive staircase."

Gerald saw the Duke's lips tighten, and he said:

"You are taking your fences too fast, Isobel. I was
informed only a few hours ago that as Ivar has much to
do, he has no intention of marrying for years."

The Duke thought with an irrepressible smile that
Gerald, ever since he became his friend, had always
been prepared to come to his rescue in a tight corner.

"That is true," he agreed. "It will certainly be years
before the Castle and the Estate are put to right and
things are restored to what they were in the past."

There was silence, and Isobel looked from one man to
the other.

"What is all this?" she asked.

Her voice now sounded a very different note, and she
went on:

"Is this a conspiracy between you two?"

"Not in the least," Gerald replied, "but it is always
wise, my dear Isobel, to face facts, and the fact is that
Ivar, for the moment, is not in the marriage-market."

"That is nothing to do with you!" she said angrily. "I
presume Ivar can speak for himself."

Then, as if she thought this attitude was unwise, she
rose from the sofa, went to the Duke, and slipped her
hand in his.

"We will talk about it when we are alone," she said
very softly.

The Duke, as was expected of him, raised her hand to
his lips.

"We will meet tonight at Carlton House."

"I am sure you will be kind enough to take me home
afterwards," Isobel said in a child-like voice which she
used when she was at her most dangerous. "Papa hates
his horses and his coachmen being kept out late."

The Duke could not think of a reasonable way he
could refuse, and she flashed a smile at Gerald but her
eyes as she looked at him were hard as agates.

Then, as the Duke hurried to open the door for her, she moved down the room with a contrived grace which made her appear like a young goddess who had just stepped down from Olympus.

As she reached the Duke, she said in a voice that only he could hear:

"*Au revoir,* my love. I shall be counting the hours until tonight."

When he had seen her to her carriage at the front door, the Duke returned to where Gerald was waiting in the Drawing-Room.

"I suppose I ought to say 'thank you,' " he said. "I do not know whether you have made things worse or better."

"I do not think they could be much worse," Gerald replied, "unless you intend to marry Isobel."

The Duke did not answer, and he said:

"You know, Ivar, I never interfere in your love-affairs, but I think you ought to know that I learnt just now when I went to White's that the reason she left Paris so quickly was not only that she was following you."

The Duke waited, with a questioning look in his eyes, and Gerald went on:

"After you left, she behaved so outrageously with the *Duc* de Gramont that the *Duchesse* was furious, and there was a highly dramatic scene at a party, where I gather the whole of Paris was present, which made it imperative for Isobel to leave the next day."

The Duke walked across the room and back again before he said:

"I am glad you have told me. I am in a mess."

"I thought you would be," Gerald replied. "I told you she was determined to be a Duchess, and I cannot imagine a worse fate for any man than to be married to Isobel."

The Duke knew this was true, but because Isobel had been so persistent, he had played with the idea of making her his wife.

Now he knew that he could never envisage her at the

Castle, caring for his people who worked for him and worrying herself as to whether their children were educated or their grandparents had medical attention.

At the same time, he had the uncomfortable feeling that he was half-committed, and that Isobel, fastening onto him like a leech, would do everything in her power to prevent him getting away from her.

As if Gerald knew what he was thinking, he said:

"For God's sake, Ivar, be careful. She is a dangerous woman, and you will find it impossible to be free of her."

"No-one, not even Prinny, can make me marry someone I do not wish to marry!" the Duke said firmly.

"Do not be too sure of that," Gerald replied, "and the last thing you want at this particular moment is a scandal."

"That is true," the Duke agreed. "It is just another problem on top of the ones I am weighed down with already."

"I will give you something else to think about," Gerald said. "You may find it even more unpleasant."

"What is that?"

"Jason is calling on you tomorrow morning, and, from all I hear, you will either have to bail him out or let him go to the Fleet."

The Duke started.

The Fleet, which was the prison for debtors, was so notorious that any gentleman who was sent there for not being able to pay his debts received a great deal of publicity in the national newspapers.

He could not imagine anything which he would dislike more than for the world to know that his relative, and a Harling, was there.

At a moment when he was preparing to take his place in the House of Lords as the fifth Duke of Harlington, it would be impossible to admit that his cousin was incarcerated in the filth, vulgarity, and degradation of the debtors' prison.

Because it upset him even to think of it, the Duke's voice was harsh as he replied:

"I have already decided to see Jason and tell him that I will give him a fairly generous allowance, as long as he behaves himself."

"It will cost you a pretty penny to rescue him in the first place. I do not suppose he will thank you for it or agree to your conditions."

"I will make him agree!" the Duke said fiercely.

"How?" Gerald asked simply.

The Duke knew uncomfortably and unmistakably that he did not have the answer to that question.

CHAPTER FIVE

THE PRINCE REGENT retired early, with Lady Hertford on his arm.

One of the few things for which Lady Hertford was liked was that she did not wish to keep the Prince up late.

She was in fact getting on in years and was only too willing to end the evening far sooner than was hoped by those who surrounded the Prince Regent.

The Duke, watching them go, looked round for Gerald Chertson and saw him deep in conversation with Viscount Castlereagh, the Secretary of State for Foreign Affairs.

As he did not like to interrupt them unnecessarily, he walked slowly through the Reception-Rooms, noticing how many additions had been made since he was last in England.

The Prince's passion for collecting was one of the bits of gossip which had percolated through to the Armed Forces, besides rumours concerning his amatory affairs.

But, while the majority of the Duke's fellow-officers had strongly criticised the pile of debts accumulating from the treasures installed at Carlton House and the Royal Pavilion at Brighton, the Duke was sympathetic.

He was quite certain that future generations would acclaim the Prince Regent as a man of exceptionally good taste, but for the moment the only things that concerned the populace were his interest in women and the huge pile of unpaid debts.

Now the Duke stopped appreciatively before some Dutch paintings which the Prince Regent had bought early in the century, and thought how wise he had been to acquire them when they were inexpensive.

There were also some outstanding statues and a collection of miniatures which he appraised carefully, thinking with satisfaction that they were not as good as those he himself owned.

When he felt that Gerald must have finished his conversation, he saw him coming down the room towards him.

"Are you ready to leave?" Gerald asked.

"I am," the Duke replied, "but I did not like to interrupt you when I saw how seriously you were talking to Castlereagh."

"He was being extraordinarily interesting," Gerald said. "I will tell you about it as we drive home."

As they moved towards the door, he said as if it was an after-thought:

"By the way, I have not seen Isobel for some time."

"Neither have I," the Duke replied. "Do you suppose she has left?"

"It seems surprising that she should do so, unless she is annoyed with you."

The Duke thought this might be the reason.

He had ignored the invitation in Isobel's eyes when the gentlemen had joined the ladies after dinner and had deliberately talked to one of the other guests.

He had known without looking round that her eyes were dark with anger, and she had been tapping her fan irritably on the arm of her chair.

However, he had no intention of parading himself in public as a captive at Isobel's chariot-wheels, which he was sure she intended he should do.

Instead, he had gone out of his way the whole evening to avoid talking to her.

Therefore, he expected she was by now in one of her black moods, with which he had become familiar, and had probably found somebody else to take her home, being quite certain it would make him jealous.

There was certainly no sign of her amongst the other ladies who were collecting their wraps, and as he and Gerald settled themselves comfortably in the carriage that was waiting for them, Gerald said:

"You look pleased with yourself, Ivar, but I am quite certain Isobel will not let you off the hook so easily."

The Duke stiffened, and his friend knew that once again he was resenting the intrusion into his private affairs.

"I am sorry, Ivar," he said, "but because I am so fond of you, I want to make quite certain that your freedom, if nothing else, is not in danger."

The Duke did not reply, and after a moment Gerald went on:

"The night is still young. I suppose you would not like to do anything amusing? The Palace of Fortune has some extremely attractive new Cyprians whose praises were being sung in the Club this morning."

"To be honest," the Duke replied, "I have not only had quite a long day but I also have a lot to think about —in fact too much!"

Gerald laughed.

"You would soon be bored if you had nothing to do! All right, we will have an early night, but tomorrow I am taking you out on the town, whether you like it or not, otherwise you will find yourself growing old and staid beyond your years."

The Duke laughed.

"Now you are frightening me," he said, "but have it your own way. I shall need somebody to cheer me up after I have seen Jason tomorrow morning."

"That is underestimating the effect he will have on you," Gerald answered.

The carriage drew up outside the house in Berkeley Square and the Duke alighted, telling the coachman to take Major Chertson to his lodgings in Half-Moon Street.

"I shall not need you anymore," he added.

The coachman saluted, touched his top-hat, and drove away.

The Duke walked through the front door, which he saw had been opened by one of the new footmen.

He was a young man who looked quite intelligent, and the Duke asked:

"What is your name?"

"Henry, Your Grace."

"And what were you doing before you came into my service?"

"I were in the Navy, Your Grace."

The Duke asked him what ship he had been in, and learnt that he was too young to have served for more than a year at sea, but on being discharged when the war was over he had found it difficult to obtain employment.

He told the Duke how grateful he was to be taken on at Harlington House and that he hoped he would give satisfaction.

The Duke, liking his bearing and the way in which he spoke, replied:

"I am sure you will, and remember to take notice of what Mr. Bateson tells you. He has been in service all his life, and there is nothing he does not know."

"I'll do me best, Your Grace."

The Duke smiled, and without going into any of the downstairs rooms started to climb the stairs to his bedroom.

When he reached the landing he looked back to see that Henry, having locked the front door, had installed himself comfortably in the round-topped padded armchair in which as night-footman he would spend the long hours until dawn.

Walking along the corridor, the Duke reached the Master Suite, which had been occupied by all the Dukes of Harlington.

Like his bedroom at the Castle, it was dominated by a huge, curtained four-poster bed which had been installed in the house in the reign of Queen Anne.

He entered the outer door into the small hallway in which a candle had been left burning in a silver sconce bearing the Harlington crest.

He saw there was a light in his bedroom, but when he pushed open the door he was surprised to find that his valet was not waiting for him.

The Duke told himself somewhat irritably that this was a slackness he could not countenance, and he walked across to the fireplace.

He had put out his hand towards the bell-pull when a soft voice from the bed said:

"I told your man I would wait up for you!"

The Duke started and turned round.

Lying in the great bed, half-hidden by the draped curtains, was Isobel.

She was wearing nothing but an emerald necklace which, even in his surprise at seeing her, the Duke realised was new.

It flashed through his mind that it might have been a gift from the *Duc* de Gramont.

Then in a slightly irritable tone he asked:

"What are you doing here, Isobel?"

"I am waiting for you, darling."

"I thought you had gone home."

It was a somewhat banal remark, but for the moment

the Duke was finding it hard to think what he should do or how he should get rid of Isobel without creating a scene.

He realised she was being outrageous and behaving in a way which, if it ever became known, would cause a tremendous scandal.

He guessed, however, that this was what she intended, and he had walked into the trap she had set for him, from which it would be difficult to extricate himself.

As he stood looking at her, she held out her arms.

"I will explain to you everything you want to know," she said softly, "but it will be much easier to do so if you are closer."

◈◈◈◈◈◈◈◈◈

Lying in the darkness, the Duke could hear Isobel's even breathing and knew she was fast asleep.

It was not surprising, as their love-making had been fiery and, from a physical point of view, very satisfying.

At the same time, he was aware that she had tempted him into a position from which it had been impossible to free himself without extremely unpleasant recriminations.

To save these, he had given her what she wanted.

The one candle which had been left alight in the room had flickered out, and now the only light came very faintly from the sides of the curtains so that the Duke thought there must be a moon in the sky.

Very softly, moving with the stealth that came from a perfectly controlled body and from the training he had instigated and insisted upon amongst his soldiers in Portugal, Spain, and France, he crept from the bed and crossed the carpet towards the door.

As he did so, he picked up from a chair the clothes he had been wearing, and still making no sound opened the door and passed outside.

His actions were as stealthy as any Tracker's, and as

243

silent as those which he had taught his men were indispensable in making a surprise attack on the enemy in order to confuse and bewilder them.

In fact, the French had often been appalled to find, when they least expected it, that they were either surrounded or infiltrated by English soldiers whom they had neither heard nor seen approaching them.

Once outside the bedroom, the Duke moved into the room where he bathed and where his clothes were kept in large mahogany wardrobes.

He dressed himself swiftly, putting on the same silk stockings and knee-breeches he had worn at Carlton House, and his evening-coat with its long tails, on the breast of which were pinned a number of diamond-encrusted decorations.

He had managed, still without making any noise, to extract a fresh cravat from the drawer of the dressing-table, and he tied it swiftly with an expertise which always infuriated any valet who looked after him.

Then, looking exactly as he had done when he dined with the Prince Regent, he went from the Master Suite along the corridor and down the stairs into the Hall.

Henry was by this time asleep, and only when the Duke deliberately stepped noisily onto the marble floor did he awake with a start.

He jumped to his feet, and the Duke said:

"I have to go out again, Henry, and I expect I shall be late, but as soon as I have left I want you to run to the Duke of Melchester's stables at the back of Melchester House in Park Lane. Do you know where I mean?"

"I think so, Your Grace."

"Wake the coachman and tell him to come round here immediately to collect Lady Isobel Dalton and take her home."

"I'll do that, Your Grace."

"When the carriage arrives," the Duke went on, "fetch the head housemaid—I have forgotten her name—and ask her to help Lady Isobel downstairs and into the carriage."

He thought the footman looked puzzled, and added:

"Explain to her that Lady Isobel is feeling ill and is therefore lying down until the carriage arrives. Do you understand?"

"I understands, Your Grace."

"Then do exactly as I have told you," the Duke said, "and try not to make any mistakes."

"I'll do my best, Your Grace."

"Good man!"

The Duke turned towards the door and Henry hastily unlocked it for him. Only as he stepped outside did the footman say, as if he had just thought of it:

"Your Grace don't want a carriage?"

"No, I am not going far," the Duke replied.

He walked away quickly, finding his way to Gerald Chertson's lodgings in Half-Moon Street, where the sleepy porter opened the door for him.

The Duke climbed a narrow flight of stairs to the second floor, where Gerald rented two small rooms for himself and one for his servant.

It took the Duke a little time to get any answer as he knocked on the flat door.

When finally it was opened by Gerald in his nightshirt his friend stared at him in astonishment.

"Ivar! What are you doing here at this hour?"

The Duke walked past him into the bedroom, where Gerald had lit one candle before responding to the insistent noise which had awakened him.

Briefly, in as few words as possible, the Duke explained what had happened.

"So that was why Isobel left early!" Gerald exclaimed. "We might have guessed she was up to some mischief!"

The Duke did not reply, and he said:

"You realise what this means, Ivar? She will tell her father tomorrow where she has been all night, and the Duke of Melchester will insist that you marry her."

"That is where you are mistaken," the Duke replied quietly. "I have sent my footman to Melchester House for her carriage to take her home, and have told him to wake my head housemaid and explain that Isobel has been taken ill and she is to help her into it."

Gerald stared at him.

"And you think she will go quietly?"

"There is nothing else she can do," the Duke replied.

"And where does that leave you?"

"It leaves me," the Duke answered, "with you at the most important party that is taking place in London to-night."

Gerald stared at him as if he had taken leave of his senses.

Then the Duke said:

"Come on, Gerald! You cannot be so stupid as not to realise that if I am seen dancing until dawn by everybody of any importance in the *Beau Monde*, it will be impossible for Isobel to tell the world that we spent the night in each other's arms."

Gerald gave a sudden shout that seemed to vibrate round the small bedroom.

"Ivar, you are a genius!" he said. "God knows, I have seen you get out of some very tight spots, but never quite as subtly or cleverly as this!"

As he spoke, he jumped up from the bed on which he had been sitting and went to the mantelpiece, on which there was a stack of white cards engraved with the names of famous hostesses.

He picked up a handful of them and flung them down on the bed in front of the Duke.

"Pick out the best while I dress," he said.

The Duke lifted up the cards one by one, holding them so that the light from the candle fell on them.

There were six parties to which Major Gerald Chertson had been invited tonight, but by far the most important of them was the invitation sent by the Countess of Jersey.

The Countess had sprung into social fame when she captured the vacillating heart of the Prince of Wales and estranged him from Mrs. Fitzherbert, who was thought secretly to be his wife.

Marie Fitzherbert, much as she adored the Prince, had realised the truth of what Sheridan had said of him:

"He is too much of a Ladies' Man to be the man of any lady."

Although she was often exasperated by his selfishness, she had always been ready to forgive him for his casual affairs in the past, but she had never been more jealous or miserable than when she realised he was falling in love with the Countess of Jersey.

The mother of two sons and seven daughters, some of whom had already provided her with grandchildren, the Countess was nine years older than the Prince, but she was a woman of immense charm and undeniable beauty.

In fact, at the time she was spoken of as having an "irresistible seductiveness and fascination."

The Prince's affair with the Countess had lasted for some years, and she had made the very most of the association by providing for herself a place in Society from which it would be impossible to tumble her.

The Duke knew now, using his instinct for self-preservation, that to have the Countess on his side would undoubtedly be a weapon that Isobel would find hard to match.

By the time Gerald Chertson, who like the Duke had dressed himself extremely quickly and without the help of his valet, returned to the room, his friend was waiting with the Countess's invitation-card in his hand.

"That is where we are going!" he said, holding it out.

"To hear is to obey!" Gerald replied mockingly, and they hurried down the stairs together.

"Have you come in your carriage?" Gerald asked, as they reached the front door.

"No, we will have to take a hackney-cab," the Duke replied.

Fortunately, there was one just outside the house, crawling slowly down the street towards Piccadilly.

Gerald hailed it, and the two friends sat side by side as the cabby whipped up his tired horse.

"I am relying on you to introduce me," the Duke said. "I do not think I have seen the Countess for eight or nine years."

"She will welcome you with open arms," Gerald replied, "not only because she has never grown too old to appreciate a handsome man, but also because you are a Duke and she will be delighted to introduce you like a shy débutante to the *Beau Monde*."

"That is what I anticipated," the Duke said quietly.

Gerald threw back his head and laughed.

"I do not believe this is happening!" he said. "It is so like you, Ivar! I have never known you without a crisis in your life, or some incredible surprise which nobody could have anticipated."

He laughed again as he said:

"I thought we were going to have a quiet night. I only wish I could see Isobel's face when your housemaid wakes her to say that her father's carriage is waiting outside to take her home!"

"I would rather not think of it."

"Mark my words, she will not give up," Gerald continued. "She will merely dig in her spurs and be more determined than ever to wear the Harlington coronet."

"Then she will be disappointed!" the Duke said grimly.

When they reached the Earl of Jersey's house it was not yet two o'clock and the Ball-Room was still crowded.

The Countess, looking resplendent and still, despite her age, an attractive woman, held out her hands with delight as Gerald Chertson approached her.

"So you have arrived," she exclaimed, "when I had despaired, you naughty boy, of seeing you!"

Gerald kissed her hand.

"You must forgive me for being late," he said, "but I have been showing my friend Ivar Harling, who has only just arrived back in London, some of the amusements he has been missing while he has been in France."

The Countess held out her hand to the Duke with what was obviously a sincere gesture of pleasure.

"I had no idea that you were in England," she said, "or I would already have sent you a dozen invitations!"

"You are the first person, with the exception of His Royal Highness, whom I have visited," the Duke said truthfully.

The Countess was delighted.

In the space of a few minutes she introduced him to a dozen people, giving them, as she did so, a potted biography of his achievements.

She made the Duke aware that while he had been abroad and out of sight, she had not been ignorant of his new importance in the Social World.

By the time he had talked to a number of people and had even danced twice round the room with his hostess, the Duke was delighted by the suggestion that they should repair to the Supper-Room.

There, at a table precided over by the Countess, he found the conversation witty and slanderous and as stimulating as the excellent champagne.

It was long after dawn when he and Gerald left, and by that time the Duke had managed to take the Countess on one side.

"I believe that only you can help me," he said simply.

"In what way?" the Countess questioned.

He was aware of the look of curiosity in her eyes.

He told her briefly of his predecessor's illness, and how he had not only expected his daughter to take care of him but had also prevented her from seeing her relations or friends and had convinced her that they were penniless.

The Duke did not go into details about what had happened on the Estate but was concerned only to evoke the Countess's sympathy for Alvina.

He told her how she had been unable to spend a penny on herself or enjoy any of the social activities that should have been hers when she had left the School-Room.

"What am I to do about her?" the Duke asked when the story was finished.

"I can see it is a problem," the Countess replied, "but certainly not an insoluble one. I imagine, as head of the family, you will now provide for her?"

"Of course!" the Duke confirmed. "But she needs a Chaperone to introduce her to Society, and somebody who could take her to the best dressmakers."

The Countess smiled.

"There should be no difficulty about that," she said. "What woman could resist the idea of ordering a whole wardrobe of new clothes, even if they are for somebody else?"

"Then you will help me find the right person?"

"Send her to stay with me first," the Countess said, "and when I have dressed her, as you suggest, and made the first introductions, I will find somebody eminently suitable to carry on the good work."

"I cannot thank you enough," the Duke exclaimed. "At the same time, I do not like to impose on your good nature."

"I shall expect my reward."

"What is that?" he asked.

"That you will come to parties and let me find you a wife who will grace the end of your table and the Harlington diamonds."

The Duke laughed.

"Could any woman, even including Your Ladyship, refrain from match-making?"

His voice was more serious as he went on:

"I will do anything you ask, except allow you to hurry me up the aisle before I have had a holiday, and a long one! Wellington has been a hard task-master these last years, and I am afraid a wife might be an even more exacting one."

"I will find you somebody soft, sweet, gentle, and very amenable," the Countess promised.

"I doubt if such a paragon exists," the Duke replied, "but in the meantime let me enjoy myself as a bachelor. I feel I deserve it."

The Countess glanced at the decorations on his breast.

"I suppose you do," she admitted. "At the same time, my dear boy, you are far too attractive and far too handsome not to have every woman in London endeavouring to get you into her clutches!"

The Duke remembered that that was exactly what Isobel was trying to do, and he said:

"It sounds very enjoyable after being a target for French marksmen for more years than I care to remember."

"Now you are far more likely to die of kisses," the Countess promised. "And here is somebody I particularly want you to meet."

As she spoke she beckoned to a very attractive Beauty who had just come into the Supper-Room.

She came obediently towards her hostess, who introduced the Duke and insisted that they should have the last dance together.

By the end of it the Duke knew he had made a new conquest, and he had promised to call on his new acquaintance the following afternoon.

"I shall be waiting for Your Grace," she said very softly as they said good-night.

The Duke and Gerald left together, and as by now the sun was golden in the East and the last stars were receding in the sky, they decided to walk home.

"I feel I need some fresh air," the Duke said.

"I thought you were behaving admirably," Gerald said approvingly. "Our hostess was wildly enthusiastic about you, and she also told me she has promised to take your cousin under her wing. That was a clever move on your part."

"I thought that myself," the Duke agreed. "Alvina will certainly get off on the right foot."

"The Countess, if I know anything of her methods, will have her married and off your hands in a few months."

The Duke did not respond, and Gerald looked at him enquiringly, then realised he was frowning.

"There is no need for such haste," he said.

As he spoke, he wondered why the idea of marriage for Alvina as well as for himself made him feel angry.

He had set the wheels in motion, but now that they were actually turning, he thought perhaps he had been too impetuous.

It might have been better if he had left things as they were, at least for a little while longer.

⚜⚜⚜

The Duke awoke and realised it was later than he had intended.

At the same time, his valet, having learnt that he had come to bed after dawn had broken, had left him to sleep.

When he had reached his bedroom it was to find that everything had been tidied, and it was difficult to believe that when he had come home earlier Isobel had been lying against his pillows wearing nothing but an emerald necklace.

As he undressed and got back into bed, he could not help thinking with a smile how shocked many of his ancestors would have been at her behaviour and, if it came to that, at his.

Somehow he had saved himself, although now, when he thought of it, he realised it had been a very "close shave."

It had been clever of Isobel to think out a situation in which it would have been impossible for him to do anything but offer her marriage.

The Duke of Melchester was a highly respected member of the aristocracy and a gentleman of the "Old School."

He would certainly have demanded that his daughter's honour be protected, and there would have been no way of refusing to obey what the whole Social World would have thought of as a dictate of honour.

"I am free!" the Duke said to himself as he closed his eyes.

Then, almost as if there were a little devil sitting on his shoulder, a voice asked:

"But for how long?"

As Gerald had warned the Duke, the interview at eleven o'clock the next morning with his cousin Jason was extremely unpleasant.

Jason arrived looking, in the Duke's eyes, over-dressed.

If there was one thing he and the Duke of Wellington disliked, it was the "Dandies" who affected ridiculously high cravats, over-square shoulders, over-tight waists, and pantaloons which had to be dampened before they could pull them up over their hips.

The points of Jason's collar were high over his chin, and his cravat made it appear as if it was difficult for him to breathe. The shoulders of his coat were too square, and the sleeves bulged high above them, making them appear in the Duke's eyes almost grotesque.

He carried a lace-edged handkerchief which was saturated with perfume and which he held delicately to his nose.

At the same time, the Duke was aware that his eyes were hard, shrewd, and avaricious.

Jason was five years older than his cousin, and the Duke thought he was increasingly anxious to ensure that his future should be a comfortable one and that he should be very much better off financially than he had been in the past.

He wondered, as he had wondered before, why Jason had not found a rich wife.

But he was sure no decent woman would marry him, and Jason was too snobby and too proud of his Harling

blood to consider marriage with some wealthy trades-
man's daughter, who might have been prepared to accept him.

He had therefore relied on borrowing from his
friends, and gambling, but he often ran up debts which,
as at the moment, he had no possible chance of paying
without the help of the family.

The Duke knew when they met in the Library that
Jason was wondering how much he could extract from
him by blackmailing him with the fear of scandal and
adverse publicity.

Somewhat coldly he offered Jason a drink, which he
accepted.

Then the cousins sat down, eying each other like two
bull-dogs, the Duke thought, each waiting for the other
to attack.

The Duke took the initiative.

"I am quite aware, Jason, of why you wished to see
me," he said. "I have already been told that you are in
debt, and I think it would be best if you were frank and
told me exactly what is the sum involved."

His cousin named a figure which made the Duke
want to gasp, but with his usual self-control his face remained impassive.

"Is that everything?" he asked.

"Everything I can think of," Jason replied surlily.

There was a short silence. Then, as if he found it intolerable, Jason went on:

"It is all very well for you, Ivar, to walk into a fortune
without having to lift a finger for it, but surely you will
admit it is the most astounding good luck, and as head
of the family you should help those who were not born
under the same lucky star."

His last sentence was spoken in a sneering tone that
was unmistakable, and the Duke said quietly:

"I admit I have been very fortunate. I am therefore,
Jason, prepared to do two things."

"What are they?"

"The first is to pay your present outstanding bills,"

the Duke replied, "the second, to grant you in the future an allowance of a thousand pounds a year."

Jason Harling's eyes lit up on hearing that the Duke would settle his bills for him, but even so he said quickly:

"Two thousand!"

"One thousand!" the Duke replied coldly. "And there is of course a condition attached."

"What is it?"

Now there was no mistaking that Jason's expression was hostile.

"You go abroad and do not come back to England for at least five years."

Jason stared at him incredulously.

"Do you mean that?"

"I mean it!" the Duke said firmly. "If you do not agree, the whole deal is off."

Jason jumped to his feet.

"I do not believe it!"

"Then you can settle your debts yourself, and I shall not lift a finger to help you!"

"I have never heard of anything so diabolical!" Jason shouted furiously.

"I think, actually, that I am being extremely generous," the Duke said. "The debts you have run up are so enormous that it would not surprise me in the slightest if you end up in the Fleet. But, as there are a great number of other calls on the family purse, it is essential that this sort of situation should not arise again."

"In other words, you want to spend it all on yourself!" Jason said spitefully.

"That is quite untrue, and I have no intention of arguing," the Duke replied. "But when you visited the Castle the other day you must have been aware that an enormous amount of money needs to be spent on the Estate: the Schools must be opened, and the Orphanages repaired or rebuilt."

He paused to say more slowly:

"More important than anything else, the tenant-farmers need funds to bring their farms back to the standard that existed ten years ago."

As he spoke, the Duke realised that all this meant nothing to Jason and he was thinking only of himself.

"I have no wish to live abroad," he said like a sulky child.

"I am sure you will find yourself very much at home in Paris or any other town in France," the Duke replied, "and quite frankly, Jason, I want you out of the country and out of people's sight when our cousin Alvina makes her début."

"I am not in the least concerned with Cousin Alvina," Jason answered, "but with my own life, and I wish to live in England."

"Then I hope you will find ways of doing so," the Duke said, rising to his feet.

Jason, looking up at him, realised that he was up against a brick wall.

There was a long silence before he said furiously:

"Damn you! I have no alternative but to do as you insist, have I?"

"I am afraid not," the Duke agreed.

"Very well!"

Jason rose and drew from the tail of his coat a sheath of bills.

"Here you are!" he said, slapping them down on a table. "The sooner they are met, the better, otherwise you will undoubtedly have the indignity of bailing me out of a locked cell!"

The Duke thought it would be far better if he was left in one, but he said quickly:

"I will pay the first part of your allowance into the branch of Coutt's Bank in Paris, unless you prefer some other major city. I shall also make it clear that you cannot draw from that account unless you present the cheque in person."

Jason did not reply, but as he stood in front of him the Duke saw that his fingers were clenched as if he would have liked to hit him.

Instead, he said in a voice that was fraught with venom:

"Very well, Cousin Ivar, you win for the moment! But never forget that the victor today is often the loser to-morrow!"

He walked towards the door, and as he reached it he looked back and the Duke thought he had never seen hatred so vehement in any man's eyes or in the expression on his face.

Then, as if words failed him, Jason walked out of the Library and the Duke heard his footsteps going down the corridor towards the Hall.

Chapter Six

Arriving back at the Castle after riding, Alvina was humming happily to herself.

It was so exciting to be in a position to engage servants for the house and men to work in the gardens, and to be able to assure the pensioners that their cottages would be repaired and their pensions increased.

Already, because news flew on wings, the villagers were aware of what was happening, and the excitement was spreading all over the two thousand acres the Duke owned round the Castle.

Alvina was quite certain that those on the Duke's other properties also had already learnt that things were changing, and that servants in every department who had been discharged after years of service were being re-employed.

"It is all so wonderful!" Alvina said to herself.

She thought the years when her father had declared over and over again that they had no money were like a nightmare from which she had at last awakened.

The Duke had been gone for five days, but time seemed to fly past and Alvina had not felt lonely.

In fact, she had so many people to see, so much to talk about, and so much to do that she was hardly aware of being alone as she had been in the past.

At the same time, although he was not there, the Duke seemed to be with her.

It was impossible not to think of him all the time and be aware that it was due to him alone that everything was changed.

If she had wanted more positive proof of his kindness, she had received it this morning when, after she had breakfasted with a choice of three dishes, which was a new experience, a Post-Chaise had arrived from London.

For a moment she thought excitedly that the Duke had returned.

But instead several large boxes were handed to one of the new footmen, who was learning his duties under Walton.

"These are for you, M'Lady," the young man said as Alvina came into the Hall, unable to restrain her curiosity as to what was happening.

"For me?" she exclaimed.

Then as she saw the name printed on one of the boxes, she had an idea what they contained.

The footman carried them up to her bedroom.

When she opened them, with the help of old Emma, who seemed to take on a new lease of life since she had help, Alvina saw that they were gowns which she had never dreamt she would have the chance of owning.

There were four of them, two for the day, two for the evening, and a third box contained a smart, thin summer riding-habit that seemed to her to have stepped straight out of a Fashion-Plate.

Almost before she had time to look at them, Alvina was joined by three of the new housemaids, who all came from the village, together with Mrs. Johnson, Mrs. Walton, and even two of the kitchen-maids.

She knew they were acting unconventionally, but she understood that because they shared with her the bad times, they now wished to share the good.

She held up the gowns for their inspection, one after another, and because she was so excited she put on the habit so that they could see her in it.

"It's just how you should look, M'Lady!" Mrs. Walton exclaimed. "Now we know the old days are back and we can all be happy again."

The way she spoke was so moving that Alvina felt the tears come into her eyes.

Impulsively she bent and kissed Mrs. Walton, saying:

"Whatever good times come to me, I intend to share them with you. You have been so wonderful these last years."

She nearly added: "when Papa was mad," but thought it would sound disloyal.

She felt anyway they were thinking the same thing and were aware that her father's mind had become deranged after Richard's death.

Yesterday two horses had arrived from London, which had been a thrill that was almost as exciting as her new gowns.

She knew instinctively that one of them had been chosen for her and was exactly the sort of horse that any Lady would wish to ride.

The other was a huge stallion, and she thought that the Duke would look magnificent on him and wanted him to come home so that they could ride together.

When she had gone to bed last night she had told herself that there would be so many things for him to do in London, so many people ready to welcome him, that she must wait patiently for his reappearance and not be surprised if he was a long time in coming.

Because she had lived such a quiet life, she knew very little about men, but she was not so stupid as not to realise how handsome the Duke was and that he had a presence that would make him stand out in any company, however distinguished.

'Perhaps,' she thought, 'he will find life in London, when he has Harlington House restaffed, more attractive than living here.'

She was aware that it would take a little time before people in the County realised that the Duke would be willing to receive them as her father had refused to do.

Therefore, he might discover that London was more congenial and certainly more amusing.

She found herself wondering what he would talk about to the beautiful women whom she was sure he would meet at Carlton House, and who would welcome him into the most distinguished and at the same time most sophisticated society in Europe.

She knew very little about the Social World of London except what she had read in the Court Columns of the newspapers or heard discussed in the village.

Strangely enough, that had been quite a mine of information.

Several of the sons and daughters of the villagers had originally gone to London to work at Harlington House.

When on her father's instructions they had been dismissed, they had fortunately obtained employment in the houses of other distinguished aristocrats.

This meant that their parents were kept informed of what was happening in London, and every letter and every piece of news which came by post or carrier was repeated round the village the moment it arrived.

Alvina therefore was well aware of the dislike the populace had for Lady Hertford because she was the latest fancy of the Prince Regent.

She had also heard over the years of the love-affairs of

Lord Byron and a number of other noblemen, many of which were positively scandalous.

Although she told herself she should not listen, and certainly should not talk familiarly with people who were not of the same station as herself, she had nobody else to talk to.

It would have been unnatural for her to refuse to listen to what Mrs. Walton's niece wrote home about what she called the "goings-on of the smart young gentleman" in whose parents' house she was at present employed.

At the time, it had merely amused her, and she had forgotten what she heard almost as soon as it was spoken.

Now she began to imagine the Duke at parties, Balls, and Assemblies, surrounded by beautiful women and finding them very alluring after the long years of war.

'Perhaps he will never come back to the Castle,' she thought dismally.

Then she told herself there was no need for such depressing thoughts.

That he had thought of her in sending her such beautiful clothes raised her hopes that she would see him soon.

Last night she had sat up late making a list of all the people in the County whom he might invite to the Ball he was planning.

She also worked hard in supervising the new housemaids and the footmen as they cleaned the Ball-Room.

It was a tremendous task to wash down the walls, but when it was done the paint looked white and clear, and the gold-leaf which ornamented the cornice shone as brightly as it had when it was first applied.

The paintings on the walls were also improved by being dusted and having the dust scrubbed from their gold frames.

However, Alvina discovered it was going to take a long time to get the polish back on the floor.

The footmen not only got down on their knees to rub

the polish in, but on Alvina's instructions tied dusters over their shoes and slid up and down until the parquet began to look very much brighter than it had for twenty years.

"The Duke when he gets back will be pleased with what I have done," Alvina told herself.

As she reached the top of the steps she turned back to watch the groom taking away the horse she had ridden that morning, and felt with a little lilt of her heart that she was sure the Duke had chosen it especially for her.

She walked into the Hall and smiled at the two footmen on duty, their newly polished crested buttons gleaming in the sunshine.

"Enjoy your ride, M'Lady?" one of them asked.

"Yes, thank you," Alvina replied.

She walked up the staircase, wondering as she did so if the Duke realised that a new stair-carpet was needed and thinking it should be one of the things to suggest to him when he returned.

She reached the top of the stairs and was just turning towards her bedroom when she saw to her surprise that at the far end of the corridor there was a man.

He was just outside the Master Suite, and for one moment she thought it was the Duke who had returned without her being aware of it.

Then she saw that it was not he, and it was also not a servant.

Feeling curious, she walked towards the man, wondering who he could be and why the footmen had not told her there was somebody strange in the house.

The corridor was long, and in that part of the building even in the daytime there was very little light.

Yet, before she had gone very far, Alvina was aware who her visitor was.

There was no mistaking the exaggerated square shoulders of what she knew was called a "Tulip of Fashion," and the high, elaborate cravat which made its owner carry his head at an almost imperious angle.

She was halfway towards the intruder, who, looking at

the paintings to the right and the left of him, was not aware of her until they were within speaking distance.

Then Alvina ejaculated:

"Cousin Jason! Nobody told me you were here!"

"I saw you riding across the Park," Jason Harling replied, "and I saw no reason to disturb your ride."

"I was not aware that you were calling," Alvina answered, "otherwise I would have been at home to welcome you."

"There is no need for us to stand on ceremony with each other," Jason Harling replied, "and as a Harling I look on the Castle as home, as of course you do."

The way he spoke made Alvina aware that he was being subtly offensive, although nothing he said in words was actually rude.

"Now that I am back," Alvina said, making an effort to speak pleasantly, "I hope I can offer you a cup of tea, or perhaps some other refreshment?"

"How kind of you!" Jason replied.

She was sure he was being sarcastic, but she turned to walk back towards the staircase.

As she did so, she wondered if she should ask Jason what he was doing wandering about the house and if he had been in the Master Suite.

She instinctively knew that he had, but she did not know quite how to put her suspicions into words.

They walked down the staircase in silence, and when they reached the Hall she said:

"Which would you prefer, Cousin Jason? Tea? Or perhaps a glass of wine . . . ?"

Before she could finish speaking, she saw that Walton was there, and Jason, without waiting for her to give the order, said to him:

"Bring a bottle of champagne to the Library!"

He spoke sharply and authoritatively, and as Alvina looked at him in surprise, so did Walton.

Then the Butler answered quietly:

"Very good, Mr. Jason, and would you require anything to eat?"

"No, just champagne," Jason replied, and walked towards the Library door.

Because she was determined not to show how astonished she was at his behaviour, Alvina said:

"The Drawing-Room is open, if you prefer."

"I am quite happy in here," Jason said, as a footman opened the Library door for them. "I suppose you are aware that every Museum in Europe would pay a fortune for the Shakespeare Folio, and the first edition *we* own of the *Canterbury Tales?*"

He accentuated the word "we" in a manner that was impossible for Alvina to ignore, and she said quietly:

"I think you are well aware, Cousin Jason, that the contents of the Castle belong to the reigning Duke only for his lifetime."

"Of course I am aware of that," Jason replied, "but it depends upon how long he reigns."

As he spoke, Alvina had an impression of evil that almost made her wince away from Jason Harling.

It was so vivid that for a moment she thought she was imagining it just because she disliked him.

Then, as she saw the expression in his eyes, she felt she must recoil as if he were a reptile waiting to strike at her.

With what was an obvious effort to control what he was feeling, Jason flung himself down in one of the armchairs in front of the fireplace.

"Well, Cousin Alvina," he said, in a different tone of voice, "you have certainly fallen on your feet, and let me congratulate you on your riding-habit. It is certainly an improvement on what you were wearing when I last came here!"

Because Alvina was aware that he was being deliberately unpleasant, she merely inclined her head, and Jason went on:

"Rooms open, horses in the stable, footmen in the Hall! The new Duke is certainly flinging his money about in a profligate fashion."

There was a pause before he continued:

"Actually, I have come here to say good-bye to you, and of course to the Castle, the family seat of the Harlings, of which I am one."

"Good-bye?" Alvina questioned.

"Has the reigning Duke, my inestimable cousin, the gallant General of a hundred campaigns, not told you of what he has planned for me?"

He was speaking now in a jeering, mocking voice that seemed to jar the very air round them, and after a moment Alvina faltered:

"Cousin Ivar has . . . not yet returned from . . . London."

"Of course not!" Jason said. "He is enjoying himself as the new 'Lion' of the Season, the pet of the Countess of Jersey, and undoubtedly a very ardent lover of the most acclaimed Beauty of the Season."

Alvina sat upright and, clasping her fingers together because she was agitated, said in a carefully controlled tone:

"I do not think, Cousin Jason, that you should speak to me like that!"

"Have I shocked you?" he asked. "Oh, well, you will have to get used to shocks where our dashing cousin is concerned. He has deserted Lady Isobel, who declares that he promised her marriage, and if her father does not call him out, then doubtless the husband of his present inamorata will not be so cowardly."

Alvina rose to her feet.

"I have no wish to listen to you saying such things, and I think, Cousin Jason, that when you have finished your glass of wine you should be on your way."

Jason laughed and it was not a pleasant sound.

"Turning me out, are you? And by what right?"

Fortunately, before Alvina could answer, the door opened and Walton came in, followed by a footman carrying a silver tray on which there was a bottle of champagne in an ice-cooler.

He set it down on the grog-table which stood in a corner of the Library, and after a glass of champagne had been poured for Jason and Alvina had refused one, the servants withdrew.

Because she thought it degrading to quarrel while the servants were in the room, Alvina said nothing until the door shut. Then she said:

"You said just now that you had come here to say good-bye. Does that mean you are leaving England?"

"So you do know!" Jason said accusingly.

"Know what?" Alvina asked in bewilderment.

"That our cousin, the new Duke, has exiled me from my own country, my friends, and my family."

He made a sound of sheer disgust.

"Oh, yes, Cousin Alvina, you may look surprised, but that is what he has done—turned me out, lock, stock, and barrel. Unless I do what he says, he will have me thrown into prison and leave me to rot there rather than raise a finger to save me from such a fate."

"I do not believe it!" Alvina exclaimed.

"It is true! You can ask him when you see him. In the meantime, make no mistake, I shall have my revenge, and it will not be a pleasant one!"

"I do not know what you are talking about."

Jason emptied his glass and walked across the room to fill it again up to the brim from the bottle in the ice-cooler.

"There have been Harlings all through history who have survived the vengeance of Kings and the enemies with whom they have come in contact," he said. "But make no mistake, Ivar Harling will not survive the curse I have put upon him—the Curse of the Harlings, which will ensure that he dies slowly and in agony."

Alvina gave a little cry.

"Do not . . . talk like . . . that! How can you say . . . such wicked things?"

"I say them because I know they will come true," Jason said slowly.

He lifted his glass and added in a voice that seemed to ring round the Library:

"To the future, and to the moment when we hear the Duke is dead! Long live the Duke!"

As he spoke he tipped the whole glass of champagne down his throat, and without another word went from the Library, leaving Alvina staring after him in sheer astonishment.

Because of the way he had spoken, and because he seemed to leave an atmosphere of evil behind him, she found it hard to move.

In fact, it was hard to do anything but feel that she had come in contact with something that was so wicked and beastly that she felt contaminated by it.

Then at last she told herself that Jason was mad, as mad as her father had been, and she would not be afraid or over-awed by him.

She walked towards the door, but even as she reached the Hall she heard the sound of wheels outside and knew that Jason was driving away.

By the time she could see him from the front door, he was crossing the bridge over the lake in a smart, lightly sprung Phaeton with huge wheels, drawn by a team of four horses which he was driving at a tremendous pace.

As he went up the drive, the dust billowed out behind him, and Alvina had the uncomfortable thought that he was driving a chariot of fire.

"How can he hate Cousin Ivar?" she asked herself.

Then she was afraid of the answer.

※※※

Two hours later, when Alvina had changed from her riding-habit and was arranging some flowers in the Drawing-Room, she heard voices in the Hall.

She had time only to put down the flowers she held in her arms and turn to the door as it opened and the Duke came in.

At the sight of him Alvina gave a little cry and without thinking ran towards him eagerly.

"You are back!" she exclaimed. "How wonderful! I have been . . . longing for your . . . return."

"If I have been a long time you must forgive me," the Duke said in his deep voice, "but I had a great deal to do in London."

"I was sure of that," Alvina replied, "but there is so much for you to see here, and your horses have arrived."

"I thought they would please you," he said. "There are several more arriving tomorrow, and I hope some others next week."

Alvina clasped her hands together.

"We have been working desperately hard in repairing the stables," she said. "I know you will be pleased . . . and I want to show you the Ball-Room . . . and the carpenters and painters have . . . started work on the pensioners' cottages."

She spoke quickly and breathlessly, having been waiting for this moment to tell him of all the things she had been doing.

Then, as if she suddenly remembered that the Duke had travelled all the way from London, she said apologetically:

"But you must be thirsty, and I am sure Walton will be bringing you something to drink."

As she spoke, Walton came in with a footman carrying a tray just as he had done a few hours earlier.

Alvina realised with a little throb of fear as she thought of it, that she would have to tell the Duke that Jason had been to the Castle.

'I will tell him later,' she thought, wanting to postpone for as long as possible something that was unpleasant.

Only when the Duke was sipping his glass of champagne did she realise that he was looking at her searchingly and with what she thought was a twinkle in his eyes.

"I suppose first," she said a little shyly, "I should have thanked you for the . . . wonderful gowns you sent me. I can hardly believe they are . . . really mine! In fact, I do not feel myself, but somebody quite different!"

"You look very lovely in what you are wearing now," the Duke said.

He paid her the compliment in his usual calm, rather dry voice, so that it did not make Alvina feel shy, and she only asked:

"How can you have been so clever as to know exactly the sort of gowns I would want to wear?"

"I cannot take all the credit," the Duke confessed. "They were in fact chosen for you by one of the most important women in the Social World, who has most graciously promised to present you to Society and ensure that from the moment you arrive in London you will be a great success."

The Duke spoke with a note of satisfaction in his voice and as he did so did not realise that Alvina stiffened.

"Whom . . . are you talking . . . about?" she asked, and her voice seemed to tremble.

"I am referring to the Countess of Jersey," the Duke replied. "You may not have heard of her, but she is a leader of London Society, and I can think of nobody who would be a more advantageous Chaperone to introduce you to all the people you should know."

There was silence. Then Alvina said in a very small voice:

"I . . . I thought . . . the Countess of Jersey was . . . at one time a very . . . close friend of the Prince Regent."

The Duke raised his eye-brows.

He had somehow thought that Alvina, living so quietly in the country, would not have been aware of the scandal and gossip there had been about the Countess.

However, it had all ended a long time ago, and he knew that it certainly would not affect now the reputation of any girl to whom she extended her patronage.

At the same time, he was suddenly aware of how innocent and unsophisticated Alvina was.

It struck him that perhaps it would be a mistake to

plunge her into the very centre of a social vortex with its intrigues, its liaisons, and inevitably its promiscuous women like Isobel and the lovely creature with whom he had dined last night.

Because he had not before considered this aspect in regard to Alvina, he walked to the window to stand staring out into the garden.

He was wondering if he had made a mistake and questioning the arrangements he had made.

It occurred to him that if she was not shocked by what she found in the Social World, contact with it might spoil her.

He was so used to the women with whom he associated taking for granted the love-affairs which filled their lives, and believing that fidelity to their husbands was out-of-date, that he had not thought of Alvina as being completely different.

Now he realised he was dealing with a very young, unspoilt, unworldly girl, and he knew that the Countess of Jersey's involvement with the Prince had genuinely shocked her.

After a moment, when he knew Alvina was waiting for him to speak and was looking at him enquiringly, he said:

"I thought when I made the arrangement with the Countess that I was doing what was best for you, since she is undoubtedly the Leader of the Social World as we know it."

"I . . . I have been thinking over your suggestion that . . . I should go to London," Alvina said, "and I would not want you to think me . . . ungrateful . . . but if it is possible . . . I would much rather . . . stay here."

She spoke hesitatingly, and after a moment the Duke said:

"I think it would be best for you to extend your horizons."

"I understand what you are saying to me," Alvina replied, "and I know how . . . ignorant and how foolish you must . . . think me . . . but it would be different if . . . Mama were with me . . . or even if I had a father on whom I could rely for guidance and . . . to prevent me from making mistakes."

She made a little gesture with her hands which was somehow pathetic.

As she spoke, the Duke thought of the conversation that had taken place at the Countess of Jersey's dinner-party.

He remembered that although it had been sophisticated, witty, and undoubtedly amusing, there had been a *double entendre* in every other word, and he now thought that a great deal had been said which was very unsuitable for a young girl to listen to.

Almost as if he could see a picture unroll in front of him, he could see the expression in Lady Isobel's eyes when she looked at him, and that look duplicated in the eyes of a dozen other women with whom he had danced, talked, and dined.

It was something with which he had grown very familiar in Paris, and he had almost taken it for granted.

Women were all the same, and they wanted only one thing from him.

But now he was aware that Alvina was very different.

He had not missed the lilt in her voice when he came into the room and the expression of joy and happiness in her eyes because he was back.

He suddenly felt that she was part of the sunshine outside, the flowers in the garden, the freshness of the air, and the birds that flew above the trees.

She was youth, she was spring. She was as clear as the sky overhead and the water silver in the lake.

Feeling almost that he was being accused of trying to commit a crime, he said as if to defend himself:

"I thought I was arranging what was best for you!"

"You are so kind, so very, very kind," Alvina said, "and you know I will do anything you really want me to . . . but please, this is where I belong . . . and there is nothing in London which could be more wonderful than being here in this . . . lovely Castle."

There was a little tremor in her voice as she spoke, as if it was already being taken away from her, and the Duke said:

"Shall we talk about it later? I want to look at all the improvements you have been making, and of course to see the Ball-Room."

At his words she made a little sound of excitement, and quite unselfconsciously she put her hand into his as she said:

"Come and look at the Ball-Room. I know it is going to surprise you, and everybody has worked so very, very hard so that you would be pleased."

The Duke's fingers closed over hers, and as they did so he told himself that he had to think about what he should do with her all over again.

One thing was more important than anything else—she must not be spoilt.

⚜⚜⚜

Dinner was over, and Alvina was wearing one of her new gowns, in which she felt like the Princess in a fairy-story.

It was white gauze, and in the new fashion was elaborately trimmed with frills and flowers round the hem.

There were also flowers on the small puffed sleeves which revealed her shoulders, the whiteness of her skin, and her long swan-like neck.

The Duke had looked at her critically as she joined him in the Drawing-Room before dinner and knew she could hold her own in any London Ball-Room.

She would undoubtedly be acclaimed as a Beauty as soon as she appeared.

There was something about her that was very distinctive and, he thought, unusual.

After scrutinising her with a connoisseur's eye, he decided that she looked different from other women he had known because there was something untouched, perhaps spiritual, about her that had been missing in all of them.

He could not exactly describe it, except that he knew it was part of the same feeling he had had about the Castle when he was young.

If he had thought of himself, as he had, as a Knight, and the Castle itself had been peopled with Knights, then Alvina fitted in as one of their Ladies, filled with the same ideals of chivalry and honour.

That was what motivated the Knights, and if they were prepared to wage war against what was wrong and evil, so in their own way the women to whom they returned with the spoils of victory had the same standards from which they never faltered.

As they talked at dinner and the candles on the table illuminated Alvina's face, the Duke thought her beauty had a subtlety that grew on the mind and on the imagination.

It was very different from a loveliness that was entirely physical.

He had grown used to knowing that every woman he met since hostilities had ceased had only one object, which was to arouse him physically into admiring and desiring her.

He knew when he considered it that while Alvina looked upon him with admiration, listened to him appreciatively, and was obviously thrilled to be with him, her feelings for him were very different.

She had no idea how to flirt, no idea how to turn the conversation so as to make it personal to her, whatever subject they might be discussing.

She did not attempt to touch him with intimate little gestures that were meant to be provocative.

Her lips did not curve to entice him, nor was there an invitation in her eyes.

Instead, she had an aura of happiness about her because she was with him, and there was a lilt in her voice with a kind of radiance about it when she talked of all she had been doing in his name on the Estate.

She made what she had to relate seem absorbingly interesting, and the Duke was quite surprised to find how long they had been in the Dining-Room.

Only when they went into the Drawing-Room, where the candles were lit and the fragrance of the flowers scented the room, did Alvina say a little hesitatingly:

"There is . . . something . . . I feel I . . . must tell you."

"What is it?" the Duke asked.

"Cousin Jason was here today."

"Jason?"

The name came from the Duke's lips like a pistol-shot.

"Yes, and he was very angry . . . and bitter."

The Duke was silent for a moment. Then he said:

"He must have been on his way to Dover. I told him to leave the country."

"He was very . . . angry!"

"That I can understand. I paid his debts—and they were astronomical—only on condition that he left England, and he will receive the allowance I promised him as long as he stays away."

"I am sure it was very generous of you . . . but he was very upset."

"And he upset you?" the Duke questioned sharply.

"He . . . he . . . cursed you!"

The Duke laughed.

"That does not surprise me. My friend Gerald Chertson said that whatever I did for him, Jason would not be grateful."

There was silence. Then Alvina said:

"He hates you . . . and I am . . . afraid he may . . . hurt you."

The Duke smiled.

"You are not to worry about me. I assure you I can take care of myself."

He saw by the expression on her face that she was really worried, and added:

"I did not survive all those years of fighting against Napoleon's Armies to be exterminated by a rat like Jason!"

"Cornered rats can be . . . dangerous!" Alvina said, speaking as if the words were jerked from her lips.

"Jason is not cornered," the Duke replied. "One of the reasons I was delayed in London was that I was making sure that all his debts were paid in full, and that his allowance would be waiting for him every quarter at a Bank in France. It will, I promise you, be impossible for him to starve."

"I am still frightened for . . . you."

"I refuse to allow Jason to worry either you or me," the Duke replied, "so forget him and let us talk of much more pleasant things."

He saw that Alvina's eyes were still clouded, and said to her quietly:

"I am very grateful to you for worrying about me, but I want you instead to think of yourself."

Alvina raised her eyes to his, and he said:

"We are not going to talk about that tonight, but I will think over what you have said, and I want you to think about it too. We must try to come to some conclusion and agree as to what would be best for you."

"You . . . know the answer to that."

The Duke was about to argue. Then he said:

"Because I did not get to bed until the early hours of the morning, and as I suspect you are too tired after all you have done, I suggest we go to bed. Incidentally, I have not asked you how Miss Richardson is."

"She is not very well," Alvina replied. "She has been laid up these last two days, but she is being looked after by the new housemaids, and I hope she will be able to get up tomorrow."

"Then I shall look forward to seeing her," the Duke said. "Now I think we should both retire and arrange to meet in the Hall at half-past-seven so that we can have an hour's ride before breakfast."

"That would be wonderful!" Alvina exclaimed. "I was so hoping you would suggest it, and I have been looking forward to seeing you on *Black Knight*."

The Duke raised his eye-brows.

"Is that the name of my new stallion?"

Alvina looked embarrassed.

"I thought you would not mind my christening him," she said. "He had a horrid name which did not seem appropriate to the Castle."

The Duke laughed.

"Then *Black Knight* he shall be, and one day I will tell you exactly why it is so very appropriate."

"Tell me now."

"Tomorrow," he said. "I need my 'beauty sleep,' and of course you have to live up to your new gowns."

"I have not thanked you properly for them."

"Thank me when the next lot arrives."

He remembered as he spoke that he had asked the Countess of Jersey to choose Alvina's wardrobe for her.

He had ordered two more gowns, which should arrive tomorrow or the next day, but he had thought it would be a mistake for her to have any more before she reached London.

Now he was wondering if all he had planned would have to be changed, and thought that perhaps he had made a mistake in enlisting the help of the Countess of Jersey before he had been certain it was what Alvina wanted.

But he did not wish to discuss it with her at the moment. So he took her by the arm and they walked up the stairs side by side, after the Duke had given orders for the horses to be ready for them in the morning.

When they reached the landing and separated, the Duke to go to his room and Alvina to hers, he said.

"Sleep peacefully, and do not worry. And I promise I will not force you to do anything you really have no wish to do."

She looked up at him as he took her hand in his.

"You are so kind . . . so very . . . very kind, and I . . . want to . . . please you."

"You do please me," he answered, "and if you feel grateful to me, I am grateful to you for all you have done."

"But we have not finished yet," Alvina said quickly.

"We have not finished," the Duke agreed.

"Then . . . good-night, and . . . thank you," she said with a little throb in her voice.

As she spoke she bent her head and kissed his hand.

Then, almost before he realised it had happened, she turned and sped away from him down the passage, disappearing into the darkness as if she were one of the ghosts of the Castle.

The Duke stood still for a second or two after he could see her no more.

Then slowly, as if he was deep in his thoughts, he walked towards his own bedroom.

❦❦❦

Alvina, lying in the darkness, found it hard to sleep.

So much had happened during the day, and yet it was as if she had moved in a dream until the Duke had come home.

Then everything had flared into life and become a pulsating, exciting reality so that she felt as if she had suddenly come alive.

"He is back!" she told herself now. "Please, God, let him stay for a very long time."

She had wanted to ask him what he had been doing in London but had felt too shy.

When he said he had been late in getting to bed last night, she supposed he had been enjoying himself with some very beautiful woman who had enthralled and amused him as she was unable to do because she was so ignorant.

She wondered what they had talked about together

277

and if the Duke had paid her compliments. Perhaps when they said "good-night" he had taken her in his arms and kissed her.

Alvina had no idea what a kiss would be like, and yet she thought that if the Duke kissed anybody it would be a very wonderful experience.

'Perhaps it would be like touching the sunlight,' she told herself, 'or feeling a star twinkling against one's breast.'

She had kissed the Duke's hand in gratitude because she had no words in which to tell him how grateful she was for everything he had done since his home-coming.

There was the happiness of the servants as they moved about the great house; the worry which had left the pensioners' eyes; and the satisfaction she had found with the farmers she had visited, once they realised they could repair their buildings and start buying and breeding new stock.

"How can one man, almost as if he were God, change everything overnight?" Alvina asked.

She thought that the Duke exuded a special light which lit up everything and everybody it touched.

"He is wonderful . . . wonderful!" she whispered.

Then, insidiously, as if it were a snake creeping into her thoughts and into the room, she heard Jason's voice cursing him.

She felt herself shiver because of the hatred with which he had spoken and the evil in his eyes which had seemed to vibrate from him.

It had left a darkness on the atmosphere that made her feel she would be afraid to go into the Library again.

"He will hurt the Duke if he can," she told herself, and she knew he wanted him to be dead so that he could be the sixth Duke.

The mere idea of it made her want to cry out in horror.

She was quite certain that there would be no improvements on the Estates if Jason was the Duke, and that in London he would merely dissipate away the money he inherited, or perhaps he would fill the Castle with his dubious friends.

"That must never happen!" she thought, and instinctively she began to pray.

"Take care of the Duke! Please, God, take care of him. Do not let Cousin Jason hurt him, as I know he wishes to."

As she prayed, a sudden idea came into her mind that made her stiffen and lie very still.

When she had found Jason in the house, he was coming from the direction of the Master Suite, and she had wondered why the footmen in the Hall had not told her when she returned from riding that he had called.

It suddenly struck her that they had not done so because they had not known he was in the Castle.

Because he had been there so often when he was a child and later as a young man, he knew the Castle as well as Richard had.

He would be aware that there were dozens of ways leading into it, apart from through the front door.

Now, almost as if somebody were guiding her back into the past, she remembered how Richard and Cousin Ivar had often climbed up the old Tower in order to show off to each other their skill and nerve.

Because the Tower had been built in mediaeval times, with the stones rough and uncovered with plaster, every one unevenly put in place, it provided easy footholds for anybody experienced at climbing.

She could see, although she must have been very small at the time, her brother and another boy with him holding on to the protruding grey stones and racing each other to the top.

She could hear an echo coming back through the years as Richard cried out:

"I have won!"

Even as she heard his voice echoing back at her, he added:

"You have lost, Jason, and you owe me a bag of sweets!"

'That is how Jason must have got in,' she thought, 'but why? That is the point.'

Even as she asked the question, she knew the answer and in a sudden terror sat up in bed.

Chapter Seven

$\mathcal{M}$OVING BY INSTINCT because it was dark and there was no time to light a candle, Alvina tore from her bedroom and along the corridor towards the Master Suite on the other side of the Castle.

It was quite a long way, and yet she was driven by an urgency that made her run more quickly than she had ever run before in her life.

Only as she finally reached the outside door did she come to a halt and draw in her breath.

Then she turned the handle and went into the small and elegant Hall off which the Duke's rooms opened.

There was one light flickering low in a sconce on the wall, which guided her to the bedroom door, which she opened without knocking.

As she entered she saw that the Duke had drawn back the curtains and the moonlight was diffusing the room with a magic iridescence which for the moment seemed almost blinding.

Then as she looked towards the bed, the curtains hanging from the heavy canopy made it appear as if there were no-one in it.

The idea that the Duke was already dead made Alvina feel a pain pierce her heart as if it were a dagger.

Strangely, even in that moment of agony, she knew that she loved the Duke.

Then there was a movement from the bed and he exclaimed incredulously:

"Alvina! What is it? What do you want?"

He had gone to bed thinking of her and worrying as to whether he was doing the right thing as far as she was concerned.

Because he was tired, sleep had come to him unexpectedly quickly, and now as he awoke at the opening of the door with the alertness of a man who was used to danger, he was not certain whether he was dreaming it was Alvina or whether she was real.

The moonlight did not reach to where she was standing, and yet he could see somebody white, ethereal, and insubstantial.

The thought passed through his mind that it was a ghost or an apparition such as he had always heard existed in the Castle.

Then he knew it was Alvina and called out her name.

She moved towards the bed.

"It is . . . Jason . . . Cousin Ivar," she said in a breathless tone so that he could barely hear what she said.

The Duke sat up.

"Jason?" he repeated. "What are you talking about?"

"I know how he intends to . . . kill you!"

The Duke stared at Alvina as if he thought he could not be hearing aright what she was saying and must be imagining it.

Now that she was nearer to him, he could see her face quite clearly in the light from the window; her eyes were dark and very large, and he was aware that she was trembling.

"I . . . I did not . . . tell you," she said, "as I . . . should have done . . . but I found him coming from

here along the corridor, and he did not enter the Castle
by the front door."

"I do not understand."

"You must remember," Alvina went on, "how you
and Richard used to climb up the Tower, and both
Mama and Papa said that if you did so you were not to
climb down again because that was too dangerous, but
should come into the house through the trap-door
which leads to the staircase inside the tower itself."

Now the Duke understood, and he said:

"Are you suggesting that Jason might enter the Castle
in such a strange way to kill me while I am asleep?"

"I am positive that is what he intends to do!" Alvina
answered. "Please, Cousin Ivar, believe me, I know that
is what he has planned . . . and I can feel the evil of
him coming . . . nearer and nearer!"

She wanted to tell the Duke how Jason, after he had
cursed him, had drunk a toast saying: "The Duke is
dead! Long live the Duke!" but she thought it would
only delay things further.

Instead, she said frantically:

"Get up! Please, get up, and be ready for him! I was
only . . . desperately afraid that I was too late to . . .
warn you!"

The terror in her voice prevented the Duke from arguing, and he merely said:

"Wait for me outside. I will not be a minute."

Obediently Alvina turned towards the door and went
out into the small Hall.

Owing to the draught that she had made when she
had opened the door—or perhaps the candle had not
been replenished as it should have been—the candle
was now extinguished and it was quite dark.

Alvina therefore left the door of the Duke's bedroom
ajar, and she could hear him moving about as he
dressed himself.

Only as she thought of it was she aware that what she
was wearing was very scanty.

She had felt like a Fairy Princess when she went down

to dinner in the new gown which the Duke had given her.

So she had, when she went to bed, felt it impossible to put on one of the threadbare and darned nightgowns she had worn for the last few years when her father would not give her any money.

Almost as if it were an auspicious occasion, she had opened the drawer to take out the last nightgown she possessed of those which had belonged to her mother.

It was certainly lovely in contrast to her own, and her mother had worn it seldom because, as she had told Alvina, it was very precious, as her husband had bought it for her on their honeymoon.

Made of soft, almost transparent material, it had frills of shadow lace round the hem, the neck, and the sleeves.

Because her dinner with the Duke had been so enchanting, Alvina had thought that if she looked as attractive in bed as she had at the dining-table, the magic which had encompassed her ever since he had returned would still be with her.

Now, because her nightgown was so transparent, she felt that he might be shocked.

All she had to cover it was a light woollen shawl she had snatched up when she had sprung out of bed.

She had long ago grown out of the dressing-gown she had had when she was a girl, and her father would give her no money with which to buy another.

So the shawl had taken its place, and now a little nervously she made it as long at the back as she could and crossed it over her breasts.

She hoped that the Duke would not notice what she was wearing, but at the same time she felt it was wrong to think of herself when his life was in danger.

She told herself reassuringly that once he had gone up the twisting stone staircase inside the Tower and bolted the trap-door at the top of it, however evil Jason's intentions might be, he would not be able to enter the Castle.

Because Richard and his cousins had insisted upon climbing the Tower, her mother had made the Estate carpenter fix an iron trap into the Tower with bolts on both sides of it.

"I insist on your promising me that when you climb up," she had said firmly, "you will come down through the Tower and back through the house. I know climbing down is far more dangerous than climbing up."

Looking back, Alvina could remember Richard grumbling because he had promised his mother that that was what he would do, and he was too honourable to break his word.

She knew that Jason would pull back the bolts on the trap-door at the top of the Tower, then climb down the twisting stone steps which soldiers had used when the Castle had been built in the Twelfth Century.

She heard the Duke close a drawer and had a sudden fear, as he was taking so long, that long before he could close the trap-door from the inside, Jason would have entered the Castle.

"Hurry!" she cried urgently. "Hurry!"

"I have only been a few minutes," the Duke replied, and opened the door behind her.

He was silhouetted against the moonlight, and she saw that he was wearing a pair of long black pantaloons and a fine linen shirt with a silk scarf round his neck.

She knew, although she could not see his face clearly, that he smiled at her as he said:

"I think, Alvina, this is part of your very fertile imagination, but to make you happy I will close the trap-door at the top of the Tower and bolt it. Then you will be able to sleep peacefully again."

"Thank you," Alvina said, "but . . . please, let us . . . hurry!"

She felt he would not understand if she told him that she could feel the evil that Jason exuded coming nearer and nearer.

The Duke opened the other door and they stepped into the corridor.

There was enough light from just one or two candles that had been left burning for them to see their way to where beyond the Master Suite there was a door that led into the Tower, which was at the extreme end of the building.

As they reached it, Alvina thought that if they found the door was locked, then the Duke would laugh at her for being unnecessarily alarmed.

But it was open, and she was aware that he thought it strange.

Then they were both inside the Tower and standing on the stone steps which led both upwards and downwards, spiralling round a stone pole which had been built in the very centre of the Tower.

There was just enough light from the arrow-slits for them to pick their way without stumbling.

The Duke went first, moving swiftly and almost silently because he was wearing, Alvina realised, bedroom slippers.

It was only as she felt the cold stone under her feet that she realised she was bare-footed.

But nothing mattered except that they should shut Jason out, and as they climbed higher and higher, she did not feel either the cold or the roughness of the stones which bruised the softness of her skin.

They reached the top, and, finding the trap-door shut, the Duke turned his head to say:

"Your fears, Alvina, were unnecessary."

As he spoke he reached up his hand and found that the inside bolts were pulled back and it was not locked as it should have been.

Then, as he pushed, the trap-door swung open and the moonlight flooded in.

"It was not bolted!" Alvina said almost beneath her breath.

Then, to her consternation, instead of bolting it on the inside as she wanted him to do, the Duke stepped out onto the roof, and turning put his hand out to pull her out too.

They now stood on the sloping leads.

These had been added very much later to prevent the water from accumulating on the top of the Tower and percolating down the sides of the new part of the house.

It was easy to stand without slipping because her feet were bare, and the Duke, having drawn her beside him, said:

"It is years since I have been up here, and I had forgotten how high it is, but of course in the daytime there is the finest view over the countryside one could possibly imagine."

As he spoke he moved away from her towards the side of the Tower to look out over the valley which lay to the right of the Castle, and which, bathed in moonlight, was very beautiful.

Even as he did so, Alvina heard a sound on the other side of the Tower and saw a man's head appear.

She made an inarticulate little sound of fear.

But before the Duke could turn round, Jason had swung himself over the parapet and was standing on the Tower, balancing himself, as the Duke had been forced to do, on the sliping leads.

"Quite a reception-party, I see!" he said sarcastically. "I suppose our interfering, tiresome little Cousin Alvina thought I might be visiting you tonight?"

"What are you doing here, Jason?" the Duke asked sharply. "You should be in Dover by now."

"I will reach Dover tomorrow morning," Jason replied, "where I shall be told that, most regrettably, my dear cousin the Duke of Harlington has met with an unfortunate accident during the night."

As he spoke he drew from his waist a long, thin, evil-looking knife of the sort Alvina imagined a brigand or a pirate might use, but which she had not seen before except in pictures.

She gave a cry of horror and realised, even as she did so, that when Jason had said that the Duke would die painfully, this was what he was planning.

Too late, she thought wildly that she should have made the Duke bring some weapon with him.

But she had never envisaged for one moment that he would come out onto the roof, but rather that he would bolt the trap-door to make it impossible for Jason to enter the Castle.

The Duke, however, was looking at his cousin with contempt.

"Do you really imagine that you can murder me and not be hanged for your crime?"

"It is unfortunate that you were foolish enough to come up to the Tower when you could have died far more comfortably in your bed," Jason sneered, "and to bring that tiresome chit Alvina with you was an even greater mistake."

"Certainly from your point of view," the Duke said. "Criminals always dislike a witness to their crime."

He was talking normally, but at the same time he was trying to work out how he could reach Jason and knock him out without being badly wounded by the long blade of the knife which was now pointing towards him.

The Duke never under-estimated an enemy, and he knew he had been stupid and foolhardy to have come up on the Tower empty-handed while Jason was sure to be well armed.

The Duke knew it was the sort of knife that could pierce deeply into a man's body, and if it entered his heart there would be no chance of anybody being able to save his life.

"Alvina will of course have an unfortunate fall from the top of the Tower," Jason replied in answer to the Duke's last remark, "while you will have impaled yourself, quite by accident, of course, on the knife, which will have only your finger-prints on it."

"Very carefully planned!" the Duke exclaimed. "At the same time, Jason, things seldom work out exactly as one wishes them to do, and I warn you that I shall fight ferociously both to live and to ensure that you do not take my place as the next Duke."

Jason's laugh sounded eerie and not human.

Now he moved a little farther up the sloping roof so as to be higher than the Duke, and he was pointing the knife at him almost as if it were a sword.

Alvina knew that in such a position it was almost impossible for the Duke to approach him without being wounded or perhaps killed in the attempt.

It was easy to see that Jason, without his fancy coat and wearing only a shirt, was far stronger and more athletic than he appeared when dolled up as a Dandy.

Alvina could see the muscles in his arms and knew, as she had told the Duke, that like a cornered rat he would fight dangerously, unsportingly, unfairly, because from his point of view there was so much at stake.

She had become so frightened while the two men were talking that she felt as if her legs would no longer support her.

Now she sank down on the leads, half-kneeling, half-sitting, feeling her heart beat tumultuously in her breast from sheer terror.

As she watched the two men eying each other, Jason waiting to strike to kill, she felt desperately that only God could save the Duke.

"Save him! Save him!" she prayed frantically. "Oh, God, let him live!"

She felt as if every instinct, every nerve in her body, was tense with the agonising plea of her prayer.

Then, because she felt almost as if she would faint at the horror of what was happening, she put out her hand to steady herself, and felt something hard lying on the leads beside her.

She thought it was a stone.

Then as her fingers closed over it, she realised it was a hand that must have become detached from one of the statues which decorated the roof of the centre block to which the Tower was attached.

Without thinking, she held on to it tightly, and as she did so, an idea came to her.

It was almost as if Richard were beside her, saying as he had in the old days:

"Come on, 'Vina, try to bowl like a man rather than throw like a woman!"

So she had learnt to do what he told her, and when there was nobody better to play with him, she had bowled to him so that he could practise his batting for the Cricket XI at Eton.

The two men were still watching each other closely, and because she loved him Alvina knew that the Duke was thinking his only chance was to spring at Jason and topple him over before he had a chance to drive the knife into his body.

It was a slender chance, a very slender one, because Jason was on a higher level than he was, and his hatred had given him in some ways a superior strength.

The Duke made one last plea.

"Put down that deadly weapon, Jason," he said, "and let us talk this over sensibly. I will even arrange that you shall have more money than I have already promised when you reach France."

"I do not want your money," Jason snarled, "I want your title, and that is what I intend to have! Then I shall be head of the family—I, Jason Harling, whom you have all despised—and you will be dead, damn you!"

As he spoke he made a stabbing gesture with the knife, and Alvina had a sudden fear that he might throw it at the Duke.

Raising her arm, she threw the stone hand with all her strength in exactly the way Richard had taught her, aiming at Jason's head.

It flew through the air, catching him on the side of his cheek below the eye with a violence that threw him off balance.

He staggered, but he was standing precariously on the sloping roof, and his feet slipped.

He tried to save himself, dropping the knife as he flung out his hands towards the higher level of the castellated parapet, but he missed and staggered again.

Then, so swiftly that it was hard to believe it was happening, he tripped over the lower part of the wall, and there was just one last glimpse of his feet silhouetted against the sky before he disappeared completely.

As he did so, Alvina gave a muffled cry and, rising, flung herself against the Duke to hide her face on his shoulder.

She was trembling so violently that he put his arms round her, for the shock and terror of what had happened had made her unable to stand alone.

Then, as he heard her gasping for breath as if she had been near drowning, he said very quietly:

"It is all right, my darling, you saved my life, and he will not trouble either of us any more!"

As Alvina felt she could not have heard him aright, she raised her face to look up at him in bewilderment.

Then as he looked down at her in the moonlight, he pulled her closer still and his lips came down on hers.

Only as he kissed her did Alvina know that this was what she had been longing for, wanting, and dreaming about, but she had never thought it would happen.

For a moment the closeness of him, the comfort of his arms, and the fact that he was alive were all a part of his lips.

Then as his kiss became more insistent, more possessive, she felt her fear vanish, and instead there was a wonder like a shaft of golden sunshine moving up from her breast into her throat.

It was so wonderful, so perfect, so much a part of her dreams and the moonlight, that she felt it was she who must have died and reached a Heaven in which there was no fear but only the Duke and the wonder of him.

When he kissed her, the Duke knew to his astonishment that he had found, when he had least expected it, what he had been searching for all his life.

As he felt the softness of Alvina's lips beneath his, he knew that she was not only part of the Castle and the ideals he had had of it when he was young, but the love he had thought was unobtainable because it only existed in fairy-stories and his dreams.

The feelings she was arousing in him were fine and spiritual, and different in every way from what he had felt for any other woman.

They were also part of the honour and chivalry that had always lain at the back of his mind, being the ideal for which all men should strive.

He knew as he held Alvina closer and still closer to him that this was what he had wanted to find in the woman he made his wife but had thought it impossible.

Only when he was aware that she was quivering in his arms, but very differently from when she had turned to him in fear and horror, did he raise his head to say:

"My precious—I love you!"

"You . . . love me?" she whispered. "And I . . . love you. I knew tonight when I thought you might . . . die that if you did . . . I must die too."

Because what she felt had been so intense, so terrifying, for a moment the fear was back in her eyes and in her voice.

Then, as if it was unimportant, she asked:

"Did you . . . really say that you . . . loved me?"

"I love you," the Duke confirmed, "and, my darling, what could be more appropriate than you should have saved my life, so that now I can dedicate it to you, and to everything you wish me to do for all time."

Alvina gave a little cry, and lifting her face to his she said:

"You are so . . . wonderful! I knew God could not let you die . . . and when I prayed . . . He told me what to do!"

As if her words made the Duke remember what they had passed through and that they were still standing on top of the Tower, with Jason dead on the ground below, he said:

"Let us get away from here. It will be easier to talk inside."

Alvina did not move. Instead she said:

291

"I shall . . . always remember that it was here . . . with your head against the stars . . . that you . . . first kissed me."

Because the way she spoke sounded as if she was enchanted, the Duke kissed her again, his lips holding her captive, his arms making it hard for her to breathe.

Yet she felt as if they were both enveloped by something sacred, something very spiritual and part of God.

Then, as if he forced himself to be sensible, the Duke said:

"Go down the stairs, my darling. I wish to be rid of that unpleasant weapon before I join you."

As she drew away from him, Alvina realised that when she had run to him after Jason's fall, she had left her shawl behind.

Now she put her hands up to her breasts, blushed, and said:

"I am sorry . . . I forgot I was only . . . wearing a nightgown."

The Duke smiled.

"You look very lovely, my darling, if a little unconventional."

Then, as if she excited him, he pulled her back into his arms and kissed her again.

His kiss was different from what it had been before, more demanding, more passionate, but at the same time he kept control of his desire, fearing to frighten her.

As he felt her surrender herself to his insistence, he knew that while the softness and warmth of her excited him, so that his body throbbed for her, it was still something very different from anything he had felt before.

Perhaps reverence was the right word, or simply love, the real love he never expected to find.

He raised his head to look down at Alvina's radiant face and shining eyes.

"I love you," he said as if it was a vow.

"I love you until there is nothing . . . else . . . in the whole world but you," she whispered.

Then as the Duke let her go, she blushed again and

bent to pick up her shawl, before she moved carefully towards the trap-door.

As she did so, the Duke climbed over the sloping roof to where on the other side of it Jason had dropped the long, sharp knife with which he had intended to kill him.

He picked it up, and then, feeling as if it was an omen of the future, he flung the knife, gleaming evilly in the moonlight, over the side of the Tower.

He knew it would fall into a clump of thick shrubs, where it would doubtless be a very long time before it was discovered.

As he did so, he felt that he threw from himself and Alvina everything that was wicked and dangerous, and that now he could protect and keep her, and all those who depended on him, safe for as long as he should live.

Then as he turned towards the trap-door, he took one quick glance over the side of the Tower.

Vaguely in the shadow of the Tower he could see, spread-eagled on the ground far below, the prostrate form of Jason Harling.

The Duke knew there was no chance that after falling from such a great height he could still be alive, and in the morning when he was found he would think up an explanation.

He could say that Jason had wished to climb the Tower for the last time before he left England, and no-body need ever know there was any other reason for such an exploit.

Turning away, the Duke followed Alvina, who was moving down the twisting staircase towards the door which led to the end of the corridor.

He pulled the trap-door to behind him, but he did not bolt it.

He felt as he left it open that it was symbolic of the fact that there was no longer anything to fear, and that not only his life but the contents of the Castle and the people who lived there were also safe.

They were under the protection of the Power that

had saved him from what he was well aware might have been an ignominious death.

He reached the door into the corridor and Alvina was waiting. He thought as she looked up at him than an inner light illuminated her face.

He put his arms round her as together they walked towards the Master Suite and in through the door they had left open.

The bedroom was still bathed in moonlight, and the Duke took Alvina to the open window.

They looked out over the lake, which was a pool of silver, and at the great trees in the Park, their leaves shining above their dark trunks.

With a little sigh Alvina spoke for the first time.

"Now we need no . . . longer be . . . afraid."

"That is true," the Duke said. "I will protect and look after you, and as my wife there will be for you no fears, only happiness."

Alvina gave a little cry that was almost child-like and said:

"Is it . . . true . . . really true that you . . . love me?"

"It will take me a long time to tell you how much," the Duke replied. "I know now that you are the ideal person I dream of, and who was always in a secret shrine in my heart."

He pulled her closer before he went on:

"I have travelled a long way to find you, my precious one, and now that I have done so, I will never let you go! You are mine!"

She turned her face up to his, and she thought he would kiss her, but instead he said:

"You will not go to London, you will not be acclaimed as a Society Beauty. You will stay here with me, and I warn you I shall be very jealous if you want anything else."

Alvina laughed, and it was like the song of the birds in Spring.

"Oh, darling, wonderful Ivar! You know I want

nothing more than to be here in the Castle with . . . you, but I still cannot believe that you . . . love me."

"I will make you sure of it."

"But I do not know how to . . . amuse you like the beautiful women you know in Paris and in London, and perhaps after a little while you will find me very boring."

The Duke smiled, and he knew as he thought back of the women in his life that like Isobel they had always ultimately bored him.

The reason why he always wished to escape from them was that they could not give him what Alvina could.

"Someday," he said very quietly, "I will make you understand that the love we have for each other is very different from anything I have ever found or known before."

"Is that true?"

"I promise you it is true," he said, "and just as when I was a boy, the Castle stood for me for everything that was fine and noble, so I have always thought in my heart that the woman who reigned here with me must be fine, noble, beautiful, and also must love me, but *nobody else*."

He accentuated the last words, thinking of how he had always loathed the idea of being married to somebody who would deceive him with other lovers.

He had also disliked the knowledge that he was not the first man in their lives, but was probably following a succession of other men who had possessed them.

Because Alvina was so different, he felt frightened that she might change, and pulling her almost roughly against him he added:

"You are mine, mine completely, and if you stop loving me I think I would strangle you, or throw you from the Tower as Jason intended to do!"

He was speaking in a way so unlike his usual iron control that it flashed through his mind that he had frightened her.

Instead, she gave a little laugh and pressed herself closer to him.

"How can you imagine I could ever look at anybody else besides you?" she asked. "I have not known many men, but I know that nobody could be kinder, or more like the Knights who used to live here in the Castle."

Because she was thinking as he had, the Duke looked at her in surprise as she went on:

"I sometimes think those Knights are still here with us, and when I have been lonely and afraid because Papa was very angry with me, they seemed to be guarding me and telling me that one day things would be different."

She gave a deep sigh that seemed to come from the very depths of her being as she added:

"Then you came, and you were a Knight in Shining Armour, to kill the Dragon that was destroying everything."

"I think you did that," the Duke said quietly, "and it is something, my precious, that you must never tell anybody, or even think about again."

"I do not think it was . . . wrong of me to . . . kill Cousin Jason," Alvina said, "because I knew that if he killed you, so many people would suffer . . . perhaps in an even worse way than they did with Papa."

"We will never talk about it again," the Duke said firmly. "Instead, I want only to think of you and to kiss you."

His lips came down on hers, and he kissed her until she felt that the moonlight was not only round them but on their lips, in their hearts, and in their very souls.

She knew that the Duke was right when he had said that together they would make the Castle a place of nobility and honour for all those who looked to them for guidance.

Perhaps too it would shine like a beacon of light to help those in other parts of the country who were in desperate need of help.

Alvina felt that the generations of people who had lived in the Castle before them were supporting them and giving them strength in the great task which lay ahead.

Because she had saved the Duke's life, she no longer felt insignificant or unsure of herself as she had done in the past.

She knew he would always be her master, her guide, and her protector, but she knew too that she had something to give him, and that was love, real love, which he said he had not found in his life until now.

She reached up her arms towards him and did not notice that her shawl fell to the floor.

"I love you . . . I love you! Teach me to do . . . exactly as you want me to do, and I know, because God has blessed us . . . that I shall be able to make you . . . happy."

"I am happy, my lovely one!" the Duke answered. "Happier than I have ever been before and we will express our gratitude by making everybody round us happy too."

He kissed her forehead, her straight little nose, her chin, and then the softness of her neck.

He felt her quiver with an excitement she had never known before, and knew she excited him to madness.

"God, how I love you," he said.

His voice was deep and unsteady as he added:

"How soon will you marry me? I cannot wait to make you my wife!"

"I am ready now . . . at this moment . . . or tomorrow!" Alvina replied impulsively.

He laughed tenderly before he said:

"That is what I wanted you to say, and I will arrange it."

"Can we be married here . . . in the Chapel?"

He knew she looked at him a little anxiously in case he should want something different, and he replied:

"Of course! I can think of nothing more appropriate than that we should be married, not with a large number of friends and acquaintances to watch us, but with those who have lived and died in the Castle and are still here, watching over us."

Because it was just what she thought herself, Alvina made a murmur of joy.

Then she asked:

"How can you think . . . exactly as I do? How can you believe as I . . . believe? And how can you . . . want what I want?"

"The answer to that is quite simple," the Duke replied. "We are one person, my precious one, and when you are my wife you will find that our life together will be very full, very exciting, and indeed very satisfying, because together we are complete."

Alvina gave a cry of sheer happiness.

Then he was kissing her again, kissing her passionately, demandingly, possessively, and she could feel his heart beating frantically against hers.

She knew as the moonlight within them seemed to intensify until it filled the whole world that there was nothing else but their love.

They had passed through great dangers to find each other, and neither of them would ever be alone again.

SECRET HARBOR

Author's Note

The slaves' revolution in Grenada under Julius Fédor ended in April 1796. In the Parish of St. George's there was no fighting.

Martinque, which was first colonized by the French in 1635, was recaptured from the British in 1802.

I visited Martinque in 1976 and found it fascinating, with every good French characteristic including delicious food. I wrote a novel about it called *The Magic of Love*.

In 1981 I paid my first visit to Grenada. "The Isle of Spice" is as lovely as the guide books describe it, and although in 1980 it became a Communist state, the only signs of it were the large posters exhorting the population to support the revolution. This I learnt had been completely bloodless, and the charming, smiling Grenadians are delighted to welcome visitors.

The tropical forests, the golden beaches, and the plantations of nutmegs, cocoa beans, and bananas are all as I have described them in this novel.

The sun shines, the shrubs are vivid patches of brilliant color, and the palm trees wave in the breeze from a blue and emerald sea.

What more could we ask?

CHAPTER ONE

❧

1795

GRANIA WALKED QUICKLY up the stairs and stood at the top listening.

The house was dark, but it was not only the darkness that made her feel frightened.

She was frightened as she listened to the voices coming from the Dining-Room, and frightened by an atmosphere that she sensed was tense, if not evil.

In the last month, she had been looking forward with an almost childish excitement to being back in Grenada, feeling that she was coming home and that everything would be as it had been three years ago when she left.

Instead of which, once they had reached the green islands which had always seemed to her to resemble emeralds set in a sea of blue, everything began to go wrong.

She had been so sure when her father said he was taking her home that she would be happy again with the same happiness which had been hers in the years when she had lived in what had always seemed a magical island.

It had been inhabited not only by smiling people but also, she felt, by gods and goddesses who dwelt on the top of the mountains, and fairies and gnomes who moved so swiftly amongst the nutmeg and cocoa trees that she only had a fleeting glimpse of them.

"It will be so exciting to be back at Secret Harbour," Grania had said to her father when they had passed through the storms of the Atlantic.

The sea smooth and clear glittered in the sunshine and the sailors as they climbed the masts sang songs that Grania remembered were part of her childhood.

Her father did not answer and after a moment she looked at him questioningly.

"Is something worrying you, Papa?"

He had not been drinking as much during the last few days as he had at the beginning of the voyage, and despite what her mother had called his ""dissipated life", he still looked amazingly handsome.

"I want to talk to you sometime, Grania," he replied, "about your future."

"My future, Papa?"

Her father did not answer, and after a moment she said as a sudden fear struck her like a streak of lightning: "What are you . . . saying? My future is with . . . you. I am going to . . . look after you as Mama did . . . and I am sure we will be very happy . . . together."

"I have different plans for you."

Grania stared at him incredulously.

Then one of the officers of the ship had come up to speak to them and he moved away from Grania in a way which told her that he had no wish to continue the conversation.

What he meant and what he had intended to say worried her all through the day.

She had wanted to discuss it with him later in the evening, but they had dined with the Captain and after dinner her father was incapable of having a coherent conversation with anybody.

It was the same the next day and the next, and only when the ship was actually within sight of the high mountains that she knew so well did Grania manage to find her father alone at the ship's rail and say to him insistently:

"You must tell me, Papa, what you are planning before we reach home."

"We are not going straight home," the Earl of Kilkerry replied.

"Not going home?"

"No. I have arranged that we shall stay for a night or two with Roderick Maigrin."

"Why?"

The question was sharp, and it seemed almost to burst from Grania's lips.

"He wants to see you, Grania, in fact he is very anxious to do so."

"Why?" Grania asked again, and now the sound that came from her seemed to tremble on the air.

She felt as if her father braced himself before he answered. Then he spoke in a gruff tone which told her he was embarrassed.

"You are eighteen. It is time you were married."

For a moment it was impossible for Grania to reply; impossible even to draw in her breath.

Then she said in a voice which did not sound like her own:

"Are you . . . saying, Papa . . . that Mr. Maigrin . . . wishes to . . . marry me?"

Even as she asked the question she thought it was too incredible to even contemplate.

She remembered Roderick Maigrin. He was a neighbour of whom her mother had never approved, and whom she had always discouraged from visiting Secret Harbour.

A thick-set, hard-drinking, rough-speaking man who was suspected, Grania remembered, of being a cruel task-master on his plantation.

He was old, almost as old as her father, and to think of marrying him was so absurd that if she had not been frightened she would have laughed at the very idea.

"Maigrin is a good chap," her father was saying, "and a very rich one."

That was not Grania thought later, the whole answer.

Roderick Maigrin was rich, and her father as usual was in a state of penury when he had to rely even for the rum he drank on the generosity of his friends.

It was her father's propensity for drinking, gambling and neglecting his plantations which had made her mother run away three years earlier.

"What hope have you, darling, of getting any education in this place?" she had said to her daughter. "We see nobody but those dissolute friends of your father's who encourage him to drink and gamble away on the cards every penny of his income?"

"Papa is always sorry that he makes you angry, Mama," Grania had replied.

For a moment her mother's eyes had softened. Then she said:

"Yes, he is sorry, and I forgive him and I have gone on forgiving him. But now I have to think about you."

Grania had not understood, and her mother had continued:

"You are very lovely, my darling, and it is only right that you should have the chance that I had of meeting your social equals and going to the Balls and parties to which your position entitles you."

Again Grania had not understood for there were no parties in Grenada unless her father and mother went to stay with friends at St. George's or Charlotte Town.

But she was very happy at Secret Harbour playing with the children of the slaves, although those of her own age were already working.

Almost before she realised what was happening her mother had taken her away, leaving very early one morning while her father was still sleeping off the excesses of the night before.

In the beautiful harbour of St. George's overlooked by the Fort there was a large ship, and almost as soon as they were aboard, it moved out into the open sea and away from the island that had been her home ever since she had been six years old.

It was only when they reached London and her

mother got in touch with several old friends that Grania learned how adventurous her mother had been when she was only eighteen in marrying the handsome Earl of Kilkerry, and six years later going out with him to start a strange new life on an island in the Caribbean.

"Your mother was so beautiful," one of her mother's friends had said to Grania, "and we felt when she left us, as if London lost a shining jewel. Now she is back to shine as she did in the old days and we are very thrilled to see her again."

But things were not the same, Grania soon learned, because her mother's father was now dead, her other relations had grown old and no longer lived in London, and they had not enough money to make a mark in the gay social life which centred around the young Prince of Wales.

The Countess of Kilkerry, however, made her curtsy to the King and Queen and promised that as soon as Grania was old enough she should do the same.

"In the meantime, my dearest," she said, "you will have to work hard to catch up with all the education you have missed."

Grania did in fact work very hard because she wanted to please her mother, and she also wanted to learn.

There was a School she attended daily, and there were extra teachers who came to the small house her mother had rented in Mayfair.

There was little time for anything but her lessons, but she did realise that her mother had a number of friends whom she was continually visiting for luncheon and dinner and who took her to the Italian Opera House and Vauxhall Gardens.

It seemed to Grania that without the insistent worry over her father's drinking and gaming her mother looked very much younger, and certainly more beautiful.

Besides which the new gowns she had bought immediately on reaching London were very becoming.

The full muslin skirts, the satin sashes, the fichus

which framed her mother's shoulders were very different from the gowns they had made for themselves in Grenada.

There was little choice of material in St. George's and Grania had worn the same bright coarse cottons which were the pride and joy of the native woman.

In London she developed her taste not only for gowns but for furniture, pictures and people.

Then, when she was nearly eighteen and her mother was planning to present her to the King and Queen, the Countess became ill.

Perhaps it was the fogs and cold of winter that she felt more acutely than her friends because she had lived in a warm climate for so long, perhaps it was the treacherous fevers which were always prevalent in London.

Whatever it was, the Countess grew weaker and weaker until despairingly she said to Grania:

"I think you should write to your father and ask him to come to us at once. There must be somebody to look after you, if I die."

Grania gave a cry of horror.

"Do not think of dying, Mama! You will get better as soon as the winter is over. It is only the cold which makes you cough and feel so ill."

But her mother had insisted, and because she felt it was only right that her father should know how ill she was, Grania had written to him.

She was well aware that it would take some time for her letter to be answered, just as during the years they had been away they had heard from him only spasmodically.

Sometimes letters must have been lost at sea, but others arrived which were long and full of information about the house, the plantations, the prices he had got for the nutmeg crop or the cocoa beans, and whether it was a good season for bananas.

At other times, after months, there would be just a scrawl, written with a hand that was too unsteady to hold the pen.

When these letters came Grania knew by the way her mother's lips tightened and the expression on her face that she was thinking how right she had been to come away.

She knew that if they had been at home there would have been the same repeated scenes over her father's drinking, the same apologies, the same act of forgiveness after the reiteration of the same promises he would not keep.

Once Grania had said to her mother:

"As we are spending your money, Mama, here in England, how is Papa managing at home?"

For a moment she thought her mother would not answer. Then the Countess had replied:

"What little money I have is now being spent on you, Grania. Your father must learn to stand on his own feet. It will be the best thing that could happen if he learns to depend on himself rather than on me."

Grania had not said anything, but she had a feeling that her father would always find somebody on whom he could depend, and if it was not her mother, it would be one of his friends who drank and gambled with him.

However badly he behaved, however much he drank, however much her mother complained of his neglect of his property and of her, the Earl had an Irish charm and fascination that everybody who knew him found hard to resist.

When he was not drinking Grania knew that he was more fun to be with and a more exciting companion than anybody she had ever known.

It was his laughter that was infectious, and the way he could find a story and a joke in everything.

"Give your father two potatoes and a wooden box, and he will mesmerise you into believing it is a carriage and pair that will carry you to a King's Palace!" one of her father's friends had said to Grania when she was a little girl, and she had never forgotten.

It was true.

Her father found life an amusing adventure which he

could never take seriously, and it was difficult for anybody who was in his company to think otherwise.

But now Grania knew the three years they had been apart had changed him.

He could still laugh, could still make the tales he told have a magical quality about them that was irresistible, but at the same time, she had known all the way across the Atlantic that he was keeping something from her, and when they actually arrived at Grenada she learnt what it was.

She had taken it for granted after the tragedy of her mother's death that he would want her to be with him and try to create a happy home together.

Instead, incredibly, he wished to marry her off to a man whom she had disliked when she was a child and knew that her mother despised.

The ship in which they were travelling, and which was to dock in the harbour at St. George's, had in the obliging manner which was usual in the Caribbean sailed a little way off course to set them down where her father wished.

Roderick Maigrin's plantation was in the adjoining Parish to St. George's that had been named by the British "St. David".

It was the only Parish on the island without a town and was in the south of the island adjoining St. George's and very similar in respect of the beauty of its landscape and the people who lived there.

At Westerhall Point, which was a small peninsula, covered with flowering trees and shrubs, Roderick Maigrin had built himself a large house somewhat pretentious in aspect which to Grania had all the characteristics of its owner, so that instinctively she disliked it.

She could never remember visiting it as a child, but now as they were rowed ashore in Mr. Maigrin's boat which came out to the ship to collect them, she had the terrifying feeling that she was entering a prison.

It would be impossible for her to escape, and she

would no longer be herself but entirely subservient to the large, red-faced man waiting to greet them.

"Glad to see you back, Kilkerry!" Roderick Maigrin shouted in a loud, over-hearty voice, clapping the Earl on the back.

Then as he stretched out his hand towards Grania and she saw the expression in his eyes, it was only with a tremendous effort of will that she did not run frantically back towards the ship.

But it was already sailing westwards to round the point of the island before it turned north to reach St. George's harbour.

Roderick Maigrin led them inside the house to where a servant was already preparing rum punches in long glasses.

There was a gleam in the Earl's eye as he lifted his glass to his lips.

"I have been waiting for this moment ever since I left England," he said.

Roderick Maigrin laughed.

"That is what I thought you would say," he said. "So drink up! There is plenty more where that came from, and I want to drink the health of the lovely girl you have brought back with you."

He raised his glass as he spoke and Grania thought that his blood-shot eyes leered at her as if he was mentally undressing her.

She hated him so violently that she knew she could not stay in the same room without telling him so.

She made the excuse that she wished to retire to her bedroom, but when a servant told her what time dinner was served she was forced to wash and change and go downstairs, making herself behave as her mother would have expected, with dignity.

As she had anticipated, by this time her father had already had a great deal of drink, and so had their host.

Grania was aware that the rum punches were not only strong, but their action was accumulative.

By the end of the dinner neither man made any

311

pretence of eating; they were only drinking, toasting each other and her, and making it quite clear that she was to be married as soon as the ceremony could be arranged.

What was so insulting to Grania was that Roderick Maigrin had not even paid her the lip-service of asking her to be his wife but had taken it for granted.

She had already learned in London that a daughter was not expected to question the arrangements her parents made on her behalf when it came to marriage.

She wondered at first that her father could think that a coarse, elderly, hard-drinking man like Roderick Maigrin would be a suitable husband for her.

Then what they said to each other and the innuendos in Roderick Maigrin's remarks made Grania sure that he was paying her father for the privilege of becoming her husband, and her father was well satisfied with the deal.

As course succeeded course she sat at the dining-table not speaking but only listening with horror to the two men who were treating her as if she was a puppet with no feelings, no sensitivity, and certainly with no opinions of her own.

She was to be married whether she liked it or not, and she would become the property of a man she loathed, a property as complete as any of the slaves who only lived and breathed because he allowed them to.

She disliked everything he said and the way he said it.

"Any excitements while I have been away?" her father asked.

"That cursed pirate Will Wilken came in the night, took six of my best pigs and a dozen turkeys, and slit the throat of the boy who tried to stop him."

"It was brave of the lad not to run away," the Earl remarked.

"He was a blasted fool, if you ask me, to take on Wilken single-handed," Roderick Maigrin replied.

"Anything else?"

"There's another damned pirate, a Frenchman,

scudding about, called Beaufort. If I see him, I'll blow a piece of lead between his eyes."

Grania was only half listening, and not until the meal had ended and the servants put a number of bottles on the table before they filled up the glasses and left the room did she realise she could escape.

She was quite certain her father, at any rate, was past noticing whether she was there or not, and she thought that Roderick Maigrin drinking with him would find it difficult if he tried to follow her.

She therefore waited until she was sure they had for the moment forgotten her existence, then quickly, without speaking she slipped from the room, closing the door behind her.

Then as she went up the stairs to the only place in which she felt assured of any privacy she wondered what she could do.

Trembling she was frantically trying to think if there was anybody on the island to whom she could go for help.

Then she knew that even if they were prepared to assist her, her father could collect her without their being able to prevent it or even protest.

As she stood on the landing trying to consider what she should do, she heard Roderick Maigrin laugh, and it sounded like the last horror to impinge upon her consciousness, and make her realise how helpless she was.

She felt it was not only the laugh of a man who had drunk too much, but also of a man who was pleased and satisfied with his lot, a man who had got what he desired.

Then, almost as if somebody was explaining it to her in words, Grania knew the answer.

Roderick Maigrin wanted her not only for her looks, and that was obvious from the expression in his eyes, but also because she was her father's daughter and therefore socially even in the small community that existed on Grenada, of some importance.

It was the reason why, she thought, he had been

attracted to her father in the first place, not only because they were neighbours, but because he wanted to be a friend of the man who was received, consulted and respected by the Governor and by everybody else who mattered.

Before she had left the island Grania had begun to understand the social snobberies which existed wherever the British ruled.

But her mother had made it very clear that she disliked Roderick Maigrin not so much because of his breeding, but because of his behaviour.

"That man is coarse and vulgar," Grania remembered her saying to her father, "and I will not have him here in my house."

"He is a neighbour," the Earl had replied lightheartedly, "and we have not so many that we can be choosy."

"I intend to be what you call 'choosy' when it comes to friendship." the Countess had replied. "We have plenty of other friends when we have time to see them, none of whom wish to be associated with Roderick Maigrin."

Her father had argued, but her mother had been adamant.

"I do not like him, and I do not trust him," she said finally, "and what is more, whatever you may say, I believe the stories of the way he ill treats his slaves, so I will not have him here."

Her mother had her way to the extent that Roderick Maigrin did not come to Secret Harbour, but Grania knew that her father visited him and they met drinking in other parts of the island.

Now her mother was dead and her father had agreed that she should marry a man who was everything she hated and despised, and from whom she shrank in terror.

"What am I to do?"

The question was beating again and again in her head, and when she went into her bedroom and locked her door, she felt as if the very air coming from the open window repeated and repeated it.

She did not light the candles that were waiting for her on her dressing-table, but instead went to look out at a sky encrusted with thousands of stars.

The moonlight was shining on the palm trees as they moved in the wind which still blew faintly from the sea.

It had dropped with the coming of night, but there was always a fresh breeze blowing over the island to take the edge off the heavy, damp heat which at the height of the sun could be almost intolerable.

As she stood there, Grania felt that she could smell the stringent fragrance of nutmegs, the sharpness of cinnamon and the clinging scent of cloves.

Perhaps she was imagining them, but they were so much part of her memories of Grenada that she felt the spices of the island were calling to her and in their own way welcoming her home.

But home to what?

To Roderick Maigrin and the terror she felt she must die rather than endure!

How long she stood at the window she had no idea.

She only knew that for the moment the years in which she had been in England seemed to vanish as if they had never happened and instead she was part of the island as she had been for so many years of her life.

It was not only the magic of the tropical jungle, the giant tree ferns, the liana vines and the cocoa plantations, but it was also the story of her own life.

A world of Caribs, of buccaneers and pirates, of hurricanes and volcanic eruptions, of battles on land and sea between the French and the English.

It was all so familiar that it had become part of herself and indivisible from her, and the education she had received in London peeled away in the warmth of the air.

She was no longer Lady Grania O'Kerry, but instead one with the spirits of Grenada, one with the flowers, the spices, the palm trees and the softly lapping waves of the sea which she could hear far away in the distance.

"Help me! Help me!" Grania cried aloud.

She was calling to the island as if it could feel for her in her troubles and help her.

※※※

A long time later Grania slowly undressed and got into bed.

There had been no sound in the house while she was looking out into the night, and she thought that if her father had come unsteadily up to bed she would have heard his footsteps on the stairs.

But she did not worry about him as she had done so often since he had come back into her life.

Instead she could only think of herself, and even as her eyes closed in sleep she was praying with an intensity that involved her whole body and soul for help.

Grania awoke startled by a noise that she sensed rather than heard.

Then as she came back to consciousness and listened, she heard it again and for a moment thought that somebody was at her bedroom door, and was afraid of who it might be.

Then she realised the sound had come from outside, and again there was a low whistle, followed by the sound of her name.

Still only half-awake Grania got out of bed and went to the window which she had left open and uncurtained.

She looked out and there below her she saw Abe.

He was her father's servant. He had come with him to England and she had known him all her life.

It was Abe who had managed their house for her mother, found the servants they could afford and trained them besides keeping them in order.

It was Abe who had first taken her out in a boat when she came to the Island and she had helped him bring back the lobsters which they caught in their own bay, and searched for the oysters which her father preferred to any other sea-food.

It was Abe who had taken her riding on a small pony

when she was too small to walk round the plantation to watch the slaves working amongst the bananas, the nutmegs and the cocoa beans.

It was Abe who would go with her to St. George when she wanted to buy something in the shops, or merely to watch the big ships come in to unload their cargo and pick up passengers travelling to other islands.

"I do not know what we should do without Abe," her mother said almost every day of her childhood.

When they had left for London without him, Grania often felt her mother missed Abe as much as she did.

"We ought to have brought him with us," she said, but her mother had shaken her head.

"Abe belongs to Grenada and is part of the island," she said. "What is more, your father could not manage without him."

After she had sent for her father and he arrived in England too late to say goodbye to her mother before she died, Abe had come with him.

Grania had been so pleased to see Abe that she almost flung her arms around his neck and kissed him.

She had only stopped herself at the last moment because she realised how much it would embarrass Abe. But the sight of his smiling coffee-coloured face had made Grania feel home-sick for Grenada in a way she had not felt all the time she had been in London.

Leaning out of the window now Grania asked:

"What is it, Abe?"

"I mus' talk with you, Lady."

He now called her "Lady", though when she was a child he had said "Little Lady", and there was something in the way he spoke which told Grania it was important.

"I will come down," she said, then hesitated.

Abe knew what she was thinking.

"Quite safe, Lady," he said, "Master not hear."

Grania knew without further explanation why the Earl would not hear, and without saying any more she put on a dressing-gown which was lying unpacked on top of her trunk and a pair of soft slippers.

Then cautiously, making as little noise as possible, she unlocked her bedroom door.

Whatever Abe might say, she was afraid not of seeing her father but their host.

The candles on the stairs were still alight but guttering low as she came down, and reaching the hall she entered the room which she knew looked out onto the garden below her bedroom.

She went to the window which opened onto the verandah and as she lifted the catch Abe came up the wooden steps to join her.

"We leave quickly, Lady."

"Leave? What do you mean?"

"Danger—big danger!"

"What has happened? What are you trying to tell me?" Grania asked.

Before he answered, Abe looked over his shoulder almost as if he was afraid somebody might be listening. Then he said:

"Rebellion start in Grenville 'mong French slaves."

"A rebellion!" Grania exclaimed.

"Very bad. Kill many English!"

"How do you know this?" Grania asked.

"Some run 'way. Reach here afor' dark."

Abe looked over his shoulder again before he said:

"Slaves here think they join rebellion."

Grania did not question that he was telling the truth.

There were always rumours of trouble on the islands which were constantly changing hands, of rebellions amongst the communities which favoured the French, or favoured the English, which were not in power.

The only thing which was surprising was that it should happen on Grenada which had been English for twelve years after a comparatively short period when it had been in the hands of the French.

But when she had been sailing in the ship from England the officers had talked incessantly of the revolution in France and the execution two years ago of Louis XVI.

"It is obvious now that the French slaves on the islands are likely to become restless," the Captain had said, "and ready to start their own revolutions."

Now it had happened in Grenada and Grania was frightened.

"Where shall we go?" she asked.

"Home, mistress. Much safest place. Few people find Secret Harbour."

Grania knew that was true. Secret Harbour was rightly named.

The house which had been built many years before her father restored it was in an obscure part of the island, and likely to be a safe hiding-place from the French or anybody else.

"We must go at once!" she said. "Have you told Papa?"

Abe shook his head.

"No wake Master," he answered. "You come now, Lady, Master follow."

For a moment Grania hesitated at the idea of leaving her father. Then she thought she would also be leaving Roderick Maigrin, and that was certainly something she wished to do.

"All right, Abe," she said. "We must go if there is any danger, and I am sure Papa will follow us tomorrow."

"I three horses ready," Abe said. "One carry luggage."

Grania was just about to say her luggage was of no importance, then changed her mind.

After all, she had not been home for three years and she had nothing to wear except the clothes she had brought with her from London.

As if he sensed her hesitation Abe said:

"Leave to me, Lady, I fetch trunk."

Then as if he was suddenly frightened he added:

"Hurry! Go quick! No time lose!"

Grania gave a little gasp, then holding up her

dressing-gown with both hands she ran back through the room and up the stairs to her bedroom.

It took her only a few minutes to put on her riding skirt and pack the gown she had worn for dinner, with her night things on the top of her trunk which had not yet been unpacked.

Just one piece of her luggage had been brought upstairs and the rest had been left below.

She was just buttoning her muslin blouse when Abe knocked very softly on the door.

"I am ready, Abe," she whispered.

He came in, shut her trunk, strapped it and picked it up.

He set it on his shoulder and without speaking moved silently down the stairs.

Grania followed him, when as she reached the hall she knew she could not leave without telling her father where she was going.

She had already seen that there was a desk in the room in which Roderick Maigrin had received them before dinner. Carrying a candle she searched for a piece of writing-paper.

She found it and also a quill pen which she dipped into the ink-well, and wrote:

"I have gone home,
Grania."

Carrying the candle she went back into the hall.

For a moment she wondered if she should leave the note on a side-table where her father would see it.

Then she was afraid it might be removed before he should do so.

Nervously, conscious that her heart was beating violently she slowly turned the handle of the Dining-Room door.

It opened a crack and she peeped inside.

She could see the table and the light of the candles

revealed the two men slumped forward unconscious, their heads amongst the bottles and glasses.

For a moment Grania just looked at the man who was her father and the man he intended her to marry.

As if she could not bear to go any nearer she slipped the piece of paper on which she had written the message just inside the door before she closed it again.

Then she was running as quickly as she could, pursued by a terror she could not suppress, to where Abe was waiting for her outside.

Chapter Two

GRANIA RODE WITHOUT speaking followed by Abe leading a horse with two of her trunks roped across the saddle while another horse carried a third trunk and a wicker basket.

She was aware as Abe pointed the way that he had no wish to travel on the road—little more than a track—which lay to the North of Maigrin House and was not only the nearest way to Secret Harbour, but also to St. George's and the other Westward parts of the island.

She wondered at his desire for concealment and thought perhaps he was afraid they would meet a band of slaves rebelling against their owner, or wishing to join those who were already rioting in Grenville.

Abe had said "many English killed", and she knew that once the slaves started looting, killing and pillaging it would be hard to stop them.

She was afraid, but not so afraid as she was of Roderick Maigrin and the future her father had determined for her.

She had the feeling as she rode through the thick vegetation that she was escaping from him and he would never be able to catch up with her again.

She knew this idea had no foundation in fact, but at least she was moving away from him, which was a consolation in itself.

There was a path of a sort which kept parallel with the sea, twisting and turning to follow the numerous bays and rugged outline of the coast.

Grania was aware that by this route it would take very much longer to reach home. At the same time she was in no hurry.

The scene around her had a strange, ethereal magic which was a part of her heart.

The shafts of moonlight seemed almost like a revelation coming down to them from the Heavens making a pattern of silver on the path ahead and on the great leaves of the tropical ferns.

They passed cascades that were like molten silver, then had glimpses of the sea with the moon shimmering on the slight movement of the water and breaking crystal on the sands.

It was a world Grania knew and loved. For the moment she wanted to forget the past and the future, and think only that she was home, and that the spirits that inhabited the tropical forests were protecting and guiding her.

After they had travelled for nearly an hour the path entered an open space and Abe walked beside her.

"Who is looking after everything at home while you have been in England?" Grania asked.

There was a little pause before he replied:

"Joseph in charge."

Grania thought for a moment, then she remembered a tall young man who she thought was some relation of Abe's.

"Are you sure Joseph is capable of looking after the house and the plantations?" she asked.

Abe did not answer and she said insistently:

"Tell me what has been happening, Abe. You are keeping something from me."

"Master not live Secret Harbour for two year!" Abe said at length.

Grania was astonished.

"Not live at Secret Harbour?" she enquired. "Then where . . . ?"

She stopped. There was no need to answer that question.

She knew quite well where her father had been living, and why they had gone to Roderick Maigrin's house rather than home.

"Master lonely after mistress leave," Abe said as if he must make excuses for the master he served.

"I can understand that," Grania said almost beneath her breath, "but why did he have to stay with that man?"

"Mr. Maigrin come see master all time," Abe said. "Then Master say: 'I go where there's somebody to talk to,' and he leave."

"And you did not go with him?" Grania enquired.

"I look after plantations an' house, Lady," Abe replied, "'til last year Master send for me."

"Do you mean to tell me," Grania asked, "that there has been nobody looking after the place for over a year?"

"Go back when possible," Abe replied, "but Master need me."

Grania sighed.

She could understand how her father found Abe indispensable, even as her mother had done, but she could hardly believe that he would leave the house locked up and the plantations to run themselves while he was drinking with Roderick Maigrin.

However there was no point in saying so. She only thought it was what her mother might have expected would happen if they left her father alone with nobody congenial to keep him company.

"We should never have gone away," she told herself.

At the same time she knew that it was only because her mother had taken her to London that she had been educated in a way which would have been impossible if she had stayed on the island, and she would always be grateful for the experience.

She had learned so many things in London, and not only from books.

At the same time she had the uncomfortable feeling that her father had paid for that experience not in money, but first by loneliness, then by being obliged to seek the company of a man who was a thoroughly bad influence in his life.

But it was too late now for regrets, and as soon as her father joined her they must make up their minds what to do about the rebellion, if it was as serious as Abe seemed to think it was.

When the islands changed hands, which they had done regularly during recent years, there were always planters who lost their land and their money, even if they kept their lives.

But after the first elation and excitement the slaves invariably found that they had only changed one hard task-master for another.

"Perhaps it is nothing very serious," Grania tried to persuade herself.

To change the subject she said to Abe:

"We were lucky when we were coming here that we did not encounter any French ships, or indeed any pirates. I hear Will Wilken took Mr. Maigrin's pigs and turkeys and killed a man while he was doing so."

"Pirate bad man!" Abe said, "but he not fight big ships."

"That is true," Grania agreed, "but the sailors on our ships said that pirates like Wilken attack cargo boats, and that is destressing for those who need the food and those who lose money they would otherwise have obtained for their goods."

"Bad man! Cruel!" Abe murmured.

"Will Wilken is English, and I hear there is also a Frenchman, but I do not believe he was about before I left for England."

"No, not here then," Abe said.

He spoke as if he did not wish to say any more, and Grania turned her head to look at him before she said:

"I think the Frenchman is called Beaufort. Have you heard anything about him?"

Again there was a pause before Abe said:

"We take path left, Lady ride ahead."

Grania obeyed and wondered vaguely why he did not seem to wish to talk about the French pirate.

When she was a child pirates had always seemed to her to be exciting people, despite the fact that the slaves shivered when their names were mentioned, and those that were Catholics crossed themselves.

Her father used to joke about them, saying they usually were not as bad as they were painted.

"They only have small ships, so they dare not attack larger vessels," he said, "and are nothing more than sneak-thieves, taking a pig here, a turkey there, and seldom doing more harm than the gypsies or tinkers would do when I was a boy in Ireland."

They rode on and now at last the way became familiar and Grania recognised clumps of palm trees and the brilliance of the poinsettias which on the island grew to over forty feet.

Now the moonlight was fading the stars seeming to recede into the darkness of the sky.

Soon it would be dawn and already she could feel a breeze coming from the sea to sweep away the heaviness of the air enclosed by the tropical plants which grew sometimes like green cliffs on each side of the path.

Then at last the jungle was left behind and they had reached her father's plantations.

Even in the dimness of the fading moonlight she had

the idea they looked neglected. Then she told herself she was being unnecessarily critical.

Now she could smell the nutmegs, the cinnamons and the chives, while mixed with the scent of them all was the fragrance of thyme which she remembered was always sold in bunches with the chives.

As they moved on she thought she could recognise the strong fragrance of the Tonka bean, which her father grew because it was easier than some of the other crops.

"The island spices," she said to herself with a smile and was sure she could distinguish allspice or pimento which Abe had pointed out to her when she was very small, their smell combining the fragrance of cinnamon, nutmeg and cloves, all mixed together.

Now the dawn was breaking and as the sky became translucent Grania could see in the distance the roofs of her home.

"There it is, Abe!" she exclaimed with a sudden excitement in her voice.

"Yes, Lady. But you not disappointed if dusty. I get women soon clean everything."

"Yes, of course," Grania agreed.

At the same time she was sure now that her father had never intended to take her home.

He had meant them to stay with Roderick Maigrin and if there had not been a revolution she would doubtless have been married very quickly, whatever she might say, however much she might protest.

"I cannot marry him!" she said beneath her breath.

She thought if her father came home alone she could explain why it was impossible for her to tolerate such a man, and try to make him understand.

It would be easier, she thought, if she could talk to him without that horrible, red-faced Roderick Maigrin listening and plying her father with drinks.

She sent up a little prayer to her mother for help and felt that she would somehow save her, although how she could do so Grania had no idea.

As they drew nearer to the house, it was easy to see that the windows were covered by wooden shutters, and the shrubs had encroached nearer than they would have been allowed to do in the past.

It flashed through Grania's mind that it was like the Palace of the Sleeping Beauty.

Bougainvillaea covered the steps of the verandah and had wound its way up onto the roof of it, while the pale yellow blossoms of the caccia and a vine which was called "Cup of Gold" had crept prolifically over everything within sight.

It was beautiful but had something unreal about it, and for a moment Grania felt as if it was only a dream that might vanish and she would wake to find it was no longer there.

Then she forced herself to say in what she hoped was a matter-of-fact tone:

"Put the horses in the stable, Abe, and give me the key of the house, if you have it."

"Have key back door, Lady."

"Then I will go in at the back," Grania smiled, "and start opening the shutters. I expect everything will smell musty after being shut up for so long."

She thought too without saying so that there would be lizards running up the walls, and if there had been a crack anywhere in the roof birds would have nested in the corners of the rooms.

She only hoped they had not damaged the things her mother had prized—the furniture she had brought from England when she was first married.

There were other treasures which she had accumulated over the years, buying them sometimes from planters who were going home, or receiving them as presents from their friends in St. George's and other parts of the island.

The stables at the back of the house were almost covered with purple bougainvillaea so that Abe had to pull it aside to find the entrance to the stalls.

Grania dismounted, leaving Abe to unsaddle the

horse she had ridden and lift the trunks from the other two horses.

She suspected that in a short while the slaves would be awake and there would be somebody to assist him, but for the moment she was interested only in going into the house.

She went up the steps to the back door seeing that they badly needed repairing, and the door itself looked dilapidated with the paint peeling from the heat.

The key turned easily and she pushed open the door and walked inside.

As she had expected, the house smelt musty, but not as badly as it might have done.

She walked in through the back premises past the large kitchen which her mother had always insisted be kept spotlessly clean, then into the hall.

The house was not as dusty as she had expected, although it was hard to see in the dim light.

She opened the door into what had been the Drawing-Room.

To her surprise the sofas were not protected as they should have been by Holland covers, the curtains were drawn back from the windows and the shutters were not closed.

She thought it was careless of Abe not to have taken more trouble over this particular room.

But it certainly did not seem to have come to very much harm, although it was difficult to see every detail.

Grania instinctively tidied a cushion that was crooked on a chair, then she told herself that before she started opening up the house she had better change.

The day was already beginning to grow warmer, and her riding-skirt which was not of a very thin material would soon become uncomfortably heavy, while the muslin blouse she was wearing had sleeves.

She thought she would have grown out of all the clothes she had left behind but there would doubtless be something of her mother's she could wear.

When they had left for London the Countess had not

packed her light cottons gowns knowing she would have no use for them there, and they would also be out of fashion.

"I will put on one of Mama's gowns," Grania told herself. "Then I will start to make the house look as it used to be before we left."

She went to the Drawing-Room and up the stairs.

A rather beautiful staircase swept round artistically and up to a landing on which the centre room had been specially designed for her mother.

As she neared it Grania was thinking of how it was to this room she had always run eagerly as a child first thing in the morning, as soon as she was dressed by the coloured maid who looked after her.

Her mother would be in bed propped against the pillows that were edged with lace and had insertions through which she would thread pretty coloured ribbons to match her nightgowns.

"You look so pretty in bed, Mama, you might be going to a Ball," Grania said once.

"I want to look pretty for your father," her mother had replied. "He is a very handsome man, dearest, and he likes a woman to be pretty and always to make the best of herself. You must remember that."

Grania had remembered, and she knew that her father was proud of herself too when he took her to St. George's and his friends paid her compliments and said that when she grew up she would be the Belle of the island.

Grania in her own mind had always connected her father with things that were beautiful, and she asked herself now how he could possibly contemplate marrying her off to a man who was not only ugly in appearance, but ugly also in character.

She opened the door of the bedroom and was once again surprised to find the shutters drawn from the large windows that covered one wall of the room.

Through them she could see the palm trees against a sky that now held a tinge of gold in it.

There was a fragrance in the room that she had always connected with her mother, and she knew that it was the scent of jasmine whose small star-shaped white flowers bloomed all the year round.

Her mother had distilled the perfume which she always used, and which in consequence now brought her back so vividly to Grania's mind that instinctively she looked towards the bed as if she expected to see her there.

Then suddenly she was very still as if rooted to the spot, staring as if her eyes must be deceiving her.

It was not her mother she could see against the white pillows, but a man.

For a moment she thought she must be imagining him. Then almost as if the light grew clearer she could see quite distinctly and unmistakably there was a man's head on her mother's pillows.

She stood for a moment staring, wondering whether she should go or stay.

Then as if in his sleep her presence communicated itself to him, the man stirred and opened his eyes, and now they were looking at each other across the room.

He was good-looking—handsome she supposed was the right word.

He had dark hair sweeping back from a square forehead, a clean-shaven face with distinctive features, and dark eyes which for a moment stared at her blankly.

Then his expression changed, and there was a smile on his lips and a sudden twinkle of recognition in his eyes.

"Who are you? What are you doing here?" Grania asked.

"Your pardon, *Mademoiselle*," the man replied sitting up against the pillows, "but I have no reason to ask who you are when your picture hangs before me on the wall."

Without really meaning to Grania turned her head to where facing the bed over the top of the chest-of-drawers there was a picture of her mother painted when she had first been engaged to her father and before she had come to Grenada.

"That is a picture of my mother," she said. "What are you doing in her bed?"

Even as she spoke she realised that the way the man had spoken to her showed that he was not English.

She gave a little gasp.

"You are French!" she exclaimed.

"Yes, *Mademoiselle,* I am French," the man replied, "and I can only apologize for occupying your mother's room, but the house was empty."

"I know that," Grania replied, "but you had no . . . right. It is an . . . intrusion for you to . . . come here. And I do not understand . . ."

Then again she stopped and drew in her breath before she said:

"I think . . . perhaps I have . . . heard of you."

The man made a little gesture with his hand.

"I promise you I am not famous, but infamous," he said. "Beaufort—at your service!"

"The pirate!"

"The same, *Mademoiselle!* And a very contrite pirate if my presence here upsets you."

"Of course you upset me!" Grania said sharply. "As I have said, you had no right to intrude because we were away from home."

"I knew the house was empty, and may I add that nobody expected that you would come when you returned home to Grenada."

There was silence. Then Grania said hesitatingly:

"You . . . speak as if you knew I was . . . coming back to the island."

The Pirate smiled at her and it not only seemed to make him look younger, but gave a touch of mischievousness to his expression.

"I should think everybody on the island knows it. Gossip is carried on the wind and in the song of the birds."

"Then you knew my father had gone to England."

The Pirate nodded.

"I knew that, and that you sent for him because your mother was ill. I am hoping that she is better."

"She is . . . dead!"

"My deepest condolences, *Mademoiselle*."

He spoke with a sincerity which did not make it seem as if he was being intrusive.

Suddenly Grania was aware that she was talking to a Pirate and he was lying in her mother's bed, his shoulders above the sheets showing that he was naked.

She had half-turned towards the door when the Pirate said:

"If you will permit me to dress myself, *Mademoiselle*, I will come downstairs to explain my presence, and make my apologies before I leave."

"Thank you," Grania said and went from the room closing the door behind her.

Outside on the landing she stood for a moment thinking that now in fact she *must* be dreaming, and this could not really be happening.

How could she have come home to find a pirate in the house, and a Frenchman at that?

She supposed she should have been frightened not only because the man was a pirate, but also because he was French.

Yet in some way she could not explain, he did not frighten her.

She had the feeling that if she asked him to leave he would do so at once, only making sure before he left that she accepted his apologies for having used the house in her absence.

"It is an intolerable thing to have done!" she told herself, but she was not angry.

She went to her own room and found it as she had expected the whole house to be after what Abe had said.

When she opened the shutters the dust was thick on the floor, on the dressing-table, and on the cover which protected the bed.

Two little lizards shot behind the curtains when she

appeared and there was a smell of mustiness which was over-powering until she opened the window.

She pulled open the wardrobe and knew she could not change into any of the cotton gowns that hung there because she had grown so much taller in the last three years, and although she was still very slim, her figure was no longer that of a child, but had the first curves of maturity.

"I must stay as I am," Grania decided and tried to feel angry because the presence of the pirate was inconvenient to her, but in fact she only felt curious.

There was nothing she could do in her bedroom and she therefore went downstairs.

As she reached the hall she heard the sound of voices in the kitchen and felt she should warn Abe that there was a pirate in the house.

Then as she went towards the kitchen-quarters she heard a man's voice saying in broken English:

"We not expect you. I go wake *Monsieur*."

"Good idea," Abe replied, "a'fore my Lady see him."

Grania walked into the kitchen.

Standing beside Abe was a white man who looked, she thought, extremely French.

He was small, dark-haired and she thought that if she had seen him anywhere in the world she would have known that he was of French origin.

He looked startled at her appearance and she thought also a little fearful.

"I have already talked to your Master," she said. "He is dressing, and coming downstairs to make his apologies before he leaves."

The little Frenchman looked relieved and moved towards the kitchen-table where Grania saw there was a large tin and beside it a tray on which there was a coffee-pot.

She guessed that the Frenchman's servant had been preparing his breakfast for him and with a faint smile she said:

"It would only be hospitable to allow your Master to

have his coffee before he leaves. Where does he usually drink it?"

"On the verandah, *M'mselle*."

"Very well. Take it there. And Abe, I too would like a cup of coffee."

She knew both men stared at her with surprise, then smiling she walked towards the front door.

As she might have expected it was not bolted, and she guessed that was the entrance through which the Frenchman came into the house.

She went out onto the verandah and now in the distance over the palm trees she could just see the tops of two masts.

The trees were so high that unless she had been looking for them they would be invisible and she knew that Secret Harbour was the perfect place for a pirate ship to hide, and wondered why she had never thought of it before.

The small bay had been given its name which described it very aptly, by its former owner.

The entrance to it was at the side and a long tongue of land covered with pine trees faced the sea.

Once the ship was in the harbour it was almost impossible to see it either from the land side or from the sea.

Unless one was actually aware of its existence, one could pass and repass a dozen times without being aware there was a ship at anchor in the bay.

"I would like to see the ship," Grania thought then chided herself for her curiosity.

She knew she should be feeling shocked, angry, and perhaps insulted that a pirate should use her home, and yet she felt none of these emotions which much surprised her.

When a few minutes later the Pirate joined her on the verandah she thought that he would have been more at home in the Drawing-Rooms and Ball-Rooms of London.

He was somehow too elegant and certainly too smart

for the verandah with its over-grown vines and the dirty neglected windows behind them.

There was a table made of native wicker-work and two chairs and before the Frenchman could speak, the servants, Abe and his own man, appeared carrying a white table-cloth with which they covered the table and placed on it a silver tray containing two cups and saucers.

They were the ones her mother kept for best, Grania noticed, and now there was the aroma of coffee and the servants set down a pot and beside it a plate of croissants warm from the oven, a pat of butter, and a glass dish filled with honey.

"*Petit déjeuner est servi, Monsieur,*" the Frenchman's servant announced and then he and Abe vanished.

Grania looked at the pirate. He seemed about to speak, then suddenly she laughed.

"I do not believe this is happening," she said. "You cannot really be a pirate."

"I assure you that I am."

"But I always imagined they were evil, dirty, greasy men who used rough oaths; men from whom women hid in terror."

"You are thinking of one of your own countrymen— Wicken."

"We are lucky he did not discover Secret Harbour," Grania said. "I heard last night that he was pillaging further down the coast."

"I have heard many things about him," the Frenchman replied, "but may I suggest that the coffee is waiting?"

"Yes, of course."

She sat down by instinct in front of the coffee-pot and as he seated himself opposite her she asked:

"Shall I pour out your coffee, or would you prefer to do it for yourself?"

"I should be honoured for you to act as my hostess."

She tried to smile at him, but there was something about him that made her feel a little shy.

So instead she busied herself by filling his cup and passing it to him.

"You must have brought your croissants with you," she said.

"My servant brought them," the Frenchman replied. "They are baked fresh every day."

Grania gave a little laugh.

"So even a pirate if he is French, worries about his food!"

"But of course," the Pirate replied. "Food is an art, and the worst hardship of being perpetually at sea is eating what I have to instead of procuring what I like to eat."

Grania laughed again. Then she asked:

"Why are you a pirate? It seems . . . or perhaps I am being impertinent . . . a strange occupation for you."

"It is a long story," the Frenchman replied. "But may I first ask why you are here, and where is your father?"

"I am here," Grania explained, "because a revolution has broken out in Grenville."

The Frenchman was suddenly tense, staring at her across the table.

"A revolution?"

"Yes. It started several nights ago, but we arrived only yesterday evening at Mr. Maigrin's house. Then in the middle of the night Abe learnt that the revolutionaries had taken over Grenville and killed a number of Englishmen."

"It cannot be possible!" the Frenchman said as if he spoke to himself. "But if there is a revolution it will have been started by Julien Fédor."

"How do you know that?"

"I heard that he was preaching sedition amongst the French slaves."

"So you think the revolution is serious?"

"I am afraid it will be," the Pirate replied.

"But surely you want the French to be the victors and take over this island again as they did twelve years ago?"

He shook his head.

"If the French take it over it will be with ships and soldiers, and not by a rebellion amongst the slaves. They may be successful for a short while, but English soldiers will eventually arrive to attack them and there will be a great deal of blood-shed."

Grania sighed.

It all seemed so unnecessary and rather frightening.

The Frenchman rose to his feet.

"Will you excuse me for one moment while I speak to my servant? He must find out exactly how much danger there may be for you."

He walked away into the house and she stared after him.

She could not help contrasting the lithe grace with which he moved with the uncouth unsteadiness of Roderick Maigrin.

His hair which was dark and thick was pulled back into a neat bow set in the nape of his neck, and his cravat was crisp and fresh, the points of his collar high over his chin in the same manner as the Beaux of St. James's wore theirs.

His coat fitted without a wrinkle, his white cloth breeches revealed his slim attractive hips and his white stockings and buckled shoes were very smart.

"He is a gentleman!" Grania told herself. "It is ridiculous to call him a pirate . . . an outlaw of the seas!"

The Frenchman came back.

"My man and yours are sending people to find out exactly what is known of this revolution. But Abe assures me that the information he received last night and early this morning is absolutely reliable, and there is no doubt that the rebels are killing the English in Grenville where a hundred slaves took everybody in the town by surprise."

Grania gave a little murmur and he went on:

"As usual, they have plundered store-houses, dragged the frightened inhabitants into the street, and set them up as marks to be shot at."

"Oh . . . no!" Grania exclaimed.

"Some escaped by swimming to the vessels that were tied up in the harbour. Others made their way south, and there were some who got as far as Maigrin House."

"Do you think . . . all the slaves on the . . . island will rise and join . . . them?" Grania asked in a low voice.

"We must wait and see," the Frenchman replied. "If the worst comes to the worst, *Mademoiselle*, my ship is at your disposal."

"Do you think that will be a safe place to hide?"

The Frenchman smiled.

"It may be a case of 'any port in a storm'."

"Yes, of course, but I am hoping that my father will join me today, and perhaps he will have other ideas of where we should go."

"Naturally," the Frenchman agreed, "and I should imagine both you and your father, and doubtless also Mr. Maigrin, will be welcome in the Fort of St. George's."

Grania could not disguise the expression in her eyes as he spoke of Roderick Maigrin.

Instead of answering, she ate without speaking the delicious croissant which she had spread with butter and honey.

There was silence. Then the Frenchman said:

"I have been told, although of course it may be incorrect, that you are to marry Mr. Maigrin."

"Who told you that?"

The Frenchman shrugged his shoulders.

"I learnt that was intended before your father went to England to bring you home."

It flashed through Grania's mind that even if her mother had lived her father might have insisted on his rights as her legal guardian and brought her back to Grenada.

Then as she thought of Roderick Maigrin the revulsion she had felt for him last night swept over her again.

Quite involuntarily without really thinking what she was saying she asked:

"What can I . . . do? How can I . . . escape? I cannot . . . marry that . . . man!"

The terror in her voice seemed to vibrate on the air and she was aware the Frenchman was staring at her intently, his dark eyes searching her face.

Then he said:

"I agree it is impossible for somebody like you to marry such a man, but it is not for me to tell you how you can avoid doing so."

"Then . . . who else can I . . . ask?" Grania said almost like a child. "I did not know until the very moment we arrived that that was what Papa . . . intended, and now I am . . . here I do not know . . . what I can do . . . or where I can . . . hide from . . . him."

The Frenchman put his knife down on the table with a little clatter.

"That is your problem, *Mademoiselle*," he said, "and as you must be aware, I cannot interfere."

"No . . . of course not," Grania agreed. "I should not have . . . spoken as I . . . did. Forgive . . . me."

"There is nothing to forgive. I want to listen. I want to help you, but I am an enemy, apart from the fact that I am also a criminal outlaw."

"Perhaps that is what I . . . should be," Grania said, "then even Mr. Maigrin would not . . . wish to marry . . . me."

Even as she spoke she knew there was nothing she could do to prevent him wanting her for herself apart from her social position.

She saw again the look in his eyes last night and felt herself shiver.

She was frightened, desperately, horribly frightened, not of the revolution, not of dying, but of being touched by a man who she knew was evil, and whose very presence disgusted her so that she felt physically sick when he was near her.

Her face must have been very expressive, for suddenly the Frenchman asked harshly:

"Why did you not stay in England where you were safe?"

"How could I after Mama died?" Grania asked. "I knew very few people, and besides . . . Papa would have . . . insisted on bringing me back . . . whatever I . . . might have . . . said."

"It is a pity you could not have found somebody to marry you while you were there," the Frenchman remarked.

"I think that is what Mama wanted," Grania answered, "she intended to present me to the King and Queen, then I would have been asked to Balls and parties. She had planned so many things but she became ill . . . so terribly ill before Christmas."

She paused for a moment before she went on:

"The weather was foggy and cold, and Mama had been living in the sun for so many years that the Doctor said her blood had become thin and she was too . . . weak to stand the English . . . climate."

"I understand," the Frenchman said in a low voice. "But surely you could tell your father that you have no wish to marry this man?"

"I have told him," Grania replied, "but he said he had it all arranged . . . and that Mr. Maigrin was . . . very rich."

She felt as she spoke that she was being disloyal, but it was, she knew, the whole crux of the matter, the real reason why her father was so insistent that she must marry.

Roderick Maigrin was rich, he could keep her father in the comfort he wanted, and the only way her father could achieve this was by handing over his daughter.

"It is an intolerable situation!" the Frenchman said suddenly in a voice that made her start.

"But . . . what can I do about it?" Grania asked.

"When I lay in bed and looked at your mother's picture," he said in a low voice, "I thought it would be impossible for anybody to be lovelier, sweeter or more attractive. But now I have seen you I know that while outwardly you resemble your mother there is, perhaps because you are alive, something which the artist failed to portray."

"What is it?" Grania asked curiously.

"I think the right word for it is that you have a *spiritualité Mademoiselle* which would be impossible to convey on canvas, except for a Michaelangelo, or a Botticelli."

"Thank you," Grania said in a low voice.

"I am not just paying you a compliment," the Frenchman said, "but stating a fact, and that is why I know it would be impossible for you to marry a man like Maigrin. I have only seen him once, but I have heard a great deal about him, and I can say in all truth; better dead then that you should be his wife!"

Grania clasped her hands together.

"That is what I feel . . . but I know Papa will not . . . listen to me . . . and when he comes here I shall be forced to marry whatever I may say . . . however much I may . . . plead with . . . him."

The Frenchman rose to his feet and walked to the rail of the verandah to stand leaning against it.

Grania thought he was looking at his ship and thinking how easily he could slip out of harbour into the open sea where he would be free and could leave behind him the troubles and difficulties of the island and her personal worries.

He looked very elegant standing there, his head silhouetted against the bougainvillaea.

But she had the feeling that instead of a ship there should be a Phaeton waiting for him, drawn by two thoroughbred horses, and that he would invite her to accompany him and they would drive in Hyde Park bowing to their friends.

Then there would be only the gossip and laughter of social London and no talk of revolutions and blood-shed or of marriage to Roderick Maigrin.

She was thinking at that moment, although of course

it seemed absurd, that the Frenchman stood for security in a world that had suddenly become for her horrifying and frightening, and in which she was completely helpless.

"What time do you expect your father?" the Frenchman asked at length.

She thought his voice had an edge on it, and it was a little louder than she expected.

"I . . . I have no idea," she answered hesitatingly. "When I left in the darkness very early this morning . . . they had . . . been . . . drinking all . . . night and had not . . . gone to bed."

The Frenchman nodded as if that was what he had expected and said:

"Then we have time. For the moment I suggest you stop worrying about the future and instead perhaps you would like to visit my ship."

"Can I do that?" Grania asked.

"I should be very honoured if you would do so."

"Then please . . . may I change? It will soon be very hot."

"But of course," he replied.

Grania ran from the verandah and up the stairs.

As she had expected Abe had already taken up her trunks and put them down in her mother's room.

He had undone the straps and opened them, and she suspected that later he would find one of the women who had served in the house before to come and unpack for her.

For the moment, all she wanted was a dress in which, although she would not admit it to herself, she would look her best.

Quickly she pulled one of the pretty gowns she had bought in London out of the nearest trunk.

She had worn it last year, but its full skirt was still fashionable, and the fichu although a little creased from the voyage was crisp and clean.

It took Grania only a few minutes to take off the clothes in which she had travelled and to wash in the basin. She was not surprised to find a ewer filled with cool, clean water.

Then she dressed herself again and ran downstairs to where she was sure the Pirate would be waiting for her.

She was not mistaken.

He was sitting on the verandah having moved his chair into the sunshine, and she knew now that his skin was so dark because unlike the Beaux in London he had allowed himself to become sunburnt.

It became him, and she thought that in a way the fact that his skin had been burnt by the sun had prevented her from being shocked when she saw him naked in bed.

He rose at her approach and she saw a look of admiration in his eyes and a smile on his lips as he took in her appearance.

It was so different from the way Roderick Maigrin had looked at her last night, when she had felt that with his eyes on her breasts he was seeing her not as she was, but naked.

"Would you like me to tell you that you look very lovely, and like the Spirit of Spring?" the Frenchman asked.

"I enjoy hearing you say it," Grania replied.

"But you must have heard so many compliments in London that they cease to be anything but a bore."

"The only compliments I received were for the work I did at School, and one or two from gentlemen who called to take my mother to a ball or to Vauxhall."

"You were too young to become a Society Beauty?"

"Much too young," Grania replied, "and now, as that is something I have missed completely, I suppose it will never happen to me."

"Does that distress you?"

"It is disappointing. Mama used to describe so often the Balls and parties I should attend that I feel as if they are familiar and I have dreamed of them."

"I assure you there are other things to do in the

world which are far more entrancing," the Frenchman
said.

"Then you must tell me about them," Grania replied,
"to make up for what I have missed."

"Perhaps that is something I should not do," he said
enigmatically.

Then when she would have asked him for an explanation he said:

"Come along. Let us go quickly and see my ship just
in case your father returns before you are able to do so."

As if she was afraid that might happen, she hurried
down the steps of the verandah with the Frenchman
beside her.

They walked through the untidy garden which had
gone completely wild since her mother had left and
found themselves amongst the pine trees.

There was just enough wind to move their leaves very
gently and then ahead Grania had her first glimpse of
the ship.

She could see the poop-deck, the fo'c'sle and the high
raking masts. The sails were furled, but she had the feeling that they could be set very swiftly.

Then the ship would be gone, and she would be left
behind never to see it again.

Ahead of them was a long narrow jetty which had
been built out into the harbour. The ship was anchored
at the very end of it, and there was a gang-plank to
connect the deck with the jetty.

She and the Frenchman walked over the rough un-
planed wood and when they reached the gang-plank he
stopped and asked:

"There are no hand-rails. Are you afraid?"

"No, of course not," Grania replied smiling.

Then he said:

"Let me go first and I will help you aboard, and of
course I will be honoured to do so."

There was something in the way he spoke the last
words that made her feel a little shy.

He stretched out his hand and she took it, and as she

touched it she felt the vibration of his fingers and it gave her a strange sensation she had never had before.

The ship was entrancing, almost like a child's toy.

The deck had been scrubbed spotlessly clean, the paint was fresh, and there were men busy with ropes who paid no attention at their approach, but Grania was certain their eyes were watching her as she walked beside their Captain.

He helped her down some steps and opened a door, which she realised led into the stern cabin.

The sun was steaming through large portholes making vivid patterns on the walls of the cabin.

She had always expected that a pirate-ship would be dirty and disorderly. In the stories she had read the Captain's cabin had been a dark hole, filled with cutlasses and empty bottles.

This cabin was like a room in a house with comfortable armchairs and in one corner a four-poster bed with drawn curtains.

Everything was exquisitely neat and she thought she smelled bees'-wax and lavender.

There was a carpet on the floor, cushions on the chairs, and on the table there was a vase of flowers which she thought must have been picked from what had been her mother's garden.

She stood looking around her, until she realised the Frenchman was watching her with a smile.

"Well?" he questioned.

"It is very attractive and very comfortable."

"It is my home now," he said quietly, "and just as a Frenchman likes his food he also likes his comforts."

"But you are always in danger," Grania said. "If you are seen by either the English or the French they will try to destroy or capture you, and if you are caught . . . you will die!"

"I am aware of that," he said, "but I find danger exciting, and I can assure you, although it seems a contradiction in terms, that I will not take any risks."

"Then why . . . ?" Grania began and realised once

again she was being curious and prying into his private affairs.

"Come and sit down," the Frenchman said. "I want to see you at ease in my room, and when you are no longer there, I can look into my mind and will see you there again."

He spoke in quite an ordinary voice, and yet she felt herself blushing at what he had said.

Obediently she sat down in one of the armchairs, the sun coming through the porthole turning her hair to gold.

Because it had been so early in the morning she had not brought a hat or a sunshade, and she felt somehow it was right for her to be sitting in this tiny room talking to a man who was more attractive than any man she had seen in London.

"Why do you call yourself Beaufort?" she enquired when the silence seemed somehow embarrassing.

"Because it is my name," he answered, "the name by which I was Christened, and it does seem an appropriate sobriquet, since I cannot use my other name."

"Why not?"

"Because it would be unseemly. My ancestors would turn in their graves, and also one day I hope to go back to where I belong."

"You cannot go to France," Grania said quickly, remembering the Revolution.

"I am aware of that," he said, "but that is not where I really belong—at least not since I was very young."

"Then where? Or is that a question I should not ask?"

"Shall I say that when we are together like this we can ask any questions of each other?" the Frenchman said. "And because I am honoured that you should be interested, I will tell you that I come from Martinique, where I had a plantation, and my real name is de Vence— Beaufort de Vence."

"It is a very attractive name."

"There have been *Comtes* de Vence in France for

centuries," the Frenchman said. "They are part of the history of that country."

"Are you a *Comte*?"

"As my father is dead I am head of the family."

"But your home is in Martinique."

"It was!"

Grania looked at him puzzled, then she gave a little cry.

"You are a refugee! The British took Martinique last year!"

"Exactly!" the *Comte* said. "I should undoubtedly have died if I had not escaped just before they seized my plantation."

"So that was why you became a pirate!"

"That is why I became a pirate, and I shall remain a pirate until the British are driven out, which they will be eventually, and I can regain my possessions."

Grania gave a little sigh.

"There is always so much fighting in these islands, and the loss of life is terrible."

"I thought that myself," the *Comte* replied, "but at least for the moment I am as safe here as I am likely to be anywhere."

Grania did not speak.

She was thinking that if he was safe she on the contrary, was in the greatest danger—danger from the revolutionaries, and more frightening still, danger from Roderick Maigrin.

CHAPTER THREE

WHEN GRANIA LOOKED around the cabin she saw, as she thought she might have expected, that there were a great number of books.

The cases had been skilfully inserted into the panelling and although they did not have a glass front, there was a bar which held them in place so that they would not fall out when the ship rolled at sea.

The *Comte* followed the direction of her eyes and said with a smile:

"I feel you are also a reader."

"I had to learn about the world from books before I went to London," Grania replied, "and then, just when I was going to step into a world I had read about in the School-Room, I had to come back here."

"Perhaps you would have found that world, which is to some women very glittering and glamorous, disappointing."

"Why should you think that?"

"Because I have a feeling, and I do not think I am wrong," the *Comte* replied, "that you are seeking something deeper and more important than can be found on the surface of a Social life that relies on tinkling laughter and the clinking of glasses."

Grania looked at him in surprise.

"Perhaps you are right," she said, "but Mama always made it sound so exciting that I looked forward to

348

making my debut, and to meeting people who now remain only names to me in the newspapers and the history books."

"Then you will not feel disillusioned by reality."

Grania raised her eye-brows.

"Is that what you have been?"

"Not really," he admitted, "and I am, I suppose, fortunate in that I knew Paris before the Revolution, and I have also been to London."

"And you enjoyed it?"

"When I was young I found it very intriguing, and yet I knew that my real place was here among the islands."

"You love Martinique?"

"It is my home, and will be my home again."

The way he spoke was very moving, and Grania said softly without thinking:

"I shall pray that it will be returned to you."

A smile seemed to illumine his face before he said:

"Thank you, and I am ready to believe, *Mademoiselle*, that your prayers will always be heard."

"Except those for myself," Grania replied.

Then she thought perhaps she was being unfair. She had prayed last night to escape from Roderick Maigrin, and for the moment she was away from him.

There was always the chance that if she was alone with her father she might persuade him such a marriage was so intolerable that he would not inflict it on her.

After all, he had loved her when she was a child—there was no doubt about that—and she was sure that it was only because her mother and she had gone away that he had fallen so completely under Mr. Maigrin's thumb and was ready to acquiesce in anything he suggested.

The expressions which followed each other across her face were more revealing than she had realised, and she felt uncomfortably that the *Comte* could read her thoughts when he said:

"You are very lovely, *Mademoiselle*, and I cannot

believe that any man, even your father, would not listen when you plead with him."

"I shall try . . . I shall try very . . . hard."

He walked to one of the port-holes before he said:

"I think you should now return home. If your father arrives and finds you not there he will be very shocked to learn that you are with somebody like myself."

"I am sure if you met Papa in other circumstances you would like each other."

"But circumstances being what they are we must remain at a distance," the *Comte* said firmly.

He walked towards the door of the cabin and there was nothing Grania could do but rise from the chair in which she had been sitting.

She had the strange feeling that she was leaving safety and security for danger, but she could not put such feelings into words and she could only follow the *Comte* up the companionway and onto the deck.

The sailors watched her from the corners of their eyes as she walked towards the gangway.

She was sure because they were Frenchmen they were admiring her, and she told herself it was impertinent of them to do so because they were outlaws and pirates who in fact, should be frightened in case she betrayed them.

Again the *Comte* must have read her thoughts for as they stepped ashore he said:

"One day I hope I shall have the privilege of introducing my friends to you, for that is what my crew are: friends who have no wish to be outlaws but have been forced to flee from your countrymen."

The way he spoke made Grania feel ashamed.

"I am sorry for . . . anybody who has been a . . . victim of war," she said, "but those who live on these islands seem to know . . . nothing else."

"That is true," the *Comte* agreed, "and it is always the innocent who suffer."

They walked through the thickness of the trees and the bougainvillaea bushes until the house was in sight.

"I will leave you here," the *Comte* said.

"Please do not . . . go," Grania said impulsively.

He looked at her in surprise and she said:

"We have not yet heard what Abe and your man have found out about the revolutionaries. Suppose they are on their way here? I could only escape if you let me come aboard your ship."

Even as she spoke she knew she was not so much frightened of the revolutionaries as of losing the *Comte*.

She wanted to stay with him, she wanted to talk to him, and most of all she wanted him to protect her from Roderick Maigrin.

"If the revolutionaries are here," he said, "I doubt if even as a pirate I would be safe."

"You mean they will think of you as an aristocrat."

"Exactly!" he said. "The reason why Fédor has started a revolution is that he has been in Guadaloupe which is the centre of the French Revolution in the West Indies."

"Is that true?" Grania asked.

"I am told that Fédor was given a commission as Commander General of the insurgents in Grenada,"

"You mean this has been planned for some time?"

The *Comte* nodded.

"They have arms and ammunition, caps of liberty, national cockades, and a flag on which is inscribed: *'Liberté, Egalité, ou la Mort.'* "

Grania gave a little cry.

"Do you mean the English do not know this?"

The *Comte* shrugged his shoulders and she knew without his saying any more that the English in St. George's had become complacent and too busy enjoying themselves to anticipate there might be an uprising.

It seemed extraordinary that they should have been taken by surprise, when the *Comte* knew so much.

At the same time she was well aware that in Grenada they often knew things that happened on other islands before they knew it themselves.

As the *Comte* had said, the very birds carried gossip

351

across the blue sea, and the fact that there were French under British jurisdiction and *vice versa* was an open invitation for the slaves who planned to rebel if the opportunity arose.

They walked through the part of the garden which had once been cultivated and now was a riot of colour and blossom.

There were little patches of English flowers which her mother had tried to cultivate and which in their very profusion seemed to have become part of the tropical scene.

The house when they reached it seemed very quiet, and Grania knew at once that her father had not arrived.

She walked in through the front door followed by the *Comte,* and she went straight towards the kitchen to find it was empty.

"Abe and your man have not returned," she said.

"Then I suggest we sit and wait for them," the *Comte* said, "and it will be cooler than anywhere else in the Drawing-Room."

"I wondered when I came here this morning why there were no covers on the furniture," Grania said. "Have you sat there very often?"

"Occasionally," the *Comte* admitted. "It made me think of my home when I was a child, and also of my house in Martinique, which is very beautiful. I would like to show it to you one day."

"I would like that," Grania said simply.

Her eyes met his as she spoke, then shyly she looked away.

"Perhaps I should offer you some of your own coffee?"

"I want nothing," he said, "except to talk to you. Sit down, *Mademoiselle* and tell me about yourself."

Grania laughed.

"There is very little to tell that you do not already know, and I would rather hear about you."

"That would be dull for me," the *Comte* said, "and as the hostess you must be generous to your guest."

"An uninvited guest who has made himself very much at home!"

"That is true, but I had a feeling when I lay in bed looking at your picture that you would be as kind and welcoming as you have been."

"I am sure Mama would have liked you," Grania said impulsively.

"You could not say anything that would please me more," the *Comte* answered. "I have heard about your mother and I know how understanding she was to everybody she met, and I am sure that she was very proud of her daughter."

"She would not be . . . proud if she . . . knew what Papa is . . . planning for me," Grania said in a small voice.

"We have already agreed that you must talk to your father and make him understand what your mother would have felt had she been here," the *Comte* said.

He spoke almost severely, as if he was instructing her like a School-Master, and expecting her to obey him.

"My father has changed . . . since we have been . . . away," Grania said. "I felt when we were sailing back that he had . . . something on his . . . mind."

There was silence for a moment. Then the *Comte* said:

"If he had stayed and attended to his plantations, I am quite certain it would have brought him in the money he needs and he need not have become beholden to other—people."

There was a pause before he said the last word and Grania knew he was about to say "Roderick Maigrin", then changed his mind.

"Papa never made very much money out of the plantation," Grania said.

"That is because he grew too many different crops at the same time, instead of concentrating on one for which there was a demand."

Grania looked at the *Comte* in surprise and he said with a smile:

"My plantations were very successful, and I made a great deal of money."

"And you have looked at ours?"

"Yes, I was curious about them and wondered why your father should make himself dependent on his friends and neglect what could be a considerable source of income."

"I have always been told that the French were practical, and yet somehow you do not look like a businessman."

"I am, as you say, practical," the *Comte* replied, "and when my father died and I took over our plantations in Martinique, I was determined to make a success of them."

"And now you have lost them," Grania said. "It is too cruel that this should happen and I am so sorry for you."

"I will get them back. One day they will be mine again."

"In the meantime, please help us with ours."

"I want to, for your sake," the *Comte* answered, "but you must know it is impossible. All I can suggest is that you persuade your father to concentrate on growing nutmegs. They do well here, better than in other islands, and there is always a demand for them all over the world, as there has been since the beginning of time."

"I think Papa finds the nutmegs unattractive because they take so long to bear fruit."

The *Comte* nodded.

"That is true—eight to nine years. But they increase in yield until they are about thirty years old and the average crop may be three to four thousand nuts per tree every year."

"I had no idea it was so much!" Grania exclaimed.

"What is more they produce two main crops," the *Comte* went on. "You have quite a number of trees already, although unfortunately they are crowded by other fruits and of course the undergrowth is restricting and stunting them."

He paused and realised that Grania was listening to him raptly, and said:

"Forgive me, I am lecturing you. But quite frankly it distresses me to see good land and what could be good crops wasted unnecessarily."

"I wish you could talk to Papa like that."

"I doubt if he would listen to me," the *Comte* replied wryly, "but perhaps you can talk to whoever runs the estate for your father."

"That was Abe, but Papa took him away because he could not be without him."

The *Comte* said nothing and there was silence between them.

Grania gave an exasperated little sigh.

"You are making me feel helpless and it is too big a problem for me."

"Of course it is, and it is unfair of me to talk to you like this. You should be enjoying life at your age and finding it all exciting and beautiful. Why should you have to worry about land that is unproductive and pirates who make use of your home when it is empty?"

The *Comte* was speaking in a low voice as if he was talking to himself and Grania laughed.

"I find pirates very exciting, and one day it will be a story to tell my children and my grandchildren, and they will think I was very adventurous."

She spoke lightly as she might have spoken to her father or mother.

Then as she met the Frenchman's eyes she knew that if she had children they would be Roderick Maigrin's and she wanted to scream at the very idea of it.

Instead because of the way the *Comte* was looking at her, she felt the colour rise slowly in her cheeks, and her heart began to beat in a very strange manner.

Then there was the sound of voices and they were both very still as they listened.

"It is Abe!" Grania cried in a tone of relief.

Jumping up from her chair she ran across the room and as she reached the hall she called out:

"Abe! Abe!"

He came from the kitchen-quarters followed by the French servant.

"What have you discovered?" Grania asked.

"Things very bad, Lady," Abe replied.

Then before he could say any more the French servant went to the side of the *Comte* who had followed Grania from the Drawing-Room and burst into a flood of such quick French that it was impossible for her to follow everything he said.

Only when he had ceased speaking did she ask nervously:

"What . . . has happened?"

"It sounds bad," the *Comte* replied. "At the same time as the rebellion started in Grenville, Charlotte Town was attacked by another band of insurgents."

Grania gave a little cry of horror.

Charlotte Town, which was on the West side of the island only a little way above St. George's, was a place she knew well.

"Many lives have been lost," the *Comte* went on, "and a number of British inhabitants have been taken prisoner."

"Do they know who?"

The *Comte* questioned the Frenchman, but he shook his head.

Abe obviously understood what he asked, for he said:

"Dr. John Hay prisoner."

"Oh, no!" Grania exclaimed.

"Doctor and Rector of Charlotte Town taken Belvedere," Abe went on.

"Why Belvedere?" Grania questioned.

"That is where Fédon has made his headquarters," the *Comte* replied. "The prisoners from Grenville have also been taken there."

Grania clasped her hands together.

"What shall we do?" she asked, "and is there any news of Papa?"

Abe shook his head.

"No, Lady, I send boy find out if Master coming."

The French servant then said a great deal more and when he finished the *Comte* explained:

"There is no sign of any trouble so far in St. George's, which is where the British soldiers are, so I think for the moment you are safe and when your father joins you you will not be unprotected."

Grania did not say anything she only looked at him, and after a moment he added, as if she had asked the question:

"Until your father arrives, I will stay in the harbour."

"Thank you."

She hardly breathed the words beneath her breath but the expression in her eyes was very revealing.

"And now," the *Comte* said, "as Abe has had no opportunity to cook luncheon for you and I believe like me you are beginning to feel hungry, may I invite you to what will be a simple meal aboard my ship?"

Grania's smile seemed to light up her whole face.

"You know I would like that."

The *Comte* gave his servant some instructions and he left hurriedly by the front door, running across the garden towards the harbour.

Grania drew Abe to one side.

"Listen Abe," she said, "I am safe with *Monsieur* Beaufort. He is not really a pirate, but a refugee from Martinique."

"Know that, Lady."

"You did not tell me!" Grania said reproachfully.

"Not expect him here."

Grania looked at him sharply.

"You knew that he had . . . come here before?"

There was a little pause and she knew that Abe debated whether he should tell her the truth. Then he answered:

"Yes, Lady, he come, not do no harm. Fine man! While here he pay for what he take to ship."

"Pay for what?"

"Pigs, chickens, turkeys."

Grania laughed.

There was a remarkable difference between a pirate who paid for what he requisitioned and other pirates like Will Wilken who stole what they wanted and killed if interfered with.

"You and I trust *Monsieur*, Abe," she said, "but Papa might be angry. Come and tell me if he is coming while I am aboard the ship so that I can be here in the house when he arrives."

She knew Abe would understand he was to station two of their slaves to watch the road and the path through the forest.

She was not really afraid of what her father's reaction would be, but rather of Roderick Maigrin's if he was with him.

She was quite certain that he would shoot first and ask questions afterwards, and she thought that if she was instrumental in causing the *Comte* to be killed or wounded she would never forgive herself.

"Not worry, Lady," Abe said. "When Master come we ready."

"Thank you, Abe."

Because it was much hotter now than it had been earlier in the morning she went upstairs to collect one of her new sunshades which she had brought back with her from London.

She came downstairs again to find the *Comte* waiting for her in the hall. She felt like a child who was being taken on an unexpected treat, and she had the idea that he felt the same.

Without speaking they walked out onto the verandah and when they started to descend the wooden steps which were slightly rickety as they needed repairing, the *Comte* put out his hand to help her.

Grania put her own hand into his and as he took it

she felt again that strange vibration that she had felt before, only this time it was more insistent.

His fingers closed over hers, and when the steps ended he still held her hand.

"I am looking forward to having a French luncheon," she said.

"I am afraid you have not given me enough time to prepare what I should like to offer you," the *Comte* replied, "but Henri, who has been with me for several years, will do his best."

"I also want to see the rest of your ship. How long have you had it, and did you build it yourself?"

The *Comte* gave a little laugh.

"I stole it!"

Grania waited for an explanation and he said:

"When the English invaded Martinique I knew that I must leave and I intended to do so in my own yacht. But when I went down to the harbour I saw the ship which you have already seen lying at anchor, and as I looked at it one of my friends who was with me said:

"'It is sad that the man whose company owns that ship is in Europe at the moment. It is too good a vessel to fall into the hands of the English.'"

"So you agreed with him and took it?"

"It seemed the proper thing to do."

"I think it was very sensible and practical, which are two things you like to be."

"Yes, of course," he said, "and it meant that I could bring more people with me than I could have done otherwise, and I also transported a great amount of my furniture and my family pictures to a place where they will be safe until hostilities cease."

"Where is that?" Grania asked curiously.

"St. Martin," the *Comte* replied.

He said no more and she thought he did not wish to discuss it.

They walked in silence through the palm trees until when the ship was in sight she took her hand from his.

It was now very hot but there was a breeze from the sea.

The ship was still, only she noticed that the sails were no longer tied down, but ready to be raised at a moment's notice.

"Once he is gone I shall never see him again," Grania thought.

She felt these moments when she could be with the *Comte* were somehow very precious and something she would always remember.

They walked across the deck and down into the cabin. The port-holes were open and the sunshine came flooding in.

There was a table laid for two with a spotless white cloth and fresh flowers in the centre of it.

There was also besides the smell of bees'-wax a delicious aroma of food, and before she could say anything the French servant who had been with Abe came into the cabin, carrying a toureen in his hand.

They sat down at the table and Jean, for that was what she had heard the *Comte* call him, filled two beautiful porcelain bowls.

There was crisp French bread to eat with the soup and when Grania tasted it she knew it was made of stock, herbs, and other ingredients which she thought were fresh from the sea.

It was delicious and she realised that the aroma of it made her hungry and she and the *Comte* both ate without speaking.

The servant brought wine that was golden like the sunshine and poured it into the glasses and as they smiled at each other across the table Grania thought suddenly that she was happy.

For the first time since she had come home she was no longer worried or afraid.

When the soup was finished Jean brought them lobsters cooked with butter. They had obviously been swimming in the sea an hour or so earlier and Grania suspected they came from their own lobster-pots which had always been set in the bay when her mother was at home.

However she asked no questions, only ate eagerly because the lobsters were so tender and delicious and the salad which went with them was different from anything she had eaten while she was in London.

There was cheese and a bowl of fruit to follow the meal, but Grania could eat no more, so she and the *Comte* sat back and sipped their coffee.

Then at last the silence was broken, even though she thought they had been communicating with each other without words.

"If this is the life of a pirate," she said, "I think I shall become one."

"This is the moment," the *Comte* said, "when a pirate rests with his Lady and forgets the danger, the uncertainty and the discomfort of travelling over the face of the earth."

"At the same time it must be exciting. You are free to go where you want, to take orders from nobody, and to live on your wits."

"As you have already said I am sensible and practical," the *Comte* replied. "I want security, a wife and children, but that is something I can never have."

He spoke as if he was telling her something of infinite importance, but because she felt suddenly shy she did not look at him, but picked up her spoon to stir her coffee, although there was no need for it.

"A pirate's life is certainly no life for a woman," the *Comte* went on, as if he was following his own train of thought.

"But if there is no alternative?" Grania enquired.

"There is always an alternative to every situation," he replied firmly. "I could give up my piracy, but then I, and the people who are with me, would starve."

There was silence—a silence that seemed full of meaning before the *Comte* said quickly:

"But why do we not talk of things that are interesting?

Of books and pictures? Our different languages? And I have a great desire to hear you speak French."

"You may think I speak it badly," Grania replied in French.

"Your accent is perfect!" he exclaimed. "Who taught you?"

"My mother, and she was taught by a true Parisian."

"That is obvious."

"I also had lessons when I was at School in England," Grania explained, "although French was unpopular, and they were surprised that I should want to learn such a 'fiendish' language spoken by the people who were killing their own kin."

"I can understand that," the *Comte* said. "But even though the English are at war with my country at the moment, I still want to learn to speak like an Englishman."

"Why?"

"Because it might come in useful."

"Your English is very good except for a few words which you mispronounce and you sometimes put the stress on the wrong syllable."

The *Comte* smiled.

"Very well," he said. "When we are together I will correct you, and you will correct me. Is that a deal?"

"Yes, of course," Grania replied, "and to be fair we must divide our time together talking partly in English and partly in French, and there must be no cheating."

The *Comte* laughed. Then he said:

"It will be interesting to see who will be the better pupil, and I have the feeling, Grania, that because you are more sensitive than I am you will take the prize."

Grania noticed that he called her by her Christian name and once again he read her thoughts as he said:

"I cannot go on calling you 'My Lady' when already we know each other too well to be conventional."

"We only met this morning."

"That is not true," he replied. "I have known and

admired you, and talked to you for many nights, and your image has stayed with me during the day."

The way he spoke made her blush again and she felt the colour burning its way up to her eyes.

"You are very beautiful!" the *Comte* went on. "Far too beautiful for my peace of mind. If I was sensible and practical, as you tell me I am, I would sail away as soon as I set you ashore."

"No . . . please you . . . promised you would . . . stay until my father . . . returned," Grania said quickly.

"I am being selfish and thinking of myself," the *Comte* replied.

"I am being selfish in doing the same," Grania admitted.

"Do you really want me to stay?"

"I am begging you to do so. I will go down on my knees, if that is what you want."

The *Comte* suddenly bent across to the table and put out his hand. Slowly, because she felt shy, Grania put her hand in it.

"Now listen to me, Grania," he said. "I am a man without a home, without a future, an outlaw both to the French and the English. Let me go away while I am able to do so."

Grania's fingers tightened on his.

"I . . . cannot stop you . . . from going."

"But you are asking me to stay."

"I want you to. Please . . . I want you to. If you . . . go I shall be very . . . frightened."

Her eyes met his, and it was impossible for her to look away. Then he said:

"As you have just reminded me, we only met a few hours ago."

"But . . . time does not . . . affect what I . . . feel about . . . you."

"And what do you feel?"

"That when I am with . . . you I am . . . safe and nothing can . . . hurt me."

"I wish that was true," he said.

"It is true. I know it is true!" Grania answered.

The *Comte* looked away from her down at her hand, then he raised it to his lips.

"Very well. I will stay, but when I do go you must not blame yourself and there must be no regrets."

"I promise . . . no regrets."

But she had the feeling as she spoke that it was a promise she would not be able to keep.

They sat talking for a little until Jean came in to take away the coffee and the *Comte* said:

"Come and sit on the sofa and put up your feet. This is the time for a *siesta* and my crew will all be sleeping either on deck or below. I think it unlikely we shall be disturbed because your father will not travel in the heat of the day."

Grania knew this was true, and she walked to the sofa as the *Comte* suggested and sat back against the cushions, putting up her feet.

He pulled up an armchair to sit beside her and stretched out his long legs in their white stockings.

Grania smiled.

"Can this really be happening?" she asked. "I think both the French and the English would be very surprised if they could see us now."

"The English would certainly be very annoyed," the *Comte* replied. "They dislike pirates because they challenge their supremacy at sea, and that is something which is uncertain at the moment with the rebellions both here and in Guadaloupe."

He paused before he went on:

"At the same time they hold Martinique and a number of other islands, so undoubtedly the port of St. George's will sooner or later receive reinforcements."

Grania knew this was true, but she thought until the soldiers arrived the rebels could do a great deal of damage.

Stories of how on other islands they had tortured

their prisoners before they killed them had lost nothing in the telling.

She felt herself tremble as she imagined the indignities and perhaps the pain that Dr. Hay and the Anglican Rector might be suffering.

The *Comte* was watching her face.

"Forget it!" he said. "There is nothing you can do, and to keep thinking of such horrors is to bring them nearer and perhaps to make one's self more vulnerable."

Grania looked at him with interest.

"Do you believe that thought is transferable, and also strong enough to attract attention?"

"I assure you," the *Comte* replied, "I am not speaking of Voodoo or Black Magic when I say that the natives on Martinique know what is happening fifty miles away at the other end of the island, long before it would be possible for a messenger to travel the distance with the information."

"You mean they are able to communicate with each other in a way that we have forgotten how to do?"

"I would never underestimate their powers."

"That is very interesting."

"As you are half-Irish it should be easy for you to understand," the *Comte* said.

"Yes, of course. Papa used to tell me stories about the powers of the Irish Sorcerers and how they could foretell the future. Of course I learnt about the Leprechauns when I was very small."

"Just as I learnt about the spirits that inhabit the mountains and forests in Martinique," the *Comte* said.

"Why could they not warn you before the English invaded the island?" Grania asked.

"Perhaps they tried to do so and we did not listen!" the *Comte* replied. "When you come to Martinique you can feel them, hear them and perhaps see them."

"That is something I would love to do," Grania replied impulsively.

"You must trust to fate," the *Comte* answered, "which

as you know has already brought you out of a very difficult situation, for which I am very grateful."

"As I am grateful to be here," Grania said. "When I
rode through the forest I had the feeling I was escaping
from a terrifying danger to something very different."

"What was that?"

She drew in her breath.

"It is what I feel when I am sitting here talking to
you. I cannot . . . describe it exactly . . . but it makes
me feel very . . . happy."

There was a moment's silence. Then the *Comte* said:
"That is all I want you to feel for the moment."

CHAPTER FOUR

❧❦❧

*T*HE HOURS OF heat passed slowly. Sometimes Grania
and the *Comte* talked and sometimes they sat in silence as
if they communicated with each other without words.

But she was aware that his eyes were on her face and
sometimes he made her feel shy in a way that was half-
pleasure, half a strange embarrassment that seemed to
have something magical about it.

Then there was the sound of footsteps overhead and
the whistling of a man who was happy while he worked,
and the *Comte* rose.

"I think I should take you back to the house," he said.
"If your father is going to arrive he should be here in
perhaps under an hour."

Grania knew that was the time it would take if her father came to her by road and not through the forest.

She wanted to stay longer and go on talking to the *Comte* or even just be with him, but she could think of no viable excuse that did not sound intrusive, so reluctantly she rose from the sofa.

She had laid her head against a soft cushion, and now she patted her hair into place feeling she must be untidy and looked around for a mirror.

"You look lovely!" the *Comte* said in his deep voice, and again she blushed.

He stood watching her before he said:

"I have to tell you how much it has meant to me to have you here and feel for the moment we have stepped out of time and are at peace with the world, or perhaps it would be better to say at peace with ourselves, for the world outside does not matter."

"That is what I think," Grania answered, but again it was hard to meet his eyes.

Reluctantly he turned to the cabin door and opened it.

"Come along," he said, "we must find out if there is any sign of your father, and you must be ready to talk to him and make him see your point of view."

Grania did not reply.

For the time being the *Comte* had given her a sense of security and as he had said, peace, and it was hard to adjust her mind to what lay ahead, or even to feel menaced by Roderick Maigrin.

The *Comte* was with her, the sun was shining, the sea was vividly blue, and the palm trees were moving with an inexpressible grace in the warm wind.

When they were on deck she smiled at one of the men who was working at the ropes and he saluted her with a gesture that was very French and smiled back.

The *Comte* stopped.

"This is Pierre, my friend and neighbour when we lived in Martinique."

He spoke in French and he said to his friend:

"Let me present you, Pierre, to the beautiful lady whose hospitality we are enjoying because Secret Harbour belongs to her."

Pierre sprang to his feet and when Grania put out her hand he raised her fingers to his lips.

"*Enchanté, Mademoiselle.*"

She thought they might have been meeting in some Salon in Paris or London instead of on the deck of a pirate ship.

She walked along the gang-plank and when the *Comte* joined her on the other side he said:

"Tomorrow, if I am still here, I would like you to meet the rest of my crew. It is best for them to remain anonymous, which is why I address them by their Christian names, but they are all men who have given up very different positions in life to save themselves from coming under the harsh jurisdiction of the English."

"Are we so harsh when we are in that position?" Grania asked.

"All conquerors seem intolerable to those who are conquered."

The *Comte* spoke roughly and for a moment Grania thought that he was hating her because she was an enemy.

Without meaning to she looked at him pleadingly, and he said:

"Forgive me, I am trying not to be bitter, and most of all, not to think of myself, but of you."

"You know I want you to do that," Grania said in a low voice.

But perceptively she knew that what he resented at the moment was that because their two countries were at war he could not offer her the safety of his estate in Martinique and they could not meet as ordinary people of different nationalities might do.

They moved through the thickness of the shrubs and pine trees until the house was in sight, then Grania stopped.

Everything was very quiet, and she was certain that her father had not returned home.

Abe would have warned her if he had been sighted before he arrived.

At the same time because the *Comte* was with her she had to be careful and make sure that she was not taking him into danger.

She thought for a moment that he would leave her and return to his ship, but instead, when she moved forward again he kept beside her and they walked up the steps onto the verandah and in through the open door.

It was then she heard Abe's voice talking to somebody in the kitchen and Grania called his name.

"Abe!"

He came to her instantly, and she saw that he was smiling and that all was well.

"Good news, Lady."

"Of the Master?"

"No. No news from Maigrin House, but Momma Mabel come back."

Grania gave a little exclamation of delight. Then she asked:

"To stay? To work?"

"Yes, Lady. Very glad to be back."

"That is splendid!"

She turned to the *Comte* and asked:

"Would you, *Monsieur* do me the honour of dining here with me tonight? I cannot promise you a meal cooked by a French Chef, but my mother always thought that Momma Mabel was the best cook on the island."

The *Comte* bowed.

"*Merci, Mademoiselle,* I have much pleasure in accepting your most gracious invitation."

Grania gave a little laugh of delight.

"Shall we dine at seven-thirty?"

"I will not be late."

The *Comte* bowed again, then turned and walked back the way they had come.

She watched him go until he was out of sight, then she said to Abe:

"Let us have a dinner-party the way we used to do it when Mama was here with the candelabra on the table and all the silver. Have we any wine?"

"One bottle, Lady," Abe answered. "I hide from Master."

Grania smiled.

Her mother when they had some really good wine, always kept a few bottles hidden for special occasions. Otherwise her father would drink it indiscriminately and share it with anybody who came to the house, whatever their status in life.

Now she was glad she had what she was sure was a good claret to offer the *Comte*.

"Make a fruit drink for before dinner," she said, "and of course coffee afterwards. I will go and speak to Momma Mabel."

She went to the kitchen and as she expected Momma Mabel's huge figure and wide smile seemed to fill the whole place.

She was an enormously fat woman, but actually she herself ate very little.

What she could do was to cook in a way which had made everybody on the island value the invitations they received to Secret Harbour.

Grania could remember the Governor complaining that they could never find anybody to cook as well as Momma Mabel, and she knew her mother suspected that he tried to entice her away with higher wages than she was receiving at Secret Harbour.

But Momma Mabel, like many of the other servants on the estate when her mother had been alive, thought of themselves as part of the family.

As long as they had enough to eat, whether they received high or low wages or none at all, was immaterial.

Grania talked to Momma Mabel in the kitchen for

some time, then went to find Abe and as she expected he was cleaning the silver.

She watched him for a moment, then said in a low voice:

"If the Master returns you must warn *Monsieur* that he must not come."

Abe thought this over before he nodded and said:

"'Morrow Bella come back."

"I thought she must have gone away."

"She not far."

Bella was the maid who had looked after Grania since she was small and when she grew older had made all her gowns.

The Countess had taught her all the arts of being a lady's-maid and Grania knew that when Bella returned she would be looked after and cosseted, and her clothes from London would last far longer than they would have done otherwise.

Then she thought that she was being over-optimistic: and her father would make her go back to Maigrin House and marry its owner, and Bella would not go with her.

Then she told herself that she must believe that when her father did arrive she would somehow convince him that she could not marry Roderick Maigrin, and that if they organised the plantation properly there would be enough money for them to live here quietly and be happy however much they might miss her mother.

"Please . . . God, make him . . . listen to me," she prayed. "Please . . . Please . . ."

She felt her prayer wended its way towards the Heavens, and because she wanted to pray and also to look her best for her dinner-party she went upstairs to her bedroom.

Her trunks had not been unpacked and she knew Abe was wise to leave them for Bella.

Nevertheless, she searched until she found one of the prettiest gowns she owned.

It was one her mother had made for her just before

she grew ill, and although she was still ostensibly at School Grania was sometimes allowed to dine with her mother's friends when there was a small party.

She held the gown up, shaking the creases out of the full skirt and knowing that the soft bodice with its small puffed sleeves was very becoming.

"I wonder if he will admire me," she thought.

She was not disappointed when she saw the expression in the *Comte's* eyes when he entered the Salon where she was waiting for him.

Although it was not yet dark she had lit some of the candles, and as he came in through the door she drew in her breath because he looked so magnificent.

She thought if he was smart and very elegant in his day clothes, in black satin knee-breeches and silk stockings with a long-tailed evening-coat and a frilled cravat no man could look more attractive.

If she found it difficult to find the words in which to greet him, it seemed as if the *Comte* felt the same.

For a moment they just stood looking at each other. Then as he walked towards her she felt almost as if he was enveloped with a light that came from within him.

It radiated out so that instinctively she wished to draw nearer and make herself a part of him.

"*Bon soir*, Grania."

"*Bon soir, Monsieur le Comte!*"

"And now let us say it in English," he said. "Good evening, Grania! You look very beautiful!"

"Good evening . . . !" she answered.

She wanted to call him by his Christian name but the word would not come to her lips.

Instead, because she was shy she said quickly:

"I hope the dinner will not disappoint you."

"Nothing could disappoint me tonight."

She looked up at him and thought that in the light from the candles his eyes held a very strange expression and that they were saying something to her she did not understand.

Then Abe came in with a fruit drink which also contained rum and just a touch of nutmeg sprinkled on top of the glass.

Grania took it from the silver tray, then once again it was difficult to find anything to say, and yet there was so much unsaid, and she felt despairingly that there would be no time to say it all.

They ate dinner in the Dining-Room which her mother had decorated with very pale green walls and green curtains so that it was as if one was outside in the garden.

The candles in the silver candelabra lit the table and as dusk came and the shadows deepened it was a little island of light on which there were only two people and nothing else encroached.

The dinner was delicious, although afterwards Grania could never remember what she had eaten.

The *Comte* approved of the claret, although he drank it absentmindedly, his eyes on Grania.

"Tell me about your house in Martinique," she asked.

As if he thought he must make an effort to talk he told her how his father had built it and how he had employed an architect who had actually come from France, to make it one of the finest houses on the island.

"There is one consolation," the *Comte* said. "I expected it, and I subsequently learned that the English have made it their Headquarters, which means it will not be damaged or deliberately burnt as some of the other planters' houses have been."

"I am so glad."

"And so am I. One day I will be able to show it to you, and you will see how comfortable the French can make themselves even when they are far from their native land."

"What about your properties in France?"

The *Comte* shrugged his shoulders.

"I am hoping the Revolution will not have affected

the South in the same way as it has the North. As Vence is a little fortified city perhaps it will escape."

"I hope so, for your sake," Grania said softly.

"Whatever happens, however," the *Comte* said, "I shall never return to France except for a visit. I have made Martinique my home just as my father did and I shall wait until it becomes mine again."

His voice deepened as he finished:

"Then I shall work to restore it to its former glory and make it a heritage for my children—if I have any."

There was a pause before the last few words, and because they were so closely attuned to each other Grania felt he was saying that if he could not have children with her, then he would remain unmarried.

Even as she thought of it she told herself she was being absurd.

Marriages for Frenchmen were arranged almost from the time they were born and it was only surprising that the *Comte* was not married already.

When he did, he would choose a Frenchwoman whose family equalled his own, and it would be almost impossible for him to take a wife of another nationality.

Her mother had often told her how proud the French were, especially the ancient families, and how those who had been guillotined had gone in the tumbrels with their heads held high, scornfully contemptuous of those who executed them.

Suddenly Grania felt insignificant and of no importance.

How could the daughter of a drunken and impecunious Irish Peer stand beside a man whose ancestors could doubtless trace their lineage back to Charlemagne?

She looked down at her plate conscious for the first time that the paint was peeling from the walls, the curtains which should have been replaced years ago were ragged, and the carpet on the floor was threadbare.

To the eyes of a stranger the whole place must look, she thought, dilapidated, neglected and poverty-stricken, and she was glad the shadows hid what she felt was her own humiliation.

Dinner was over and the *Comte* pushed back his chair.

"We have finished. Shall we go into the Salon?"

"Yes, of course," Grania said quickly. "I should have suggested it."

She moved ahead and when they entered the Drawing-Room the *Comte* shut the door behind them and walked very slowly to where Grania was standing by the sofa, feeling uncertain and unsure of herself, her eyes very large in her small face.

He came to her side and stood looking at her for a long time, and she waited, wondering what he was going to say, and yet afraid to ask what he was thinking.

Finally he said:

"I am leaving now. I am going back to my ship and tomorrow at dawn we shall set sail."

She gave a little cry.

"Why? Why? You . . . said you would . . . stay!"

"I cannot do so."

"But . . . why?"

"I think you are woman enough to know the reason," he said, "without my having to explain."

Her eyes widened and he went on:

"You are very young, but you are old enough to know that one cannot play with fire and not be burned. I have to go before I hurt you and before I hurt myself more than I have done already."

Grania clasped her hands together, but she could not speak and he said:

"I fell in love with your picture when I first saw it, and I dare not tell you what I feel for you now because it would be unfair."

"Un . . . fair?" Grania barely murmured.

"I have nothing to offer you, as well you know, and when I have gone you will forget me."

"That . . . will be . . . impossible."

"You think that now," the *Comte* said, "but time is a

great healer, and we must both forget, not only for your sake, but also for mine."

"Please . . . please . . ."

"No, Grania!" he said. "There is nothing either of us can do about the position in which we find ourselves. You are everything that a man could dream of and thinks he will never find. But you are not for me."

He put out his hand and took Grania's in his.

For a moment he stood looking down at it as if it was a precious jewel. Then slowly with an indescribable grace he bent his head and kissed first the top of her hand then, turning it over, the palm.

She felt a sensation like a streak of lightning flash through her to be followed by a warm weakness which made her long to melt into him and become part of him.

Then her hand was freed and he walked towards the door.

"Goodbye, my love," he said very quietly. "God keep and protect you."

She gave a little cry, then the door was shut and she heard his footsteps crossing the verandah and going down the steps into the garden.

Then she knew this was the end and there was nothing she could say or do to prevent it. . . .

⚜⚜⚜

A long time later Grania slipped into bed, and thought as she did so that this was where he had slept last night.

Abe had changed the sheets and they were cool and smooth, but she felt as if the impression of the *Comte's* body was still on them and the vibrations that had always passed from him to her were there. So it was almost as if she lay in his arms.

She could not cry, but she wanted to. Instead there was a stone in her breast that seemed to grow heavier and heavier every minute that passed.

"I have lost him! I have lost him!" she said to herself and knew there was nothing she could do about it.

She closed her eyes and went over the day hour by hour, minute by minute; the things they had said to each other, what she had felt, then finally the feelings he had evoked in her when he had kissed her hand.

She pressed her lips to her own palm, trying to remember an ecstasy that had been so swift that it was hard to believe it had happened.

She wondered what he had felt. Had it been the same?

Although she was very ignorant about men and love, she was sure he could not evoke such a response in her without feeling the same himself.

"I love him! I love him!"

The words seemed to repeat themselves over and over again in her mind and she wished that she could die, the world come to an end, and there would be no tomorrow.

She must have dozed a little, for suddenly the door burst open with a resounding crash and she gave a cry of fright as she woke and sat up in bed.

There was a light in her eyes and for the moment she could not see what was happening, then standing in the doorway, holding a lantern in his hand she saw Roderick Maigrin!

For a moment Grania felt she must be dreaming, and it could not be true that he was there, big and solid with his legs apart as if he balanced himself, his face crimson in the light of the lantern, his blood-shot eyes black and menacing as he glared at her.

"What the devil do you think you're doing," he asked in a furious voice, "running away like that? I've come to fetch you back."

For a moment it was impossible for Grania to reply. Then in a voice that did not sound like her own she asked:

"Wh-where is . . . Papa?"

"Your father was not capable of making the journey," Roderick Maigrin replied, "so I've come in his place, and a great deal of trouble you've put me to, young lady!"

Grania managed to straighten her back before she said in a voice that was clearer:

"I am not coming . . . back to your . . . house. I want . . . Papa to . . . come here."

"Your father will do nothing of the sort!"

He walked further into the room to stand at the end of the bed holding with one hand onto the brass knob of the bed-rail.

"If you hadn't been such a little fool as to run away in that cowardly manner," he said aggressively, "you would have learned that I have dealt with the rebels who I suppose frightened you, and there will be no more rebellions on my estate."

"How can . . . you be . . . sure?" Grania asked because it seemed the obvious question.

"I am sure," Roderick Maigrin replied, "because I made damned certain by killing the ring-leaders. They won't be able to spread any further sedition amongst my slaves!"

"You . . . killed them?"

"I shot them there and then before they had a chance to do any more damage."

He boasted of it in a manner which told Grania he had enjoyed the killings, and she was sure without asking that the men he had shot had been unarmed.

She wondered how she could make him leave.

Then as she felt for words she saw the way he was looking at her and became uncomfortably conscious of the transparency of her thin nightgown and that she was only covered by a sheet.

As instinctively she shrank back against the pillows he laughed the low, lewd laugh of a man who was very sure of himself.

"You'll look damned attractive," he said, "when I've taught you to behave like a woman. Now hurry up, and get dressed. I've a carriage waiting for you outside, although after the way you've behaved, I ought to make you walk."

"You . . . mean for me to . . . come back with you now . . . at this moment?" Grania asked, thinking she could not understand what he was saying.

"With the moonlight to guide us it'll be a romantic drive," Roderick Maigrin said jeeringly, "and I've a Parson waiting to marry us tomorrow morning."

Grania gave a little cry of horror.

"I will not . . . marry you! I will not . . . come! I . . . refuse! Do you understand? I refuse!"

He laughed.

"So that's your attitude! I suppose, Miss High and Mighty, you think I'm not good enough for you. Well, that's where you're mistaken! If I didn't bail your drunken father out of debt he'd be in prison. Get that into your head!"

He paused for a moment before his eyes narrowed and he said:

"If you are not prepared to accompany me dressed, I'll take you back as you are and enjoy doing it!"

It was a threat which he looked like putting into operation, for he moved around the bed-post towards her, and she gave a cry of sheer terror.

Then there was a knock on the open door and Roderick Maigrin turned his head.

Abe was standing there.

He carried a glass on a silver tray, and his face was impassive as he walked forward to say:

"You like drink, Sir."

"I would!" Roderick Maigrin replied, "but it's just like your damned impertinence to follow me up the stairs!"

He took the glass from the tray, then as Abe did not move he said:

"I suppose I have you to thank for helping your Mistress to run away in that blasted foolish fashion! I'll have you whipped in the morning for not informing your Master where you were going."

"I try wake Master, Sir," Abe said, "not move him."

Roderick Maigrin did not answer.

He was drinking the rum punch eagerly, that Abe had brought him, pouring it down his throat as if it was water.

He finished the glass, then set it down with a bang on the silver salver that Abe still held in his hand.

"Get me another!" he said, "and while I'm drinking it you can take your Mistress's trunks downstairs and put them on my carriage."

He paused before he added:

"She's coming back with me. You can follow and bring your Master's horses with you. You'll neither of you be coming back here."

"Yes, Sir," Abe said and turning walked from the room.

Grania wanted to call out to him not to leave her, but she knew that if Roderick Maigrin whipped or killed Abe there would be nothing she could do about it.

However it seemed that Abe's appearance had diverted Maigrin's worst attentions from herself, for he wiped his lips with the back of his hand and said:

"Hurry up and get dressed or you will find I'm not joking when I say I'll take you as you are. When you're my wife you'll be obedient, or you'll find it a painful experience to defy me."

As he spoke he walked towards the door.

Only as he reached it did he realise that if he took the lantern with him Grania would be left in the dark.

He put it down noisily on top of the chest-of-drawers, then holding onto the banisters he started to go down the stairs shouting as he did so:

"Light the candles, you lazy servant! How do you expect me to find my way in the dark?"

Grania felt as if she was paralysed into immobility, and she thought wildly that there was only one person who could save her now, not only from being taken back to Maigrin House, but from being married in the morning.

Even as she thought of the *Comte* she knew it was impossible to reach him.

The house had been built with only one staircase since the servants slept outside in cabins, one to each family.

The only way of escape would be through the hall and whether Roderick Maigrin sat in the Dining-Room or the Drawing-Room he would see her pass and undoubtedly follow her.

Then he would not only find out where she was going, but she would also have betrayed the *Comte* to a man she was certain would be vindictive in a manner that might end in the death of all those who were on his ship.

"What . . . can I . . . do? What can . . . I do?" Grania asked frantically.

Because there was no alternative she got out of bed.

She did not underestimate Roderick Maigrin's threat that he would take her dressed as she was, and she realised that he would positively delight in humiliating her and in proving his mastery over her and over her father.

Tomorrow she would be married to such a man!

When she thought of it she knew that she could never marry him. If that was the fate that was waiting for her she would kill herself before she actually became his wife.

And if she did kill herself he would probably still go on helping her father because he was an Earl, and his threat of letting him go to prison would never be put into operation while he still had some use for him socially.

"I will die!" Grania told herself firmly and wondered how she could do it.

Slowly, because time was passing, she began to dress.

She had just taken from the wardrobe the gown she had worn that day and slipped it over her head when Abe appeared.

He had walked so quietly up the stairs that she had

not heard him, and now as he came into the room she looked at him as she had done when she was a child and gone to him in trouble.

"Abe . . . Abe!" she murmured. "What . . . can I . . . do?"

Abe put his finger to his lips, then as he crossed the room to close one of her trunks and strap it up he said in a whisper she could hardly hear:

"Wait here, Lady, 'till I fetch you."

Grania looked at him in surprise wondering what he meant.

Then he picked up her trunk, put it on his shoulder and walked down the stairs, making no effort to walk quietly but seeming to accentuate the noise of his footsteps.

He must have passed through the hall, then a few minutes later Grania heard him say in his quiet, respectful voice:

"Another drink, Sir?"

"Give it me and get on with the luggage," Roderick Maigrin snarled, and Grania knew he was sitting just inside the Drawing-Room door.

"Three more trunks, Sir."

"Tell your mistress to come down and talk to me. I find it boring sitting here alone."

"Not ready, Sir," Abe replied, and by this time he was halfway up the stairs.

He closed a second trunk, and took it down.

Once again Grania heard him give Mr. Maigrin another drink.

She thought perhaps Momma Mabel was preparing them in the kitchen, but there was no sound of their voices and Abe came upstairs again. This time he was not empty-handed.

He was carrying a large washing-basket in which clothes after they had been washed were taken out to be attached to the line on which they would dry.

Grania looked at him in surprise as Abe set it down on

the floor and without speaking motioned her to get inside it.

She understood, and crouching down in the basket waited while he fetched a sheet from the bed and put it over her, tucking it down round her without speaking.

Picking up the basket by its two handles he started down the stairs.

Now Grania's heart was beating frantically as she knew that there was every chance even though he had had a lot to drink, of Roderick Maigrin thinking it strange that her clothes which had come from London should be in an open washing-basket.

She was however, aware that there was nothing else in the house in which she could be carried and Abe had taken a chance on the fact that Mr. Maigrin would not be expecting her to escape in such an undignified manner.

Abe reached the last step of the stairs.

Now he was walking across the hall and passing the open door of the Drawing-Room.

Through the open wicker-work Grania could see the lights from several candles and vaguely she thought she could distinguish the large body of the man she loathed sprawled in one of her mother's comfortable armchairs, a glass in his hand.

She was not sure if she really saw this with her eyes or with her imagination.

Then Abe had passed the door and was walking down the passage to the kitchen and she held her breath, just in case at the very last moment she would hear Roderick Maigrin shouting at them to stop.

But Abe walked on and now he carried her out through the back door and still not stopping moved into the thickness of the bougainvillaea bushes which grew right up to the walls of the house.

Only as he put the basket down on the ground did Grania realise that he had rescued her, and now she could reach the *Comte* without Roderick Maigrin knowing where she had gone.

Abe pulled off the sheet which had covered her and in the moonlight Grania could see his eyes looking at her anxiously.

"Thank you, Abe," she whispered. "I will go to the ship."

Abe nodded and said:

"Bring trunks later."

As he spoke he pointed and Grania saw that the two trunks he had already brought downstairs were hidden under the bushes, where it would be difficult for anybody who was unsuspecting, to see them.

"Be careful," she warned and he smiled.

Then as the terror which enveloped her swept over her like a tidal wave, she started to run frantically, wildly, as if Roderick Maigrin was already pursuing her down through the bushes and trees towards the harbour.

Chapter Five

Although it was dark between the trees Grania could not stop running. Then suddenly she bumped into something and realising at once that it was human, she gave a little scream of fear.

But even as it left her lips she knew who it was.

"Save . . . me! Save . . . me!" she begged frantically, speaking only in a whisper for fear her voice would be overheard.

"What has happened? What has upset you?" the *Comte* asked.

For a moment Grania was too breathless to speak.

She was only aware that she was close to the *Comte* and without really thinking of what she was doing she moved closer still hiding her face against his shoulder.

Slowly, almost as if he tried to prevent himself from doing so, he put his arms around her.

To feel him holding her was an indescribable comfort and after a moment she managed to say:

"He has . . . come to fetch me . . . away . . . I am to be . . . married tomorrow . . . and I thought I would . . . never escape."

"But you have," the *Comte* said. "My look-out saw lights in the windows of your house and I was coming to investigate in case something was wrong."

"Very . . . very wrong," Grania replied, "and I thought I could not . . . get away . . . but Abe . . . carried me out in a . . . washing-basket."

She thought as she spoke it ought to sound amusing, but she was still so frightened and so breathless with the speed at which she had run that what she said was almost incoherent.

"Is Maigrin in the house?" the *Comte* asked.

"He is . . . waiting for . . . me."

The *Comte* did not reply, he merely turned her round so that she faced in the direction of the ship and with his arms round her shoulders he led her through the trees to the harbour.

Because he was with her and was actually touching her she felt her agitation gradually subside.

At the same time she felt too limp and weak to think for herself any longer.

As if he understood, when they reached the gangway the *Comte* steadied her on it then walked behind her with his hands on her arms in case she lost her balance.

They stepped on deck and for a moment Grania thought there was no one about.

Then she saw a man halfway up the mast and

supposed he was the look-out of whom the *Comte* had spoken.

Now she was on deck she turned to look back at the house and realised that the trees and shrubs made it completely invisible. Only the man on the mast could have seen the lights in the windows which had made him alert the *Comte*.

They went down the steps to the cabin and she saw that when this had happened he was already in bed.

The sheets were thrown back and she saw now by the light of a lantern that he was wearing only a thin linen shirt open at the neck and dark pantaloons.

He stood looking at her and for the first time she was conscious of her own appearance and that her hair was hanging loose over her shoulders. She had made no effort to tidy it when she had dressed on Roderick Maigrin's instructions.

The *Comte* did not speak and Grania said the first thing that came into her mind.

"I . . . I cannot . . . go back!"

"No, of course not. But where is your father?"

"He was not . . . well enough to . . . come with Mr. Maigrin."

She did not look at the *Comte* as she spoke, but they both knew it was because the Earl was drunk that he had stayed behind at Maigrin House.

"Sit down," the *Comte* said unexpectedly. "I want to talk to you."

Obediently and also gladly because her legs felt as if they could no longer support her, Grania sat down in one of the comfortable armchairs.

There were two lanterns hanging in the cabin and she saw that the port-holes were covered by wooden shutters that she had not noticed earlier in the day, and she knew that no light could be seen from outside.

The *Comte* hesitated a moment. Then he said, still standing looking down at Grania:

"I want you to think seriously of what you are asking me to do."

She did not answer. She only looked at him appre-hensively, afraid he would refuse.

"You are sure," he went on, "there is not somebody else on the island with whom you could hide from your father? And could also keep you safe from the rebels?"

"There is . . . nobody," Grania said simply.

"And nowhere on any other island where you could be with friends?"

Grania hung her head.

"I know I am being a . . . nuisance to you," she said, "and I have no . . . right to ask you to . . . protect me. But at the moment it is difficult to think of . . . anything except that I am . . . terribly afraid."

She thought as she spoke she was stating her feelings very badly, and what she really wanted to do was to beg the *Comte* to keep her with him.

Then she knew it was a very reprehensible way to behave when she had only just met him, and he had made it quite clear that she could have no part in his life.

Because she thought he must know what she was thinking she looked up at him and said:

"I am . . . sorry . . . I am very . . . sorry to ask . . . this of you."

He smiled and she felt as if a dozen more lights illu-minated the cabin.

"There is nothing to be sorry about from my point of view," he said, "but I am trying to think of yours."

He paused before he went on:

"You have your whole life in front of you and if your mother had been alive you would have taken your place in London Society. It is hardly a reasonable alternative to be the only woman aboard a pirate ship."

"But it is where . . . I want to . . . be," Grania said almost beneath her breath.

"Are you quite sure of that?"

"Quite . . . quite . . . sure."

She felt an irresistible impulse to rise and go close to him as she had been a few minutes before. She wanted

387

his closeness, his strength, the feeling of security he gave her.

Then, because her yearning to do that was so intense that she felt the colour come into her face, she looked away from him shyly.

As if she had told him what he wanted to know the *Comte* said:

"Very well. We will leave here at dawn."

"Do you mean that . . . do you really mean it?" Grania asked.

"God knows if I am doing the right thing," he answered, "but I have to protect you. That man is not fit to associate with any decent woman."

Grania gave an exclamation of horror.

"Suppose he . . . finds us? Suppose when he . . . realises I am not in the house he comes . . . here?"

"That is unlikely," the *Comte* said, "and if he does I will deal with him. But it will be impossible to sail before morning without a wind."

"He will not . . . suspect there is a ship in the . . . harbour," Grania said as if she was reassuring herself, "and if he does come this way, Abe will warn us."

"I am sure he will," the *Comte* agreed.

"When Mr. Maigrin has . . . gone, Abe will bring my . . . trunks from . . . where he has . . . hidden them."

"I will tell the man on watch to look out for him," the *Comte* said and went from the cabin.

When he had gone Grania clasped her hands together and said a prayer of thankfulness.

"Thank you, God, for letting me stay with him! Thank You that the ship was here when I most needed it!"

She thought how terrifying it would have been if to escape from Roderick Maigrin she had had to run off into the jungle alone and hide amid the tropical vegetation.

She had the feeling if she had done so he would

somehow have found her. Perhaps with dogs, perhaps instructing his own slaves to search.

"Thank You . . . God . . . thank You for the . . . *Comte*," she said as she heard his footsteps returning.

He came into the cabin and once again Grania resisted an impulse to run to him and hold onto him to make sure he was really there.

"There are still lights burning in the house," he said, "so I imagine that your unwelcome visitor has not left."

As he spoke there was a faint whistle from outside.

"I think that is to tell us that Abe is arriving," he said.

Grania jumped to her feet.

"I hope he is all right. I am terribly . . . afraid that when Mr. Maigrin finds me . . . gone he will vent his . . . rage on Abe."

She followed the *Comte* out on deck carefully shutting the cabin door behind her.

It was however quite easy to see by moonlight and when she walked over to the side of the ship she saw Abe walking along by the water's edge, carrying one of her trunks.

When he came on board she was waiting for him.

"What is happening, Abe?"

"Everything all right, Lady," Abe replied. "Mister Maigrin asleep."

"Asleep!" Grania exclaimed.

Abe grinned.

"Put little powder in last drink. He sleep now 'til morning. Wake with bad head!"

"That was clever of you, Abe."

"Very clever!" the *Comte* agreed.

"I bring luggage," Abe said. "You go 'way, not come back 'til safe."

"That is what I want to do," Grania replied, "but what about you? I am afraid Mr. Maigrin will whip you."

"I all right, Lady," Abe replied. "He not find me."

Grania knew there were many places on the island where Abe could hide, and she knew that however

much her father needed him it would be impossible for
him to face Roderick Maigrin's anger and the cruelty
with which he treated all those who served him.

"I fetch other trunks," Abe said, "and Joseph take
carriage."

Grania was surprised.

"Where will he take it?"

Abe's smile was very broad and she could see the flash
of his white teeth in the moonlight.

"When Mister wake he think you go Master. Joseph
leave horses and come back."

"That is a brilliant idea," Grania exclaimed, "and
even if he thinks I am hiding, Mr. Maigrin will look for
me near his own house."

Abe smiled with an almost childish delight. Then he
said again:

"I fetch other trunk."

"Wait a minute," the *Comte* said, "I will send somebody with you."

He spoke to the man up the mast who slid down onto
the deck. The *Comte* told him what to do and he followed Abe across the gang-plank.

The *Comte* picked up Grania's trunk and carried it
towards the cabin.

She ran ahead to open the door for him but when
they were inside she said:

"I cannot take your cabin. There must be somewhere
else I can sleep."

"This is where as my guest, you *will* sleep," he said
firmly, "and I hope you will be comfortable."

Grania gave a little laugh of sheer happiness.

"Very comfortable . . . and very safe," she said.
"How can I thank you for being so kind to me?"

He did not answer, but as they looked at each other
she had the feeling that he was telling her that he was as
happy as she was and there was no need for them to
express what they felt in words.

Because his expression made her feel shy Grania said
quickly:

"I must give Abe some money. I have some money with me which I put in one of my trunks."

She had hidden the money she had brought with her from England because she was afraid that her father would take it from her and she would be penniless.

When her mother had become ill and then grown weaker and weaker, she had said to Grania:

"I want, dearest, to draw out from my Bank all the money I have left."

"Why should you want to do that, Mama?" Grania had enquired.

There had been a long pause as if the Countess was considering what she should say.

Then as if she felt it was a mistake to tell Grania anything but the truth she said:

"You must have some money of your own which is not to be thrown away on the gaming-tables or the drink your father finds indispensible. It will not only pay for your trousseau when you marry, but you will be independent—if things go wrong!"

She did not elaborate on what she meant and because her mother was weak Grania knew how important it was to do what she wanted and not ask too many questions.

"I understand, Mama. You do not have to explain to me. I will do exactly what you wish me to do."

She had gone to the Bank the same day, and drawn out the few hundred pounds that her mother had left.

"Are you wise, My Lady?" the Manager had asked, "to carry so much money about with you?"

"I will put it in a safe place," Grania promised.

She knew he thought she was being reckless, but now it was a joy to know that she could give Abe enough to support himself and pay old servants and the slaves who were still supposed to be in their employment, though they had probably received no wages.

"Let me do that for you," the *Comte* said.

"Of course not," Grania replied, "I have my pride. Actually I have some money and this is the way I want to spend it."

She thought as she spoke that when her mother was speaking of her trousseau she had no idea that her daughter might have been married to the man she had always despised and disliked.

The *Comte* undid the straps of her trunk and opened it for her, and she found the money she sought at the bottom of it.

She counted out fifteen golden sovereigns, and thought Abe would think that was a large sum and it would last him a long time.

The *Comte* had left the cabin and when she placed the money in a small bag which had also come from the Bank she went on deck to join him.

He was watching for Abe and when he appeared with the Frenchman also carrying a trunk, Grania had the feeling that the *Comte* had been anxious just in case Roderick Maigrin had not been asleep and might have followed them.

The trunks were brought aboard and Grania took Abe to one side.

"Here is some money for you, Abe," she said. "It is for yourself and for anyone else on the plantation you think has earned it."

She put the bag into his hand and went on:

"When Mr. Maigrin gives up looking for me get the slaves to clear the undergrowth around the nutmeg trees. When things are better we will plant more of them and hope to have a crop that will make more money than we have had in the past."

"Good idea, Lady."

"Take care of the house, Abe, until I come back."

"You come back—Master miss you."

"Yes, of course I will," Grania answered, "but only when it is safe."

As she said the words she looked over her shoulder and saw that the *Comte* was not far away.

"How will we know when it is safe for us to return?" she asked.

"You will want news of your father," he replied, "but

we must be sure that the rebels have not taken St. George's as well as the other parts of the island."

"If safe, Sir," Abe said. "I leave sign."

"That is what I was going to suggest."

"If safe come here," Abe said as if he was thinking aloud, "I put white flag outside entrance."

"And if there is danger?" the *Comte* enquired.

"If rebels or Mister Maigrin in house, I leave black flag."

Grania knew the flags would be only white or dark rags tied to a stick, but the message nevertheless would be very clear.

She put out her hand to Abe saying:

"Thank you, Abe, you have looked after me ever since I was a child, and I know you will not fail me now."

"You safe, Mister Beaufort, Lady."

He shook her hand and turned to leave.

"Please, Abe, take good care of yourself," Grania pleaded. "I cannot lose you."

His smile was very confident and she knew that in a way he was enjoying the excitement and even the danger of what they had just passed through.

Then as he disappeared amongst the pine trees the *Comte* said:

"You are now under my command, and I am going to give you your orders."

Grania gave a little laugh.

"Aye, aye, Sir! Or is that only what the English sailors say?"

"Tomorrow I will teach you what to say in French," the *Comte* replied, "but now you are to go to bed and sleep. I think you have been through enough dramatics for one night."

She smiled at him and he walked ahead of her to open the cabin door. The man who had fetched the trunks with Abe followed and put them tidily against one wall.

"Do you want me to open them now?" the *Comte* asked.

Grania shook her head.

"I have everything I need in the one you have opened already."

The *Comte* extinguished one of the lanterns which were hanging from the ceiling and lifted down the other to place it beside the bed.

He undid the little glass door so that it was easy for her to extinguish it.

"Is there anything else you want?"

"No, nothing," she replied, "and thank you. I am so happy to be here that I just want to keep saying 'Thank You' over and over again."

"You can thank me tomorrow," the *Comte* said, "but now I think it important for you to rest. *Bonne nuit, Mademoiselle, dormez bien.*"

"*Bon soir, mon Capitaine,*" Grania replied.

Then she was alone.

When Grania awoke it was to feel the rolling of the ship, hear the creaking of the boards, the straining of the wind in the sails, and somewhere far away in the distance the noise of voices and laughter.

For a moment she could not think where she was, then she remembered that she was at sea, far away from Roderick Maigrin and from the fear that had been like a stone in her breast.

"I am safe! I am safe!" she wanted to cry, and knew she was happy because she was with the *Comte*.

She had gone to sleep very conscious that her head was on his pillow, that she lay on the mattress on which he had slept, and was covered by the sheet that had been his.

She felt close to him as she had felt when she ran into him in the darkness and had hidden her face against his chest.

She was conscious then of the warmth of his body

even before she had known the strength of his arms and felt in her dreams, he was still holding her.

She sat up in bed and pushed her hair back from her forehead.

She was sure that she had slept for a long time and it must be late, yet it did not matter if it was.

There was no Parson waiting for her, no Roderick Maigrin trying to touch her, no horrors lurking amongst the trees or in the house.

"I am safe!" Grania said again, and got out of bed.

By the time she was dressed she knew she was hungry. At the same time she did not hurry.

She found a small mirror amongst her other things and took a long time brushing her hair and arranging it in the way she had worn it in London, and which her mother had thought was very becoming.

Then she found a gown that was one of her prettiest, and only when the tiny mirror told her that she looked very elegant did she open the cabin door to the blinding sunshine.

The deck that had seemed deserted before was now full of activity.

There were men at the ropes, men climbing up and down the masts, and the sails were billowing out in the sea breeze.

The sea was dazzlingly blue and the gulls were whirling overhead and making a great deal of noise about it.

Grania stood looking around. She knew that she was looking for only one man and when she saw him she felt her heart give a leap as if she had been afraid he would not be there.

He was at the wheel, and she thought that with his hands on the spokes, his head lifted as if he searched the far horizon, no man could look more handsome or more omnipotent, as if he was not only Captain of his ship, but master of everything he surveyed.

She would have gone towards him, but he saw her

and gave the wheel over to another man and came walking towards her.

As he joined her she saw his eyes travel over her, and there was a faint smile on his lips as if he realised the trouble she had taken to make herself look attractive and was appreciative.

"I am so very late," Grania said because she felt he was waiting for her to speak.

"It is almost midday," he replied. "Would you wait for luncheon, or would you like to have the breakfast you missed this morning?"

"I will wait," Grania replied, because she wished to stay with him.

He put his arm through hers and led her along the deck stopping every few steps to introduce her in turn to men working at the ropes.

"This is Pierre, this is Jacques, this is André, and this is Leo."

Only later did Grania know that three of the men on board had been very rich when they left Martinique.

Two were planters in the same way that the *Comte* considered himself one, and had owned a large number of slaves, the third, Leo, was a Lawyer with the biggest practice in St. Pierre, the Capital of Martinique.

She was to learn that they showed their courage in the way they were never bitter about the fate that had swept their possessions from them, but merely optimistic that one day their fortunes would change and they would return home to claim what they had lost.

The rest of the men aboard were the personal servants of the *Comte* and his friends together with several young clerks from Leo's office, all of whom were deeply grateful for the privilege of escaping with him when they might have been imprisoned or forced to work for their conquerors.

In the next two days while they were at sea Grania learned it was not only a busy ship but a happy one.

From first thing in the morning until last thing at

night the crew sang, whistled and laughed amongst themselves as they worked.

None of the men were trained seamen, and the mere running of the ship required not only all their intelligence, but the use of muscles they had not employed before.

It appeared to Grania as if they made it a game, and she would lean over the rail of the poop-deck watching them, listening to them singing and cracking jokes with each other, and often tossing a coin to decide who would climb the tall raking spars to trim the sails.

She noticed that even amongst his friends the *Comte* appeared always to be in command, always the leader.

She had the feeling, and was sure she was not wrong that they trusted him just as she did. He gave them a sense of safety, and without him they too would have been afraid.

She had thought when she went aboard the ship that she would be alone with the Comte, but this was something that did not happen.

Always there seemed to be so much for him to do, always too he appeared to be looking out for danger.

Whenever the look-out reported a ship on the horizon they made off in another direction, and Grania was not certain at first whether this was something he would have done if she had not been on board.

She had also thought that they would have meals together, but she learned that the *Comte's* three friends always had dinner with him and when they were at sea luncheon was a meal through which everybody went on working.

Henri the Chef prepared cups of soup which the men drank as they performed their duties. There was also cheese or pâte, placed between long pieces of French bread, sliced horizontally.

Grania ate like the others, either on deck or, when she was tired of the sunshine, alone in her cabin while she read a book.

She found the *Comte's* books not only interesting but also intriguing.

She had guessed that he would enjoy Rousseau and Voltaire, but she had not expected that he would have a large collection of poetry books, and English poetry at that, or that he would also have several religious books on the shelves.

"I suppose he is a Catholic," she said to herself.

Perhaps it was due to the air or the movement of the ship, or maybe because she was content and happy, that Grania slept in the *Comte's* bed deeply and dreamlessly, as if she was a child, to wake with a feeling of excitement because it was the beginning of another day.

Then late one afternoon, after the heat was over they came in sight of St. Martin.

At dinner the previous night the *Comte* and his friends had told Grania that the smallest territory in the world was shared by two sovereign states.

"Why?" Grania had asked.

Leo, who was the Lawyer, laughed.

"According to legend," he said, "the Dutch and the French prisoners of war who had been brought to the island in 1648 to destroy the Spanish Fort and buildings came from their hiding-places after the Spanish had been routed and realised they had an island to share."

"By peaceful means," Jacques interposed.

"They had had enough of fighting," the *Comte* added, "and so the boundaries were decided by a walking contest."

Grania laughed.

"How can they have done that?"

"A Frenchman and a Dutchman," Leo explained, "started at the same spot and walked around the island in opposite directions, having agreed that the boundary line should be drawn straight across the island where they met."

"What a wonderful idea," Grania cried. "Why can they not do something so simple on the other islands?"

"Because the others are much larger," Leo replied.

"The Frenchman's walking-pace was stimulated by wine, so that he went faster than the Dutchman who was actually slowed down because he preferred his own Dutch gin."

All the men laughed, but Leo said:

"Whatever the origin of the boundary, the French and Dutch have lived in harmony ever since."

"That is what I call very, very sensible," Grania said.

For the first time since she had come aboard the *Comte* stayed behind after his three friends had left the cabin.

Grania looked at him enquiringly and he said:

"I have something to suggest to you, but I am rather afraid you will not like it."

"What is it?" Grania asked apprehensively.

The *Comte* did not answer for a moment, and she realised he was looking at her hair.

"Is . . . anything wrong?"

"I was just thinking how beautiful you are," he said, "and it would certainly be wrong for me to change you in any way, but it is something which I think is important."

"What is?"

"I have to think of you," the *Comte* said, "and not only your safety but also your reputation."

"In what way?"

"When we arrive at St. Martin, even though my house is very isolated you can well imagine that in the space of only twenty-one square miles everything is known and gossiped about."

Grania nodded.

"That is why I think you must change your identity."

"You mean . . . I must not be . . . English?"

"The French, even in St. Martin, are very patriotic."

"Then can I be French, like you?"

"That is of course what I would like you to be," the *Comte* replied, "and I thought I could introduce you as my cousin, *Mademoiselle* Gabrielle de Vence."

"I shall be delighted to be your cousin."

"There is one difficulty."

"What is that?"

"You do not look in the least French, but, if I may say so, very English."

"I always thought that my eye-lashes, which are dark, I owe to my Irish ancestry."

"But your hair which is like sunshine is as obvious as any Union Jack."

Grania laughed.

"I think I am insulted that you should think it is red, white and blue!"

"What I am suggesting is that it should be a different colour," the *Comte* said quietly.

She looked at him in astonishment.

"Are you asking me to . . . dye my hair?"

"I have talked to Henri," he said, "and he has distilled what he calls 'a rinse' which is easily washed out when you wish to revert to your own nationality."

Grania looked doubtful, but the *Comte* went on:

"I promise you it is not black or anything unpleasant. It will just change the shining gold of your hair to something a little more ordinary, the colour that a Frenchwoman could easily own, although she would never, I am afraid, have a skin so clean and soft that it is like the petals of a camelia."

Grania gave a little smile.

"That sounds very poetic."

"I find it very difficult not to be when I am talking to you. At the same time, Grania, as you have pointed out before, the French are sensible and realistic, and that is what we both must be."

"Yes . . . of course," she agreed.

But she was reluctant to dye her hair, feeling that perhaps she would not look so attractive in the *Comte's* eyes.

Henri came to the cabin to explain to her what she must do, and first of all he dipped a tress of her hair in a liquid he had in a jug and she saw that it took away the gold and darkened it considerably.

"No, no! I cannot do it!" she exclaimed.

He put down the small jug and brought another one filled with fresh water, and dipping her hair once again he swirled it round then held it up.

The brown had vanished.

"That is very clever of you, Henri!" Grania cried.

"It is a very good dye," Henri said with delight. "When there is no more war I will put it on the market and make my fortune!"

"I am sure you will"

Henri explained to her that if they used a walnut dye, or even one distilled from nutmegs, it would take months to remove, and the hair would have to grow out before she was absolutely free of it.

"This is different," he said proudly, "and one day, you see, *M'mselle*, everyone in Paris will be asking for 'Henri's Quick-Change Colour'!"

Grania laughed.

"I am delighted, Henri, to be the first to try it."

Henri brought a basin and towel and dyed her hair for her.

When she looked at herself in a much larger mirror than she had used before, she thought at first she looked like a stranger and one she did not particularly admire.

Then she knew that if her skin had seemed white before, now it glowed like a petal, and in a way she thought that the darkness of her hair made her look intriguing and perhaps a little mysterious.

She came on deck the next morning somewhat self-consciously, but the *Comte's* friends had no inhibitions.

They complimented her so vociferously that she blushed and ran away from them! When she reached the *Comte* who once again was at the steering-wheel he smiled and said:

"I see I have a very pretty new relative! You will certainly embellish the annals of the *Comtes de Vence!*"

"I was afraid you might be ashamed of me."

He merely smiled at her and there was a look in his eyes which told her far better than words that she had not lost his admiration which was all she wanted to know.

She stayed beside him and soon he realised that she wanted him to show her how to steer the ship.

It was not so much the excitement of doing something that gave her a feeling of power, but that to make certain she did it properly he stood behind her at the wheel putting his hands on the spokes above hers.

She could feel the closeness of his body and felt as they looked out towards the horizon that they were sailing over the edge of the world and the past was left behind them.

It was only when the *Comte* had walked away from her that she suddenly felt alone.

She had been so happy these past days and she was afraid when they reached St. Martin that things would change.

She was watching him on the deck below and for a moment she lost control of the wheel and the ship keeled over in the breeze.

Instantly one of the men came to help set it to rights.

She gave the wheel to him and walked onto the deck to follow the *Comte*.

It was then she knew quite suddenly that she wanted to be near him, that she wanted to feel him close to her and that it was an agony when he was away.

"What is the matter with me?" she asked herself. "How can I feel like this?"

Then she knew the answer.

It was as if it was being fired at her in an explosion from one of the cannons which stood along the sides of the deck.

She was in love!

In love with a man she had known only for a few days; a man who meant safety and security to her, but was in fact a pirate, an exile, a man with a price on his head, outlawed not only by the English, but also by the French.

"I love him whatever he is!" Grania told her heart.

Because she could not bear to be away from him for one moment longer she went to his side.

CHAPTER SIX

GRANIA SAW THAT St. Martin was not as beautiful as Grenada with its mountains and its tropical vegetation, but it was certainly very attractive with its golden beaches.

She had also noticed as they sailed alongside the island many small attractive bays.

They dropped anchor, and although she realised it was not as secluded as Secret Harbour it was nevertheless a good place for a pirate ship to hide.

While the crew were busy furling the sails the *Comte* took Grania ashore and they walked a little way up the low cliffs until in front of them she saw a very attractive house.

It was quite small but resembled the older plantation houses in Grenada and had the usual verandah over which vines were growing profusely.

The *Comte* did not say anything and she wondered if she should tell him how pretty she thought the house looked, but she felt he was thinking of his real home in Martinique and wishing they were there.

He opened the door with a key. Then as they walked through a small hall into a Sitting-Room at one side of it, she gave an exclamation of surprise.

The room was furnished with exquisite inlaid French

furniture including some very fine marble-topped commodes with gilt handles and beautiful embellished feet.

On the walls were portraits which she knew without
being told were of the *Comte's* ancestors, and guessed
these were the possessions he had brought to safety
from his house in Martinique.

There were also many china ornaments, among
which she recognised some pieces of Sèvres, while on
the floor was laid a very fine Aubusson carpet.

"So this is where you hid your treasures!" she exclaimed.

"At least they should be safe here," he answered.

"I am so very, very glad you were able to bring them
away."

She wanted to go round looking at the pictures and at
the china, but the *Comte* said in a very different voice:

"I want to talk to you, Grania, so please listen to me."

She looked up at him enquiringly and he went on:

"You came to me for protection, and that is what I
want to give you. I am going now to find the woman
who looks after this house in my absence and ask her if
she will come here to sleep."

"But . . . why?" Grania asked. "And . . . where
will . . . you be?"

"You must be aware that it would be quite wrong for
me to stay here with you," the *Comte* replied. "I shall
sleep in the ship with my crew and there will be nothing
to frighten you."

Grania said nothing and after a moment he went on:

"I do not have to tell you that you must play your
part of being a Frenchwoman at all times, and to do so
you must speak French, think French and to all intents
and purposes *be* French."

"I will try," Grania said in a low voice, "but I thought
now we were here we could be . . . together."

She spoke pleadingly, but to her surprise the *Comte*
was not looking at her, but had turned his face away and
she had the feeling he was going to say that was impossible.

Then at that moment there was a sudden shout from the front of the house, and the next minute they heard footsteps running across the verandah and Jean came bursting into the room.

"*Vite—vite! Monsieur!*" he said urgently. "*Un bateau en vue!*"

He pointed as he spoke in the direction of the sea.

"Stay here!" the *Comte* said abruptly to Grania.

Then he had gone from the house, closing the door behind him.

She went to the window to see him running towards the cliffs and Jean just ahead of him.

When he had gone she stood looking out and although she could see nothing, she was frightened there was danger, and she wished she was with the *Comte* and not left behind.

To see a ship at sea, she knew, always spelt danger for him, and she had been well aware how all the way from Grenada the *Comte* had a look-out posted on the mast, and at the first indication that there was another ship in sight had immediately changed course.

She wondered if they had been seen coming into the bay, or perhaps it was an English Man o' War intent on invading St. Martin.

The *Comte* and his friends had been quite certain this would not happen, but there was always the chance that the English would change their minds and wish to add to their conquests amongst the islands.

It was all very perturbing and although Grania stood for a long time at the window hoping she could see some sign of their own ship or the one Jean had come to warn them about, there was only the blue horizon.

It grew more and more indistinct as the afternoon merged into evening and the sun began to sink.

She wanted to go to the top of the cliffs to see what was happening, but the *Comte* had told her to stay where she was and because she loved him she wished to obey him.

After a little while she started to look around the small

house, but it was hard to concentrate on anything but the fact that the *Comte* might be in danger, and she would not know what was happening.

Slowly she went upstairs and found one large important bedroom which she knew must be his, and several others.

They were all beautifully furnished, but the *Comte's* bedroom had a magnificent French bed with curtains falling from a gold corola.

She knew he must have brought it here from Martinique and she admired the painted dressing-table which was more suited to a woman than to a man.

There were small commodes on either side of the bed which she thought were the work of one of the great French craftsmen, and the pictures which were not of his ancestors were she realized painted by Boucher.

It was all so lovely that she thought it was a room for love, then blushed at her own thoughts.

She moved restlessly about until she went downstairs again to discover a small Dining-Room with more of the Comte's ancestors on the walls and a kitchen which she was sure must delight Henri.

There was also a small room lined with books, and she told herself that at least here she would have plenty to read.

She had however, no wish to read at the moment. All she wanted was to be with the *Comte* and again she went to the window, frightened because he was away for so long.

Now the sun was sinking in a blaze of glory and when the last crimson light disappeared night came swiftly.

Although the stars were coming out one by one and a new moon was climbing up the sky Grania thought she was encompassed by the darkness of despair and was afraid she would never see the Comte again.

Supposing he had sailed out to sea to investigate the enemy ship, and there had been a battle? Supposing he had been defeated and was either drowned or taken prisoner?

She did not know what would happen to her if she was never to see him again.

She wanted to cry out at the agony of knowing he had disappeared and there would be no one to help her.

What was more, she knew despairingly, since her luggage had not been brought ashore, that she had no money and no possessions. But that was immaterial beside the fact that she had lost the *Comte*.

Now she thought her agony was like a thousand knives piercing her heart and making her suffer in a way that was almost unbearable.

Because her eyes ached from staring into the darkness she moved across the room feeling her way to a chair and sat down.

She put her head in her hands, half-praying, half just suffering helplessly like a small animal caught in a trap.

"Send him back to me . . . please, God, send him . . . back to me," she prayed.

She felt as if the darkness suffocated her and she was completely and utterly lost!

Suddenly when she felt she could bear it no longer and must go to the bay and look for him, the front door opened and he was there.

She could not see him, but she gave a little cry that seemed to echo round the walls and ran instinctively finding him.

She threw herself against him, put her arms around his neck, holding onto him and crying as she did so:

"You . . . have come . . . back! I thought I had . . . lost you! I was frightened . . . so desperately . . . frightened that I would . . . never see you . . . again!"

The words fell over themselves, and because she had been so frightened and her relief at his return was so overwhelming she cried not quite involuntarily:

"I love you . . . and I cannot . . . live without . . . you!"

The *Comte* threw something he was carrying down on the floor and put his arms around her.

He held her so tightly that she could hardly breathe, then his lips came down on hers.

As she felt his mouth hold her captive she knew that this was what she had been wanting, what she had been yearning for and what she thought she would never know.

His kiss was fierce, demanding, insistent, and she felt as if she gave him her heart, her soul, her whole self.

The agony of fear she had been feeling was gone. Instead there was an indescribable rapture, an ecstasy that seemed to fill the room with a light which came from within themselves.

The wonder of it told her that this was not just human love, but something more perfect and part of the divine.

When the *Comte* had kissed her until she felt that she was no longer herself but utterly and completely his he raised his head to say in a voice that was unsteady:

"My darling I did not mean this to happen."

"I love . . . you!"

"And I love you," he answered. "I fought against it and tried to prevent myself saying so, but you have made it impossible."

"I . . . thought I had . . . lost you."

"You will never do that as long as I am alive," he replied, "but *ma cherie,* I have been trying to protect you from myself and from my love."

"You . . . love me?"

"Of course I love you!" he said almost angrily, "but it is something I should not do any more than that you should love me."

"How can I help it?" Grania asked.

Then he was kissing her again, kissing her until she felt as if he carried her into the sky and there were no problems, no difficulties, nothing but themselves and their love.

A long time later the *Comte* said:

"Let me light the candles, my precious. We can hardly stay here in the dark for ever, although I want to go on kissing you."

"That is . . . what I want . . . you to . . . do," Grania said breathlessly.

He kissed her again. Then with an effort he took his arms from her and walked a few steps to a table at the side of the stairs.

He lit a candle and Grania could see him. She thought his face in the light was illuminated as if by some celestial fire.

His eyes were on her but as if he forced himself not to take her in his arms he lit a taper from the candle and went into the Sitting-Room to light the candles there.

Only when the room was illuminated and looking very beautiful did he say:

"Forgive me for upsetting you, *ma petite*."

"What happened? What was the . . . boat you went to . . . investigate? Was it . . . English?"

The *Comte* blew out the taper.

Then he walked towards Grania and put his arms around her again.

"I know what you have been thinking," he said. "It was an English boat which my crew had sighted but it constituted no danger to us."

Grania gave a cry of relief and put her head against his shoulder. The *Comte* kissed her forehead before he went on:

"But in a way it may concern you."

"Concern me?" Grania asked in surprise.

"There must have been a battle not far from here," he said, "perhaps two or three days ago."

It was difficult for Grania to listen because she was so content to be in his arms.

"He is with me and I am safe," she kept thinking to herself.

"I imagine," the *Comte* went on, "that an English Man o' War, H.M.S. Heroic, was sunk, because the boat which Jean came to tell us about was from that ship. It contained an Officer and eight ratings."

"They were . . . English?" Grania asked nervously.

"They were English," the *Comte* replied, "but they were all dead!"

It seemed wrong, Grania knew, but she could not help feeling relieved that they could therefore constitute no danger to the *Comte* and his crew.

"There was nothing we could do for them," the *Comte* continued, "except bury them at sea, but I took their papers which will prove their identity should it ever be necessary."

He paused before he added:

"The Officer's name, and he was a Commander, was Patrick O'Kerry."

Grania stiffened.

"Patrick O'Kerry?" she repeated.

"I thought he might be some relation of yours, and I have brought you his papers and also his jacket and cap in case you would wish to keep them."

There was a little pause. Then Grania said:

"Patrick was . . . my cousin . . . and although I hardly knew him . . . Papa will be very upset."

"We will have to let him know sometime."

"Yes . . . of course," Grania agreed, "and he will be upset not only because Patrick was his . . . nephew, but he was also . . . his heir . . . and now there are . . . no more O'Kerrys and the . . . title will die out."

"I can understand how that would upset your father."

"There is certainly not much to inherit," Grania said, "but Papa was the fourth Earl, and now there will never be a fifth."

"I am sorry about that," the *Comte* said softly. "I did not want to upset you, my darling."

Because his arms were around her again and his lips were on her cheek, it was hard for Grania to feel anything but the joy that he was touching her.

At the same time it seemed such a waste of life.

Her Cousin Patrick who had called to see her mother

when they were in London, had been so excited at being posted to a new ship and going out to the Caribbean. It seemed tragic now to think that he was dead.

She remembered how he had talked to her mother about the West Indies and she had thought him a pleasant young man, but he had not paid her much attention as she was only a School-girl.

"What I think very surprising," the *Comte* said, "is that your cousin was dark. Somehow I expected that all your relations would be fair like you."

Grania gave him a faint little smile.

"There are fair O'Kerrys like Papa and me, and there are also dark ones who are supposed to have Spanish blood in them."

She thought the *Comte* was surprised and explained:

"When the ships of the Spanish Armada on their way to invade England, were wrecked on the south coast of Ireland many of the Spanish sailors never returned home."

The *Comte* smiled.

"So they found the O'Kerry ladies attractive."

"I suppose they must have done," Grania replied, "and they certainly left their imprint on the future generations."

"No wonder some are dark and some are fair," the *Comte* said, "but I prefer you fair, and one day, *ma belle*, you can revert to looking English. But I am afraid whatever the colour of your hair you will be French."

Grania looked up at him questioningly and he said:

"You will marry me? I thought I could pretend you were my cousin, and keep you at arms' length, but you have made it impossible."

"I do not . . . wish to be at . . . arms' length," Grania murmured, "and I want . . . to be your . . . wife."

"Heaven knows what sort of life I can offer you," the *Comte* said, "and you know I have nothing to give you but my heart."

"I do not want anything else," Grania answered, "but

411

are you quite . . . quite sure I shall not be an . . . encumbrance and you will . . . . regret marrying me?"

"That would be impossible," the *Comte* said. "I have
been looking for you all my life and now I have found
you, whatever is the right and proper or sensible thing
to do, I know I cannot lose you."

Then he was kissing her again, and it was impossible
to think, but only to feel.

⟨⟨★⟩⟨★⟩⟨★⟩⟩

A long time later the *Comte* said with a sigh:

"As soon as Henri arrives to prepare our dinner, I
will go and see the Priest and arrange that we shall be
married first thing tomorrow morning."

He kissed her before he asked:

"You will not mind a Catholic wedding, my darling?
It would look very strange if my bride belonged to another church."

"As long as we are married, I do not care what sort of
Church it takes place in, but as it happens I was baptised
a Catholic."

The *Comte* looked at her incredulously.

"Do you mean that?"

Grania nodded.

"Papa was a Catholic, but Mama was not. They were
married in a Catholic Church, and I was baptised in
one."

The *Comte* was still looking astonished and she went
on:

"I am afraid Papa was not a very good Catholic even
when we lived in England, and when we came to Grenada he realised that the British were very much against
Catholicism because of their anti-French feelings and so
he did not attend any Church."

She thought the *Comte* was shocked and went on
quickly:

"When Mama was in St. George's she attended the
Protestant Church and sometimes she took me with her

412

on a Sunday, but it was a very long way to go and because it upset Papa when we left him alone it did not happen very often."

The *Comte* held her close to him.

"When you marry me, my precious," he said, "you will become a good Catholic, and together we will thank God that He has enabled us to find each other. I have a feeling that from now on He will protect us both and keep us safe."

"I feel that too," Grania said, "and you know I will do . . . anything . . . anything you ask me to."

The way she spoke made the *Comte* kiss her again, and they only drew apart when they heard Henri come into the kitchen and knew he was preparing the dinner.

When the *Comte* left to visit the Priest Jean arrived with one of Grania's trunks and she started to change her clothes.

She had a bath which was very cooling after the heat of the day, and although she protested to Jean that she should not be taking the *Comte's* bedroom from him he told her that those were his Master's orders and after that she did not argue.

She only remembered as she undressed that tomorrow they would be together and she knew that God had not only saved her from marrying Roderick Maigrin but had given her the man of her dreams.

"How can I be so lucky?" she asked herself.

Then she was saying fervently Catholic prayers which she knew were the ones that the *Comte* said and which would be hers in future.

When he returned she heard him go to another room where Jean had laid out his evening-clothes.

By this time Grania had found a pretty gown into which she could change, and she arranged her hair in the smartest fashion she knew.

She could not help wishing that it was fair again, but she knew nothing mattered as long as the *Comte* loved her and that she must remember what he had said to

413

her, to think French and to be French, so that nobody would suspect for a moment that she was an enemy.

"Once I am the *Comtesse de* Vence there will be no need for pretence," she said to her reflection in the mirror, "for then I shall have the most beautiful title in the world."

She was still looking in the mirror, but thinking of the *Comte* when there was a knock on the door and he came into the room.

"I thought you would be ready, my precious."

Then as she rose from the stool in front of the dressing-table he held out his arms and she ran towards him.

He did not kiss her but there was an expression of infinite tenderness in his eyes.

"It is all arranged," he said. "Tomorrow you will become my wife. We will sleep together in the bed which belonged to my grandfather and was so much a part of my home that I could not leave it behind."

"I thought that was what it must be."

He came a little closer and Grania asked:

"Are you really going to marry me?"

"You will be my wife and we will face all the problems and difficulties together."

He looked around the room as he said:

"I was thinking as I was coming back from the Church that at least for a little while we will not starve."

His eyes rested on the Boucher picture as he spoke and Grania gave a cry.

"You do not mean that you intend to sell that picture?"

"I shall get a good price for it from the Dutch on the other side of the island," the *Comte* replied. "Being neutral, they have gained from the war rather than otherwise."

"But you cannot sell your family treasures!"

"I have the only treasure which really matters to me now," he answered.

His lips swept away any further protest that she might have made.

They went downstairs hand-in-hand, and Jean served them the delicious dinner that Henri had cooked and when it was finished and they were alone the *Comte* said:

"I have arranged for the Housekeeper who looks after the Priest's house to sleep here tonight so that you will be chaperoned. I would not want us to start our married life by shocking the French matrons of St. Martin whose tongues wag like those of women in every part of the world."

"You will sleep in the ship?"

"In the bed in which you slept last night," the *Comte* replied, "I will dream of you, and tomorrow my dreams will come true."

"And I shall be dreaming too."

"I love you!" he said. "I love you so much that every moment I think I have reached my fullest capability of love, suddenly I love you infinitely more. What have you done to me, my darling, that I should feel like a boy in love for the first time?"

"But you must have loved so many women," Grania murmured.

The *Comte* smiled.

"I am French. I find women very attractive, but unlike most of my countrymen I resisted having an arranged marriage when I was young, and I have never, and this is the truth, found a woman until now with whom I would wish to share the rest of my life."

"Suppose I disappoint you?"

"You will never do that. I knew when I looked at what I thought was your portrait that you were everything I wanted in a woman, and when I actually saw you I knew that I had under-estimated both my need and what you can give me."

"You are . . . sure of that?" Grania enquired.

"Absolutely sure," he replied. "It is not so much what you say or even what you think, my precious, but what you are. Your sweetness, which I recognised the first time I set my eyes on you, shines like a beacon and envelops you with an aura of purity and goodness that could only come from God."

Grania clasped her hands together.

"You say such wonderful things to me. I am only so desperately afraid that I will not be able to live up to what you expect of me then perhaps you will sail away and leave me."

The *Comte* shook his head.

"You must know that I have now ceased to be a pirate. After we are married I will talk to my friends and we will think out some other ways that we can all make a living."

He thought before he went on:

"As I have said, I will sell some of my possessions so that we will not starve, and because I know God will not fail us perhaps it will not be long before we can return to Martinique."

The way he spoke seemed somehow inspired so that the tears came into Grania's eyes and she put out her hands towards his.

"I shall pray and pray," she said, "and darling, you must teach me to be good, so that my prayers are heard."

"I know that you need no teaching in that respect," the *Comte* replied, "but there are many other things that I intend to teach you, my adorable one, and I think you can guess what those lessons are."

Grania blushed. Then she said:

"I only hope you will not be . . . dissatisfied with your . . . pupil."

The *Comte* left the table and drawing Grania to her feet put his arms around her and they moved into the Sitting-Room.

It looked so lovely in the candle-light that Grania thought they might be in a Château in France, or one of the Palaces that she had read about in the books which her mother had bought to make her more proficient in the French language.

She wanted to say that she could not bear any of the

things in the room to be sold, but she knew it would be a mistake to upset the *Comte* and make him realise even more fully than he did already the sacrifices he had to make.

"At least I have some money," Grania thought.

She knew that English sovereigns when changed into French francs would amount to quite a considerable sum of money.

She smiled because she was glad she could contribute to their life together, and the *Comte* asked:

"What has made you smile, except happiness, *ma petite*?"

"I was thinking I am so glad that I have some money with me. Tomorrow it will be yours legally but, before you tell me you are too proud to take it, I suggest it could contribute to what you have to spend on your friends and the other members of the crew. After all, it is my fault that they can no longer continue to be pirates."

The *Comte* put his cheek against hers.

"I adore you, my lovely one," he said, "and I am not going to argue because, as you said, it is your fault that we shall have to settle down and behave like respectable Frenchmen. But before we sell the ship, which will undoubtedly fetch a very good price, you must sail back to Grenada to tell your father of the death of your cousin, and also to see that he himself is safe."

"Can we do that?" Grania asked. "I am worried about Papa, especially when he is with Mr. Maigrin."

"We will go together because it is the right thing to do. I also think your father should know that his daughter is married, although he will perhaps not be very pleased that it is to a Frenchman."

Grania gave a little laugh.

"My father will not mind that. You must remember he is Irish, and the Irish have never liked the English."

The *Comte* laughed too.

"I had forgotten that! So if your father will tolerate me as a son-in-law perhaps when things are better than they are at the moment he will be able to come and stay with us in St. Martin and you will be able to go and stay in Grenada."

"It is kind of you to think like that," Grania said, "because I feel in a way I ought to look after Papa."

She knew as she spoke it was only a day-dream, for as long as her father persisted in his friendship with Roderick Maigrin it was impossible for them to be together.

She was quite certain that if Maigrin learnt that she was married to a Frenchman he would try to destroy the *Comte* either by shooting him as an enemy, or having him pursued and persecuted by the English.

Yet she must have news of her father, and perhaps if he was still at Maigrin House she would on some pretext or other be able to inveigle him to Secret Harbour.

There she could at least say goodbye to him before she returned to live at St. Martin.

Then it flashed through her mind how fine the *Comte* was once again to anticipate her wishes almost before she had thought of them herself.

Because she wanted so desperately to kiss him she could only move closer into his arms and feel his lips seeking hers.

⁕⁕⁕⁕⁕⁕

Grania was awake very early because she was so excited and also because she heard movements downstairs and knew that Jean or Henri were already up and about.

Then she thought of the room next door where the Priest's Housekeeper, an elderly woman with a kind face, was sleeping.

She had arrived last night carrying a lantern to light her way through the rough land which lay just behind the house.

"I am delighted to meet you, *M'mselle*," she had said to Grania. "Father Francois sends you his blessing and is looking forward to marrying you to *Monsieur le Comte* at nine-thirty tomorrow morning."

418

"*Merci, Madame,*" Grania replied, "and thank you too for coming here tonight to keep me company. It was very kind of you."

"We all have to do what we can for those who have been stricken by the cruelties of war."

The *Comte* said goodnight, as the Housekeeper was there, and kissed Grania's hands before he returned to the ship.

When he had gone the Housekeeper said:

"That's a fine man and a very good Catholic, *M'mselle.* You're very fortunate to have such a man for your husband."

"Very fortunate indeed, *Madame,*" Grania agreed, "and I am very grateful."

"I shall pray for you both," the Housekeeper said, "and I know *le Bon Dieu* will give you great happiness."

Grania was certain that was true, and she lay awake in the beautiful bed with its gold corola thinking how wonderfully lucky she was and feeling that her mother knew of her happiness.

"How could I have known . . . how could I have guessed that I would be . . . saved at the . . . last moment from that terrible Mr. Maigrin?" Grania asked.

Then once again she was praying disjointed prayers of gratitude, disjointed because even to pray about the *Comte* made her feel again the rapture and the ecstasy he evoked in her when he kissed her and made her aware of strange feelings that were different from anything she had ever known before.

Then finally when she fell asleep it was to feel that God was watching over her and making tomorrow come quickly.

CRRRRRRRR

As the sunshine filled the room Grania thought it was an omen of what her life would be like in the future.

Outside birds were singing and the vivid colours of the bougainvillaea in the garden vied with that of the

vine climbing over the verandah and the emerald of the
sea against the horizon all seemed part of a dream.

"But it is true . . . really true!" Grania cried, and
knew this was her wedding day.

She did not have a wedding-dress, but amongst the
things her mother had bought for her there was a gown
specially to wear when she was presented at Court.

It was white, which was correct for a Debutante, and
it had been delivered after her mother had died.

Grania had in fact debated whether she should try to
sell it back to the dressmaker because she felt she would
never have a use for it.

Then she thought it would be humiliating to say that
she not only would be unable to wear it, but could not
really afford to pay for it. So she reluctantly handed
over the money and had brought it out with her to Grenada.

As she drew it out from the trunk she knew that while
it was a trifle over-elaborate it would be suitable for a
bride, and perhaps would make her look beautiful for
the *Comte*.

She had no veil and when she explained this to the
Housekeeper who had come into her room to help her
dress, the woman had sent Jean hastily to the Priest's
house.

"We have a veil which we sometimes lend to young
brides," she said, "if they arrive at the Church with only
a wreath on their heads and Father François does not
consider that respectable enough in the House of God."

"I should be very happy if I could borrow it," Grania
replied.

"It will be a pleasure!" the Housekeeper said. "And I
will make you a wreath which will be far prettier than
anything you could buy."

She sent Henri hurrying into the garden and when
he came back with a basket full of white flowers, she had
sat in Grania's bedroom arranging them skilfully in the
form of a wreath.

When she had finished nothing could have been

prettier than the fresh white flowers with their green leaves which were more becoming than any artificial wreath could ever have been.

The veil was of very fine lace and fell over Grania's shoulders, giving her an ethereal appearance, and when the wreath was arranged over it the Housekeeper stood back to survey her work and said in awe-struck tones:

"You make a very beautiful bride, *M'mselle*. No man could fail to appreciate such a lovely wife."

"I hope you are right," Grania said simply.

When she went downstairs to the Sitting-Room where the *Comte* was waiting she knew by the expression on his face that she was everything he had expected, and more.

He looked at her for a long moment before he said very quietly:

"I did not believe anyone could be so beautiful."

She smiled at him through her veil.

"I love you!"

"I will be able to tell you later how much I love you," he answered, "but now I dare not touch you. I only want to go down on my knees and light candles to you, for I not only love you, but worship you."

"You must not . . . say such things," Grania protested. "It makes me . . . afraid that I am not . . . good enough."

He smiled as if she was being absurd. Then he kissed her hand before he said:

"Our carriage is waiting at the back of the house. Because the crew did not think the horses pulling it were fine enough, they themselves are going to draw us to the Church."

Grania gave an exclamation of surprise and when she walked outside she saw that the light open carriage was horse-less while the shafts were ready to be pulled by all the young members of the crew.

The carriage itself had been decorated with the same white flowers that had made her wreath, and there was also a bouquet of them on the seat.

As they moved away Grania thought that it was just the sort of fairy-tale wedding that she wanted to have.

The *Comte* held her hand tightly in his as they were pulled down a narrow road which led to the small village.

It consisted only of a few West Indian "ginger-bread" houses with wrought-iron balconies.

They were built on the edge of the sea and inland behind them Grania could see several steep hills forming a very lovely view.

The small ancient Church was full and, as the Priest met them at the door and led them inside, the *Comte's* friends and all those who had not been pulling the carriage were waiting to watch the marriage take place.

To Grania it was a very moving service and she felt as if the fragrant incense rising towards the roof carried their prayers up to God and that He Himself blessed them and their love for each other.

She was very conscious of the wedding-ring on her finger, but more than anything else of the *Comte* kneeling beside her and his voice repeating his vows with an unmistakable sincerity.

Last night she had said to him a little nervously:

"If I am to be . . . married as your . . . cousin will it be . . . legal?"

"I thought you might ask that question," he said. "As you know we shall only be called by our Christian names, and therefore I have already told the Priest that you were Christened 'Teresa Grania'."

"I thought I was to be 'Gabrielle'?"

"I thought Gabrielle Grania sounded too much of a mouthful," the *Comte* replied, and they both laughed.

"Teresa is a very pretty name, and I am quite content with it," Grania said.

She found out at the Service that her husband had other names, when as he repeated his vows he said:

"I Beaufort Francis Louis."

When they left the little Church and were drawn back in their carriage to their own house, Grania could think of nothing except the man beside her and the words of love that he whispered in her ear.

Then they were joined by everybody who had watched the ceremony, and some friends too who lived on the island. There was wine in which to drink their health and food which Grania was sure Henri must have spent most of the night preparing.

It was all very happy and gay, with a laughter that seemed part of the sunshine.

Then at last somewhat reluctantly the people began to leave.

First the friends who lived on the island, then the Priest and his housekeeper, and finally when it was time for *siesta* the crew said they must go back to the ship.

It was then Grania realised that she was alone with her husband, and she turned to look at him, raising her face to his.

"I think," he said, "we would both be more comfortable if we had our *siesta* without being encumbered by our smart clothes, and I am very much afraid of spoiling that beautiful gown."

"It was meant to be worn at Buckingham Palace," Grania replied, "but it is much, much more appropriate that I should wear it on the day I was married to you."

"I agree with you," the *Comte* smiled. "Why should we worry about Kings and Queens when we have each other?"

He drew her up the stairs and when they reached the bedroom Grania realised that somebody, she expected it was Jean, had lowered the sunblinds so that the room was cool and dim.

It was fragrant with flowers which Jean must have arranged for them when they came back from the Church, and they stood in great vases on the dressing-table and on either side of the bed.

"My bride!" the *Comte* said very softly.

Then he took the wreath from her head and lifted the veil.

He looked at her for a long moment before he took her in his arms.

"You are real!" he said almost as if he spoke to himself. "When I was marrying you I was half afraid that you were a goddess who had come down from the top of one of the mountains or a nymph from a cascade."

"I am . . . real," Grania whispered, "but I feel like you that this is all a dream."

"If it is," the *Comte* said, "then let us go on dreaming!"

Chapter Seven

*G*RANIA AWOKE AND felt her heart was singing like the birds outside the window, and she looked adoringly towards the *Comte* sleeping beside her.

She knew that every day and every night she spent with him she loved him more.

But today was special because they were leaving for Grenada.

They had been married for over three weeks and yesterday the *Comte* had said:

"I think, my darling, we must take our last trip in the ship before I sell it."

Grania looked at him in a startled manner and he had explained:

"I intend to sell the ship first. That will give all the crew and myself enough money for us to look around and plan our futures. After that, if no one is settled, other things will have to go."

The way he spoke of "other things" told Grania how much he minded the thought of having to part with his pictures and treasures which she had learned had been collected by his ancestors over many centuries.

"They were so fortunate that they were able to bring them away from France, before the Revolution," he had said. "Otherwise everything we owned would either have been confiscated or burnt by the peasants."

There was a little silence and Grania knew that he was thinking he would have liked to keep them intact for his eldest son, but that would not be impossible.

She moved away from him to say after a moment:

"Sometimes I feel I should have left you . . . roaming the sea as a . . . pirate."

The *Comte* laughed and it had swept the expression of regret from his eyes.

"My darling, do you think I would really want to be a pirate if it meant I had to leave you? I am so happy that I thank God every day that we are together and you are my wife. At the same time we have to live."

"Yes, I know that," Grania said, "but . . ."

To keep her from apologising any further he kissed her and the rapture and wonder of it took everything else out of her mind.

Now knowing the ship was for sale, she prayed that it would fetch enough money for it to be a very, very long time before the *Comte* had to sell anything else.

She knew also that he was right in saying that before they were marooned on St. Martin with no means of getting away she must find out how her father was and if possible tell him of her marriage.

Because it meant leaving even for a little while, the *Comte's* small house and the happiness she had found there, she pressed herself against him.

He awoke and without opening his eyes he put his arms around her to hold her close, and she said:

"We will not take any risks, will we? If it is not safe to go ashore at Grenada, you will turn back?"

The *Comte* looked at her.

"You do not think, my adorable wonderful little wife, that I would take you anywhere where there was danger? I promise that if Abe's white flag does not tell us everything is safe we will turn back immediately."

"That is all I want to know," Grania said. "If anything should happen to you now I would want . . . to die!"

"Do not talk of dying," he answered. You are going to live, and we will see our children and our grandchildren running the plantations at Martinique before we either of us leave each other or this earth."

He spoke prophetically and Grania put her arm round his neck to draw his lips close to hers.

"How can I tell you how much I love you?" she asked. "Like this!"

Then he was kissing her, his heart was beating against hers, and as she felt the fire rising in him she knew the flames he evoked were rising in her too.

Then it seemed to Grania there was the music of the angels and a celestial light which covered them like the blessing of God, and they were one. . . .

⚜️⚜️⚜️

The sea was vividly blue and emerald, the sky was dazzling with the sunshine, and as the sails billowed out in the breeze the ship seemed to be skimming over the smooth water rather than sailing through it.

The crew were whistling and singing as they worked and Grania had the feeling that like the *Comte* they were content to give up the risky, dangerous life of piracy and return to what he called "respectability".

Every night over dinner they talked of what they could do.

"It is a pity there are not more people on St. Martin and that there is no crime," Leo said, "otherwise they would need my services."

"No crime?" Grania questioned.

He shook his head.

"If anybody stole how could they get away with the

spoils? And everyone is so good-natured that nobody wants to murder anyone."

"It seems a waste of your intelligence," the *Comte* said, "but when we get home I am sure there will be hundreds of cases waiting for you to deal with them."

They always talked optimistically of the time when they would return to Martinique, and the clerks who had worked in Leo's office were, Grania knew, studying in the evenings so that they would not be behind in preparation for their Examinations however long they had to wait before they took them.

She had by now a real affection for the three men who were so close to her husband, and she also found that the rest of the crew not only admired her but sought her help with their problems and wanted to talk to her about their future.

"I am sure every woman in the world would envy me if they knew I had so many delightful men all to myself," Grania said to the *Comte*.

"You belong to me, *ma petite*, and if I find you so much as looking at another man, you will find I am very jealous!"

She pressed herself nearer to him as she said:

"You know I could never look at anybody but you. I love you so much that sometimes I am afraid you will be bored with my telling you so and go in search of somebody less predictable."

"I want your love," he said, "and you do not love me yet half as much as I intend you to do."

He had then kissed her fiercely and demandingly as if he would force her to realise how much he needed her.

As they saw no ships on the voyage towards Grenada it took them less time than they had taken when they had left it for St. Martin.

The afternoon before they reached the island Henri came to the cabin after the *siesta* to help Grania wash the rinse out of her hair.

She had to apply it again every time it was washed,

but this time it had to be washed out thoroughly so that when she landed on Grenada she looked English.

She dried her hair in the sunshine and when it was dry she left it hanging over her shoulders.

The *Comte* had been busy on deck steering the ship, and when he came into the cabin as the sun was sinking he saw Grania standing by a port-hole and for a moment stood still looking at her.

Then he smiled and said:

"I see I have an English visitor! I am delighted to meet you, Mrs. Vence!"

Grania laughed and ran towards him.

"That is perfect!" she said. "Now you speak English far better than I speak French."

"That would be impossible," the *Comte* replied, "but I am glad your lessons are having an effect."

"You speak just like an Englishman," she said, "but I feel that you look almost too smart to be one."

"You flatter me," the *Comte* answered. "But, darling, whatever you may look like remember you are my wife, my very fascinating, alluring French wife."

He kissed her. Then he drew up her hair across her face and kissed her through it.

"You are my golden girl again," he said. "I am not certain how I like you best, dark and mysterious like the dusk, or shining and golden as a spring morning."

The *Comte* had planned that they should draw near Grenada well after sunrise—not too early in case Abe did not have time to change the flag. But they were slowed down by lack of wind, and when they finally arrived within sight of the island it was about eleven o'clock.

Grania was on the poop-deck beside the *Comte* and they were both waiting for the signal from the look-out on the mast.

He held a telescope to his eye and nobody on deck spoke until finally they heard him cry:

"A white flag! I can see it quite clearly!"

The *Comte* swung the wheel over, the sails filled with the breeze and they shot ahead.

It was quite a feat to enter the bay of Secret Harbour, but the *Comte* managed it brilliantly and Grania felt a little tug at her heart when she saw the jetty, the pine trees and the brilliant bushes of bougainvillaea that she had known ever since a child.

They let down the anchor, the gang-plank joined the deck to the jetty and the *Comte* helped Grania onto it.

They had arranged to go ahead while the others stayed on the ship ready to move away quickly if it was necessary.

"If Papa is here I want him to meet everybody," Grania said.

"We will have to see what your father thinks of me first," the *Comte* replied. "He may disapprove violently of your marrying a Frenchman."

"No one could disapprove of you," Grania answered, and the *Comte* laughed and kissed the tip of her nose.

Now he was carrying over his arm Patrick O'Kerry's uniform coat, and the papers he had taken from him before he was buried at sea were in the pocket.

"Papa will want to keep them," Grania said, "and one day when the war is over, if she is still alive, I am sure his mother would wish to have them."

"That is what I thought," the *Comte* answered.

"How can you be so kind?" Grania asked. "I cannot believe that any other man would think of such things in the middle of a war."

"A war which I pray will not concern us in the future," the *Comte* said beneath his breath.

Because she was so closely attuned to him Grania was aware that he was in fact apprehensive as to what sort of reception he would receive from his father-in-law.

But she was confident that, unless Roderick Maigrin was with her father, he would be glad that she had found somebody to love and who loved her.

If her father was not at Secret Harbour she was

wondering how she could manage to send for him so that he came alone.

It was not possible to predict exactly what would happen when they arrived, but what was important was that she should see Abe and find out what the position was.

They walked through the pine trees and she glanced at the *Comte* before they left their shelter for the garden.

She knew he was looking serious but, she thought, exceedingly handsome.

Because it was so hot he was wearing only a thin linen shirt, but his cravat was tied in an intricate fashion which always fascinated her, and his white cotton breeches were the same as the crew wore, only better fitting.

"He is so smart," Grania thought to herself, "but at the same time so masculine."

She blushed at her own thoughts.

They walked through the overgrown flower-beds which had been her mother's pride.

Then, just as they reached the centre of the garden and the house lay straight ahead of them, a man appeared on the verandah.

One glance at him and Grania felt her heart stand still, for he was wearing British uniform, and was, she saw, a Colonel.

Both she and the *Comte* stopped and neither of them moved as the Colonel came down the steps and walked towards them.

Then behind him Grania saw Abe and knew by the expression of consternation on his face that the English Officer's visit was unexpected.

The Colonel came forward. Then as he reached them he held out his hand to Grania and smiled.

"I think you must be Lady Grania O'Kerry," he said. "May I introduce myself? I am Lieutenant-Colonel Campbell and I have just arrived from Barbados with a transport of troops."

For a moment Grania thought it was impossible to speak.

Then she said in a voice that did not sound like her own:

"How do you do, Colonel? I am sure you were very welcome at St. George's."

"We were," the Colonel replied, "and I think we can soon get the trouble here cleared up."

He glanced at the *Comte* and Grania knew he was waiting to be introduced.

Then as she wondered frantically what she should say she saw the Colonel's eyes resting on the naval officer's coat that the *Comte* carried on his arm.

Almost like a message from Heaven Grania knew what she could do.

"May I, Colonel, introduce my cousin, who is also my husband? Commander Patrick O'Kerry!"

The *Comte* and the Colonel shook hands and the Colonel said:

"I am delighted to meet you, Commander. Strangely enough the Governor was speaking about you today and wondering how he could get in touch with you."

"What about?" the *Comte* asked.

He sounded, Grania thought, completely composed while her heart was beating frantically.

The Colonel turned again to her.

"I am afraid, Lady Grania," he said quietly, "I am the bearer of bad news."

"Bad news?" Grania repeated almost beneath her breath.

"I am here to inform you that your father, the Earl of Kilkerry, was killed by the revolutionaries."

Grania drew in her breath and put out her hand towards the *Comte*.

He took it in his and she felt as if the clasp of his fingers gave her strength.

"What . . . happened?"

"Ten days ago the slaves on Mr. Roderick Maigrin's plantation were determined to join the other rebels," the Colonel replied. "However, he became aware of it and tried to prevent them from leaving."

Grania was sure that he had killed them as he had killed the others, but she did not say anything and the Colonel went on:

"However they disarmed him and shot your father, who died instantly. But they tortured Mr. Maigrin before they finally murdered him."

Grania did not speak. She could only feel relief that her father had died without suffering.

Then the *Comte* spoke.

"You will understand, Colonel, that this has been a great shock for my wife? May I suggest that we go into the house so that she can sit down."

"Yes, of course," the Colonel agreed.

The *Comte's* arm went round Grania and as they walked across the garden and up the stairs she realised that he was limping most convincingly.

She wondered vaguely why he was doing so.

When they were seated in her mother's Drawing-Room and Abe without being told had brought them rum punches the Colonel said:

"I suppose, Commander, you are anxious to get back to sea?"

"I am afraid that will be impossible for some time," the *Comte* replied. "As you are doubtless aware, I was on H.M.S. Heroic which was sunk, and I, with a number of other men, was wounded."

"I noticed you limped," the Colonel said, "but apart from your wound as your circumstances have now changed, I am hoping we can perhaps persuade you to stay here."

The *Comte* looked surprised and the Colonel explained:

"As I think you must be aware, you are now the Earl of Kilkerry, and the reason that the bodies of the murdered gentlemen were discovered was that the Governor was anxious that the plantations should be put back into order and the slaves set to work."

Grania raised her head to say:

"I think . . . perhaps now we have . . . very few slaves . . . left."

"I expect that is true, as it is on most of the plantations where many of the slaves have run away to join the rebels, and the rest are hiding. But we shall soon take Belvedere, and once Fédon is in our hands the rebellion will be over."

"So the slaves will go back to work and will be anxious to do so," the *Comte* remarked.

"Exactly!" the Colonel agreed. "And that is why, My Lord, I would like you to stay here and run the estate for your wife. It is important to the island, and perhaps until we can find somebody to take over Mr. Maigrin's plantation you might have time to keep an eye on his land as well as your own."

There was a moment's pause while Grania knew the *Comte* was thinking. Then he said:

"I will certainly do the best I can for you, and I am certain I can see that our own slaves are content and forget any rebellious feelings they may have had."

The Colonel smiled.

"That is exactly what I want to hear, My Lord, and I am sure the Governor will be delighted by your attitude."

He paused before he added:

"By the way, Lady Grania, I know you will be sorry to hear that the old Governor, who you knew well, was killed by the rebels, and the present Governor is new to the Island. He will I know be happy to make your acquaintance later. I need not add that at the moment he is far too busy for any social engagements."

"Yes, of course," Grania said. "We will be busy too. I am afraid my father has rather neglected the plantation in the last two or three years and there is a great deal to be done."

"I am quite sure your husband will manage admirably."

The Colonel finished his rum punch and rose to his feet.

"Now, if you will forgive me," he said, "I must be on my way. I have to get back to St. George's. The Governor asked me as I was clearing up certain difficulties in St. David's to call here on my way home, and I was exceedingly fortunate to find you."

"We shall hope to see you again," Grania said holding out her hand.

"I shall hope so too," the Colonel replied. "But as soon as our plans are clarified we will go into action!"

He shook hands with the *Comte* saying:

"Goodbye, My Lord. The very best of luck! I am delighted, may I say, that you are here. You may not know there were very few survivors from H.M.S. Heroic."

The *Comte* saw the Colonel to the door where his horse was waiting and a dozen or so troops were mounted.

He watched them ride away, then went back to the Drawing-Room.

As he came through the door Grania ran towards him, to fling her arms round him.

"Darling, you were wonderful!" she said. "He had not the least suspicion that you were not who you said you were."

"Who *you* said I was," the *Comte* corrected, "and I thought it was very quick and clever of you."

He drew her to the sofa and sat down beside her holding her hand in his.

She looked up at him enquiringly and he said very quietly:

"This is a decision which you and only you can make. Are we to stay or are we to leave?"

Grania did not pause before she asked:

"Would you be willing to stay here and run the plantation as the Colonel suggested?"

"Why not? It belongs to you, I am quite certain it will be hard work, but with the experience I have we could make it pay."

He did not wait for Grania to say anything, but went on:

"If we are here we can also find work for all our friends, and your job, my darling, will be to make them proficient not on a plantation, but in the English language."

He smiled as he went on:

"After all, they are all intelligent Frenchmen, and it should not be hard for Leo eventually to find plenty of work in St. George's and if we are clever André and Jacques can take over Roderick Maigrin's plantation."

Grania gave a little cry.

"That would be wonderful, and in a way poetic justice after that man was so horrible and such a bad influence on Papa."

"If I could risk being a pirate I can certainly risk being an English Planter," the *Comte* said. "It is entirely up to you. But if, my lovely one, you would rather go back to St. Martin, I will agree."

Grania smiled.

"To sell your precious treasures?" she asked. "Of course not! We must stay here, and because you are so brilliant I am quite certain we shall never be found out. Besides, there is no O'Kerry to accuse you of usurping his title."

The *Comte* bent forward and kissed her.

"Then it shall be as you wish," he said, "and you can choose, my darling, in the future as to whether you are a Countess or a *Comtesse* and match the colour of your hair to your choice!"

Grania laughed. Then she called Abe.

"Listen Abe," she said. "You and only you will know that the gentleman here is really a Frenchman. I expect you heard what the Colonel said."

"I listen Lady," Abe replied. "Very good news! We be rich. Everyone happy!"

"Of course we will be," Grania said.

"One bit bad news, Lady."

"What is that?" Grania asked.

"New Governor take Momma Mabel. Give big money. Her gone St. George's!"

435

Grania laughed.

"That means there will be no embarrassment in asking Henri to take over the kitchen."

Her voice rose excitedly as she said:

"Go quickly to the ship, Abe, and ask Henri to come and prepare luncheon. Tell everybody else to come here too, and 'His Lordship' will tell them what has been decided."

She laughed again as she gave the *Comte* his new title.

Then as Abe without saying anything ran from the Drawing-Room and down the steps of the verandah and across the garden the *Comte* put out his arms and drew her close to him.

"I suppose you know what you are taking on," he said. "You are going to have to work very hard, my darling, and so shall I."

"But it will be exciting to work together," Grania said, "and I have thought of a new name for you—an English name."

The *Comte* raised his eye-brows as she said:

"I shall call you 'Beau' on English soil, and 'Beaufort' on French. After all, Beau can be applied to Englishmen like Beau Nash, and who could look the part better?"

"As long as that is how I appear to you, then I am satisfied."

He drew her closer still as he added very quietly:

"How can we be so lucky or so blessed to find a place where we can work, and I can make love to you until we can go home?"

"Suppose when the time comes I want to stay here?" Grania asked.

He looked at her to see if she was serious, then realised she was teasing.

His lips were very close to hers as he said:

"Let me make it quite clear once and for all that where I go you will go. You belong to me! You are mine, and not all the nations in the world could divide us or prevent us from being together."

436

"Oh, darling, that is what I want you to say!" Grania sighed. "And you know I love you."

"I will make you sure of it every day, every hour that we are together," the *Comte* said.

He pulled her almost roughly closer to him.

Then he was kissing her and she knew that once again he was proving his supremacy and domination over her.

It made her adore him because he was so much a man, but at the same time so sensitive and understanding to her feelings.

She knew that with him she would always feel safe and protected. It would not matter where they were, on what island or what part of the world.

His arms were a secret harbour which kept her safe, a harbour that was made of love.

Then as the *Comte's* kisses grew more demanding she turned her face up to his to say, and her voice trembled:

"Darling, the others will come in a minute. Please do not excite me until . . . tonight."

She saw the fire in the *Comte's* eyes but he was smiling.

"Tonight?" he enquired. "Why should we wait until tonight? After luncheon there will be a *siesta* and I intend to tell you, my wonderful, brave, courageous little wife, how I fell in love with a picture, but fate brought me the reality and she is the most exciting thing I have ever known."

Then he was kissing her again, kissing her until they heard the sound of voices coming from the garden.

It was the sound of men talking excitedly in a language which was not their own.

But to Grania and the *Comte* there was only one language they both understood and which was the same wherever they might be—the language of love.

⁂

The sunblinds were down and the room which smelt of jasmine, was very dim. On the lace-edged pillows two heads were very close together.

"*Je t'adore, ma petite,*" the *Comte* said hoarsely.

"I love you . . . I love you, darling."

"Tell me again, I want to be sure."

"I adore . . . you."

"As I adore and worship you, but I also want to excite you."

"How can I . . . tell . . . what I . . . feel?"

Grania's voice was low and breathless. The *Comte's* hands were touching her and she knew his heart was beating as frantically as hers.

"*Je te desire, ma cherie, je te desire!*"

"And I . . . want you . . . O wonderful, marvellous, Beau . . . love me."

"Give me yourself."

"I am . . . yours . . . yours . . ."

"You are mine, all mine, now and for ever."

Then there was only love in a secret harbour which was theirs alone and where no one else could encroach.

About the Author

❧

BARBARA CARTLAND, the world's best known and bestselling author of romantic fiction, is also an historian, playwright, lecturer, political speaker and television personality. She has now written over five hundred and sixty-one books and has the distinction of holding *The Guinness Book of Records* title of the world's bestselling author, having sold over six hundred and twenty million copies all over the world.

Miss Cartland is a Dame of Grace of St. John of Jerusalem; Chairman of the St. John Council in Hertfordshire; one of the first women in one thousand years ever to be admitted to the Chapter General; President of the Hertfordshire Branch of the Royal College of Midwives, President and Founder in 1964 of the National Association for Health, and invested by her Majesty the Queen as a Dame of the Order of the British Empire in 1991.

Miss Cartland lives in England at Camfield Place, Hatfield, Hertfordshire.